BLACK STONE HEART

THE FIRST STEP ON THE OBSIDIAN PATH

by
MICHAEL R. FLETCHER

BLACK STONE HEART

BLACK STONE HEART

This is a work of fiction. Names, characters, business, events and incidents are the products of the author's imagination. Any resemblance to actual persons, living or dead, or actual events is mostly coincidental.

BLACK STONE HEART Copyright © 2020 by Michael R. Fletcher

All rights reserved. No part of this publication may be reproduced, distributed, or transmitted in any form or by any means, including photocopying, recording, or other electronic or mechanical methods, without the prior written permission of the publisher, except in the case of brief quotations embodied in critical reviews and certain other non-commercial uses permitted by copyright law.

Editor: Sarah Chorn
Cover Art by: Felix Ortiz

Books by Michael R. Fletcher

Ghosts of Tomorrow
Beyond Redemption
The Mirror's Truth
Swarm and Steel
A Collection of Obsessions
The Millennial Manifesto
Smoke and Stone (City of Sacrifice #1)
Black Stone Heart (The Obsidian Path #1)

Upcoming releases

Ash and Bone (City of Sacrifice #2)
She Dreams in Blood (The Obsidian Path #2)
The Adventures of Dyrk Ashton's Pants

For Rich, who was there when this story first began

THAT WHICH KILLS YOU MAKES YOU STRONGER

PROLOGUE

Every day we do the things we think we have to do. So rarely do we stop to question our choices. We don't even see deciding that we 'have to do something' is itself a choice. We blunder through life, writing our failures and excuses as we go, defending every choice with justifications made up after the fact. The truth is, we never really consider the consequences.

My choices had consequences. Vast consequences.

A kingdom fell. No, I shouldn't belittle their efforts just because they fall well short of my own accomplishments. An empire fell. People died. A lot of people. Some died peripherally, as a result of my choices. Many died by my own hand. I tore souls from innocent victims to summon and bind hellish creatures. Demons, you'd call them.

I did terrible, terrible things trying to do the right thing.

I sought a god trapped in a sword, the End of Sorrow, and I found it.

I went in search of the ancient god I worshipped all those thousands of years ago, and I found her. I had a vision of remaking the world as it once was. She tore out my eyes and replaced that vision with one of her own.

So much death. So much violence.

In finding everything, I lost the one thing that mattered.

I'll start at the beginning, but know that it's not *the* beginning, just *my* beginning. All this started thousands of years before my story. You're not going to understand, at least not at first.

CHAPTER ONE

For an eternity I was nothing but animal hunger. Small lives, crawling, twitching, and slithering, fed me. I wanted more, needed more. Always more. Buried in earth and stone I fed off the grass above me. When the roots of an ancient tree that started life millennia after my death reached me, I drank its life too. I was voracious, insatiable, a devourer. Squirrels and mice crossing my ravenous grave stiffened and fell dead.

With each life I grew.

Blood.

Blood soaked through the earth. This was a large life, a bright spark of existence, wounded and dying. It collapsed upon me. Even buried I felt its weight impact the soil above. Sucking the life from it, I regained some shred of what I was. What I had been.

I woke, suffocating in the earth, choking on dirt and clawing in mad panic. I fought free of my prison. Roots hung from me, the veins through which I fed. I watched them squirm and writhe their way back into my flesh, and wondered what I was.

BLACK STONE HEART

A lone wolf stood a score of strides away. Gaunt from a hard winter, its fur hung in tatters. It watched me, waiting. For a moment I couldn't decide whether I should flee, or try and run it down so I could feed off it. I turned toward it and the starved beast disappeared into the trees.

I had no name, no memory of self, and yet still this seemed strange.

Naked and filthy, I stood in the morning sun. A circle of dead grass, a dozen strides across, surrounded me. Thousands of tiny corpses, husked and dried, littered the ground. Translucent shells of insects. Fragile birds, skeletal and empty. Countless remains of squirrels and rodents, twisted with agony. The corpse of a man, long rotted to bone and gristle, lay nearby. He wore armour, decayed leather and scraps of rusted chain. His throat had been torn out. A cleared path through the corpses suggested he'd been dragged onto my grave. At the edge of the dead circle stood an ancient tree towering far into the sky. Rot hollowed its trunk. A good wind would bring it down.

Dew beaded my arms and torso, bright gems of rainbow light. I admired their beauty as a cool breeze puckered my skin. I was empty, a vessel waiting to be filled. With memories. With life. With death.

The ground cracked beneath me, a thin crust of dirt still frozen after the passing of winter. I remember the joy of standing in the sun, the feel of the air, of life buzzing and croaking all around me. Birds flitted through the trees, chasing each other in an endless game. I was nothing, and that nothing was beautiful. I think, even then, I had some inkling of what I once was, what I must once again become. If I could have stayed there forever in that empty state, I would have.

I should have.

When I did finally move, stepping toward a rabbit who wandered out of the bush to stare at me, I collapsed to my knees. The rabbit bolted and I scrambled after it, crawling, tearing my hands and knees on sharp sticks and stones. It soon became clear that I would never catch the little beast. I lay panting in the dirt, grinning at the sky.

Hunger drove me back to my feet and I padded barefoot through the forest, limping and whimpering.

At the time, the direction I chose seemed random. I now know I followed some instinct writ deep in my tainted blood. I walked south, stopping to eat worms and beetles and the occasional plant. I needed life. Large life. I was too weak, too slow, to catch it.

When the sun sank I collapsed to the soil and slept, dreamless and innocent. I should have been cold. I wasn't. I woke to find the shrivelled corpses of slugs and leeches spotting my body. Picking one off, I crushed its brittle shell before tossing it aside.

Had my flesh drained them of life?

I walked south for two days. Sleeping, drinking icy water from the snowmelt of a winter just ended, and eating what small lives crossed my path. On the morning of the third day I found a cabin. It was a crude structure of sticks and mud. For the first time since waking, I knew an emotion other than endless hunger: Curiosity.

Furs hung stretched across sticks driven into the trampled mud. The bones and skulls of hundreds of animals sat piled against one wall. Yellow and furred brown with clinging strands of rotten meat, they looked to have been well-gnawed. Moving closer I saw the hut was made as much from bone as from sticks. This was a home of death.

The air stank of decaying flesh and rancid fur.

Another feeling grew in me: Fear.

Up until this moment I had always been the hunter, the killer, devourer of lives. Whatever lived here was a more successful murderer than I. The desire to flee pulsed through me and yet, even more powerful, was the need to move closer, to see who or what was within this hut.

The door swung open on leather hinges and an old man, swaddled in furs, stood framed by wood and mud and death. He was bone thin, ropes of hard muscle and veins stretched over an angular frame. His skin was a ruddy pink, wind-burned.

Lifting an arm, I examined my own flesh, black, darker than night.

Something hung in his fist and I recognized it as a weapon. Where my feet were bloody and raw from walking the forest, his were encased in hard leather.

I wanted that weapon. I wanted *my* feet to be warm and protected. I wanted his crude hut and his furs.

I wanted everything he had.

He said something, and I tackled him, crashing into the hut. We wrestled until I smashed his head against a rock lodged in the mud floor. Over and over I slammed his skull against stone until he became still and limp.

I took everything he possessed and made it mine.

Everything.

CHAPTER TWO

Years passed in that hut. I was alone and it never occurred to me I could be anything else. I remembered flashes of some distant past and words like *axe* and *boots*. I found his shortbow and learned how to use it, fashioning rough arrows when the last of his disappeared into the forest lodged in the haunch of a deer. By following the old man's tracks in the mud, I found his traps. After studying them, I was able to reset them and make a few of my own.

Sometimes wolves would visit me. They'd stay in the trees, watching with knowing eyes. Perhaps they recognized a fellow predator. They never bothered me, never came closer. I grew accustomed to the attention and soon ignored them. They were a small, unhealthy pack, clearly eking out a desperate survival. Sometimes their fur hung off them in ragged clumps. No matter how awful they looked, they never moved closer, never stole meat from my kills, even when I left it outside.

Time passed, unnoticed by the emptiness of me.

I killed. I ate.

Winters were cruel and I often went hungry. Each spring my traps filled with squirming life and I gorged myself.

Early one morning, as I sat outside enjoying the feel of the sun on my face, something woke in me. I felt a presence growing nearer. I didn't know what it was, but felt in my blood that it was important, that it had something I wanted.

Returning to my hut I collected my hatchet and stood waiting. A wolf came to the edge of the treeline to wait with me. He watched with infinite patience.

Hours passed before a naked youth staggered from the trees. Unlike the trapper I killed, we were the same colour. Long coils of greasy blue-black hair hung to his shoulders like matted snakes. A tangled scruff of beard muddied his features. I reached up to touch the matted riot growing on my own chin. My hair matched his, though I tied mine back with a leather thong.

He stared at me, blinking. Eyes of black, set deep in a sunken and filthy face, watched me. He moved closer, tentative like a baby deer.

I waited, hatchet held behind my back. He had something. Inside him. It was mine.

I wanted it.

Stopping a stride away, he touched his chest over his heart, he then pointed at the same spot on me.

I nodded, understanding.

"It's inside you," I said, my voice cracking from disuse. "I need it," I told him. "Whatever it is that's in there, I need it."

He showed no sign of understanding my words.

I repeated his gesture, touching his chest.

When he glanced down, I split his skull with my hatchet. He dropped, face first, to the mud. I had to stand on his neck to wrestle the blade free of bone.

I rolled him onto his back and he blinked up at me, tremors running through his body, his feet kicking in little twitches as he died. I saw comprehension in those eyes, understanding of what I'd done to him.

Three times I chopped into his chest before the ribs split. Each time, he blinked, his mouth opening a little as if struggling to speak.

Working my fingers into him, I cracked him open.

The bastard was skin and bone and my subsistence-level diet left me weak. After opening him, I pulled his heart from his chest, hacking at the veins and arteries with my axe to free it.

"You'd have done the same to me if you got here first," I joked. But he was dead, empty eyes staring into the endless blue sky. My voice, unused in years, rang harsh in my ears.

I tore his heart apart with my teeth, searching. I found what I sought, buried deep at the centre. A tiny flake of black stone barely the size of my smallest fingernail.

"Who are you?" I asked the corpse. "What do you remember?"

I blinked in surprise at the strange question.

The stone sank into my flesh. Following an artery, it tore through me, tunnelling its way to my heart. Agony took the world away and I lay screaming in the mud.

I woke, staring up at the stars. The body lay beside me, cold and still. The blood I'd splashed over myself while tearing this man apart had dried to a hard crust. I stank of death and murder. Somewhere inside me, the sliver of stone I took from his heart met the flake already residing in my own.

Turning my head, I studied his slack features and black flesh, and knew him for who he was.

Me.

Pushing myself from the bloody mud, I stood grinning at the night sky.

The wolf was gone.

"I have a name," I told the stars. They shimmered and shivered in terror.

It wasn't much, but it was something.

As fragment of stone met fragment of stone, memory coalesced. Meaningless on their own, together they told a story, albeit one with huge gaps.

"Khraen," I said, testing the sound of my name.

I needed more. How many more shards of stone were out there? Where were they? Who did this to me? Why had they broken me apart and scattered me?

I had to know.

Staggering back into my mud hut, I collapsed on the stinking pile of furs I called a bed.

Nightmares tore my sleep that night. I dreamed of a colossal fleet, ships littered from horizon to horizon. I stood on the prow of the flagship, the Habnikaav. Red sails snapped in the wind. Red robes. Red armour. A red sword sheathed at my side.

I was blood.

They came out of the sun. White ships. Sails bleached harsh and blinding. A pretension of purity. A lie.

A wall of water rose up between the fleets, elementalists waking the ocean itself and turning it against me. They were insane. No one could hope to control an elemental as huge and ancient as an ocean. Waking it was a move of utter desperation. But their recklessness spelled the end of the Imperial Navy of… of… I couldn't remember.

I watched the ocean destroy my ships. I watched the elementalists crack and lose control, and I watched the ocean turn on the white fleet. It was awake now, and angry. Next it would scrub any nearby coasts free of offending life.

The next morning, I packed my meagre belongings. My clothes were from the trapper I killed several winters ago. I couldn't remember how long I'd been here. Time in this lonely cabin had a way of sneaking past. The trapper's hatchet I wore in a loop in my rope belt. His short-bow and collection of crude arrows, I slung over my shoulder. After putting what remained of my cured meat from the winter into my backpack, an awkward burlap contraption which also belonged to the trapper, I left my reeking little hut. I stood in the mud, the trapper's too-large boots on my feet. They were falling apart now, wouldn't last another winter. Something took the sundered corpse during the night. Probably the wolves. They were welcome to it.

Though it had been my sanctuary for years, I thought to never see that hut again. I was wrong. There was so much I didn't know.

It felt strange to remember murdering that naked man. Chopping into his skull, his dull look of astonishment, the axe rising and falling, the splash of blood as I hacked his chest apart.

His skin was black, like mine.

Somehow, he was me. Or a piece of me.

That was the first time I saw myself since waking, alone and naked, four or five years ago. Had I not found the trapper and his shack of mud and sticks, gods know what would have become of me.

Gods?

I shrugged the thought away.

This shack, mud, and death, had been my world for too long. It was time to move. I had a name, and a name meant a history. Though I knew next to nothing, I was damned sure people weren't supposed to have shards of obsidian in their hearts.

Turning my back on that hut, I set out. After a dozen strides I stopped.

Everything I knew lay behind me. My whole world. I was safe there, if not comfortable. I knew where the rabbits ran and where wild potatoes grew. I knew a stream where the fish were plentiful. I knew where all the dead and dying trees were within three days walk. I could stay there forever.

Tremors of fear shook me, hunched my shoulders.

Turn back. Go home.

What dangers lay waiting in the world beyond? How long had I been dead? Did I still have living enemies, or were they long gone? I had no way of knowing. What if they came looking and found me cowering in my hut?

Tears ran free and hot. My eyes burned.

"I'm scared," I said. I didn't even know what language I spoke.

I was terrified. The path ahead was too much. Too strange, too different from my lonely shack.

I looked south. Something drew me there.

If I stayed here, what was I? A shaggy wild man waiting to die.

If I left…

Would I let fear define me? Was that the kind of man I was?

I walked south.

CHAPTER THREE

On the second day, I finished what remained of my cured meat and lived off insects and leaves. On the fourth day, I shot a rabbit and ate it raw. This being early spring, the little beast was still scrawny. A starved rabbit is a thousand times better than a plump maggot.

On the fifth day, I smelled smoke and cooking meat.

My fear returned. I wanted to run and hide. The familiar security of my shack called to me: Come home, you'll be safe. Hide here forever.

Lies and false promises. Someone broke me. I had enemies, powerful enemies. I didn't know who or where, but they were out there. I would not cower.

Nocking one of my arrows, I crept into the brush, staying low and moving slow. Each footstep taken with care. I was in no rush. If it took half a day to reach the fire unseen, that was fine. I'd done enough hunting over the years to know that stealth lay in patience. The eye often failed to track something moving slowly enough. If you were careful, willing to take your time, you could sneak up on just about anything.

The wind was with me, carrying smoke past. It would hide my scent, carrying it away from the fire.

I found a youth, straight dark hair falling past his shoulders. His skin, a pale brown, was darker than the trapper's, but much lighter than my own. He crouched by the fire, turning a spit with three impaled rabbits. These were fatter than the one I killed. I watched as grease dripped into the fire, heard it sizzling. My mouth watered at the smell. Stabbed into the earth, a spear stood at his side. A shortbow and quiver of arrows leaned against the spear. A long knife, curved and vicious, hung in a soft leather scabbard at his hip. He wore deerskin pants and no shirt. I guessed his age at twelve.

One boy. Three rabbits.

While confident I could eat all three, I doubted this youth planned to do so. There had to be others.

I waited.

The youth fussed with the fire, prodding at it and adding small twigs just to see them burn. I watched him raise a tent made of hides stretched on a wood frame. The tent was large enough for several men.

Where were they?

I took the morning to work myself around the camp. I found no footprints and no sign of anyone other than this lone youth. He seemed unconcerned, and not at all impatient. He gave no hint that he awaited the arrival of others. Did that mean he didn't expect anyone for some time?

Deciding I'd rather face this boy than a group of unknown numbers, I slung my bow over my shoulder and slipped from the trees. Hopefully he'd be friendly. Or at least not immediately murderous. Somehow, I knew he had no stone in his heart, and I had no pressing drive to kill him. I figured, however, it would be best to get close enough before he saw me so he couldn't shoot me with his bow.

I took my time approaching the boy, moving slow, examining the ground before placing each foot, all the while keeping an eye on him as he puttered about the camp. Lost in his chores, he failed to notice me.

When I stood a stride away, I said "Hello," my voice cracking.

I was ready for him to spin in surprise. I was even ready for him to go for the long knife hanging at his belt or to scream or make a mad dash for the trees. What I wasn't ready for was what happened.

The boy hurled himself at me, teeth bared in a feral snarl. He slammed into me, toppling me backward. Stumbling, I fell. He landed atop me, driving two fast and hard punches into my left eye. The pure animal savagery startled me, but I'd been an animal myself for too long not to react in kind. When he tried to hit me again I caught his arm and threw him off me. He rolled, coming back to his feet, knife drawn, and hurled himself upon me once again. He caught me as I struggled to regain my feet and we rolled, growling and snarling, in the mud, fighting for possession of the knife.

He was strong for a boy, but I had several years on him. In spite of my state of near-starvation, I was the stronger.

The fight left him as I drove the knife into his belly. Dragging the blade free, I rose to stand over him as he curled about his wound, keening like a savaged animal.

I was somehow sure it wasn't a mortal wound. If I stopped the bleeding he'd likely live. At least assuming infection didn't get him. These thoughts felt strange to me, distant.

What then? What if I bandaged his wounds?

At some point, whoever he shared this camp with would return. Would they be grateful for me stabbing, but not murdering the boy?

That seemed unlikely. I struggled to see this from their perspective, and failed. The boy attacked me; he brought this on himself.

Should I leave him here to bleed out, head for the trees? I wanted to be moving, to continue my path south. Maybe the others would return before he died. They could save him. That bothered me, the idea of leaving an enemy—even a wounded child—behind me. At the least, he'd be able to point out which direction I went.

What was I, that this made sense?

He was just a boy, not even in his teens.

Reaching down I took his hair in my fist. He whimpered in fear and pain. Pulling his head back I cut his throat. It felt no different than killing a rabbit.

Standing over the boy I had turned into a corpse, I wondered who I was. I hadn't wanted to kill him, but now that I had, I felt no regret.

"Am I a murderer?"

Was that why they killed me—whoever they were—and scattered the stone of my heart?

Kneeling by the boy, I touched the smooth skin of his chest. There was no stone in there. If I cut him open, all I'd find was the heart of a child. No compulsion moved me to split him wide.

I took his curved knife and leather scabbard. Grabbing the three spitted rabbits, I fled south into the forest like a coyote stealing a wolf's kill.

CHAPTER FOUR

I ate the first rabbit as I walked, fat dripping down my chin. I cracked its bones and sucked out the marrow, denuded them of meat and sinew, and tossed them aside. It was the best meal I'd eaten in a week.

I ate the second rabbit as the sun fell and the sounds of the night grew in volume. The third rabbit, I ate while sitting on a rock. Sated, belly full, I scraped together a pile of leaves and twigs and crawled in, burying myself. They were dry and served to both shelter me from the cool of night, and hide me from sight. The *scriiiitch scriiiiitch* of crickets filled the air and for once I wasn't using the sound to track and devour their bitter little bodies.

I woke to silence, the forest dark, the stars occluded by heavy cloud. The air tasted of rain, a dank damp.

Remaining still, I listened.

Nothing.

Squinting into the night I searched for even a hint of movement, some clue as to what silenced the crickets. There were two possibilities. Either some animal was nearby, or someone had tracked me from the camp. I realized then that I was unaccustomed to being prey. I'd walked south, thoughtless of the spoor I left behind. I'd tossed rabbit bones aside as I walked, made no attempt to hide my tracks.

If it was an animal, I might be able to startle it, scare it away. With luck, it might even be something I could kill and eat. If it was human, I needed to be a lot more careful.

Burying myself in leaves seemed clever when contemplating the night's chill. Now, however, it looked foolish. Even the slightest movement caused a loud rustling. I couldn't move without giving away my location. Though my bow lay nearby, I dared not reach for it.

A slice of something, a sliver, a shadow in the night. Details grew as it moved closer, the rounded shoulders, hunched gait of a man with a bow stalking prey. He made no sound. I saw his path would bring him within a stride of me. I could do nothing without him hearing me. I couldn't reach to ready a weapon, couldn't gather my legs under me in preparation of an attack. Even drawing breath rustled the leaves. When he got close enough, would he hear me?

Six strides away, he paused, hesitating, head moving side to side, as he listened. Lifting the bow, he drew back on an arrow. It was too dark, I couldn't tell if he aimed at me or merely near me.

I couldn't chance it.

Rolling from my hiding place, I came to my feet and charged, screaming, hoping the noise and shock would spoil his aim. An arrow hit me from behind, punching into the meat of my thigh, changing my battle-cry from a deep roar to a wail of agony. I hit him, shoved him sprawling to the dirt, and continued past. Fear drove me through the pain. I'd misjudged, there was more than one.

An arrow hissed past my ear, an evil sound. A hand-span to the right and it would have embedded itself in the back of my skull. Ducking, I ran in a staggering zig zag. If they loosed another arrow. I didn't hear it.

I stumbled through the dark for what felt like hours, falling often, cursing and crying at the pain. The arrow juddered in my leg with every step but terror kept me moving.

I considered stopping, trying to ambush whoever chased me, but I'd left the shortbow and quiver behind when I fled my sleeping place. Raw animal fear drove me on.

When I finally stumbled to a halt, I heard no signs of pursuit over my own wheezing. Light-headed, I stood shaking until I had my breath back. The forest heaved and sighed about me as the wind picked up. It sounded like the laboured inhalations of a great beast. I had this image of a colossal dragon towering over me, glaring down with wise eyes of gold and fire. It flinched away as I raised my hand toward it, and was gone, just a figment of my imagination.

A drop of icy water made it through the canopy above to land on the back of my neck and trickle down my spine. In a score of heartbeats, the *drip drip* of rain grew to a steady patter and then to a roaring deluge. The sky cracked harsh blue-white with lightning and, for an instant, I saw the forest in brutal detail. Purple after images haunted the ensuing black.

In moments I was soaked through, shivering. Though my breathing calmed, I heard nothing over the torrential downpour. In that instant of light, I saw no sign of pursuit. Had I lost them in the forest? How many were there?

Gritting my teeth, I reached back and touched the arrow still lodged in my leg. Pain staggered me to my knees and I found myself on all fours in the mud. Whimpering, I felt around the wound. I tried not to think about how dirty my hands were. Running hadn't done me any favours and it felt like a gaping chasm in my flesh. My hand came away sticky and hot and another flash of lightning showed it splashed in blood and filth.

I had to keep moving. My pursuers were out there. Leaving this arrow lodged in my leg, however, was not an option. I had to get it out and stop the bleeding before I lost consciousness. Gripping the shaft, I clenched my jaw against the pain and dragged it from my leg. The arrow came free. Too dark to see much, I felt the arrow shaft and found the blunt end of wood. Shreds of the sinew that once attached the arrowhead to the wood, hung loose. I groaned in pain. Had the arrowhead fallen in the mud, or did it remain within my leg? Was it stuck in the muscle, or lodged in bone? Praying for an illuminating bolt of lightning, I turned and squinted awkwardly at the wound in the back of my thigh. The lightning didn't cooperate and I saw only black. A wave of nausea doubled me over and I retched partially digested rabbit into the mud.

The arrowhead. I had to get it out. It would fester. I'd be dead in days if whoever hunted me didn't find me first.

Drawing the knife I took from the boy, I sat back, my ass soaked as silty rainwater swirled around me. Bone-shaking shivers rocked me and left my hands twitching. I felt like all my body's warmth leaked out the hole in my leg.

Feeling about in the dark, I found a stick and jammed it in my mouth. I bit down hard. It tasted like dirt and worms, flavours I was all too familiar with. Gripping the blade near the tip, I used it to dig about within the wound. I worked by feel, waiting for the sensation of steel on stone.

Lightning slashed the sky, tore the world a bright wound of its own, and I screamed in agony as I fumbled the blade, dropping it into the muck. Cursing the gods, the sky, and the earth below me, I fetched the knife from the dirt. Wiping it on my shirt, I returned to searching for the arrowhead.

I dug at my flesh.

The stick in my mouth crumbled, shedding rough bark, and I thought I'd chew through it. I felt the arrowhead, steel on stone! Clenching my eyes shut, useless in the dark, I levered it free, screaming past the wood. The stone plopped into the water running past me as I fell backward with relief, sighing, and spitting out the branch.

Rain fell on my face and I opened my mouth, letting it fill with water.

Time to get up, I told myself. You have to keep moving.

I couldn't. I was tired, weak from blood loss. The cold of the water faded, became a distant discomfort. After digging about in my thigh with a knife, everything felt good.

I woke, hollowed and frozen, shivering uncontrollably in the dawn light. To the east the clouds shone red, lit by the rising sun.

"Red sky in morning," I said. I couldn't remember the rest.

The sky above, free of clouds and making that imperceptible transition from the black of night to the blue of day, promised warmth. The wound had crusted closed, the damp cotton of my pants having dried over it like a filthy bandage. Clambering to my feet pulled the material from the wound, and blood ran.

What were the chances I got the entire arrowhead free? What were the odds some threads of cotton or clods of dirt remained in the wound?

I was a dead man. Infection would kill me.

An owl hooted to the north, and then another further to the east. I realized infection might not get the chance to end me. Those were no owls.

Setting off into the trees, I set the fastest pace I was capable of. My leg ached, numb and leaden, and I limped badly, falling often.

The owls followed, their calls growing ever closer.

Glancing behind me I saw the scuffed trail of a wounded man stumbling through the bush. It wasn't subtle. A blind child could follow me.

Dying of infection or no, I didn't want to take another arrow. I pushed myself faster.

Some part of me woke to the realization that these were likely the parents of the boy I killed. If they caught me, my death would be neither pleasant nor quick. Again, I wondered at myself, at my casual murder of a child.

Never leave an enemy behind you. How could such obvious wisdom be wrong? It felt like an ancient lesson learned the hard way.

I pushed myself faster, sobbing at the pain, opening the wound and leaving a trail of blood as if the marks of my passing weren't already easy enough to follow.

One of the owls hooted, its call so close I spun, expecting to see someone. I was alone in the forest. Instead of an answering owl call, a man screamed, a wet tearing gurgle cut short. I froze in indecision. That lone owl hooted again.

Nothing answered.

Again, a plaintive hoot.

Listening, I heard nothing, the unnatural quiet of the forest. That decided me. Praying the scream came from one of my hunters, I set off toward the sound. Hopefully whatever killed him wasn't still there and I could loot the body for weapons. If whoever it was had a bow, maybe I could even kill the one still tracking me.

I found where my pursuer died, the dirt scuffed and kicked by a brief struggle. Sprayed blood spattered leaves for several strides and the gory trail in the dirt said his corpse had been dragged away. His weapons must have been taken along with him. I found nothing.

The taint of rot tickled my nose. I'd seen wolves and predators roll on the corpses of their victims to disguise their scent, and whatever this beast rolled on had been ripe indeed.

The other parent would come to investigate.

I scrambled up the nearest large tree and settled in to wait. If they saw me, I'd be an easy target. Hopefully they'd be more focussed on the ground and finding their friend.

I didn't have to wait long before a woman slipped from the trees. She wore skins like the boy, a shortbow held ready with an arrow nocked. She prowled like an animal, making no sound and leaving no track. Straight black hair hung to her waist. I couldn't begin to guess her age.

Her path would bring her near enough. I could drop on her with a bit of a leap. I didn't relish the prospect of landing with my leg in this condition, but anything was better than suffering another arrow wound. I watched her slow, studying the trail left by whatever dragged her partner away. She tested the air, sniffing. Turning, she raised her head and I knew she'd see me.

I jumped, and the shortbow came up, the arrow drawn, her eyes widening in surprise even as she acted to kill me. Crashing into her, I sent us both slamming to the dirt. We scuffled, punching and clawing, and she rolled away, coming to her feet, long knife drawn. I rose more slowly, groaning, and drawing the knife I took from the boy. She recognized it and a look of purest hatred, utter animal rage, crossed her features. She bared teeth, spitting strange words I couldn't understand.

The shortbow lay shattered between us. I'd broken it when I landed on her. The arrows with their evil sharpened flint heads lay scattered in the dirt, having spilled from the quiver.

We circled each other, measuring, but also alert in case whatever took her partner returned. The forest remained eerily silent, our breathing, her staccato spat hate, the only sounds. What could kill an armed man and drag him away so quickly? Why had it taken him instead of eating him right then and there? It was like the creature had fled, though I couldn't imagine whatever it was had much to fear from me.

The woman stepped close, stabbing at me, and when I lashed out with my own knife she ducked under my swing and kicked my wounded leg out from under me. I screamed, rolling away, my movement taking me over the littered arrows. I collected one in my left hand, keeping it concealed behind my forearm as I rose.

She followed, calm as death, eyes like a raptor. Her rage promised a slow demise. She wanted to hurt me before she killed me.

Because I hurt her. I saw it now. The boy was her son, I knew it to be true. I'd killed her child, and now she was going to dissect me.

"I'm sorry," I said. "I couldn't leave him behind."

She showed no hint of understanding my words.

It didn't matter. It was a shit apology anyway.

That razor-sharp knife snaked out, opening a long cut across my ribs, steel on bone. Instead of retreating, I lashed back with my own knife and once again she easily avoided it, swaying back and then leaping forward to leave a line of hot fire across my arm as she cut me again. My knife fell away, spinning to the dirt. But she hadn't seen the arrow clenched in the other fist, hidden from sight. I stabbed her in the throat, driving the arrow deep. Eyes wide, she gurgled and sputtered, pulling away. I held on to the shaft and the arrow came free, leaving that shard of flint in her. Blood fountained from the hole.

I stood watching, detached and distant, as she fought to stanch the bleeding. She collapsed to her knees, bloody teeth bared in a snarl of hatred as she realized she wouldn't get to kill me.

"You already killed me," I told her. "Infection will end me soon enough."

It was, apparently, no consolation.

She spat harsh consonants, mouth frothing red, and then fell to her side.

I watched until she stopped moving.

Then I collected her knife, and the one I dropped. I had no doubt infection would kill me. Until then, I would walk south.

Something there called me.

I had to move.

CHAPTER FIVE

My wounds healed quickly and I felt better with each passing day. No fever tortured me and somehow, miraculously, infection never set in. Whether this was luck or because of who—or what—I was, I had no idea.

I left behind the ancient arboreal dark of the old forest and found myself in newer, younger growth. The sun rose and fell, cycles of light and dark, warmth and cold. The land around me sank and flattened. Walking from the trees I found myself looking down over sprawling farmlands. Rolling hills, gentle like the curves of a young woman, her hair and eyes in dark contrast to pale skin so unlike the ebony of my own, lips quirked in a knowing half-smile. I blinked and lost the thought.

Who was she? Someone I once knew? A lover? Or was this nothing more than the lonely yearning of a man who'd only met four people in living memory and killed every single one of them? She felt too detailed, too real, to be imaginary. I wanted more, but she was gone.

Much as I would have preferred to avoid humanity, these lands had been well-hunted and I hadn't eaten anything beyond bugs and leaves in days. Desperate hunger drove me to the first farmhouse I saw. Banging on the door, I backed away, hands held clear of my weapons. A man opened the door, his wife and child peering at me from behind him. All three were pale and pink, hair so blond as to be almost white. I mimed eating and he waved me away, scowling. I turned to leave.

"Oh, for fuck's sake," said his wife. "Feed the boy."

Boy? That stopped me. She was right. I knew I couldn't be more than nineteen years old, physically, but felt infinitely more ancient. I waited.

"He looks dangerous," said the farmer.

"He looks hungry."

She ducked inside, returning moments later with a loaf of bread and a cup of fresh water. Pushing past her grumbling husband, she approached.

"Your family are trackers in the north?" she asked, noting my tattered attire.

I nodded.

"Damned ebony souls," muttered her husband. He fell quiet when she shot him an angry look.

"You're alone," she continued. "No wagon loaded with furs. You've had a rough go of it."

"Yes, Ma'am," I said, voice raw.

"Strange accent," she said. "You're from the islands?"

Was I? I nodded again, not knowing how to answer.

She watched, hands on hips, head to one side as I wolfed down the bread and drank the water. A solid woman, I wasn't at all sure I could best her in a fair fight. She showed no hint of fear. When I finished the last crumb, she sent her grumbling husband back inside to fetch more food. He refused to look at me, refused to meet my eye. She sent me off with another loaf of bread, a brick of white cheese, and a half dozen carrots.

I cried as I walked, undone by her charity.

The next day I found a well-trod dirt path and followed it south. Around noon, I saw the town. Standing atop a shallow hill, I looked down upon a walled community of no more than a thousand souls. The town had grown beyond the confines of the original wall and houses littered the landscape. A lone stone tower stood within the wall. It wasn't a defensible position, had no crenellations. Four stories of moss-covered field stones, it didn't even have windows. A single door of black iron the only entrance, it looked ancient.

I hated that tower, wanted to topple it, to break it to nothing. I wanted to melt the stones to slag.

I wanted to hide from whatever lurked within. I had no idea why.

Forcing myself forward, I descended into the town. The gates set into the wall sat open. Rusting, flaking and overgrown, they looked like they hadn't moved in centuries. In town, I found the people pink-skinned and fair-haired like the farmer and his family. My black skin and long tangle of midnight hair stood out and they stared as I walked the street, crossing to avoid me. No doubt the fact I hadn't bathed in a year and my ill-fitting tracker's clothing, crumbled and falling apart, did me no favours. Armed as I was, hatchet in its loop, a curved long-knife hanging at each hip, I doubt I looked like the kind of person you'd invite to a diplomatic feast.

I stopped in the street. Diplomatic feast? The thought slid away before I could grasp it.

'Darker,' I heard someone call me. Others whispered 'black soul,' or 'stained.'

Did they think my skin colour the result of some dye?

Homes of wood and stone towered over me, some even with a second story. My mud shack suddenly felt pathetic and small, embarrassing in its crudity. And people. So many people. Dozens walked the street, shopping or going about strange and unknown tasks. I felt their gazes, their loathing, saw it in the way their lips curled in disgust, the way they pointed when they thought I wasn't looking.

Trying to ignore them, I continued into town.

A caravan of a dozen wagons lined the main street. Men and women bustled about, loading supplies. Several of the wagons already bore burdens of baled wheat and other assorted grains. Seeing as there was nothing north, it seemed a safe assumption they'd travel south.

It would be a lot safer travelling in a crowd.

I followed the bellowing of the loudest, deepest voice to its source, a fat, balding man standing atop the grain bails piled onto the lead wagon. People rushed about, flinching when he turned his voice upon them.

Standing beneath him, I craned my neck to shout up at him. Not sure what was normal, I settled on a blunt approach.

"I seek employment!"

I had to yell a second time before he heard me over his own booming voice. The fat man scowled down at me, running a hand over the bright pink dome of his head.

"Where you from, boy?" he called.

I gestured north.

"Before that."

I shrugged.

"Secrets, eh? Fine." Eyes narrowed, he squinted at me. "Those knives. Show me one."

I drew a curved long-knife from its scabbard and held it up.

"Where you get that?"

I considered lying, but didn't know enough about anything. "I took them from the people who tried to kill me."

"You killed two Septks?"

I nodded, deciding not to mention that one was a child.

"You and how many others?"

"Just me."

He eyed me. "Don't recognize that accent."

I shrugged, sheathing the knife.

"You're a long way from home, I think. And that means you're running from something."

I waited.

"Help load the wagons, and I'll buy you dinner and a pint of beer."

"Two pints," I said, the words escaping without thought.

"Fine."

"And I want to go south with you."

"I already have enough guards."

"Not if I kill a few."

He laughed, a loud, belly-shaking guffaw. "Fine. I pay three bronze a day. If you get drunk while we're on the road, I'll leave you there, alone."

Was that supposed to be a threat? I'd always been alone. "Fair enough."

"Then get to work," he said, turning to scream orders at someone else.

I spent the rest of the day loading the last wagons. True to his word, the caravan master—Paulak, he said his name was—bought me dinner and two pints. A leg of lamb and a mountain of mashed potatoes swimming in gravy, the meal dwarfed even the memory of the cooked rabbits. The beer, dark as mud, tasted of burnt oats and left my head swimming.

Paulak sat across from me, waiting until I finished before speaking. "You were hungry."

I belched, sitting back and resting a hand on my belly. "I haven't eaten anything but bugs and roots in a week."

Sipping from his own pint, he eyed me over the rim of the clay mug. "Whatever you were hiding from up there won't be a problem for me, right?"

I shook my head. "My problems are long dead." I wasn't sure if I lied.

"You don't look old enough to have 'long dead' problems."

I shrugged. "No one is looking for me, if that's what you're worried about."

"Good. You getting a room?"

I laughed.

"That's what I thought. Sleep on one of the wagons."

That night I dreamed of flames. A hundred thousand warships, red and white alike, burned. Wreckage clogged the ocean. Floating corpses. Burnt men clinging to the shattered remains of ships. Screams of agony, lonely and forlorn. The elementalists dead and broken, the ocean turned to vent its anger elsewhere. No waves slapped the hulls of those few vessels yet to sink.

This was the death of a dream, the death of an empire.

The corpses of colossal creatures, called from the deep by shamans, floated alongside the blasted remains of slain demons. Sharks and all manner of sea monsters fed on their flesh.

My own vessel, the Habnikaav, was surrounded by white ships populated by ancient men and women in white robes.

They thought they had me.

They thought they'd won.

I laughed. This was not the only battle.

Calling upon my demons, I left my enemies to their hollow victory.

The morning sun found me awake and waiting for the others to rise. Men and women trickled out of the inn and nearby homes, or crawled from under other wagons, stretching and groaning. A big woman, face flushed and pink, bustled about with a tray, bringing strips of dried meat to everyone. It was chewy and salty, but left me sated.

Selecting the wagon at the rear of the train, I clambered aboard to discover a blond woman already sitting up there. She wore armour of boiled leather, a hard vest and skirt, which hung past her knees. A sheathed sword lay in the hay at her side. Her hair was cropped short and brutal. She examined me with pale blue eyes. I guessed she was in her early twenties.

"May I join you?" I asked.

Scratching at her chin with blunt fingernails, she finally shrugged.

I sat a few strides away so as not to bother her. Down below, the teamsters were busy tethering teams of four oxen to each wagon.

"You done this route before?" the blond woman asked.

I glanced at her. Though armour concealed everything, my imagination immediately went to work trying to figure out what might be beneath. It was so strange, to feel so ancient and yet, in truth, be so young. It didn't hurt that she was easily the prettiest girl I'd seen since leaving my hut. Not that she had much competition.

"I don't think so," I said.

She laughed, but I wasn't sure at what. "I'm Shalayn." She offered a hand and I crawled closer to shake it.

"Khraen," I said.

We sat in silence for several minutes before the wagons lurched into motion.

"Where are we going?" I asked.

"You signed on to a caravan without even asking the destination?"

"I want to be south," I said. "Beyond that, I don't much care." It was a small lie.

"We're going to Taramlae."

"Is it big?"

"It's the capital."

"Of?"

She stared at me now, eyes incredulous. "What do you mean?"

"What is it the capital of? Some kingdom? A duchy?"

"Everything," said Shalayn. "It's the capital of everything."

"It can't be. The world…" I wasn't sure what I wanted to say. I knew nothing.

"You grew up in the far north, didn't you? And no one taught you anything of the rest of the world? Your parents told you nothing?"

"They're long dead," I said, remaining carefully vague.

"That's a strange accent. Where were your folks from?"

Ignoring the question, I asked, "Taramlae is the capital of the world?" The thought twisted something in my gut.

"The Guild rules from Taramlae."

"Guild?"

"Now I know you're messing with me."

"My education has been sadly lacking." I shrugged, helpless. "And I've been in the far north, tracking."

"For the last three thousand years?"

I didn't know. How long was I buried?

Guild. I hated that word, but didn't know why. "What guild?" I asked again.

"The Wizard's Guild."

Wizards.

My head hurt. Rage pounded through my veins. Only when Shalayn reached for her sword did I realize I'd bared my teeth in a savage snarl. Closing my eyes, I breathed deep, calming myself.

"Sorry," I said. "I think I don't like wizards."

"No one likes wizards," she said. "Even when they're family."

I opened my eyes to see pain in hers. The wizards had somehow hurt her too. This, I saw, was a fresh wound. She blinked away tears.

To change the subject, I pointed at the windowless tower as we rumbled past. "What's that?"

"Really?" she asked, eyeing me.

"Yes."

"It's a wizard's tower."

I wanted to tear it down with my bare hands.

CHAPTER SIX

We spent the day riding the wagon. After weeks of walking, sitting on baled hay as the world passed beneath me was the highest luxury. Once the town disappeared behind us, I realized we were still very much in wild country. A crude dirt path, little more than rutted wagon tracks, wended south through thick forest. Trees crowded our route, hanging over us like looming wraiths. Even with the sun high, the woods remained dark, the heavy growth blotting the sky. Things moved in there, inhuman shapes, following us.

The guards stayed sharp, eyes on the trees at all times.

"That was a frontier settlement," I said, speaking to myself.

"Chorn," said Shalayn. "It's the northern-most settlement."

Remembering the ancient wizard's tower, and the homes spilling past the dubious protection of the wall, I said, "But it's old."

"Everything is."

"How can a frontier remain the frontier for that long?"

"The Septks rule everything north of Chorn. Only the mad and desperate enter their lands."

"Which are you?" I blurted. There didn't seem to be much for anyone who didn't live there.

"A little mad, a little desperate." She stared off into the dark of the forest. "I came north with another caravan."

Of all the people in Chorn, all the other men and women hired on with this caravan, only Shalayn didn't seem to notice my skin. Only Shalayn looked at me like I was human, a man, and not some foul stain.

That evening the caravan rumbled into a clearing. The trees had been hacked back to create room enough to form a circle with the wagons. The oxen were freed from their harnesses and brought to the centre of the ring. Fires were lit and a fat man bustled about preparing a huge pot of soup. Paulak wandered the camp barking orders and assigning everyone their watch duties. Anyone caught sleeping on their shift, he said, would walk home alone. With the caliginous woods hiding whatever followed us all day, no one wanted to chance that. People went about their chores, darting glances at the treeline whenever something moved in the deep dark.

He assigned Shalayn and I to the same watch. I think the wagon master fancied himself something of a match-maker. I caught a poorly hidden wink tossed in Shalayn's direction. She blushed pink and punched him in the shoulder. The blow, so fast that neither Paulak nor I saw it coming, sent him staggering. He laughed and wandered away, rubbing his arm and wincing.

"You two know each other?" I asked.

"I've done this route a few times."

The men and women on the other wagons shot hostile looks in our direction. They didn't like that we stood together, that I talked with her.

Shalayn either didn't notice, or didn't care. Maybe both.

The sun dropped, lighting the clouds from below and washing the horizon in a gorgeous swirl of orange, purple, and red. A brisk wind blew down from the north. It stank of rot.

When Shalayn saw me huddled against the cold, she dug into her pack and tossed me a heavy cotton shirt. It smelled of woman, something I had not scented in living memory.

"I'll wash it before I return it," I promised, knowing how filthy I was and how bad I must smell. "And thank you."

She shrugged. "Don't want you freezing to death and leaving me to do the watch alone."

The next two hours passed in silence. When our replacements found us—two rough looking men with pale skin, shocks of bright yellow hair, and leather armour—Shalayn suggested we retire to one of the fires. The men watched us leave, lips curled in distaste.

"Why don't they like me?" I asked, once we were out of earshot.

"Ignore them."

We sat at the fire the two men had left. Paulak came around with bowls of warm soup, a broth with chunks of vegetable matter and chewy goat. I devoured it like a dog terrified someone might take it.

Shalayn watched. When I finished, she held out her bowl. "Here."

"Thank you," I said. "But I'm fine."

"Eat it. You look like a starved rat."

I nodded acceptance and finished her soup.

Paulak came around to collect the bowls. Seeing both in front of me, he grinned at Shalayn. "You softy," he said, staying out of punching distance.

She bared white teeth at him and he wandered away, laughing to himself.

Sated, I curled up by the fire and slept. For a while I was dimly aware of Shalayn singing, a soft, throaty tune of incomprehensible syllables, heavy with mourning. The song was loss and regret, too deep for words.

We rode south for days, the caravan moving at a slow but steady pace, oak wheels rumbling on the earth when it was hard and squelching through muck when it wasn't. Stops were made each day to feed and water the oxen, and let the caravan guards stretch their legs and relieve themselves. Whatever was in the trees followed us, lurking in the shadows. When someone went to piss, they never went alone, and never beyond sight of the wagons.

There was, I learned, something of a pecking order among the guards. Those at the top rode the front wagons, breathing fresh air and enjoying the view. Those at the bottom rode at the back, breathing road dust and enjoying the stench of ox dung. The beasts shat constantly as they walked. Shalayn and I rode the last wagon. Paulak didn't assign it to us, but the other guards made it clear we wouldn't be welcome elsewhere.

In the evening I set my sleeping roll—Shalayn gave me one of hers when she realized I didn't have my own—away from the others. While none of the light or heat from the fire reached me, I was tired of being stared at, tired of the whispered hate.

Darker.

Ebony soul.

Stained heart.

The last made me smile. If they knew the truth, they'd either run screaming or kill me. The way they watched through slitted eyes made me wonder if they planned that anyway.

Shalayn wandered over and set her sleeping roll near mine. A minute later she was fast asleep and snoring quietly.

It wasn't until the third day that I realized I'd misread the situation. Shalayn they were fine with. It was me no one wanted on their wagon.

She sat with me out of choice. Or maybe pity. While grateful for the company, anger built in me. This was wrong. I was no one's dog.

Shalayn acted like it was nothing, like she was unaware of the slight, didn't notice the way the others stared at us.

On the fourth day, we rode together in silence. I'd asked about her family, and she'd become quiet. Unsure what I said wrong, I watched the trees and the shapes moving within. While whatever followed us made no attempt to impede our slow progress, it also hadn't given up.

"Is it always like this?" I asked.

"Stupid people fear the different," she answered. "Ignore them."

"I meant things in the trees."

"Oh. Sorry. No, I've never seen anything like this. I've been on caravans attacked by Septks before, but whatever is in there isn't human."

"Monsters?"

She shrugged. "Whatever it is doesn't want to be seen. Whenever someone heads towards the trees, it fades away."

"So, it's intelligent?"

"The little forest dragons can be pretty smart, but they don't travel in packs."

For an instant I saw a dragon, colossal wings stretched wide, spewing great twisting sheets of blue flame as it flew low over a gathered host of grey-skinned giants. I blinked and the vision vanished.

"When we stopped for lunch," continued Shalayn, "I went to the edge to do my business. It stank like rotting meat."

I considered several jokes but kept them to myself.

"Really?" she said. "Nothing? I drop a line like that and you just sit there staring at me?" She shook her head in disgust. "Whatever is in there, let's hope it stays there."

That night, I once again set my sleeping roll away from the fire. Without a word, Shalayn set hers up beside me. For an hour she told stories of various caravan routes she'd worked. Most were up here in the north, but occasionally she did the southern routes, guarding wagons hauling goods north from the coast. She talked about fighting Septks, finding her fellow guards skinned alive and partially eaten. She once saw the site of an ancient battlefield, the earth ravaged and bent like it had been liquefied and then turned to stone. The corpses of giants and dragons and all manner of strange creatures were trapped in there, sheathed in rock, forever frozen in their moment of torment. She spoke of boulders the size of castles wandering the foothills of the Deredi Mountains, awakened thousands of years ago by elementalists, and now unable to find peace.

I woke with a hand clamped over my mouth and a figure kneeling at my side. For an instant I thought I'd been stabbed before I realized I'd fallen asleep against a cold rock.

"Quiet," breathed Shalayn. She removed her hand. "There's something in camp."

Some*thing*, not some*one*?

Still kneeling, she drew her sword, steel sliding from scabbard like a lover's sigh.

I wanted a sword. I wanted *my* sword.

My sword?

Rolling over, I pushed myself into a crouch.

Clouds must have scudded in during the night. The moon and stars were gone, the sky an impenetrable dome of black. The campfire had been allowed to dwindle down to dull, throbbing embers. No doubt Paulak would be yelling at someone come morning.

Something moved in the dark, low and menacing. I squinted, but lost the shape. "Wild dogs?" I whispered. "Wolves?"

"I don't think so," Shalayn hissed back, eyes scouring the night. "Too many people. Watch my back." She rose. "Stay close."

Drawing my hatchet, I nodded. Another shape slunk past, a sinuous shadow in a world of night. I caught the brief glint of firelight reflected in predator eyes, and a foul stench washed over us.

"That smells like—"

"Death," said Shalayn. "Bad. Very bad." Her head swivelled, pale eyes searching.

Rotting meat. Liquefying brains and decaying fur. A miasma of gut-churning putrescence enveloped us.

"We have to get to the fire," whispered Shalayn, "build it up. Follow."

She moved like a stalking cat, coiled muscle, low and deadly, balance perfect, weight centred. I felt like a lumbering oaf in comparison.

Something leapt out of the dark, long and lean. It looked like a mountain lion and stank like the grave. Shalayn rolled under it, slashing with her sword, as it passed above her. Guts spilled and the stench got worse. The cat disappeared into the night, its organs trailing along behind. Other than guts dragging in dirt, it never made a sound.

Shalayn swore, something in a language I didn't understand. The meaning was clear enough. "Necromancer," she said, again moving. "Somewhere, out there in the dark, is a damned necromancer."

A scream shredded the night air, a pure note of terror and agony. The wail choked to silence with the wet crunch of bone.

Movement, all around. The fire, only twenty paces away, seemed unreachably distant. The north wind gusted and flames danced, turning everything into a menacing nightmare. Every stunted tree was the corpse of a hunting cat. Every rock was a crouched wolf, ready to pounce.

"We have to kill the necromancer," I said. "To end the spell."

Would that work? I wasn't at all sure.

Even in the dark I saw Shalayn's look of incredulous disbelief. "Are you insane? At the fire, we can hold them off; we can see them coming."

Something slunk past, the reek of death wafting in its steps.

"Follow!" she commanded, setting off.

For a moment I stared at her retreating shape, anger flashing through me. No one ordered *me* around!

An ear-splitting roar rent the air, guttural and deep. It shook me to my bones. I knew that sound. Anyone who lived in a shack of mud and sticks had quaked in fear at that sound.

Grizzly bear.

No. Undead grizzly bear.

I watched Shalayn head for the fire. Against a pack of undead wolves and a mountain lion, perhaps we stood a chance. Maybe enough of their old lives remained, they'd avoid the flames. I had doubts. If it came to a fight, maybe we could immobilize them, break their legs. Even that seemed a weak hope.

But an undead grizzly bear? It would smash us, tear us apart. Our knives and swords would be useless.

Turning, I ran into the dark.

This was a terrible plan. A stupid plan. It wasn't a damned plan at all. It was suicide.

Putting more distance between myself and the fire, I crouched low, knife and hatchet ready for violence. To preserve my night vision, I faced away from the light. Another man screamed and I heard the grunting and swearing of pitched battle, steel on flesh and bone. I hoped Shalayn was safe.

The dark beckoned. Escape. Leave the camp behind. Abandon Shalayn and Paulak, and the men and women who loathed me. Head south. Run.

I couldn't imagine this necromancer had any interest in me. Most likely he was after the goods on the caravan. One man running away was one man he wouldn't have to worry about.

Shalayn. I didn't know her, not really. I owed her nothing.

That wasn't quite true. She gave me a shirt and a sleeping roll, shared food. She showed kindness. So had Paulak.

I hesitated.

Shalayn would be at the fire by now. I heard her calling out to me. There were others there too. They'd die. They'd all die.

I remembered stumbling upon a pack of timber wolves while checking my traps. They were dead, broken and bloody, scattered across the snow. Claw marks ripped them to the bone. I saw the tracks. They'd been desperate, starving, and attacked a grizzly.

The bear Shalayn faced was dead. It felt no pain, knew no fear. Wounds wouldn't slow it unless you broke bones. She was going to die here.

"I don't know you," I whispered, unsure if I meant me or her.

I took a step into the dark.

Run away.

Save yourself.

Who was I? The kind of person who thought only of themselves? The kind of person who abandoned those in need?

I realized I'd asked the wrong question. Why let my unknown past define me?

It wasn't, 'Who was I?' but rather, 'Who *am* I?'

And still, I hesitated.

CHAPTER SEVEN

The wolves decided me.

Not the ones here, dead and lurking in the dark, prowling just beyond the desperate light of the fire. It was those wolves I found in the snow, shattered and bloody, bodies riven. Life torn from them by dagger-like claws.

Imagining Shalayn like that kicked me into motion.

I crept through the night, relying more on my hearing than sight. My black skin would hide me, unlike these pale people who stood out like beacons in the dark. Those skills I'd learned hunting from my mud shack would serve well. Move slow. Stop. Listen.

A living animal might catch my scent, depending on the wind, but I suspected these dead creatures lived in a world of muted senses. If they felt no pain, what were the chances they could taste or smell? Slim, I hoped.

I moved, careful with the placement of each foot, bringing it down slowly, lest there be a twig to snap or a rock to twist my ankle. I stopped often, listening, doing my best to filter out the sounds of those by the fire. If I rushed to their aid, we'd all die.

I had to find the necromancer.

Why was I so sure his magic would end when I killed him? The thought paralysed me for a moment. I knew nothing of necromancy! What if I killed him, and the undead creatures remained? Would they continue following his last command, or would they revert to more animal behaviour and flee?

I pushed my fear away. Doubt achieved nothing. Fear achieved nothing.

Only violence.

The reek of death grew stronger and I followed it.

I heard muttering in the inky black. The voice, soft and gentle, was higher pitched than I expected. Feminine. A sliver of moon breached the clouds and I saw the outline of a petite woman, slim, shoulders hunched. Black hair, tangled and greasy, hung to her waist, concealing her face.

Not a man after all. I don't know why I'd expected one. It didn't matter. I had her.

The all-pervading stench of rot filled me, became my world. Death surrounded me, polluted everything. For an insane instant, I had this thought: I'd have to apologize to Shalayn for the smell of her shirt when I returned it. No way my clothes could ever not stink. I tasted decay, it filled my lungs with every breath.

Creeping closer, I paused, alert. This necromancer would have something nearby, something protecting her.

A sound. Guts dragging in dirt.

I dropped, rolling away as the mountain lion passed above. Its spilled organs slapped across me, wet and bloody. The blade of my hatchet caught in a loop of intestine and was yanked from my hand. I thought I'd escaped, unharmed. Then, agony lit my back. It felt like I'd been opened to the spine, cool night air on bone.

Move. Keep moving. I would not become the next victim of this necromancer. The thought of existing in service to another—being a slave—terrified and enraged me. That would not be my fate!

Driven by fear, I rushed the necromancer. She glanced up as I tackled her and I caught a glimpse of ashen features, delicate and porcelain pale, black eyes rimmed in shadow. She was beautiful, heartbreakingly vulnerable.

I crashed into her, smashing her to the dirt. She hissed and clawed, fingernails raking my face. I punched her, snapping her head hard to the side. She fought with wild strength, bucking and kicking. I hit her again, and it felt like I was beating a side of raw beef. My hand ached.

Her eyes locked on my face and widened. She went limp, staring up at me. Beautiful eyes, calm, and unafraid.

"Call off your creatures," I said. "Or I'll kill you."

She laughed. With her free hand she pulled open the wretched ruin of her black robes to expose pale, perfect breasts. And the jagged wound between them, stapled closed with twists of rusting wire. I saw white bone where our struggles had opened her.

"The dead fear no death," she said.

Remembering my knives, I drew one and held it aloft. "Do they fear being hacked to pieces and scattered about the land?" The threat bothered me, struck too close to home.

She examined me. Under all that filth, beneath the stench of death, she was gorgeous. She reminded me of someone, but I couldn't find the memory.

"Yes," she said, eyes flinching away, showing fear for the first time.

Her vulnerability stabbed me.

"If I hear one of your beasts come at me, I'll take your head off." I had no idea if I was capable of such a blow, but prayed she didn't either.

The night fell silent. All sounds of battle faded to nothing. What the hell was I going to do now?

Hell? A thought for later, I decided.

Facing her from my position atop this dead girl, seeing terror in those dark eyes, robes still open exposing her, my plan suddenly felt foul.

"You're dead," I said, struggling to formulate a new plan. I knew nothing.

"Yes."

"Are all necromancers dead?"

She stared at me until I lifted the knife in threat.

"Yes. It's part of the ceremony that creates us. Our master cuts our heart out during the casting of the creation spell."

I glanced at the scar on her chest, eyes lingering. "Your heart?"

She shrugged one shoulder. "My master has it. A means of control. As long as he has it in his possession, he can command me." She looked up at me, dark eyes terrified. "I am his slave."

She was like me, her heart stolen. I couldn't wrap my head around this moment, the similarities in our situations. Nothing made sense. "Why did you attack us? Do you sell the goods?"

"Yes." She hesitated.

"And?"

She hid her face behind a pale hand, struggling to turn away. I held her trapped, easily overpowering her slight frame. Broken bone showed through the torn flesh where one of her fingers had snapped.

"And?" I said again.

"I'm so alone," she said in a small voice. "For so long, alone." But there was still some hesitation.

"Tell me the truth," I demanded, pulling her hand away.

Sagging beneath me, she met my gaze with purest heart-rending misery. "I can't go into town. I can't buy supplies. I can't…" She closed her eyes.

I thought I understood. This lonely girl craved companionship, but no doubt the locals knew her. They probably hunted her, hoping to destroy this fragile beauty. Beyond that, she needed someone who could venture into the nearest town to purchase whatever supplies she required. She needed someone she could trust, someone who wouldn't betray her.

No. Someone who *couldn't* betray her. An important distinction, and one I understood on a deep, primal level.

Had I been like that, distrusting and desperate for control, in my relationships?

"If I let you up," I said, "if I let you have one of the dead…" Gorgeous eyes lit with desperate hope. "You can use him to get whatever you need from town?"

She nodded, just the tiniest movement. "If the wizards find me they'll burn me to ash."

Wizards. A knot of anger built in me. Anything they hated was something I wanted to preserve.

She studied me, gaze roving about my face like she sought to memorize every line and detail. "Better to hide," she whispered.

"You can't have these people," I said, nodding at the survivors surrounding the fire.

She looked away, staring off to the side. So young. She looked no older than I. Or at least no older than I looked. She couldn't have been more than nineteen when someone cut her heart out. I felt something for her, an affinity. I couldn't end her unlife. Of all the people in the world, this dead girl might understand me.

"If I get off you, will your creatures attack?"

She looked at me. I saw no hope in her eyes, just an eternity of emptiness. How long had she been dead? Who would do this to a girl? Why? What had the necromancer who created her hoped to achieve?

"No," she said.

I rolled off her and stood, shoulders hunched, waiting to die.

Nothing happened. I heard the voices of those gathered around the fire. Shalayn called out to me.

"You can have those who are already dead," I said, deciding. "Take them and leave."

Midnight eyes, bright and unblinking, stared up at me. She seemed unaware that her robes remained open.

"I am evil," she whispered. "Damned." She pushed herself into a sitting position, one shoulder slumped and low. "You should hate me. Loathe me." She looked away again, glancing toward the fire, eyes narrowing. "You should fear me."

I didn't. I couldn't. I saw something of myself in this broken soul.

"Don't attack caravans," I said. "Too many people. Too dangerous. There are homesteads with small families. Much safer." I thought about the woman who fed me, and hated myself. Why did I care more about this dead girl than those simple souls living out here on the frontier?

Simple souls? Why did I belittle their existence? What was I, that I thought myself above them?

With a start I realized I had none of the loathing for necromancers that I bore for wizards. Necromancers paid a high price for their power. For some reason that mattered. It made a difference.

I offered her a hand. When she took it, I pulled her to her feet. Her skin was cold, damp. She stood close to me. I had a head of height on her.

BLACK STONE HEART

Pulling her robes closed I said, "You have to take better care of yourself. You might not feel pain, but you have to learn to avoid danger. Don't break so many bones." I gestured at her mangled hand. "How did you do that?"

"My wolves and I were hunting the mountain lion. It got past them and attacked me."

"Always keep at least two at your side. Had you done that, I never could have taken you down."

A grin flashed across her pale features. "I'm glad you did." She licked her lips, not moving away, staring up at me. "Who are you?" she asked. "Why help me?"

"I'm Khraen. And…I don't know. You and I are, somehow, the same." It wasn't quite true. I had this inkling, the beginning of an idea tickling at the back of my thoughts, that a necromancer would be useful.

"I'm Henka." She hugged me, wrapping her arms around my waist and burying her face in my chest. Corpse cold, she held me like we were old friends, lovers long separated, moulding herself to me.

Flustered, I waited until she let go.

"Sorry," she said, retreating, hurt crumpling her features.

Feelings I didn't understand scattered my thoughts, hints of memories of a girl with dark hair and white skin. Those eyes.

"Some of those you killed tonight have armour," I said. "Wear it." I choked down a surge of emotion, anger that this girl had to live like this. "I have something I must do, but after, I will return. I will find you. Please stay alive—" I laughed. "You know what I mean. Still *exist* when I return."

She tilted her head, examining me. "Why?"

"We're going to find the bastard who did this to you. We're going to get your heart back." I felt like a fool making such a rash promise to this girl I didn't know, but I meant it.

"I'll see you again" she said. "You'll come back to me. I know you will." Her eyes held no trace of doubt.

I left her, limped to the campfire and the caravan guards huddled there. One of them almost shot me with a bow, but I called out. The wounds in my back burned.

"What happened?" asked Shalayn, as I warmed my hands at the fire.

I didn't want to talk about it. These people lost friends here. They'd never understand why I let Henka go. And, as they so clearly hated me, I felt no compunction to explain my choices.

"I found the necromancer," I answered.

"Are we safe?" asked Paulak, who miraculously survived unscathed.

I nodded. "She's dead." It wasn't a lie, though I knew they'd misunderstand.

Shalayn put a hand on my shoulder. After Henka's cold embrace, she was warm with life. "She?"

"Just a girl."

"Are you alright?"

Again, I nodded.

"Your back!" she said when I shifted, wincing.

Grabbing a water skin, she cleaned my wounds as we talked.

"Turn your back to the fire," she said, "so I can see what I'm doing."

"It's not that bad, looks worse than it is." I didn't want them seeing what the necromancer's creature did to me. Having survived an arrow in the leg and what should have been guaranteed infection, I was strangely unworried about this. But if they saw clearly the extent of my wounds, there'd be questions.

"You can keep the shirt," Shalayn said. It was torn and filthy, splashed with blood, stinking of rot.

"Thanks."

"Should we bury her?" asked Paulak. "Or burn the corpse to make sure she doesn't come back?"

"No. Too dangerous." I prayed I hadn't made a colossally stupid mistake by leaving her alive, and hoped she wouldn't return to finish what she started. "Let's get out of here," I said. "Best if we're gone before light. The bodies will attract animals."

Everyone seemed happy to put some distance between us and the grizzly scene no doubt hidden by the dark.

CHAPTER EIGHT

We travelled south, the cold fading into an unpleasant memory. The days were long, the sun crawling across the bowl of the sky like it had not a care in the world. Farming communities came and went. Small towns were replaced by big towns, then sprawling villages, and eventually cities. We passed them all, taking the long way around.

The wounds in my back healed fast. Shalayn, who cleaned them each day and changed the bandages for me, raised an eyebrow at that but didn't comment

She also gave me another shirt that smelled of her, throwing the other one in the fire.

We always rode together now. If the rest of the surviving guards no longer glared quite so much hatred and disgust at our proximity, they still avoided me, communicating in grunts, if at all.

I missed my hatchet but had been unable to find it in the dark. The two Septk knives were my only weapons. Sometimes, at night, I dreamed of a red sword.

I thought of Henka often, her face haunting my dreams, so beautiful, so fragile. I couldn't shake the idea that I'd known someone like her before.

"Why don't we stop at any of these?" I asked Shalayn as we rolled past yet another city.

She looked up from sharpening her sword. The woman lavished great affection on her arms and armour. I'd only bathed at a stream we camped near because she informed me I smelled like a wet dog that had been sprayed by a skunk and then killed and left in the sun. I felt strangely light after, like I'd shed several pounds of filth.

Glancing at the city in question, she shrugged. "These northern grains make the best ales and will fetch the highest price in the capital." She gestured at the city. "Everyone stops there because it's close, convenient, and easy. Demand will be low."

"You ever kill anyone?" I asked, abruptly changing the topic.

She frowned at the blade of her sword, rubbing at some offending blemish I couldn't see. "Yes." She looked up. "People like us don't usually ask such questions."

People like us? Who or what did she think I was? Not that I knew the answer, but I wondered what she thought.

"You?" she asked. "I saw those Septk knives. You kill to get those?"

"I thought people like us didn't ask such questions."

She arched an eyebrow.

"I did," I admitted. "They attacked me," I added, though I wasn't sure why I needed to clarify. "I had no choice." I remembered killing the boy and swallowed the bile of the lie. Why did I feel worse for the lie than the murder?

"Septks don't much like southerners," she said. "They don't even like each other." She grunted a laugh. "So, only a couple of Septks?"

"No." How could I tell her of the trapper I killed for his clothes and boots? How could I tell her I murdered myself for the fragment of obsidian lodged in my heart?

She didn't ask.

That evening, after the guards finished their meal and those on picket duty walked their rounds, Shalayn and I sat by a fire. We'd taken to lighting our own rather than sharing the one the rest of the caravan folks sat around. Everyone seemed fine with this arrangement, happy to put some distance between themselves and us.

"Why do you think some women are drawn to bad boys and dangerous men?" she asked.

I wondered which she thought I was.

"I didn't know they were," I admitted.

We sat in silence, watching the flames.

"You move very slowly," she said.

A fly buzzed past and I snatched it out of the air. I held it up for her to see. "Not so slow."

"Not what I meant."

Releasing the fly, I watched it wobble drunkenly away. "I'm not sure—"

"We sit and talk every night."

"You're the only one who will talk to me. Except maybe Paulak."

"And yet you have not once made an advance. Did I misjudge you? Are you not the trouble I was hoping you might be?"

"Oh," I said. "It's been a while. It seems like a thousand years."

She glanced at me, pale blue eyes twinkling. "Are you planning on it being a thousand more?"

I'd been so focussed on survival, on moving south, it never occurred to me there could be more to life. For the first time I really looked at this woman I'd spent so many hours talking to. She was sturdy and strong, but not unattractive.

She punched me in the shoulder. "I know that look. You're trying to decide if you want to, if it's been long enough, you're that desperate."

"No," I said. "I was trying to figure out what you look like under that armour."

She showed me.

Shalayn was a lot stronger than I realised. She hurt me several times, though I never complained. I figured if I somehow survived being mauled by an undead mountain lion, I had some slight chance of surviving her attentions.

After, as we lay tangled in her sleeping roll, her head on my chest, she said, "Definitely trouble."

The next morning found me bruised and feeling more alive, more human, than I ever had. The savage creature that wandered down from the far north seemed distant and strange. I couldn't believe the things I'd done. Violence. Murder. Hacking my own chest open to get at the shard in my heart. These were someone else's memories.

Though the sun had yet to rise, the eastern horizon glowed gold. Shalayn lay beside me, pale and freckled skin gleaming. One hand against my chest, pale pink on deepest black, she seemed lost in the contrast of our complexions.

I met those blue eyes. "Yes?"

"How old are you?" she asked.

Physically, I'd guess that she had maybe two or three years on me. "No idea," I said. "Older than you."

She looked sceptical. "The bath helped, but that scraggly scruff of a beard is a disaster."

"And?"

"Can I trim it?"

"Sure."

Sitting before me, wearing nothing but a shirt, she spent an hour trimming and carving with a knife so sharp I was amazed to survive. She was tender, gentle, moving slowly and stopping often to consider the next cut. The other caravan guards watched, their looks of disgust returning. It wasn't her they didn't like, it was me. Or maybe it was her with me.

When she finished, Shalayn leaned back to examine her work. "No way you're older than me."

"How old are you?"

She punched me in the shoulder again. I winced as she connected with the bruise left by her previous blow.

"You can't be more than nineteen," she said.

Rather than tempt an explanation, I shrugged.

"Fine," she said. "Have your secrets."

She rose and I watched, laying back, as she dressed. She took her time doing that too, carefully setting each piece of armour, adjusting its weight, and strapping it tight. When she finished, she kicked me in the ribs and walked away, hips swinging in an exaggerated strut.

I lay there for a while, trying to decipher my feelings for her, before giving up. When Paulak strode about the camp, bellowing marching orders for the day, I got dressed. He saw me clamber from Shalayn's sleeping roll and raised an eyebrow. If he said nothing, I think it was more for respect of Shalayn than out of any fear of me.

We were hours into the city of Taramlae, the supposed capital of everything, before I knew it. What I took to be a sprawling town, turned out to be the outskirts. Hour after hour, the homes became more numerous, the space between each, smaller. Soon we wandered cobbled streets, the wagon wheels clattering loudly on stone. The buildings were all either attached or so close together only the skinniest child could slip between. People watched the passing caravan, eyes widening when they caught sight of me. The looks of disgust and hate were either ill-concealed, or not hidden at all. I ignored them as best I could.

Something in Taramlae called to me. I wanted to hop off this wagon and go in search of it, but decided entering the city as just one more caravan guard was probably safer. I clearly stood out.

"It stinks, but I expected it to be worse," I said to Shalayn. We sat together atop the baled grains stacked on the last wagon.

"The Guild runs everything. There's a magical aqueduct system under the city."

The Guild. Wizards. I ground teeth at the mention. Something deep in me loathed wizards.

"Today is the last day on this caravan," she said.

I considered that. The tug of whatever pulled me south grew stronger with every passing day. Now, it was a constant pressure in my skull. Ahead, I saw a colossal wall towering the height of one hundred men, each standing on the head of the man below. Huge portcullises, bars of iron as thick as a man's waist, were raised. A line of wagons awaited entrance to the inner city. Beyond the wall, the only buildings tall enough to be seen were evenly spaced towers running its circumference. None had windows.

Shalayn noted my attention. "That's the inner wall, ringed by wizard's towers. It's old. Dates back to the Great War, when the wizards threw off the yoke of the demonologists."

I wanted to tear it down. I wanted to topple those towers and raze the city, salt the earth with the blood of thousands.

Her earlier words made it past my anger. "Our last day? What are you doing after?"

Shalayn examined the row of towers fading into the distance. "Maybe sign on to another caravan. Preferably one going somewhere interesting."

What did *I* want to do? After years of living alone, the thought of Shalayn leaving suddenly terrified me. I didn't want to be alone again, but there was something here, somewhere in Taramlae, that I wanted more than anything.

"You leaving right away?" I asked.

"Nah. I'll sample some of what the capital has to offer—food, drink, silk sheets—first." She gave me a crooked smile. "I don't like staying in one place too long. I get bored quickly."

"Ah," I said.

"Not bored of you."

"I'm glad."

"Yet." She grinned. "Bathe every day, and we'll see how long we can make this last."

I made a mental note to hunt down a bath at the first chance.

A dozen guards in bright chain armour and liveries of white lounged around the gate. To either side of the entrance to the inner city stood a figure in gleaming white plate armour. Each held a huge sword, point down, hands resting on pommels. At first, I took them as statues of worked metal but one moved, just the slightest shift of weight. As the day had grown warm, I imagined how much they must stink in that armour. I pointed them out and Shalayn smacked my hand down.

"Don't point. They watch everything."

"Who are they?" I asked. The slap stung. She was damned fast.

"Battle Mages. I heard they're immortal and that any one of them could level a city."

That stank of hyperbole, but I kept the thought to myself. What kind of brain-dead oaf would spend their immortality standing guard at a gate? I wanted to test one, wander over and see if I could kill him with my knife. I must have moved because Shalayn grabbed me.

"Don't be an idiot," she said.

Paulak called a halt to the convoy as we joined the line of wagons entering the gate. He hurried forward to talk with the Gate Master, an even fatter bald man with robes of sweat-stained white.

"I don't like white," I told Shalayn.

"It's the wizard's colour. It's supposed to represent purity of thought, clarity of mind, and honesty of intent. Or something. I can't remember." She shot me a glance, jaw clenched, eyes hard. "In my experience, wizards lie just like everyone else."

I watched Paulak hand a heavy pouch to the Gate Master. The man pried it open with greedy fingers, peered inside, licked his lips with a quick dart of pink tongue, and nodded.

"Do the wizards have enemies?" I asked.

"Like the sorcerers or the elementalists? Supposedly the Great War killed them all off. You always hear rumours about sorcerers in the deserts or elementalists riding mountains, but no one actually believes that stuff. Before the other day, I'd never actually seen proof that anything other than wizards remained. Now…" she shrugged. "I don't know. Maybe some of those rumours are true."

"And all wizards are Guild members?" I asked, trying to understand this world.

"There's always going to be people who live on the fringe. Thieves." She darted a quick look at me. "Whatever. Not every mage is a member of the Guild."

"What about the demonologists you mentioned?"

"Gone. Wiped out. Exterminated."

"Impossible."

"For a thousand years after the Great War it was death to be even accused of being a demonologist."

"Why?"

"Seriously," she said, "where have you been that you don't know this?"

I shrugged, helpless.

"There are lots of traces left by the demonologists," she said. "Entire cities no one dares enter. There are weapons and armour and artefacts of all kinds with demons in them. But because no one knows how to control them—"

"Bind them," I corrected without thought.

"Whatever. No one knows how to use them. Touching a demonic object almost always leads to death. I heard a farmer picked up a shiny stone he found outside an abandoned city. He killed hundreds before the Guild brought him down."

The wizards, again.

"There are the bones of an empire out there," continued Shalayn. "The island of PalTaq is said to have been the capital of the demon empire. Apparently, the city still stands, untouched by thousands of years, empty."

Under Paulak's orders, the caravan tightened formation as we rolled through the gate and into the heart of Taramlae. Chainmail-clad guards, liveried in bright white, patrolled the main thoroughfare. The streets were crowded, a press of humanity. Not everyone was quite as pale as the blond folks I'd been travelling with. Here and there I caught sight of light, sandy brown hair. No one looked like me. Those who noticed me, perched atop the wagon with Shalayn, stared in undisguised disgust, sometimes nudging companions and pointing.

"They don't much like me," I said to Shalayn.

"Ignore them. They're just ignorant."

"But why?"

"People like you never travel this far north."

People like me? So there were more of us, somewhere to the south? I liked the idea of fitting in, of not being an object of loathing.

"It doesn't bother you?" I asked.

"No. I've travelled more than most. I've been to the ports on the southern coast. I've met sailors and islanders who come to trade."

Islanders. Isle of PalTaq. Far to the south. I wanted to go there.

But not yet. There was something here, in Taramlae, I had to have.

Nodding toward one of the guards I asked, "Does the city guard work for the mages?"

"They *are* mages. Albeit, probably minor wizards. Maybe Battle Mages in training."

"So why is Paulak so worried now that we're under their watchful eye?" I couldn't keep a little of the barb from my voice.

"Like I said, not all mages are white-wearing Guild members. Some hire out as assassins." Again, that darted glance, jaw tight. "Some are thieves."

"They're all thieves."

"For someone who doesn't know anything, you carry an awful lot of hate for wizards."

She wasn't wrong. But how could I explain?

A tower, smaller than those lining the inner wall, caught my eye. Like the others, it too had no windows. The base was lost behind a block of shops selling bright clothes. I wanted inside. I *needed* to get inside that tower.

Later, I decided. For now, I filed away its location. Not that I'd have trouble finding it. The incredible pull of the tower made thinking of anything else difficult.

We entered a huge open square and Paulak called a halt to the wagon train. At his signal, Shalayn and I clambered from our perch. Squads of what looked like street-children mobbed the wagons, and began the task of unloading. Watching them struggle under the weight of the bales, I wanted to help. When I suggested it, Shalayn told me the kids would likely tear me apart for trying to steal their jobs.

Paulak wandered from guard to guard, one of his personal retainers at his side. Each time he handed over a pouch of coins, said a few words, shook the guard's hand, and moved on.

After he paid Shalayn and I, I showed her my pouch of coins and asked her how long this would support me.

"In some little farming community," she said, "that would keep you for a month or two. If you leave now, and walk fast, you might make it out of Taramlae before falling deep into debt."

Then, she took several minutes to mock my haggling skills.

"Come," she said, "I'll buy you dinner and we'll have a drink. Or two."

She led me from the open area which, she informed me, was called the Grain Importers Market. There were, she said, other similar squares such as the Grain Exporters Market, the Silk Importers Market, and on and on.

After years alone in the north, and a week or so with Shalayn as my only real company, Taramlae was too much. The city crushed me. People everywhere. Sweat, breath, and thick cloying perfume. The stink of horses and dung and fresh-sawn wood intermingled in an all-encompassing miasma. Glancing up I saw what looked to be eagles or large hawks circling above us. It was difficult to make out much detail at this distance, but they looked ragged and unhealthy, their wide-spread wings tattered. They wobbled often, as if having difficulty riding the up-draughts.

It was one thing to have a couple of wagon guards glare their hate at me, but this was an entire city of loathing. Everyone I passed flinched away from me, eyes wide. Some spat on the ground and made a sign over their hearts. Though I had no idea what it meant, I didn't bother asking Shalayn. There was no way the answer would be pleasant. On the high side, it made travelling through the crowded streets easier. No one wanted to be anywhere near me.

Except Shalayn. She ignored all of this, acted like she didn't even notice.

I tried to watch everyone. I tried to see everything. Hate like this had to lead to violence. Eyes everywhere, lips curled in revulsions. I was nothing here, a filthy savage out of his depth. I didn't fit in, never could.

To distract myself, I dug a coin from my pouch to examine it. Their money, these little wedges of bronze, meant nothing. I had no idea who the woman was whose face graced one side. The other side was a swirling mess that looked like entwined snakes.

"What's that?" I asked Shalayn, holding up the coin.

"Chaos," she said, glancing at the object in my hand. "Mages use chaos to feed their magic."

Filthy chaos magic. Power for nothing.

"And this?" I flipped the coin.

"That's the Empress. She toppled the demon empire, built a new world. A world of brightness and sense and logic. A world not ruled by demons and slavers." She spoke like she was rattling off something memorized in childhood, eyes glazing over at the litany.

I kept my doubts to myself. This Empress may have ended the demonologists and built Taramlae atop the bones of the old empire, but I seriously doubted she was a paragon of purity and logic. More likely, she was a power-hungry tyrant hiding behind a veil of rewritten history.

"If you're going to look like a murderous lunatic every time we talk about wizards," said Shalayn, "we are going to talk about something else."

She made a show of considering her options as she pushed through a crowd of children who parted before her. The kids paid no attention to her sword and armour. They also didn't seem to notice me. Only the children didn't care that I was different.

"Perhaps," she said, "you could start by telling me why you hate them?"

"The truth is, I don't know. I remember very little of my old life."

"The truth is," she said, "I learned long ago that sentences beginning with 'the truth is' are always lies."

"Yours wasn't," I pointed out.

This time when she tried to punch me in the shoulder I was ready and slid away from the blow.

"Missed!"

She punched me in the other shoulder.

Twice.

Shalayn led me to an inn she knew called the Dripping Bucket. I asked about the name, and she shrugged, said they were everywhere, and ordered us a round of pints and two plates loaded with savoury lamb pie. The man who brought our food almost dropped the plates when he saw me. He looked ready to spit into our lamb. Eyeing Shalayn, he decided to drop it loudly to the table and stalk away, shoulders hunched.

"Great service," I said.

"Eat."

Pastry.

I lived off bugs, sometimes for weeks on end. I ate beetles and spiders. I ate snakes and frogs and chewed roots from the ground still caked in mud. I ate raw eggs that smelled like the farts of a dead rat and spent days after, puking. I sucked snails from their shells and choked down their gritty nasty little bodies.

Pastry.

Never once, not since waking surrounded by death, did I think of pastry. I'd been an animal. Since leaving my shack, the time I spent with Shalayn, I was finding myself, rediscovering something of who I'd been. Somehow, I knew what pastry was. Some memory lay buried deep within. This delicious pie, rudely delivered, brought some of it out.

"I like pastry," I told Shalayn.

"Did you even chew?"

"I'm going to eat pastry every day."

Those pale blue eyes examined me. She looked different now. I couldn't explain it. That brutal haircut, strawberry blond hair hewn short, was her. The broad shoulders, the loose way she moved when relaxed, the coiled speed of a viper when she wasn't. The way her eyes closed and her freckled chest flushed warm pink when she orgasmed, body bucking and twitching.

"Will you eat pastry with me tomorrow?" I asked.

"Sure."

"And the day after that?"

Her eyes narrowed. "Maybe."

I grinned at her. It was good to be alive. Good to be here, with her. The loathing of an entire city meant nothing while I was with this woman. Though some people still glared, for the most part, the patrons of the inn decided to ignore me. They focussed instead on singing loud off-key drinking songs.

For the first time, I wasn't alone.

"You were in the north for a really long time, weren't you?"

I nodded.

"Were you born there?"

"Kind of."

She raised an eyebrow but let it go. "Let's wait until you've seen some other women before planning years of pastry eating."

"All the other women hate me."

Except Henka. She hadn't cared about the colour of my skin, didn't seem to notice.

Shalayn looked away as a band made their way to the stage. The room subsided to a low rumble of conversation. A lute, two strange flutes, and a singer, they entertained us with songs of love and tragedy.

I laughed, and I cried, and we drank.

Shalayn joined in the choruses of some of the songs, her voice rough and beautiful, and we drank more. Either the patrons got used to me and stopped pouring their hate in my direction, or I became so blearily focussed on Shalayn, I stopped noticing. She was beautiful. The soft pink of her skin, the dusting of freckles across her cheeks and nose. Pale blue eyes that danced with humour.

Later, we stumbled upstairs into a room she rented. We fucked drunk. If I have previous experiences, I can't remember them, but I can honestly say: You haven't fucked until you've fucked drunk.

CHAPTER NINE

I woke with a world-ending hangover and Shalayn draped across me. She'd fallen asleep on one of my arms and it had long since lost all feeling. She drooled into my armpit. Waking her seemed like effort so I lay there, moaning in quiet misery.

"Someone kill that fucking cat," she muttered, falling immediately back to sleep.

I moaned quieter.

My second attempt at facing the world proved marginally more successful. I managed to roll Shalayn off me without getting stabbed or otherwise murdered. She scowled at me through one bloodshot eye, the other apparently not ready to open.

"Whiskey," she croaked.

"You're mad."

"It's our only hope."

After puking in the shared soilroom in the hall and marvelling at—and hating—the water system that flushed away my rancid bile, I stumbled downstairs.

The innkeeper backed away from the bar as I approached, bumping into the counter behind him. He regarded me with nervous eyes and I wondered if I'd done something terrible and violent the night before. Though hazy, I couldn't remember doing anything worse than trying to sing along with Shalayn.

Two whiskeys wiped out what bronze I had, and I staggered back upstairs, trying not to spill or puke in them. I found Shalayn sitting up, the sheets bundled about her waist. Her pale skin, freckled and pink, was laced with scars gleaming white in the sun forcing its way through the ratty curtains.

"It's too bright in here," I said.

She took one of the whiskeys and downed it. Then she took the other and drank that too.

"You should have got yourself a couple," she said, handing me the empty glasses.

"Maybe next time."

Much to Shalayn's amusement, I puked twice more before we managed to get dressed and make it downstairs for breakfast. Apparently being dead for a long time, and then living on a diet of worms and roots, had done little for my alcohol tolerance.

Breakfast, served with darted looks of hostility shared evenly between Shalayn and I, was more lamb pies, no doubt leftover from last night.

"I'll never eat another pastry again," I said, eyeing the food before me. My guts rumbled complaint and threatened rebellion.

"So, we're not having pastry together tomorrow?"

What amounted to my drunken profession of love, returned to me. "If you're there," I said, hoping to salvage the situation, "I'll eat anything."

She grunted and loosed a gut-churning fart. "That was the whiskey," she said, as if having something to blame rendered her free of culpability.

"I think I've gone blind."

I watched her wolf down her pie. Then, seeing I hadn't touched mine, she ate that too.

"I have to do something today," I said, hoping she wouldn't ask what.

"Yeah? What?"

"Probably something stupid."

Eyes narrowed. Pale shards of ice-blue examined me. "Sounds fun. What kind of stupid?"

I was too hungover for subtlety or deceit. "There's something in a wizard's tower that I want."

"Oh. You meant *stupid* stupid and not fun stupid. What is it?"

"I don't know. Not exactly." It wasn't quite a lie. I had an idea, but couldn't know for sure.

She stared at me, unblinking.

"It'll be a small chip of black stone." I held my fingers apart to show her what I guessed its size to be. "They won't even notice it missing."

"Right."

"Today, I just want to look at the tower. I'm too hungover to attempt anything more."

"So, the islands man who wanders out of the far north and who has never heard of Taramlae and didn't know it was the capital or what wizard's towers are…" She drew breath. "…suddenly wants to break into one to steal something, though he's not sure what?"

"Essentially."

"Essentially." Pale eyes examined me.

I'd seen moments of softness. Sometimes the way she looked at me made me want to forget whatever drew me south. Now, she was iron.

"Have you been lying to me?" she asked. "Has everything you've said been a steaming boot-load of pig shit?"

"No." I tried to remember everything I'd said, as best as my muzzy brain allowed. "Though I can't promise I never exaggerated or left out an unflattering detail."

"Why do you want this little piece of stone? And if you lie, I'm leaving."

I was pretty damned sure I could lie convincingly enough to fool her, but didn't want to.

"I don't want to tell you," I said. "You'll think I'm lying."

"I'm leaving." She stood.

"Every time I find a piece of this stone I remember more of my past."

Shalayn leaned forward, bunched fists on the table. "What *do* you remember?"

"I woke in the north. I lived there, alone in a mud shack, for maybe five years. Then I came south. You were the first person I really talked to." I was leaving out a lot, but the details seemed increasingly insane. "My name really is Khraen. I know that. Otherwise, I have no idea who I was."

"Sounds like magic."

I shrugged, looking up at her. "Yeah, it does."

"And you want to break into a wizard's tower."

"That's where the stone is."

"If you don't know anything, can't remember anything, how do you know it's there?"

"I just do. I can feel it. I'm drawn to it." I struggled to find the words without sharing exactly what it was. "It's part of me."

"I've seen all your parts. And while some were rock hard, none were made of stone."

I shrugged again.

Shalayn sat. "Fuck."

"What?"

"Do you have any idea how much women love mysterious men?"

"No."

She looked like she wanted to punch me. "Today we'll stroll past the tower. We're looking, nothing more."

"You don't have to do this."

"I know that. I'm curious. I can't help it. It'll be the death of me."

"Just looking," I agreed. "Once we've seen it, we can plan."

"Right. Plan to break into an impregnable wizard's tower." She tilted her head to one side and ran a hand through her rough-cropped hair. "You regain memories with each piece of stone?"

"Yes."

"How many do you have?"

"Two, so far."

"How many are there?"

"No idea."

She thought this over. "Do you change as you find pieces? Do you become more like whoever you used to be?"

"I suppose so."

She stared at me.

"Yes," I added. "I think I do. Maybe. I don't know, because I can't remember who or what I was, or what that person was like." I reached out to touch her hand. "I know I changed a lot after I met you. Before, I was…trapped inside."

"What if you're going to become someone who doesn't like me?"

"Then he's an asshole."

Her lips quirked in a smile. "Can this be undone? What if you discover you're someone you don't like, or don't want to be? Can you go back?"

I thought about the shards of obsidian gathering in my heart. "Not easily."

"But it's possible?"

Sure, if you hack me open, cut out my heart, and shatter whatever you find in there. "Yes."

"Okay. Fine." She drew a deep breath. "This really is too much for a hungover morning."

"Agreed."

She pushed her plate away and waved at the innkeeper to bring us two pints of ale. He dropped them on the table, sloshing foam onto my lap, and stomped away.

"Lovely chap," I said. "Has a real way with people."

Shalayn downed hers in one fast go, whereas I sipped mine over several minutes. While it didn't cure the hangover, it did somewhat lessen the pain.

Had I dreamed of a dark haired, dark eyed woman last night? Was she real, or a construct of my imagination?

Brisk but warming fast, the morning air felt good. I wanted it to be warmer, however. A lot warmer. People about their business wore short-sleeves and seemed unaware of the cold. Was I from the tropics? How far south would I have to travel before I met people like me?

Once again, I received more attention than I wanted. Ill-concealed looks of venomous animosity, dashed in my direction. Revulsion. Shalayn ignored all of it. She walked fast, long muscled legs carrying her in a hip-swinging stride somewhere between sexy and the walk of those people who drive the oxen. It was, I decided, the stomping purpose which separated one from the other. When she wanted to be, she was graceful, light on her feet. When her mind was elsewhere, she clomped about like a five-year-old.

A five-year-old? Where did that come from?

I hurried to keep up with her.

We crossed a long bridge spanning a great river upon which cargo ships road the currents west. A few boats came east, travelling against the current. They bore no sails and no banks of oars. Wizardry, no doubt. All were painted harsh white, reminding me of my dream. Many were stained yellow, particularly those coming from the west. I hid my satisfied grin from Shalayn.

Making my way to the rail, I paused, looking out over the river. Something looked wrong. "No warships?"

Shalayn joined me. "Who would we war against?" She watched a barge, loaded with crates and bails of pale straw, pass by beneath us, a crooked, wistful smile teasing her lips. "I've never been west. We always go south and east."

We? I didn't ask.

The wizards had no navy? Had they truly conquered the world so utterly? I couldn't believe it.

Grunting, she turned away and continued across the bridge. I followed.

"Which way?" she asked, stopping at an intersection on the far side of the bridge.

I turned a full circle. A butchery called Medium Rare sat on one corner. Gutted goats and rabbits hung glistening in the open front. The scent of salt and curing meats wafted past me. A dusky skinned woman —though still far paler than I—carved long slices from a smoked lamb and wrapped them in sheets of brown paper. An accountant, Whadehra and Daughters, took another corner. Pillars of white marble framed the door and smoked glass hid the interior. The other two corners were held by what looked like a candy shop, painted in red and white swirls, and a bootery.

I glanced down at the trapper's decaying boots, still laced tight to my feet. They didn't have many miles left in them. I needed money. Unfortunately, beyond killing children and Septk women, I had no marketable skills. At least none I was aware of. I considered the bootery, tried to imagine myself repairing shoes. I had no idea where to start. Though from the way Shalayn spent coin on food and booze, there was decent money to be made from killing some folks and protecting others. As long as you didn't get attacked by a necromancer, it seemed like pretty easy work and a decent way to see the world. The idea held its attractions. Forget my stone heart, travel the lands with Shalayn.

"Well?" she asked.

"What?" For a second, I thought she'd read my mind or maybe I'd accidentally spoken aloud. "Oh." I pointed. "That way."

She set off, and once again, I followed. Whereas I still felt like an incontinent donkey took a rancid shit in my skull, Shalayn seemed to have fully recovered. She set a hard pace, bright eyes sweeping the street, right hand resting casually on the pommel of her sword.

I wanted a sword. But not just any sword. I wanted *my* sword.

"I have a sword?"

"What?" she asked.

"Nothing."

I had a sword. Maybe.

I found my fist clenched with the memory of gripping something. I felt its familiar weight in my arm.

At the next intersection I pointed north.

We traversed several blocks of ancient stone homes falling just short of being castles in their own right. Many had turrets and crenellations. A few even gave modest nods at moats, though they were more like manicured streams that could be easily hopped by someone whose hangover wouldn't murder them for jumping.

"Who lives in these huge houses?" I asked.

"Bankers. Exporters." She glanced at me without breaking stride. "If I say 'wizards,' are you going to get all weird?"

"No," I lied.

"Liar."

I shrugged and flashed her an apologetic grin, which she ignored.

After the luxury of the castle district—I have no idea what it was really called—we entered block after block of smiths and tanneries. It stank like rusting iron and blood. Huge sheets of tanned hide hung flapping in the morning breeze. The air reeked of rancid meat and flayed flesh. Somewhere to the east, the eerily human screams of pigs at a slaughterhouse echoed like nightmares on stone.

Different screams, those of horror and defeat, echoed in my thoughts.

White sails. Blood on the water.

"Sometimes I feel like I'm on the edge of remembering something."

"Yeah?" said Shalayn. "If you ever remember that you prefer redheads, keep it to yourself."

I decided cowardice was the best part of valour, and didn't ask.

After the stench of the tanneries, the rows of homes closer to the wall, still large and well-maintained, possessed a much more human ordure. The wizards may have supplied the city with a miraculous underground water system, but if you pack people together, they stink.

The wall, hazy and distant when we were in the Grain Importers' Square, loomed large. It towered above us, throwing the nearby homes into perpetual shadow. These houses were small, crude, and constructed mostly of wood. At some point, someone painted most of them white, but now that paint was stained and flaking. A leprous yellow, the neighbourhood looked like it had somehow managed to piss itself.

Leprous.

"I remember lepers."

"Lovely. They're more common in the islands."

I pointed out a squat tower in the shadow of the wall. It wasn't one of the huge towers ringing the inside of the wall, but still stood several stories tall.

Shalayn lashed out like a striking viper and slapped my hand down. "Don't point."

"There are no windows," I said, shaking the sting from my hand.

"Wizards can still see out. They see everything."

"That, I doubt."

I squinted at the tower. Like the others, it was ancient, the stones grey with age. Ivy grew thick and green along one side, but only reached half way up. A shame, as that would have made scaling it easy. A single door, a slab of iron banded with yet more iron, sat in the base.

"Let's do a walk around and see if there's another entrance," I said.

"Let's not."

Shalayn followed me in spite of her words.

We circumnavigated the tower doing our best to look casual and disinterested. The hangover helped. Mostly, I wanted to go back to bed.

"How tall is that?" I asked.

"Why are men always asking women how big something looks?"

"Forty feet?"

"It's always smaller than you think."

"Thirty?"

"Thirty-five," she said.

The roof looked to be flat from down here. I couldn't tell what was up there. It might be a trapdoor leading in, a lovely patio so the wizards can have drinks and spit down on the people they ruled, or featureless impenetrable stone.

"What would you put on the roof?" I asked.

"If I was a wizard, I'd have somewhere to sit and drink beer in the sun where no one can bother me."

"My thoughts exactly."

We returned to the Dripping Bucket to plan our attack.

"It's hopeless," said Shalayn. "It would be suicidal if it wasn't already impossible."

"Has anyone tried?"

"No one is dumb enough."

"Wizards are just people. There's nothing special about them."

"Except they tap untold sources of power to twist the world to their desire."

"Except that," I agreed. "And it's not 'untold,' it's chaos. They shape chaos."

"So, you do know something."

"Something. The point is, they're human. They're fallible. What are the odds the wizard remembers to lock a door no one can reach?"

"I would," said Shalayn.

"But you are both perfect and paranoid." And just maybe, judging by how quickly she agreed to my mad plan to break into a wizard's tower, something of a thrill-seeker and a thief.

"You say the nicest things." Strong fingers drummed the table top in a rapid staccato. Pale blue eyes narrowed in thought. "I couldn't climb that tower, even without my armour."

"We need help."

BLACK STONE HEART

"We need a drink."

Shalayn waved at the barkeep and he brought us two tankards of frothing ale. He placed hers gently on the table before her, and slammed mine down once again splashing a good portion on my lap.

"Thanks so much," I said as he stomped away.

The ale was deep gold and held hints of citrus and tasted much better than the barkeep's hate.

I leaned forward, elbows in puddled beer. "You said not all wizards belong to the Guild. You said some were thieves. Do you, by any chance, know one?"

Her eyes said yes, and for an instant I saw a flash of quickly hidden pain. "All the more reason to lock a rooftop access. If there even is one."

"And you know where we can find such a wizard?" It galled me to have to ask a wizard for help, but I saw no other choice.

Blue eyes examined me.

"I thought so," I said, sipping beer. Another problem occurred to me. "I spent my last coins buying whiskey this morning."

"I have some money," she said, "but not enough to hire a wizard."

"We'll have to steal something else while we're in the tower. Something we can sell." Aside from Shalayn's charity, I'd been living in poverty my entire life. Or at least what I could remember of it. Perhaps we could steal several things to fund my search for the rest of my heart. "We're going to need money."

"We?" asked Shalayn.

"I hope so. Though if you're just here for the moment, I understand."

"Do you?"

"Not really. I hope you don't leave."

"Hmm." The drumming fingers stopped. She stared at the table, reached across to draw lines in the beer pooled before me. She looked distant, lost in memory, seeing things I could not. Finally, she nodded to herself, some decision made. "Tomorrow morning I'll take you to meet Tien." She didn't look happy about the decision.

"A wizard?"

"A wizard."

"Is he powerful?"

"She. And not terribly. She's… a thief."

"Is she good?"

I saw Shalayn's jaw tighten. "As a person, she leaves something to be desired. As a thief, she's good enough."

There was something she wasn't telling me. She and this Tien shared some past Shalayn wasn't altogether happy about. Seeing as I had no other options, didn't know anyone else in the city, I let it slide.

Shalayn examined me, gnawing on her bottom lip. "Maybe I should meet her alone."

"Why?"

"You seem to have some issue with wizards."

She wasn't lying, but she wasn't telling the entire truth either. She had other reasons for wanting to do this alone. But this was my heart; I needed to be involved. And no way I was going to trust a wizard without even meeting her.

"I'll be fine," I said, waving away her concern. "I promise to behave."

She breathed deep, sighed, and nodded. "First thing in the morning, then. There's a coffee shop. If she's not dead, she'll be there."

That night we tangled in the sheets, biting and clawing and making enough noise people pounded on the walls and told us to shut up. Having endured their barbed glances and scorn all evening, I ignored them.

We went somewhat easier on the booze, and woke only slightly hungover. When I asked Shalayn if I should fetch whiskeys, she asked if I was some kind of barbarian.

The kitchen wasn't yet open when we descended to the main floor so we made do with a fistful of peanuts left out in a bowl on the bar. We ate as we walked, cracking the shells and devouring the nuts. We tossed the empty husks to the birds who didn't seem at all disappointed with their meal. The sun, peeking over the city wall, took the edge off the morning chill.

I found myself smiling as I walked. Something other than the sun warmed me, a feeling I couldn't remember ever having felt before. Contentment. Shalayn was a good woman. Better than I deserved. It felt good to be with her, good to be near her. I felt light and alive.

"What the fuck are you grinning about?"

"I'm happy."

"Hmm." She turned away, but not before I caught a glimpse of her own smile.

"You have beautiful lips."

She flushed bright, freckled pink.

"Can I kiss you?"

Stopping, she turned. Grabbing me by the back of the head she pulled me in for a hard kiss and bit my bottom lip. I tasted blood. The morning crowd parted around us. Locked in this tight embrace, hands roving and exploring, tongues doing battle, I couldn't see their hate.

When we parted, she punched me in the shoulder and walked away.

"Ow," I said, unsure if I meant the kiss or the punch.

Shalayn led me off the main street and into a mad tangle of back alleys. If there were street signs, I couldn't find them. Where the rest of Taramlae was relatively clean, and altogether too white, this dark underbelly was everything but. Trash lay strewn everywhere. The stones beneath my feet were sticky. I couldn't tell if it was piss, spilled blood, puke, or a mix of all three. A spider's web of clothes lines clogged the sky above us, sometimes hanging low enough, we had to duck to avoid being garrotted.

Turning a corner, Shalayn pointed to a set of shallow, well-worn steps leading down beneath a building that looked well on its way to toppling over like a drunkard.

"Is that safe?" I asked.

Shalayn cocked an eyebrow at me. "You'll get stabbed in there long before the building falls over."

The coffee house was a murky blend of stained brass and threadbare velvet. The bar, huge, oak, and lined with scratched and dented rails, wouldn't have looked out of place in a fine restaurant. At least, if that restaurant had burned in a terrible fire and then partially caved in. A dozen small, round tables were scattered about the floor with anywhere from two to six people standing at each. There was nowhere to sit. No chairs.

Shalayn weaved through the room, nodding to some, ignoring others. Our feet made damp squelching sounds on the carpet. Narrowed eyes followed our progress.

At the back of the room we found a table with three women leaning against it. All sipped black sludge from chipped white cups little bigger than thimbles. One of the women, short and in her mid-twenties, with bright red hair cropped short and emerald green eyes, fluttered her fingers. The other two departed without a word, looking me over as they passed.

"Tien," said Shalayn as we arrived at her table.

"Shalayn," said Tien, rubbing at a petite nose. She examined me, making no attempt to disguise her curiosity. "An islander boy? A bit young for you, isn't he? Another charity case?"

Shalayn grimaced in embarrassment. "I—"

"I don't suppose you've reconsidered my offer?"

"No," said Shalayn with utter finality. "We need your help."

"Really? We?" Tien looked from Shalayn to me, wriggling her little nose. "He's cute in a starved rat kind of way, but darkers are trouble." She darted a mischievous grin at Shalayn. "And we *know* how much you like trouble."

Shalayn flushed pink.

Some guy who looked like he'd been trampled by an entire herd of horses brought us chipped mugs of sludge and disappeared back behind the bar. He wiped at its surface with a filthy rag that made no difference to the stains there. I sniffed at the contents of the mug and found the scent more appealing than the appearance.

Regaining her normal pale complexion, Shalayn leaned forward on the table. "We need to get into a wizard's tower."

Tien's eyebrows went up. "Why?"

"To steal something."

"I figured that much."

"The wizards took something from me," I said. "I want it back."

Once again Tien glanced back and forth between Shalayn and I. "This true?" she directed at Shalayn.

"I'd give it fair odds of being true. If it's a lie, it's the most insane one ever told."

Back to me. "What did the wizards take?"

"That," I said, "is not for discussion."

"Interesting. Well, if you won't tell me what we're stealing, there's more risk for me. If the risk is higher, the price is higher." She put a hand on Shalayn's. "You know I'm sorry about what happened. I didn't plan that. It just…"

Shalayn slid her hand away. "Great. Fine."

Tien looked hurt, disappointed. Shalayn, on the other hand, looked angrier than I'd ever seen.

"What if you didn't have to come," I said to Tien, hoping to distract them. "We only need help getting to the top of the tower. After that, we don't need you."

Tien had eyes only for Shalayn. "Really?"

"Hopefully," said Shalayn, ignoring the other woman's attention.

"Which tower?"

Shalayn described the location of the tower as I took a moment to examine the other patrons in the coffee house. They ignored us. For the first time in weeks, no one shot looks of hate at me. It was like we didn't exist. It was nice.

"We don't know which wizard owns it," continued Shalayn. "For all we know, it's abandoned or hasn't been used in decades."

"I know the tower," said Tien. "No one *owns* it. The Guild uses it as a depot of sorts." She eyed me. "There is something you want in there?"

"Yes."

"In that tower specifically."

"Yes."

"Interesting. I'll help you."

Shalayn rapped a knuckle on the table top. "We can't afford your normal rates."

"And yet here you are. I'm going to help you for free."

"Why?" I asked.

"Because," she glanced at me with an evil grin, "there just so happens to be something in that tower that I want." She looked all too pleased with herself.

"And that is?" I asked.

Tien leered at me. "You show me yours and I'll show you mine." She stretched, languid and sinuous. She was small and lithe, but softer than Shalayn. "Otherwise, no questions."

That sounded fair to me, but Shalayn looked less convinced.

"Is it dangerous?" she asked.

"Everything in that tower is dangerous. If you can get in and get out with whatever the cute stained-soul wants," she nodded at me, "then grabbing something for me will be easy." She grinned at the two of us, pug nose wrinkling. "I think you're going to die in there, but I've been wrong before." She tilted her head toward Shalayn. "Once."

Shalayn's blue eyes hardened to chips of ice. "No wizard lives there?"

"Nope."

"There goes the 'slip in the unlocked roof door the last wizard forgot to lock the last time he was up there having drinks' plan," said Shalayn.

"Shalayn my dear," said Tien, "not everyone is a drunk."

"Everyone I know is," answered Shalayn.

"Sure, but you only hobnob with the dregs of society."

"Thanks," I said.

"If you had any idea what being seen with the likes of you is doing to Shalayn's reputation, you'd leave now and never come back. At least if you cared for her, you would."

Shalayn ignored Tien's words. "What are we getting for you?"

"A trinket. A bauble. It's a gold ring with some stuff engraved on it." Leaning forward, Tien drew swirling lines on the table top with a fingertip. She left behind glowing red traces and I remembered then that she was a wizard. It had been easy to forget. The lines were letters and words and teased at my memory. I couldn't understand them, but felt like I should. It wasn't a human language.

"Bring me the ring with this written on it," said Tien, leaning back, "and I'll consider us even." She eyed the two of us. "It's magic," she added. "Obviously. If Shalayn touches it, the ring will destroy her." She looked to the other woman, eyes softening. "Don't touch it, Shal. Please don't touch it."

Shal?

"So only I can touch it," I said. "I'll be safe?"

"If I'm right about the ring, and…" Tien shrugged. "You should be."

I eyed the wizard with distrust and she flashed a sweet smile dripping innocence.

"Bring me any other ring," she continued, "and I'll boil his stained blood."

While Shalayn rolled her eyes at the threat, I found myself grinding my teeth. Rage bubbled up from somewhere deep and dark. Wizards should know their place. They were servants, tolerated at best.

Shalayn reached over and squeezed my hand. Hard. "Sounds fair," she said.

Tien either didn't notice or didn't care. "Come back tomorrow. I'll have something that will get you to the roof and through the door you'll find up there."

"Tomorrow, then," said Shalayn. "Come." She used her grip on my hand to pull me away from the table.

"Sweetie," I heard Tien whisper as we left, "you orchestrate your own failures." She watched us leave, eyes sad.

Once on the street Shalayn released me and walked away. I hurried to catch up.

"Are you going to be able to work with Tien?" she demanded. "Will this be a problem?"

"No problem." Much as I loathed wizards, I knew I had no other options.

"Why do you hate them?"

"I don't know. I can't remember. But if a piece of my memory is in that tower, does it not stand to reason that wizards broke me. They stole who I was."

She walked fast, hips swinging. "You don't know that."

"I don't," I admitted. "But I think I'm right. And if I am, does that not give me some reason to hate?"

She stopped abruptly and I narrowly avoided running into her.

"You see how people look at you?"

I nodded. Even now, everyone eyed me as they passed. Sometimes I caught whispered words. Darker. Ebony soul. Stained.

"Is it fair that they hate everyone who has dark skin? They haven't met you. They don't know you, yet they loathe you. Your hate is no better."

She strode away, and once again I was forced to rush after her. Was she right? Did my hatred of wizards make no more sense than the hate of these pale people who didn't know me?

As I caught up with her she said, "Hating all wizards for the actions of one or two is madness. If a woman breaks your heart, do you hate all women?"

The mention of a broken heart silenced me. That, and the fact she wasn't wrong. Maybe my hate was unreasonable. And yet, I couldn't get past it. Wizards took something from me. They took my life and my history. They *broke* me. They would pay.

"How much will you change when you have your memories back?"

I shrugged. "I don't know." I thought about it. I needed to be more honest with her. "This tower doesn't hold all of me," I said, unable to remember how much I'd told her while drunk. "There are more pieces out there."

She said nothing, but I saw the measured look, understood it.

She worried she wouldn't like the me I'd become. But what if *I* didn't like that me, either?

"I'm sorry," I said. "You're right."

"Of course I am."

"That's what I just—"

She cut me off with a raised hand. "I saw the way you looked at Tien. Like skinny little women with small tits, do you?"

Did I? I didn't know how to answer. Since entering Taramlae I'd seen thousands of women and, while they all seemed to hate me on sight, they also all looked good. I'd been alone in the north for a long time. I didn't think I had a preference, but there was that shadow of a memory. A slim girl with black hair, pale skin, and dark eyes, large and bright with humour.

Shalayn laughed at me. "I'm just messing with you. Tien flirts with everyone. It's how she keeps people off balance and distracted. It guarantees men underestimate her."

And not women? I kept the thought to myself. Shalayn and the wizard shared some past. The details were none of my business.

Was I jealous? Did that contribute to my dislike of Tien? Maybe.

One thing I knew for certain: I didn't trust her.

CHAPTER TEN

Back at the Dripping Bucket, Shalayn selected a table in the darkest corner and collapsed into a chair, back to the wall. She scratched at the table top with a blunt fingernail, eyes narrowed in thought.

We'd completed the long walk in silence, and I had no idea if it was a comfortable one. Judging by the look on her face, I thought not.

I sat across from her, felt the eyes in the room on my back. She looked up from the table and flashed a quick grin. I felt a little better. Shalayn waved two fingers at the innkeeper and a moment later two mugs arrived. He must have been distracted because he forgot to drop mine and splash me with beer.

"What did Tien call the tower?" she asked,

"A depot, of sorts, I believe." I watched her down half her pint in a single go. "Maybe we should take it easy tonight. If Tien comes through for us, we're going to need to be sharp tomorrow. Not hungover to rat shit."

"We are likely going to die tomorrow." Shalayn took another drink. "I'm not missing out on one last chance to enjoy a few drinks."

I wasn't sure if that was wisdom or insanity. I downed my pint, finishing as she finished hers. She ordered two more, and a platter of cheese and sausages.

"What would wizards store in a depot?" she asked.

"Things they don't want, or can't use?"

"Stuff that's too dangerous to be left lying around."

"We put grain in depots," I pointed out. My god, I loved those blue eyes. "Are you worried this thing we're getting for Tien might be more trouble than it's worth? You think maybe it's too dangerous?" I realized I had absolutely no problem with the idea of betraying the wizard, but cared very much how Shalayn felt about the idea.

"Nope."

"Well, then..." I understood. "Me. You think I might be dangerous once I know who I am."

She nodded.

I took her hand. "I promise, I will never be a danger to you. I would never hurt you." I meant it.

Her expression never changed. "You don't know that. You can't."

"Look, I might be dangerous to the wizards, though I can't really imagine how. But I don't believe I'm a bad person. I can't believe I'm evil." I touched my chest over my heart. "This me, this is who I am. I'll still be me, but with more memories." I struggled to explain. "This me is constant. He doesn't get replaced, he just remembers more of his past."

"Our memories define us."

I didn't know how to argue with that, wasn't even sure if it was true. I wanted to tell her I was falling in love with her, but some part of me hesitated. The truth was, no matter how I felt about her, I barely knew her. She kept surprising me. She walked, armed and armoured, through a city where the populace went unarmed. She was chummy with thieves and wizards, and knew where they took their morning coffee.

The entire city hated me for the colour of my skin, and yet she didn't care. She killed and regretted it. And most damning of all, here she was planning to break into a wizard's tower—suicide if Tien was to be believed—to steal something for a man she barely knew. I'd wondered if she was a thrill-seeker, drawn to danger. Now, I wondered if maybe she was suicidal. If the wizards broke me apart and scattered me around the world, there had to be a reason. It surely wasn't because they loved me.

Why would Shalayn involve herself? Clearly, the reasonable course of action would be to walk away. Hell, she should probably go to the wizards and report me. Yet here she was, getting drunk with me. Again. Did she feel for me what I was beginning to feel for her? Why? Who did she think I was?

Why do women love bad boys and dangerous men? She'd asked that, though as a rhetorical question. Was that it? Was she with me because she thought I was dangerous? Was Tien right, was Shalayn orchestrating her next failure?

I watched her inhale a second pint and flag the innkeeper. Popping a chunk of sausage into her mouth, she asked him to bring us a bottle of whiskey and leave it on the table.

She certainly seemed to have something of a self-destructive streak. Was this an elaborate suicide?

The innkeeper arrived with the whiskey. After blowing the dust off the bottle, he peeled the wax from the top and worked free the cork. Setting the bottle on the table, he placed a small steel cup in front of each of us. Looking like he wanted to spit in mine, he somehow resisted the urge. Likely because Shalayn would kill him.

We watched him waddle back to the bar. Someone said something as he arrived and both darted glances in our direction.

"Would they hate me less if I wasn't with you?" I asked.

"Probably. But then they might also just drag you into the alley behind the bar and murder you too."

"I need a drink."

Shalayn poured us each a healthy measure. Lifting the cup, she said, "To tomorrow. May we drink so much, and fuck so hard, we don't care if we die." She winked at me. "Life to the full!" And downed the whiskey.

"To the full," I said, tossing mine down my throat. It was golden fire, caramel and dark chocolate, and warmed me to my balls. I had no memory of ever eating caramel or dark chocolate. "This whiskey is too good to drink like that."

"Old man," she said, mocking.

"You have no idea."

She poured another round.

Hours later we stumbled upstairs, half tripping over each other we were so intertwined. I clawed at the straps of her armour and was defeated. Once inside the room, she undid the buckles with the speed and agility of a master. Kicking the leather aside, she tackled me. Bouncing off the edge of the bed, we ended up on the floor.

Shalayn tore her shirt off me, bit my neck, and swirled her tongue around my ear.

At some point we made it onto the bed and her knees were hooked over my shoulders. Hands planted flat on the headboard, she kept panting "Harder, fucking harder."

Morning came about a week sooner than I was ready for. I peeled my face off her pale and freckled ass, which I'd been using as a pillow, and gave it a half-hearted slap.

"Fuck off," she muttered.

Looking at that ass, the curve, the line where ass met leg, half of me wanted another go. The other half wanted to die. Anything to escape the hellish putrescent shitstorm ravaging my skull.

"Whiskey," she said.

I kissed one ass cheek and bit the other. Then I shuffled downstairs, relying on the walls for support, and fetched us two whiskeys each. The innkeeper was too tired to hate me.

This was mad. No one could maintain this pace. I hadn't even recovered from the previous evening's festivities before we commenced on a second night of debauchery. Sure, I was grinning like an idiot. I felt spent, mauled. And yeah, the sex got better and better as we learned each other's bodies. But a couple more nights like this would end me.

What a way to go.

Four whiskeys in hand, it took me six times as long to make it back up the stairs as it had to come down.

Was I some kind of distraction for Shalayn, a diversion from something she didn't want to think about? She'd been sober on the caravan ride south, but our two days in Taramlae had been a drunken tornado.

Opening the door, I stood half in the hall, examining the room. The place was a dump and we hadn't done it any favours. Sleeping on her side now, back to me, Shalayn's naked curves drew my eye.

"Shut the damned door," she said.

Two hours later I sat on the edge of the bed watching Shalayn strap on her armour. Her blue eyes were rimmed red with exhaustion. She grinned evilly at me, and I wanted to tell her to strip off the armour and forget Tien.

"Maybe we can see your wizard friend tomorrow," I suggested.

"Friend." She laughed without humour. "No. Tien will..." She scowled, focussing on the straps of her leather skirt.

Interesting.

Miraculously, I pulled on my pants without falling over and stood there blinking stupidly at her.

"Where's your shirt?" she asked.

We discovered it under the bed with a pair of lace panties neither of us recognized.

We found Tien in the same coffee shop drinking the same sludgy coffee. It rained during the night and the shallow steps leading into the basement cafe had become a cascading waterfall. The customers plodded through it like this was a regular occurrence, not even worth noticing.

Tien watched our approach, green eyes narrowing when she spotted me. It wasn't the look of loathing I got from most folk, but it certainly wasn't welcoming. More like she had a different, entirely personal, reason for disliking me.

"You two look like puked up dog turds," Tien said as we arrived.

"We had some drinks," said Shalayn. "A little celebrating." She leaned heavily on the table like without it she might topple to the floor.

"You're ready to do this?" asked Tien, eyeing us with some doubt.

"Yes," I lied.

Shalayn nodded and then looked regretful.

Tien slid a ring across the table to Shalayn. "Put that in your pocket and don't put it on your finger until you're at the base of the tower."

Shalayn pocketed the ring. "What is it?"

"There's a levitation spell with enough juice in it to get the two of you to the top of the tower."

"Two?" I asked. "And one ring?"

"It creates a field-effect, but she'll have to carry you."

"I could carry her," I suggested. Though the days of decent food filled me out a bit, I remained bone thin. Years of near starvation wouldn't be erased that fast.

"No," said Tien. "It'll only work for her. Suck up your manly pride and deal with it."

I shrugged.

"There's a trigger phrase," she told Shalayn.

Tien wrote the words 'I deserve better,' on the table top with her finger. They glowed for a moment before fading.

"Don't say them aloud until you have the ring on, and the stained-soul here in your loving arms. If you do—"

"Stained-soul," I interrupted. "I've heard that before. Why do they call me that?"

She looked annoyed at being interrupted, but answered. "Darkers—islanders—were at the heart of the old empire. Some were demonologists, stained-souls making dark deals. Now, if I may continue?"

Dark deals. I nodded.

"The ring will bear you up at a comfortable speed, but if it isn't carrying your combined weight, it'll take off pretty fast. You'll have some control. Say forward, back, left, right, to direct it. When you're over the roof, remove the ring to drop down."

"What will happen to the ring?" I asked.

"It'll disappear straight up."

"After, how do we get out of the tower?" asked Shalayn.

"Through the front door," answered Tien. "From the inside, it should be easy."

"Should?" I asked. "You ever been inside one of these depot towers before?"

"Of course not. It's suicide."

Great.

"You remember what I want, right?" She directed her question at Shalayn.

"We do."

"And the writing?"

Shalayn glanced at me and I nodded. "We remember," she said.

And I did. I remembered it perfectly. It was branded it into my brain, too teasingly familiar to ever forget. I felt like I should know what it said but couldn't quite recall, a language once learned, and now forgotten.

Tien glared at Shalayn. "Remember, you are not to touch it. It'll kill you." For a moment, I thought she was going to reach out and grab Shalayn's hand. "It has to be a man," she finished.

"I remember," said Shalayn.

The wizard turned her attention on me. "Do you love her?" She pinned me with green eyes.

Did I? I thought I might. I wanted to be with her, and I wanted her to be with me.

Shalayn groaned and closed her eyes.

I nodded to Tien.

"Then don't do this," she said. "Take her away from here. Take her away from this life. Make her stop drinking. Give her a reason to live forever."

Conflict tore me. I wanted that, but I *needed* what was in that tower.

"Shalayn," I said, touching her arm. She remained still, eyes closed, jaw clenched. "Is that what you want?"

"No."

I wanted to ask if she was sure. I wanted her to look at me, to tell me the truth, but I got the answer I'd hoped for. I hated myself a little, then.

"That's not what she wants," I said to Tien.

The petite wizard's shoulders sagged. She shook her head, sighing with disappointment.

Shalayn rapped the table with a knuckle. "We'll be back with your bauble." She wore an impenetrable mask of calm, a wall between her and the world.

Tien nodded, her own gaze hooded. I saw through her. There were cracks in her defences. Pain hid behind those green eyes.

Shalayn spun and left, stomping across the wet floor.

I realized we hadn't got everything yet. "How do we get through the door?"

Tien handed me a key. "Give this to Shalayn. There'll be a keyhole. Tell her to insert it. It'll fit any lock." She examined me. "It has to be her. It won't work for you."

"Fine."

"If you come back and she doesn't…"

"You'll boil my blood?"

"You'll wish."

Pocketing the key, I turned to leave.

"Please, if you care about her at all, don't let her touch the ring in the tower."

"I won't."

"You're a selfish asshole," said Tien. "I know, because I'm one too."

I followed Shalayn out of the basement cafe.

CHAPTER ELEVEN

I caught up with Shalayn a block later, my head feeling like it might burst like an over-ripe melon from the jog.

"Where are we going?" I asked, when I got my breath back and thought I might not vomit.

"To the tower," she said, eyes ahead.

"Shouldn't we go back to the inn, plan this a little?"

"Why? We don't know what's in there. We don't know what we're facing. What can we plan?"

"Well… maybe we should do this at night."

"No. Now."

"People will see us."

"When they see us levitate up to the roof, they'll assume we're wizards. They'll find something else to look at. No one messes with wizards." Finally, she did snap a glance at me. "No one except you, apparently."

"We don't look like wizards."

"Does Tien?"

She had me there. "Speaking of Tien…" I fished the key out of my pocket and offered it to Shalayn. "She says it'll open any lock and only works for you."

"Typical." She took the key and stuffed it into the same pocket as the ring.

"She also said that if I loved—"

"Don't want to hear it."

We walked in silence for several blocks until I spotted a shop with candles and lanterns on display.

"We should grab a couple of lanterns. Who knows what it's like inside the tower. There are no windows."

After purchasing one each, and flint steels, char cloth, and tinders for lighting them, we continued on our way.

"We're going to have to leave Taramlae after, aren't we?" I asked.

Shalayn grunted. "Probably best."

"We'll need funds. I'd like some new clothes, boots that fit. A sword, maybe some armour."

"Yay," she dead-panned. "A shopping spree."

"I can't keep sponging off you."

"Need to be self-sufficient, eh? Your own man?"

I wasn't even sure what she was angry about.

"Once you have whatever is in the tower you won't need me anymore."

Ah. "That's not—*We* are going to need money."

She turned a corner and I followed.

"I think we should take a couple of things while we're in the tower," I said. "Sell them to fund our trip to wherever we're going next."

"And where is that?"

Good question. "I don't know yet. I just know there's a piece of me in that tower. It's calling so loud I can't hear anything else. Until I have it in…" I didn't want to explain the heart thing. "Once I have it, I think I'll know where the next piece is."

"Have you been lying?" demanded Shalayn. "This whole time, has all this been about robbing a wizard's tower to steal a bunch of forbidden magical items?"

"No. There is only one thing in that tower I want. If you'd rather, we can walk out of there with nothing else."

She kept walking, jaw muscles working.

I grabbed her arm and dragged her to a halt.

"You decide," I said. "You decide what we take."

"If I walk away right now? If I take the key and the ring and leave?"

What would I do? "I'll watch you go."

"And?"

Damn. I decided to be honest. "And try and find another way into the tower."

"And if I ask you to walk away with me?"

I swallowed. This close to the tower, the draw was intense, a constant pressure battling the hangover. Who did I want more, me or her?

"We're going to the tower," she said, not waiting for an answer. "We'll find your memories. Somehow. We'll steal a few magical trinkets while we're at it. Then, we'll escape and live happily ever after." She laughed, a humourless chuckle. "Right. I forgot. This isn't the only piece. Somewhere, there is more of you." She shook her head. "Let's go."

It was midday by the time we reached the tower. My hangover deepened, festering in my skull, and infusing my spine. I couldn't keep doing this.

The cool breeze of the morning died, replaced by a still heat. I was almost comfortable. The pale people of Taramlae turned pink and red and dripped sweat and found a new reason to hate me.

From a couple of blocks distance, a thirty-five-foot-tall tower of mortared stone doesn't look terribly imposing. Standing at its base, lost in its shadow, you come to realize just how a fall from that height will break you. The tower was also much wider around than I realized. Walking its circumference took several minutes.

Grey and black, the stones looked damp. When I touched one, my hand came away dry. I peered up. The slightly conical shape of the tower, tapering in a little toward the top, didn't help.

"Let's not fall," I said.

Shalayn nodded agreement. "Stop looking around to see if anyone's watching. We're wizards. We're going to fly to the top of our tower."

I focussed on her and she grinned at me. I felt off balance, confused by her rapidly shifting moods. Running fingers through her close-cropped hair, she leaned back to stare at the top of the tower.

"Are you afraid of heights?" she asked.

"No."

She punched me in the shoulder, a playful jab that only stung a bit. "How do you know?"

That stumped me. "I just do." I imagined riding something high above the ground. Clouds, white and fluffy yet strangely solid-looking, flashed past beneath me. Cold air chilled my face while the rest of me remained comfortably warm. We banked, wings spread wide, and the world tilted and I gloried in the sheer joy of the moment.

"What are you smiling about?"

I blinked away the memory, if that's what it was. "Daydreaming about flying."

Shalayn removed the ring from her pocket and slid it on her finger. "Get over here and hold on tight."

I stepped close and wrapped my arms around her. "You sure you want to do this?" I asked.

"I deserve better," she said, and we rose up off the ground.

As long as I stayed close, the field enveloped me, but I suspect if I pushed away I'd drop like a stone. I decided not to experiment.

"Remind me to thank Tien for her excellent choice of trigger phrase," I said.

"She always does that."

Always? I wondered how many times Shalayn had been in similar situations, and with whom.

By mumbling 'forward' at regular intervals, she kept us close to the tower wall as it sloped inward. As soon as we crested the top she moved us forward again and then removed the ring from her finger. Releasing it, it shot straight up.

We dropped a foot or two and landed on the tower's roof. I held her a moment longer and she gave me a quick kiss on the cheek. Glancing up, I couldn't find the ring.

"Let's rob these bastards blind," she said.

Releasing her, I surveyed the rooftop. "We were right."

CHAPTER TWELVE

The roof was flat with an iron trapdoor in the middle. A heavy table, wrought of twisted black iron, sat surrounded by six similar chairs. A short length of chain attached each chair to the roof.

"So they don't blow away," said Shalayn.

"An iron chair falling on you from thirty feet would ruin anyone's day."

Shalayn collapsed into one of the chairs and grinned at me. "We should have brought something to drink." She waved an arm at the scene below. "Look at the view. This is the best patio in the city."

Too damned hungover to even think about booze, I turned in a complete circle. Taramlae, while orderly and clean enough, at least from up here, nonetheless seemed somehow crude. Something was missing, and I couldn't imagine what. There weren't enough people, I decided. For what was supposed to be the capital of the wizard-run world, Taramlae was too damned small.

"Where are all the people?" I asked. "If this is the capital, it should be bigger."

Shalayn frowned at the city, shrugging. "It's huge."

She was right, and yet I still expected *more*.

"In school," she said, "we learn that the Great War killed seven in ten people. The following wars, as the various schools of magic battled for supremacy, killed three in ten of what was left."

"Let me guess, the wizards run the schools."

"They run everything." Seeing my face, she held up a stalling hand. "The wars brought us to the edge of extinction. The wizards saved humanity." She gestured at the city. "They built this from the ashes of the old world."

"History is written by the winner. That wall," I said, abruptly changing the subject. Even at our elevation, the outer wall towered over us. "What was it built to keep out? Dragons?"

"Dragons would fly over the top," she said. "Anyway, the big ones are all but extinct, except around the Deredi Mountains, and that's thousands of miles from here."

"Right."

"I heard it was built during the Great War as a defence against the demon armies. Apparently, there are wards built into the wall. Huge circles of wizards powered them."

"Circles?" Why did I remember some things, but not others? Sometimes it felt like whoever broke me did so with an eye to what memories this fragment retained.

Slumped in the iron chair, looking like she ought to be sipping beer on a patio bar, Shalayn examined me with narrowed eyes. "Wizards meditate to draw power from chaos, which they can then shape. Tien told me it can take years of meditation to fuel a really serious spell. But they can work in circles, pooling their resources. Instead of one wizard spending power built over hundreds of hours of meditation, one hundred wizards can spend one hour's meditation each."

For reasons I couldn't explain, that only made me hate them more. It bothered me that cooperation was their strength.

I glanced into the sky. "How high do you think Tien's ring will go?"

Shalayn gave a disinterested shrug.

"Do spells wear off? Will it eventually fall back to earth? Are the clouds littered with wizard junk?"

"For someone who hates wizards, you're awfully fascinated by them."

Know your enemy. I kept that thought to myself.

Shalayn pushed herself out of the iron chair and stretched, a languid twisting of her torso doing all kinds of interesting things, even with armour on.

"Let's do this," she said, approaching the trap door and scowling down at the iron slab. Kneeling over the door, she found the keyhole and inserted Tien's key. I heard a dull *click* the instant the key entered.

"Let's hope the rest of this is that easy," I said

Shalayn swung the door open with ease, despite its being half a foot thick.

"Don't know if that was magic," she said, peering down into the stairwell. "Good thing I thought to get lanterns. It's damned dark down there."

I joined her. The sun overhead lit the room beneath. Everything else was black. "Yeah. Good thing."

Drawing her sword, Shalayn descended. I followed, not bothering with my knives.

The room we entered looked like a kitchen in a well-appointed inn. There was a large wood-burning oven and enough firewood to cook several weeks' meals. Huge countertops finished in thick slabs of white marble seemed to stretch on for miles. Shelves, mounted above the counters, were stacked with flour, grains, and jars of fruit and vegetable preserves. One wall was a massive wine rack holding thousands of bottles.

"No," I said, "leave the wine."

"You're no fun." She stole a long plaintive look at the wall of wine, one arm lifting a little as if she wanted to touch one, just for a moment. "I bet some of those are worth a fortune."

"Do you know which ones?" Wine seemed like something pretty safe to sell without drawing wizardly attention.

"Nope."

"Would you actually sell them?"

She flashed a grin. "Nope."

Stairs followed the outer wall, spiralling into darkness.

"Let's give the kitchen a quick look," I said, "and then we'll—"

The trapdoor above us swung closed with a soft click, plunging us into utter black. No hint of light made it through. Climbing the steps to the door, I gave it a tentative push. It didn't budge. Running fingertips across the ceiling, I searched for seams and found nothing, though I did discover what I assumed to be a keyhole.

"I don't suppose you grabbed that key before we came down?" I asked.

"Fuck."

I took that as a no.

Sparks slashed the dark as she worked to light a lantern. I closed my eyes to save my night vision and then realized how pointless that was. With there being absolutely no light in here—not even a whisper made it past the trap door—no matter how much my eyes adjusted, I'd never be able to see. I gave up searching the ceiling. Other than the key hole, I found nothing. Not even hinges. I couldn't remember seeing them when we were outside, but couldn't figure where else they'd be. Damned wizards. I heaved my full weight against the door a few times but it was an immoveable slab of iron. I might as well have thrown my scrawny and still slightly malnourished body against a stone wall.

As I descended back to the kitchen, Shalayn got the first lantern lit. Yellow light filled the room and set shadows dancing as she started on the second lantern.

With both lanterns lit, she lifted one to examine the ceiling above. "We aren't getting out that way."

I agreed. Being able to see didn't change the fact that this was a magically locked door and we were on the wrong side of it.

She passed me one of the lanterns and then once again drew her sword.

"I don't think you'll need that," I said. "I'm guessing we're alone in here."

"Sure, but when we get hungry because we can't escape, I may have to kill and eat you."

I took in the extensive larder. "There's enough in here to keep us fat and drunk for years."

"That doesn't sound all bad," she said, looking wistful as she again eyed the wine racks.

She was right. It sounded a damned sight better than what I had planned.

I felt the pull of my heart from somewhere beneath us. This close, it filled me, thrummed through me like a deep bass note.

"It's below us," I said. "My... My memories."

Sword drawn, lantern raised, Shalayn approached the steps down. Again, I followed.

"We're definitely coming back for some of the wine before we leave," she said over her shoulder.

I knew better than to argue.

Sword held before her, lantern raised to light the way, Shalayn descended. She hugged the outer wall to give herself as much warning as to what awaited around the bend as possible. Moving slowly, she took her time with each step, waiting for something to leap out and attack.

At the bottom of the stairs, she paused. A long hall cut the tower in half, with doors on either side. At the far end, another set of stairs continued down. The doors—five on each side—were labelled in a strange, jagged script that glowed like fire in the lantern light. I joined her.

"Can you read that?" I asked.

"Nope. Guild Cant. Secret language."

"Fucking wizards."

Ignoring me, she moved to the first door. Reaching for the knob, a round ball of shiny glass, she hesitated. "What if it's trapped?"

"We could leave it and keep going down?" This close to a shard of my heart, I itched to keep moving. It still lay somewhere below us.

"I don't like leaving doors behind me. Leads to surprises later."

"Up to you."

"Screw it." She opened the door, peering in. "Whoa!"

I leaned to look over her shoulder. A palatial suite lay beyond. A bed large enough for a half dozen folks to sprawl comfortably lay against one wall. Sheets of grey silk glowed lustrous in the lantern light. Huge armoires of oak and mahogany lined another wall. An open doorway led to a spacious office with a colossal desk and rows of shelves lined with books. Sheets of paper, ink pots, and a selection of quills lay neatly arranged upon the desk. Another open door led to what looked to be a water closet finished in brass and marble.

Shalayn entered the bedroom, and I followed close behind. Crossing to the office, she ran a finger across the surface of the desk.

"No dust," she said, holding up the finger like I might not believe her.

"Fucking wizards."

She turned a complete circle. "Is this... Isn't this too big?"

"For one person, yes." Though somehow, I felt immediately at home in the luxurious surroundings, like this was what I was accustomed to.

"No, for the tower."

"It's pretty big."

She passed me on her way back into the hall. Crossing, she opened the door on the opposite side. An equally large room lay beyond. Whoever decorated this one preferred gold and purple.

"Wizards are a crass and tasteless bunch," I said.

"No way it's this big." She held up a hand, interrupting me. "I know, fucking wizards."

"That's not what I was going to say," I lied.

In rapid succession, Shalayn threw open the rest of the doors. Each opened to a suite including a massive bedroom replete with a huge bed, secondary offices, walk-in closets, and a room for toiletries. Even wizards, it seemed, had to shit.

After throwing open the last door, she went in to explore. Whoever decorated this room liked forest-green and deep velvet.

"If we're stuck here," she said, "at least we'll be comfortable."

"You see lanterns or candles anywhere?"

"Nope. Maybe that stuff is downstairs."

I blew out my lantern. "We should conserve oil," I said, "just in case. It'll be awfully dark in here."

Shalayn headed into the water closet, and again, I followed. It looked oddly clean. A marble toilet sat next to what looked like a knee-high water fountain. Water ran continually, climbing to mid-thigh height.

I glanced into the toilet, expecting to see more water but only impossible black lay at the bottom. Sheets of soft paper, no doubt meant for wiping wizard ass, sat piled nearby. Selecting one, I dropped it into the toilet. The sheet disappeared the moment it touched the black.

"What do you suppose happens to wizard turds?" I asked Shalayn, who'd stopped to watch me.

"They probably teleport it somewhere."

"Could this be our escape?"

"Into a huge underground repository for wizard shit? No thanks." She tilted her head, thinking. "Anyway, it's just as likely they incinerate it, or it leads to the bottom of the ocean."

It did seem unlikely they'd leave a handy escape portal in their tower.

At the far end of the water closet was a separate room, again finished in white marble. Perfectly spaced holes riddled the ceiling and a drain lay in the centre of the slightly concave floor.

Shalayn stuck her hand in and water immediately rained from the ceiling. "It's warm," she said, wiping her hand.

"We won't starve or die of thirst."

"And," she said, "we'll sleep in majestic comfort."

"In eternal dark."

"Doesn't sound all bad."

It didn't. But there was something in this tower I wanted. Something I *needed*. This close, its call was deafening.

"If nothing else," said Shalayn, "we can sell some of these silk sheets. The bedding alone is worth a fortune."

I wanted to stuff them all in the toilet to be incinerated or teleported away just to annoy whatever wizards slept here. I kept that thought to myself.

"There's that look," she said, rolling her eyes. "You want to crap on the beds or shove the sheets in the shitter or something."

"Let's keep going," I said, getting impatient. More of me waited below. It felt it like the tug of a fish hook in flesh. I wanted to know what I was, why the wizards broke me.

"No sense of adventure," said Shalayn, pushing past me and heading back into the hall.

We walked to the far end, peering down into the dark where the curve of the stairs went beyond the light of our lantern. Shalayn was right. This tower was much bigger on the inside than the outside showed to be possible.

We descended.

The next floor looked like a museum. Rows and rows of shelves and tall cases turned the space into a maze. Assorted objects from rocks, to armoured helms, to kitchen implements, to feathers and damned near anything else I could think of, lined the shelves. That strange, jagged script—Guild cant—labelled everything with eerily glowing letters.

"We're going to be rich," said Shalayn.

"You're going to be dead," said the wizard who appeared before us as the entire ceiling suddenly glowed bright.

CHAPTER THIRTEEN

Shalayn, who still had her sword drawn, put it in the wizard's throat even as I started to say "Don't kill him!"

Her sword was faster than my mouth.

The wizard blinked in surprise like it never occurred to him someone might have the audacity, the utter gall, to put steel in him. He coughed bright blood. His lips moved as if trying to speak. A hand rose, fingers twitching. Shalayn severed it and then stuck him in the chest.

"I think he was trying to cast a spell," she said, as he crumpled at our feet.

The mage coughed more blood and she neatly slid the blade between the fourth and fifth ribs. He went rigid like all his muscles contracted at the same time, shivered, and relaxed, sagging loose.

"Dead," I said.

"Good."

"I hope we don't need him to get out," I said. "Couldn't you have knocked him unconscious instead?"

"No." She shot me an annoyed look. "An even halfway decent wizard can cast with nothing more than concentration and a few gestures. Only acolytes run around screaming spells like you see in the plays."

Having no memory of ever having seen a play, and knowing next to nothing about wizards, I decided to let it go.

"My—" I caught myself before I said heart. "The piece of stone with my memories is somewhere in this room. Let's find it and get out before another wizard shows up."

I prayed Tien was right and we'd wander out the front door without difficulty. The fact that the rooftop door didn't open easily from the inside, however, hadn't filled me with confidence.

Shalayn glanced at the many shelves lined with stones of every shape, size, and colour. "How do we find it?"

"I'm drawn to it. Shouldn't be too difficult."

"We'll split up," Shalayn suggested. "You get the stone, I'll look for that ring Tien wants." She flashed a fast grin. "At least we can see now." She doused the lantern.

I glanced at the glowing ceiling, half expecting it to begin fading. It didn't. "Let's move fast."

Picking an aisle with shelves loaded with trinkets and jewellery, Shalayn set off.

"Don't touch anything!" I called after her. "Specially the ring!"

She replied with something rude.

Turning away, I followed the pull of my heart. Passing several aisles of swords, assorted weapons and armour, I found one where the shelves were covered in rocks. From tiny shards little more than grains, to skull-sized boulders, they came in every colour imaginable. Chips of slate-grey shale lay next to nuggets of gold. Crystals of purple amethyst caught the light and sparkled the ceiling in rainbows. Diamonds, rubies, and emeralds lay everywhere. If we could carry out even a fraction of this, we'd be set for life.

I stopped, staring at a fist-sized diamond with thousands of facets. Glinting hard and bright, it was somehow menacing. Why didn't the thought of an easy life of luxury appeal to me? I realized I was more interested in the wealth as a means to fund my search, than as an end in itself. I liked Shalayn, a lot. Maybe I even loved her. But did I want to be with her forever? Did she want to be with me?

"But I'm happy with her," I whispered.

So why not leave it at that? What could be better than being happy and wealthy with a good woman at my side? I remembered the speed and utter lack of emotion with which she killed the wizard. Could I do that? I wasn't sure. I'd murdered the trapper because I had to, and I'd been more animal than man at the time. And I'd split my own skull, though again it seemed like I had no choice; one of us had to kill the other to get at his heart.

What about that youth, the Septk? Him, I didn't have to kill.

I pushed the memory aside.

I found the shard of my obsidian heart lying amidst a mix of equally nondescript black stones. Had they thought to hide it from me? Did the wizards think I wouldn't immediately know which one was me?

I reached for the stone and stopped. The last time I touched one it sank into my flesh and tore through me on its way to my heart. After, I spent an unknown amount of time sprawled on the ground, unconscious. Much as I wanted what was in this stone, I couldn't do that without first warning Shalayn. And this probably wasn't the best time for unconsciousness.

"You find the ring?" I shouted.

"No!"

"I found my memories!"

"Hold on," she called. "I'm coming."

A moment later Shalayn appeared. She bit her bottom lip, chewing nervously as she eyed the arrayed stones. "There's a fortune in here."

I nodded agreement. "One of those little black ones," I pointed at the shelf, "is me."

"Okay." She studied me now.

I decided to tell her. "When I pick it up, things will happen."

"Bad things?"

"Well, painful things. It'll sink into my skin. I'll probably flop around on the floor screaming in agony as it moves through me."

Pale eyes narrowed. "Where is it going?"

"To my heart, where it will join the chunk of stone already there."

She looked from the flake of rock, to me. "You're telling me you have a heart of obsidian, black and brittle and sharp."

"It sounds bad when you say it like that."

Shalayn snorted an unladylike grunt.

"Last time," I said, "I lost consciousness for a while. A day, maybe two."

"A wizard could pop in at any moment," she pointed out. "The ceiling," she glanced up, "might go dark. I'd rather not be trapped in a pitch-black wizard's tower with an unconscious guy."

"I'll take the stone, but make sure it doesn't touch my flesh. That should do. Then, once we're somewhere safe, I'll touch it."

"Fine."

Shalayn dug a kerchief from somewhere and handed to me. I used it to collect and wrap the stone and dropped it into a pocket.

We stood, staring at each other.

"Now what?" I asked.

"Let's find Tien's ring and get out of here."

"Do you trust her?"

"She would never hurt me." She winced. "Well, not physically. That said, she *is* a thief."

"Right. Let's not touch anything we don't have to. I have a bad feeling about this place. I think everything in here might be dangerous."

"Like your obsidian heart?"

I let that slide without comment.

It took us an hour to find the ring. During that time, no wizards arrived, and the glow of the ceiling remained unchanged. Careful not to touch it, we wrapped the ring in fabric and I pocketed it.

"Let's make sure we can open the door to get out," I said. "Then we'll decide what we're taking and rob the wizards blind."

"Good plan. And we're taking at least one bottle of wine."

"Deal."

Circumnavigating the outer wall, looking for the door, we found it, a slab of plain iron with glowing script scrawled all over it. We found no hint of hinges and nothing to grip or pull. There was also no keyhole, not that we had a key.

"I don't think we should touch it," said Shalayn.

I agreed. Even being close to it made the hairs on my neck and arms stand straight and filled my mouth with a metallic tang.

Without getting too close, we examined the door.

"There isn't even room to wedge the tip of a sword between the door and the wall or floor," I said.

"You try and do that to my sword, and I'll smack you."

We spent hours looking over the slab of steel. Then we searched the rest of the room, still careful not to touch anything. Shalayn kept her sword drawn, ready for violence. We found nothing to aid our escape. No other wizards appeared.

"Do we touch it?" I asked.

"Not yet."

"I'm hungry."

"I'm thirsty," she said, sheathing her sword.

"There's news."

We returned upstairs to the kitchen area. While I put together a meal of preserved fruits, and vegetables soaked in olive oil, Shalayn selected a bottle of red wine that was, according to the label, over sixty years old.

There was no dust on anything. It felt like someone finished cleaning moments before our arrival.

"How long does olive oil last?" I asked.

"About a year," answered Shalayn as she hunted through drawers, looking for a bottle opener.

"Do they restock every few months?"

"That, or this stuff is magically preserved."

Finding what she sought, she had the bottle open seconds later.

"Want wine glasses?" I asked, eyeing the many cupboards.

"Nah." Taking a long drink from the bottle, she sank cross-legged to the floor.

Carrying the food I'd gathered, I sat across from her.

We ate and drank, passing the bottle back and forth, in comfortable silence. The fruit tasted juicy and fresh and the wine had a soft musty flavour with hints of strawberry and chocolate in the bouquet.

"I could get used to this," said Shalayn, finishing the last of the wine.

I could too. "We can't stay," I said. "Eventually—"

"Don't ruin it."

"—another wizard will come. We can't kill him this time. Somehow, we have to use him to get out. We have to force him to bring us with him when he leaves."

"Won't work," said Shalayn, shaking her head. "The only reason I got that one was because he appeared within stabbing distance and I already had my sword drawn. Unless you surprise a wizard, you're pretty much fucked." She glanced around, eyeing the thousands of wine bottles. "And I'm betting they can appear anywhere in here."

"If we stay alert, maybe we can get the drop on one. If we hide in one of the bedrooms, we can jump him when he enters."

"If he's an idiot."

"Got another plan?"

"We try the door downstairs."

After trooping back down the stairs, I reached tentatively toward the door, ready to snatch my hand away. Pressure built as I got closer and then with a *snap* a bright spark arced out and stabbed my hand. Howling in pain, I flinched away. Once she realized I wasn't seriously harmed, Shalayn had a great time laughing at my expression as I sucked on the palm of my hand. I hadn't got closer than a foot.

"I think if I tried again, if I threw myself at it, it would blast me to ash."

That had been a little warning. I felt sure the door was capable of much worse.

Shalayn calmed down. "Right then. Let's try your brilliant 'jump a wizard' plan."

We picked one of the bedrooms and hid in two different armoires, shoving aside the clothes hanging there to make room.

Several hours passed in tedious silence before Shalayn started making jokes about how we could better pass the time if we both hid in the same armoire. Finally, after the third hour, she said, "I'm getting a drink."

Rather than feel like an idiot in an armoire, I followed her back to the kitchen and watched her select another bottle of red wine.

"Are we going to hide again?" I asked.

"Go ahead."

We ate paper-thin sheets of salted ham wrapped around olive-oil soaked artichoke hearts with slabs of crumbling cheddar, and washed it down with more wine.

When the wizards failed to show up and kill us, we picked another room and went to bed.

"We could die at any time," said Shalayn. "A wizard could teleport in while we're sleeping."

"True, but I'm too tired to stand guard."

"I don't want to die sober, and I don't want to die horny."

"Oh. I'm awake enough for that."

We took care of both those issues, and still the wizards failed to show up and kill us.

In the morning, she told me she didn't want to die hungover.

For a week we searched the tower for some means of escape while the dead wizard on the ground floor stank worse with each passing day. We found nothing other than that dangerous door which neither of us was willing to try to touch again. The one discovery we did make was that each time we returned to the bedroom, it had been tidied and the bed remade. I also learned that if anyone stayed in the room trying to learn how that happened, nothing got cleaned. I suppose whatever magic the wizards worked to achieve this effect was set only to function in an empty room so as not to disturb its occupants.

"Fucking wizards, eh?" said Shalayn, grinning, when I shared my discovery.

At some point she noted that I still wore the mouldering old clothes she found me in and that the armoires were filled with pristine clothing in a wide range of colours, styles, and sizes. Much as I hated wizards, they did seem to appreciate quality. I selected for myself a pair of black cotton pants, a loose shirt the hue of dark blood, and comfortable leather shoes. What I really wanted was a long robe of all red, but couldn't find it. Every other colour was available except the one I wanted. Like the wizards had some aversion to that one choice. Weird.

I transferred the ring and the wrapped shard of my heart to a pocket in my new pants.

Shalayn eyed me as I displayed my choices.

"What?"

"Red suits you. You look good."

"Yeah?"

She shrugged.

With no windows, we had no way of knowing if it was day or night and soon lost track of time. We ate. We drank. We made love in every bedroom.

Shalayn shed her armour and found a set of silk robes that accentuated her curves to great effect. Pale blue, they matched her eyes.

As we sat to eat yet another meal and drink more wine I drew the shard of my heart from its pocket. I lay it on the floor between us, unfolding the material to display it.

"We might be here for a while," I said. "I want to know more of who I am."

Shalayn stared, unblinking, at the stone. "I don't want to be stuck in here with an asshole."

"It won't change how I—" I stopped, uncomfortable. I wanted to tell her it wouldn't change how I felt about her, but I was never really sure what she felt about me. "I'll still be me." That sounded pathetic.

"I know you really want this. Thank you for waiting as long as you did. That must have been difficult."

She had no idea. Many nights, after she fell asleep, I sat up staring at the shard. So many times, I almost touched the stone and robbed her of any choice in who she shared this tower with. I didn't want to be that kind of person. I wanted to be someone she could rely on. Someone she could trust.

Someone she could love.

She'd been hurt, I was sure. Who hurt her, I didn't know. Maybe it was Tien, they definitely shared some history. Being with the two of them in that underground cafe felt like interloping on old friends. I decided that if Shalayn wanted me to know, she'd tell me.

"We're in this together," I said, "and together, we'll make decisions."

"Good. So how does this work?"

"When I touch it, it'll enter my flesh. It'll make its way through my body to my heart."

She nibbled on her bottom lip, looking thoughtful. "Is it painful?"

"Incredibly."

"Why don't you push it against your chest over your heart so it doesn't have to tear through your entire body to get there?"

I blinked at her. "Because I'm an idiot."

She flashed a quick smile. "And you said you were unconscious for a while afterwards?"

"At least a day. Maybe two."

"Right. Let's get you into bed—"

"Oh, here we go again. Always thinking with your—"

"So I don't have to drag you there. And you'll be more comfortable."

After retiring to one of the bedrooms—this one was deep earthy tones and down comforters big enough to lose yourself in—I sat on the bed. I lay the tiny shard of obsidian on the sheets before me.

"You're sure?" said Shalayn. "You don't want to smash it to dust or toss it down the hole in the water closet?"

I couldn't tell her how tempting that was, or how terrifying. The idea of just being me, *this* me, of spending my days with her... I wanted that. Taking on new memories would change me—how could it not?

"I need to know," I said.

She nodded and I picked up the stone and held it against my chest.

For a moment, nothing.

I screamed as it split the skin and bore through one of my ribs. This was not less painful.

I lost Shalayn. She must have been there, but the pain became everything. Searing agony.

CHAPTER FOURTEEN

A man, cloaked in blood, stood on a hill. An icy wind, rushing down from the Deredi Mountains, snapped and tugged at his robes, blew the cowl back exposing hard features shaped by hard choices. His hair, once black, now shot with iron grey, hung in long, ropey braids. His eyes were gone, torn from his skull, replaced by two differently shaped and sized stones that looked to have been forced into the sockets. Ridged scars like melted flesh surrounded the stones.

Down below, in the Melechesh Pass, arrayed armies faced off against each other. Stone eyes surveyed the scene.

Battalions of giants, armoured in the scales of slain dragons, held colossal great swords. Sorcerers spent themselves, ageing at a furious rate, growing old and weak, to fuel their crude but powerful spells. Elementalists stood surrounded by armies of trees and rocks. The very earth did their bidding.

The man watched distant elementalists work to wake the mountain upon which they stood. This was madness. Size and age determined an elemental's power. If they succeeded, they could never hope to control something so large, so ancient.

Even the western tribes had come. Shamans in stinking animal skins clawed themselves bloody, called ancient and long-dead ancestors and spirits.

He saw armies of corpses surrounding the necromancers. Dead knights mounted on rotting horses. Giants, reduced to decaying sinew and bone, rode undead dragons, their massive wings like wind-tattered sheets. Anything falling in the coming battle would rise up against the man in blood.

And there, safe at the back, cowering behind the vast armies they plotted and manipulated to bring against him, stood the wizards. Legions of Battle Mages twisted the world with their filthy chaos magic. The air stank of change and unfettered potential. Standing in huge rings, thousands of women and men holding hands, they pooled their resources to work world-shattering spells.

"This is too much," said the man with the stone eyes. "They damage the world with their mad quest for power and domination."

He turned to the demon standing at his side and asked, "Can we interrupt whatever spell they're working? If we break a circle that big, the backlash will destroy most of their army."

The demon, in robes of ink, looked like a gaunt old man, bald, bent and near skeletal. "If we break that circle, it might crack the earth to its core. Lava. Ash in the sky for years."

"I'm fine with that."

"The elementalists have succeeded in waking that mountain. It will be angry."

"Perfect. Break the circle."

The demon squinted at the distant mage-circle. "Whatever the cost?"

"Whatever the cost."

Icy wind dragged at the creature's black robes and it pulled them tight. "You can't win, old friend. The world is against you. The wizards have won. The Empire will fall."

"Perhaps I can't win," said the man. "But I can make their victory expensive." He turned to survey the ranked demons behind him. "Maybe I can cost them everything."

Creatures called from a hundred different realities stood waiting. Massive beasts, some dwarfing even the Deredi giants, held formation beside winged nightmares from some distant hell. Many, hailing from closer realities looked human, differing only in some small detail. Purple skin, horns, claws, too many or two few fingers. With this army, he had bound the world under a single rule: His. And now, with this army, he would lose the world.

Ten thousand years ago, when he first rose to power, there had been no Wizard's Guild. The many branches of magic, mages, sorcerers, necromancers, shamans, elementalists, and demonologists squabbled like children.

He brought the demonologists together, unified them in purpose. With him at the helm, the demonologists conquered the world, created the first true empire. The wizards were jealous of his power and built their guild, mimicking the unity of the demonologists. He tolerated it; chaos magic had its uses. They were leeches, feeding off all he wrought, always worming their way into every aspect of the Empire.

Ten thousand years was too much. Increasingly he left details of the Empire to be run by underlings. Conquering kingdom after kingdom, the Empire swelled beyond the scope of one man. It was too large. And that, he knew, had been its weakness.

Size killed the Empire.

Size, and the machinations of the greedy, power-hungry wizards.

They'd learn.

The wizards might win. Tomorrow, the Empire might be theirs to rule. But it was also theirs to lose. And lose it, they would. Short-sighted, they had no idea just how much the Empire relied upon demons. Demons the wizards had no means of controlling.

"We fight to the end," said the man. "To the death."

The demon beside him nodded, wizened face sad.

Commands were sent out and the demonic host, bound in servitude to the demonologists, had no choice but to obey.

That night the Empire fell, and the world sank into a thousand years of darkness.

CHAPTER FIFTEEN

I woke to find Shalayn in a silk nightie with a spread of food, cheeses and oil-soaked vegetables, laid out on the bed. She sat cross-legged, a bottle of red wine between her freckled thighs.

She watched me surface, cocking an eyebrow. "You started twitching and groaning. I figured you'd wake up soon."

"You look amazing." And she did. I was so used to seeing her in armour I still had trouble equating this woman to that warrior.

"I am." She passed me the bottle. "You were out for two days and one night," she said as I drank.

She examined me, reclaimed the bottle and took a long swig.

"I'm still me," I said. "I still... My feelings for you haven't changed."

"You remember your past?"

I considered her question. There was so much in there, swirling about my thoughts. I couldn't be sure which parts were real and which were fragments of a strange dream. Frankly, none of it seemed terribly real. The past, I decided, was like that. Even the most cherished moments faded, became memories of memories, as we focussed on the parts we liked, and forgot the rest. But where individual moments lacked clarity, knowledge was something different. I *knew* things. Impossible things. I remembered ancient symbols written in blood, pacts between men and creatures from other realities. I remembered one of the earliest bindings I learned as a young demonologist.

The majority of my past, however, remained lost to me.

"I think I know why the wizards did this to me."

Shalayn waited.

I hesitated. Should I tell her? She believed the history the wizards taught, that all demonologists were evil, that the wizards saved the world. I didn't remember much, but I knew she was wrong. The wizards lied. Their treachery destroyed the empire that kept the world peaceful for millennia. They destroyed an ancient civilization in their thirst for power.

"Well?" She raised an eyebrow.

"I'm worried you won't like it. I'm afraid you won't understand, that the wizards poisoned you."

"Poisoned? So, you're a demon, or something?" she joked. "I guess that would explain the stone heart."

"Close."

She blinked at me.

"I think I was a demonologist."

She leaned away, subtly distancing herself. That hurt.

"I know some very minor demonology spells. Nothing big, nothing world-shaking."

Shalayn pushed herself off the bed, stood there in her nightie, staring at me, bottle clutched in one hand.

"I'm not evil," I said. "I'm the same man you knew. I haven't changed."

She drank.

"You can't believe everything the wizards taught you. They lied about a lot. They rewrote history to make themselves look good."

She drank again, emptying the bottle.

"I still…"

Turning away, she left the room.

"I still love you," I said after she'd gone.

I sat, wondering what to do. Should I chase her, try to explain? Would she even listen?

In the end, I decided to wait, to give her time to come to terms with what I told her.

Hours later she returned, quite drunk, still wearing that sexy nightie. I was happy to see she hadn't gone to fetch her sword. Instead, she held another bottle of wine clutched in her fist. It was full.

"You're a fucking demonologist," she slurred.

"Technically, you've been fu…" Her look stopped me. Not a time for jokes. "A very minor one," I said. "No great earth-shattering magic, here. I doubt I could actually summon anything." I left out the fact that I was quite sure I'd learn more as I found more shards of my heart.

"You're likely the only one in all the world." She sat on the edge of the bed, but stayed beyond arm's reach.

"I don't believe that." I couldn't see how the wizards could possibly have wiped out every single demonologist. Somewhere, they were hidden away. Probably far to the south, in the islands.

"Demonologists are evil. Were evil," she corrected. She blinked at me, eyes red. "Are evil."

"I'm not evil."

"I have the worst taste in men. Tien…" She laughed, a snort of derision. "She managed to do it again. Ruined another one." She drank, spilling wine down her chest, wiping at her lips with the back of her hand. "So stupid."

I wasn't sure who she meant, me, her, or Tien. I shuffled closer on the bed and she didn't move away.

Reaching out, I touched her arm, the softest, most tentative caress. "I haven't changed. I'm still me. I haven't suddenly become some blood-swilling soul-sucking monster."

She studied me, eyes miserable, wanting to believe me, tormented by a life-time of wizard propaganda.

"The wizards lied to you," I said, moving closer, putting an arm around her. "They lied to everyone."

"It can't all be lies."

"You're probably right," I admitted. "But I don't know everything they taught you. I don't know their history. And it's not like all wizards are good and honest people, either. A wizard helped us break into this very tower so we could steal something for her."

She nodded, wanting me to still be the man she knew. I pulled her close and she leaned against me.

"I will never become a man you don't like," I swore. "If I do, you can cut me open, and shatter my heart, break me back to the man you love."

Nightie soaked in red wine, she pressed herself against me, staring up into my eyes. "You promise?"

"I promise."

"I knew," she said. "I knew there was something different about you. When that dead mountain lion clawed you, the wounds were terrible. I didn't think you'd last the night, but you didn't even seem worried. I cleaned your wounds, and by morning they were already starting to heal. I *knew*," she said, like somehow this was all her fault.

I held her while she slept, snoring and drunk.

In the morning, she changed into a long silk dress she found in one of the armoires. We ate our breakfast, more preserved vegetables, sitting on the floor in the kitchen. The ground floor and the dead wizard stank so bad we no longer went down there.

She was quiet and tense, but not distant. I think that while she accepted what I was, she hadn't yet decided what it meant. She was willing to give me the benefit of the doubt. At least for now. I promised myself I wouldn't let her down.

"I have an idea," I told her. "It's a terrible idea, and probably dangerous, but I'm not sure we have much choice."

Pale eyes hardened. "You're going to summon a demon."

I considered the idea, searching my memories. "I'm not sure I know how. Anyway…" I grinned, "I don't think I need to. If my theory is right, most of the objects in the museum downstairs already have demons bound to them."

"You think this tower is where the wizards piled all the demon junk they didn't know what to do with?"

"Exactly."

"Then why was that piece of your heart here?"

"Probably got mixed up with all the other demon stuff. There hasn't been a demonologist in thousands of years, right? I doubt anyone alive has any idea who I am. Or was."

"I suppose." Shalayn selected a chunk of red pepper from the jar of preserved vegetables and popped it into her mouth. She washed it down with some white wine. "So, you're going to muck about with a bunch of unknown demons until you find one that can get us out?"

"When you put it like that, it sounds dangerous."

"Just a little."

"But hopefully not. I have no way of knowing what's in any given object. I think a more skilled demonologist could, but I know only the most rudimentary binding. If I try that on a powerful demon, it will devour my soul."

After taking another sip of wine, she returned the bottle to me.

"Wine for breakfast?" I asked.

"Shut up."

I drank.

"I want to know what's in the ring Tien wanted," I said.

"Why that one?"

"I think she knew what was in this tower. Maybe not everything, but what *kind* of stuff we'd find here. Think about it. She showed us the writing. She must know what it is. It's something she wants for some reason."

"Or she figured it'd kill you the moment you touched it."

I hadn't thought of that. "Maybe. I bet she knows more about demonologists than either of us. I think she knew I was one—even though I didn't—and assumed I'd be able to command it to obey her. Her reaction, her lack of surprise, there must be other demonologists out there. Just more proof the wizards are lying."

"Maybe," she said. "Are you sure there's a demon in that ring?"

"Yes. The writing on the ring. I still can't read it, but I recognize it. I figure there's no way she'd mess with a powerful demon. It has to be pretty minor."

Shalayn looked unconvinced. "So, what do you need for this?"

I consulted my memories. "It depends on who bound the demon, how it was bound, and its last command. But…blood. Human blood."

"There's only two of us here, and if you come near me with a knife, it's going to be your blood all over the floor." She said it jokingly, but there was a brittle edge to her.

I held up my hands, placating. "Maybe I can bleed myself, a little at a time." The idea didn't particularly appeal.

Shalayn eyed me. "Where does the blood usually come from?"

"Sacrifices."

"Human sacrifices."

I grimaced. "Yes."

"And demonologists aren't evil?"

"Not all of them."

"This new you, or rather the old you, the person you were, sacrificed people to summon and control demons."

"I…" I couldn't imagine doing that, but I may have, at some point deep in my forgotten past, done that. "Not that I can remember. And maybe people volunteered?" I said, cringing at how pathetic I sounded.

"Maybe," said Shalayn, making no attempt to hide her doubt.

"I'm not that person."

"Yet."

"Look," I said, frustrated, "if you have some other plan for getting us out, now is the time to share it."

"Is it so bad in here, with me?"

"You know that's not what I meant. But we can't stay here forever. Someday another mage will come and we won't be ready. Even if that doesn't happen, eventually we'll run out of food."

"I know." She sighed, and took another long drink of wine. "I've enjoyed having you to myself, pretending we are the entire world. Forgetting the last year. It's been nice."

"More than nice." I grabbed her hand, spilling wine. "This has been a dream. A few months ago, I was a wild animal in the north. I'm still discovering myself. I don't know who I was. I don't even know who I *am*. You've helped me so much. You brought me back."

"I know who you are," she said. "You're a good man. Who you were…" she shrugged. "The demonologists were evil. That's why the wizards had to rise up against them. The old Empire sacrificed countless souls every year to feed its need for demons. The wizards stopped that."

"The victors of any war write the history books. I don't believe the intentions of the wizards were quite so pure."

"Human sacrifice hasn't taken place in thousands of years."

"I have memories of wonders you wouldn't believe. Their Empire spanned the entire world. This capital, Taramlae, would have been an outpost then, barely worthy of note. One man, above bribery and petty manoeuvring, decided the path for all humanity. The Emperor ruled fairly. People were happy, prosperous."

"Were they? How about the people being sacrificed?"

"Criminals," I said, guessing.

Shalayn looked unconvinced. "It's all ancient history. I suppose we'll never know. All my life, I've heard about how evil the demonologists were, how the Emperor was insane. I've seen the ruins of the old cities, the sites of ancient wars. Yes, they're huge. Yes, they put Taramlae to shame. But I heard that inside those cities are huge public squares lined with blood troughs so hundreds could be sacrificed at once. They worked terrible magic, tore reality and summoned evil demons from a thousand hells." She swallowed. "I can't believe *all* those stories are wrong."

"Someday," I promised, "you and I will visit one of those cities and see for ourselves."

"Someday. So," she said, abruptly changing the subject. "What else do you need for this demonic dalliance?"

"The soul of a virgin," I joked.

"Well, you're fucked there."

"If I were summoning the creature, I'd need souls to offer it. Since I'm just going to attempt a binding, blood will do. I'll also need either paint or chalk."

"For drawing evil symbols on the floor?"

"Pretty much. I need to trap the demon before I attempt to bind it."

"Isn't it already trapped in the ring?"

"Kind of. I need to wrap it in my own binding so it has to obey me rather than whoever bound it to the ring. Once bound, I'll be able to question it, discover its powers."

"And if it can't get us out of the tower?"

"We keep living the dream. At least until we get hungry or you're forced to sober up."

She glared at me in mock anger and drank more wine. "Keep doing that thing with your tongue and we'll be fine."

"I realize I've been asleep for two days," I said, "but I'm exhausted. I'll do the binding in the morning."

She raised an eyebrow, tossed the empty bottle aside, and crawled on top of me.

Apparently two days alone was more than enough. We killed another bottle of wine and I did that thing with my tongue.

That night I dreamed of a strange hell where demons were immaterial spirits that could be bound to steel and iron. They thirsted for death, fed off the essence of the living as it fled the dying body.

I wanted to summon one, to bind it to a sword. But not just any demon, I wanted their master, the Lord of the entire Hell. He had a name, and it was the End of Sorrow.

CHAPTER SIXTEEN

The next day we found powdered chalk in one of the bedrooms. I had no idea what the wizards would have used it for, but it would work perfectly.

Shalayn watched, shaking her head in disgust, as I bled myself into the chalk bowl. She bound my wound, and I set about stirring the concoction into a thick paint. Once the consistency felt right, I drew a circle on the floor with my finger. Using the kerchief so I didn't touch it, I laid the ring in the centre of the circle.

"Next come the Accords," I explained, as I wrote unearthly text around the perimeter of the circle. "They're sort of a set of rules, an agreement, a contract set down to bind all parties."

"What does it say?" she asked.

"No idea. Though I think I used to know."

"So you're basically signing a contract you can't read."

"Basically."

"Brilliant. Who wrote the first ones? Who created the contracts? Who enforces them?"

That stopped me. "I think I used to know that too."

"Doesn't that seem like an important detail? Who would have the power to enforce something like that?"

"Gods?"

"There are no gods."

"There aren't?" That surprised me. I realized I'd never heard anyone mention a god, nor had I seen a church in any of the small towns we passed. It felt wrong.

"The wizards say religion was a tool of the demonologists to control people. They say the gods, and all their many hells, were meant to scare people into behaving."

That definitely sounded wrong, but I had no memory of that time and knew little of this one. It was frustrating, like someone hand-chose which memories I reacquired, deliberately keeping me ignorant of some things while returning knowledge of others.

"No one worships gods?" I asked, stunned.

"Not in thousands of years. At least no one civilized. The Septks worship trees, animal spirits, and their dead."

Civilized. I hated that word. The demonologists had a world-spanning civilization, I was sure of that. They achieved wonders that made the cities of the mages look like crude farming communities. While I couldn't remember their gods, I also couldn't believe they weren't real.

"Demonologists summon things from other realities, from other worlds," I said. "How can you be sure there aren't gods?"

"Then, where are they?" she asked. "Why did they suddenly all disappear when the demonologists were defeated?"

I didn't know. "What if, like demons, the gods required demonologists to gain entry to this world?"

Shalayn stared at me, expression flat. "Is that what you want, to bring back ancient gods? To see tens of thousands sacrificed to feed them?"

"No, of course not. But if the demonologists called gods through into this world, it was for a reason."

"Yes, evil."

"No one does something just to be evil," I said, frustrated. "There's always a reason that—at least to them—seems sound. It's only other people, coming along thousands of years later with nothing but history books written by wizards to rely on, that call them evil."

"Sacrificing people is evil. You can't possibly defend that."

"What if sacrificing one person will save an entire city?" I asked. "Would you not make the evil choice for the greater good?"

Seeing the trap I set, she glared at me.

"Do I seem evil?" I asked. "Did *I* stab that wizard in the throat? Did I even ask for some of your blood? No." I took a calming breath. "I just want to understand. I want to know the truth."

Shalayn gave a half-shrug that might have been her conceding the point, or saying she remained unconvinced. "You finished with the circle?" she asked, changing the subject.

"Yes." I stood back to examine my work. "Whatever you do, don't cross the paint or scuff the circle. The demon should be trapped in there."

"Should."

"Should. Break the circle, and it's free. That would be bad."

"How bad?"

I shrugged, helpless. "No idea. I don't remember that."

"Great."

I ignored her sarcasm. "If this works, maybe I can try some of the other objects in here." Though in truth, the thought scared the hell out of me. I stifled a laugh. Next, she'd tell me there were no hells. "At least we can try the ones we think might hold minor demons." I had no way of knowing what was in each object. There was no reason a Lord of Hell

BLACK STONE HEART

couldn't be bound to a cheap trinket, if a powerful enough demonologist did the work.

"At least until you run out of blood," she said.

I walked the circle, making sure it was perfect. One small flaw, one missed character, would spell our doom. Finally, without thought, I moved to stand before one of the characters. It felt right. I'd painted it from memory with no understanding of what it was.

"Hold on," said Shalayn, leaving at a jog.

She returned a moment later with her sword, drawn. "Just in case it takes you over and I have to kill you."

"How will you know?" I asked.

She shrugged. "Maybe I can give you the stab test."

"Stab test?"

"If you don't die, you're a demon."

"Right then. Stand back," I said, though the advice was probably pointless. If I messed this up, nowhere in this tower would be safe.

I chanted the words I remembered, throat twisting and harsh, until my voice cracked.

Nothing happened.

"Well?" asked Shalayn.

I didn't know. Was something supposed to happen? I had no idea. Had I missed something, made a mistake somewhere? Again, I didn't know.

"It worked," I said, feeling less confident than I sounded. "I'm going to pick it up now." What the hell was I doing?

She clutched her sword, ready. "Is that a good idea?"

I grinned at her. "Only one way to find out. If I start acting strange—"

"Stranger than some young man who claims to be a demonologist reborn after thousands of years whose heart is made of obsidian which has been shattered by the wizards and scattered around the world?"

"Yes, stranger than that, then you should probably kill me."

"I will."

I'd been joking, but maybe it wasn't bad advice after all.

Bending over the circle, I picked up the ring.

Nothing happened.

"I think it worked!"

I slipped the ring onto my finger.

I stood, alone.

The rock beneath my feet was jagged and black, mirrored like obsidian. Smoke, oily and thick, coiled from cracks in the stone. The rock rose up on my left, becoming a mountain of glistening jet. To my right it fell away to a sharp ledge. A long path wended away from me and ended in a castle hewn from the mountain. Piles of bright white littered the path here and there. The sky above was an endless dome of purple and black swirling around what appeared to be a dark red sun. The sun ate the clouds.

The air stank.

A hot wind pulled at my clothes.

I felt heavy, like something invisible weighed me down. I stared up at the black castle. Windows, dark and sunk in shadow, stared back. Aside from the curling smoke and the sinkhole spiralling of the sky, nothing moved.

"Shalayn," I called.

Nothing.

"Shalayn!"

Nothing.

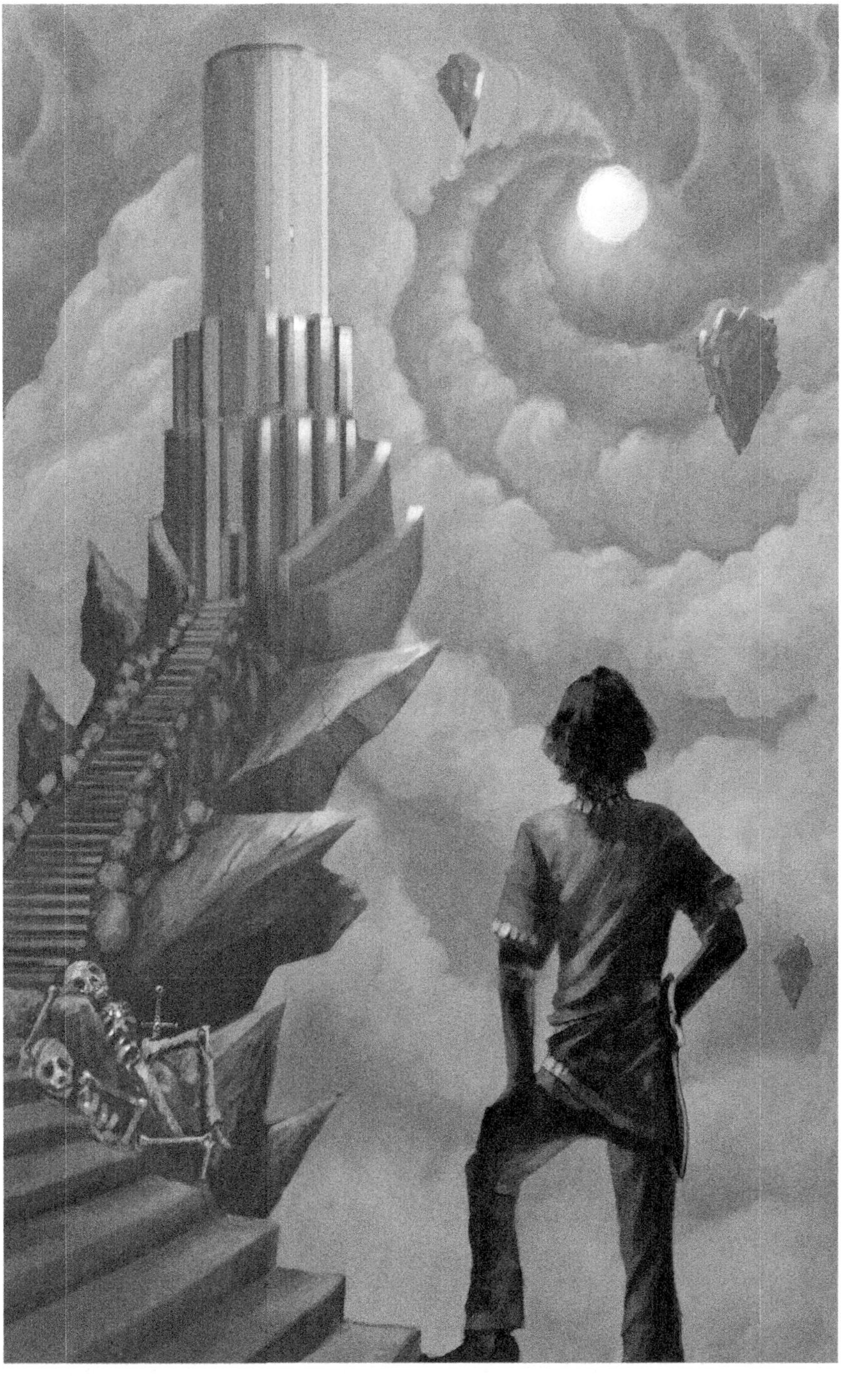

I glanced at the ring on my finger. If it was anything other than a ring, I couldn't tell.

"Hello?" I said.

The ring ignored me.

I had to get back. Somehow.

First, I needed to understand where I was. Picking my way across the obsidian, careful not to trip and fall for fear of cutting myself and bleeding to death, I walked to the edge. Looking down, I saw nothing. The same purple and black swirl of sky continued below. Movement caught my eye. An obsidian rock floated past. With nothing to compare it to, it was impossible to judge size or distance. My best guess put it at half a mile away, but it easily could have been much farther and larger than I thought. It disappeared behind the mountain I stood on. Was it circling? Would it appear again if I waited long enough?

Curiosity almost caught me.

"I have to find a way back to Shalayn."

Turning away from that purple and black infinity, I made my way back to the path. When I reached the spot I first stood upon, I realized the path started there.

"Who puts a path from an empty spot to a castle?"

Whoever owned the castle must know that arriving guests would stand where I stood. Was that promising? It seemed unlikely.

With little choice, I walked toward that black keep.

I inventoried what I had with me. While Shalayn often padded barefoot around the wizard's tower, I always felt more comfortable in shoes. Thank the gods—whoever and wherever they might be—for that foible. My only weapon was one of the Septk knives I still wore at my side. I never thought I'd miss that decrepit old hatchet. Aside from my black pants and crimson shirt, that was it.

I noticed the chalk and blood still drying on my fingers but decided that didn't quite qualify as inventory.

The first pile of jagged white I came across, was a corpse. It was ancient, nothing remained but bone. All the white piles dotting the path were corpses. Ribs, rounded by millennium of exposure to that hot wind, clawed the air like dull fingers. The most recent corpse still bore sunken black flesh stretched over pale bone.

I saw no signs of violence. Had they starved?

That wasn't good.

The glint of gold caught my attention. There, on the finger of a corpse, was a ring identical to the one I wore. A quick search showed that all the corpses had an identical gold ring. I was careful not to touch them. The rings had brought them here just as this one brought me.

They died out here, all of them.

"Tien," I said. She sent us for that ring. I remembered her telling Shalayn not to touch it. "She knew." I was sure. Maybe the wizard didn't know exactly where the ring would take me, but she knew it would take me somewhere I'd never return from.

'I deserve better,' That had been the trigger phrase for the levitation ring. Tien didn't like me, wanted to separate Shalayn and I.

She succeeded. The thieving bitch effectively murdered me to remove me from Shalayn's life.

Fucking wizards.

Rage built in me, cold like obsidian. I'd find my way back to Shalayn, and then pay the diminutive wizard a visit. She would regret the day she made me her enemy.

I was going to kill her. Whatever she was to Shalayn in the past, I was Shalayn's future.

Setting aside my anger, I turned from the littered corpses.

The tower was larger, and farther away, than I thought.

The sun devoured the sky, the constant swirl leaving me nauseated.

By the time I reached the first tower, a colossal turret reaching hundreds of times the height of a man into the spinning sky, I was exhausted and desperately thirsty. I felt like I'd eaten a bowl of chalk. Dust choked my throat and tongue.

Leaning back, I shaded my eyes from the hard, red sun. The lowest window was easily fifty feet above me. While, from a distance, the tower looked to have been carved from obsidian, up close, it was much stranger. Surprisingly smooth, the walls looked like a smoky mirror. I saw myself reflected back, dark and evil, warped by imperfections in the stone. I stopped, caught by the sight of myself. My hair had grown longer and fell in tight curls past my shoulders. The weeks in the wizard's tower, eating and drinking with Shalayn had filled me out. I was no longer the gaunt, half-starved animal I remembered. My eyes, even in the dark glass of the stone, glinted bright, their own shards of obsidian.

I knew that face.

I didn't know that face.

The features were strange to me, unlike Shalayn's or any of the people I met since leaving the north. Where they had small noses and soft, rounded faces, mine was all angles and planes.

Pulling myself away, I followed the wall to the main gate. A portcullis of iron, bars as wide around as my legs, separated me from a door into the castle. Even if I managed to pass through this first obstruction, the door beyond, a monstrosity of oak and iron, would easily stop me.

With few choices, I called out, "Hello!"

I waited, listening.

When I got bored, I turned a complete circle, again taking in the obsidian mountain, the sky-devouring red sun. Another mountain floated past, this one either smaller or farther away.

I stood screaming and bellowing at the tower for hours. The sky never changed. The red sun sucked in the purple and black clouds and never moved. Mountains floated by, some bigger, some smaller. Distance was impossible to judge. I couldn't tell if I was seeing the same ones over and over, maybe at different distances, or if it was new mountains each time.

If I ran and jumped, assuming I didn't plummet to my death, could I make it to one of the other mountains. What if I missed, would I float forever? What if there was nothing on that other rock? At least here there was a castle, some sign of habitation. Though all these ancient corpses hardly filled me with hope for gaining entrance.

Come to think of it, I couldn't see any small debris floating between the rocks. That seemed to make falling the likely answer. But then fall to where? I'd looked down. There was nothing there.

I wasn't that desperate. Not yet. How many others jumped?

I yelled and screamed at the tower until I lost my voice. I was so thirsty my throat felt like I'd gargled obsidian dust.

At some point I wandered back to where I first appeared on this rock and searched for some clue as to how I got here, and some way back to Shalayn.

Nothing.

Giving up, I returned to the castle, staggering from exhaustion, weak from thirst and hunger. How long had I been there? Hours? Had it been a day? Longer? I croaked ever quieter pleas to whoever remained hidden within. Desperate to be heard, I grabbed the portcullis, shaking them. Nothing. I decided to try and lift it high enough to wedge a little rock under. Maybe I could slowly create enough space I could crawl through.

The portcullis lifted easily, sliding silently up to disappear into the stone above.

I stood staring for a moment, stunned. Had none of the others tried to lift it? I couldn't believe that. I stepped forward and it slid down behind me without a sound. I turned and gave it a tentative lift, worried I'd now trapped myself in the castle. It rose easily. What the hell was the point of a portcullis someone could simply lift?

The huge iron door beyond opened with equal ease. While, from the outside, the tower looked to have been carved from the obsidian mountain, the interior was finished in normal stone. It could have been any tower I passed on my caravan ride south.

Thinking of that reminded me of Henka, the young necromancer, and my insane promise to return and help her find her heart. A promise it looked increasingly unlikely I'd be able to keep. What would Shalayn have thought? Would she understand? Would she come north to help me? Did I want her to? The thought of the two meeting left me uncomfortable.

A heavy layer of black dust coated the stone floor. There were no foot prints. Nothing had disturbed this dust in a very long time. That didn't bode well. If the castle was deserted, I'd die here. A long hall disappeared into the dark, torches sitting in brackets every half-dozen strides. I had nothing to light them with, but hoped I might find something in the keep. Blundering around in the dark held no appeal.

As I stepped through the door, the first torch sputtered to life. The dry stench of burnt dust filled the air, a strangely familiar scent. The fire looked odd, too red, too even. The flames danced, but I saw none of the chaos inherent in fire. It looked choreographed, predictable. Structured.

Curious, I took several more steps down the hall. The door swung silently closed behind me, but as I approached the next torch, it too sparked to life. This flame looked identical to the last. I stood entranced, watching. They cavorted together to the same unheard rhythm.

Turning back, I headed deeper into the obsidian castle. As I reached each torch, it burst into flame, joining the rest. The hall ended in a huge cathedral of delicate black pillars reaching sixty feet up to meet the stone ceiling. Looking back the way I came, I saw the torches, flames identical.

When I stepped into the great hall, a thousand torches sputtered to life and joined the dance.

CHAPTER SEVENTEEN

I spent hours—maybe days—exploring the castle. I found chambers for hundreds of guests, bedrooms so fantastically laid out it made the wealth and comfort of the wizard's tower look pathetic by comparison. Walls of colossal murals and hangings portrayed strange scenes. Men and demons working together. Battles where wizards, guarded by phalanx of demons, called rocks from the sky to crush their enemies. Elementalists rousing mountains and burning entire forests to birth fire elementals of incredible power. They reminded me of my dreams.

I remembered something then, something I knew in another life. Everything is alive. Every tree, every rock, every body of water, and every fire. Oceans were mammoth water elementals as old as the world. The larger and older an elemental was, the more powerful, the more difficult to awaken. And the more difficult to control.

I remembered a man, a master elementalist, though his name escaped me. He smashed elements together to create strange new blends. He commanded lava and mud and clouds. He made something for me—dust and wind and debris—something I left roaming in… I couldn't remember.

I put the thought aside. There'd be no answers, that elementalist would be long dead now.

Thirst and hunger drove me. I found kitchens, devoid of food. I found libraries filled with thousands of ancient books, pages dry to the touch, but miraculously preserved. Shelves reached up to thirty-foot ceilings, packed with knowledge, information, and gods knew what else. I wanted to stop here, to spend my last days reading, to lose myself in their pages.

Self-preservation pushed me on. I couldn't surrender, not now.

I climbed spiralling stairs. Everywhere I went torches, mounted in brackets, burst into flame to light my way. Fire writhed its perfect dance, winked at me with the joy of being alive. Silence echoed long halls. I left wandering trails in the dust.

I found rooms with huge wood tables where scores could meet in discussion. Leather chairs, blanketed in thick dust but still supple to the touch, surrounded every table.

I found water closets with no water.

I found pantries of dust.

On the top floor of the castle, I found a single bedroom. Though huge, it was simple. One large bed. One oak desk, papers laid out as if whoever worked here had been interrupted but moments ago. A wall hanging depicted a woman caught in the act of turning away. Her hair, long and black, flew in the wind. One hand, skin white and porcelain perfect, trailed behind her as if she'd just released mine. So familiar, and yet I knew nothing of her.

I stood, staring, until exhaustion cracked me. Stumbling, I made it to the bed. Clouds of dust billowed up around me as I collapsed onto it. I was too tired to care. Tomorrow I'd explore downward.

I thought sleep would be an escape from thirst and hunger. Instead, I dreamed of fountains and feasts.

The torches must have gone out as I slept. They sparked back to life the moment I woke and pushed myself, groaning, into a sitting position. Struggling from the bed, I rose. I felt weak, dry. Thirst clawed at me. Dust caked my throat closed.

I found a small room, devoid of purpose, with a single table, empty, against one wall. There was no chair. No decoration.

I searched on.

Spotting a doorway I'd missed in my exhaustion, I went to explore. A second room awaited beyond. A suit of crimson armour, plates formed of some strange material, sat on a steel-frame mannequin. Accords, ancient bargains, a thousand times more complex than those on the ring Tien wanted, were carved into the material. The armour terrified me, exuded a presence I didn't understand. It felt like death, like standing in a mausoleum of souls surrounded by husks of devoured ghosts. I wouldn't touch it, not for anything.

Above the armour hung an oil painting. A man, dark and brooding, stood in a field of battle. He wore the bloody armour. Corpses surrounded him. The sky burned. Rolling fields of torn earth and shattered trees. He leaned on a red sword, huge and splashed in gore, as if exhausted. I knew how he felt. Like the armour, the sword bore twisted runes snaking the blade.

I saw his face. Midnight skin. Features sharp and chiselled. But the eyes were wrong, too confident.

"He knows who he is," I whispered.

A dusty croak of a laugh escaped my dry throat. It was me. Some other me from gods know when.

This was *my* castle on *my* floating mountain.

I'd found myself and I'd found nothing.

"I'm going to die in my own tower."

I wanted to laugh, to scream and cry.

Choking down my emotions, I turned from the painting.

The armour was here, but where was the sword? A nonsensical string of words stumbled through my thoughts, something about how I can't lament the End of Sorrow. What the hell did that mean? Was death the end of sorrow?

Much as I wanted to stay, to examine the armour and the painting in minute detail, search through that desk and read every book, thirst drove me on. I retraced my steps, descending stair after stair, torches coming alive as I went. Thirst pushed my pace, shoved me past tapestries screaming to be admired and studied, drove me from libraries of enticing tomes. On the ground floor, in an otherwise unremarkable pantry, I found stairs down I had not seen the previous day. With no other choice, I descended.

Steps led me deep into the mountain, torches sparking to life, stinking of burnt dust, as I went. The stone ended abruptly, replaced by raw obsidian, surface mirrored and smoky in the torchlight.

Smoke.

I stopped.

The torches emitted no smoke. Moving closer, I raised a hand to the perfect flame. I snatched it back, hissing in pain. Definitely fire. Sucking at a burnt finger, I leaned as close as I dared. The wood of the torch wasn't being devoured by the flame, showed no sign of heat damage. Glancing back up the steps, I realized the torches had been winking out behind me.

Thirsty.

I continued down.

At the bottom of the steps stood an iron door adorned in in symbols like those on the sword and armour. They looked like they'd been painted in blood but moments ago. I reached forward to touch the blood, to see if it was as wet as it looked, and the door swung open before me. Beyond lay more rooms. Here, strange runes were carved deep into the floor like gutters. I imagined them filling with blood. They looked like what I'd drawn on the floor in chalk and blood when I tried to bind the demon in the ring, but infinitely more complex.

I glanced at the ring. "You alive? Take me back to the tower."

Nothing.

I screamed at it then. I broke down and I begged and screamed and threatened.

Nothing.

Thirst. I couldn't manage much more than a dust-clogged whisper.

Exploring deeper, staggering, sheer will driving me on, I found room after room of increasingly alien script carved into the obsidian floor. The air felt heavy down here, with the weight of countless millennium.

I passed through a room filled with strange things. Chalks in every colour. Buckets of dark earth. Bowls rimmed with salt like they once held sea water, which I would happily now drink. Alongside these, sat jars stained brown and stinking of ancient blood. Bright metallic tools, knives and blades, devices for spreading flesh and ribs, were laid out, orderly and neat, on a long table. Sheets of tanned paper hung from one wall as if left there to dry. Moving closer, I spotted the wrinkles and whorls of flesh. Not paper. Sheets of human skin. Reaching out to touch one, I found it soft and warm. I would have puked then, had there been anything in me to vomit forth. Instead, I retched thick sour drool into the dust.

"Is all this mine?" I whispered to the room.

Implements of torture. Flayed flesh. Was this me, had *I* done this?

The oak doors at the far end of the room swung open at my approach. Beyond, I saw another library, this one smaller than those on the floors above. Rows of dark oak shelves held tightly packed books of all shapes and sizes. As I entered, torches along the perimeter came to life, danced their synchronized jig. A single leather chair, big enough to swallow a man, sat in front of a fireplace loaded with dust-covered wood. It was cosy, inanely sane in comparison to the room I just passed through.

Could one man flay flesh from his victims, and then come here to read and relax?

A grey statue of an old man stood off to one side of the fireplace, covered in a heavy blanket of thick dust. No door led out. Barring hidden passageways, I'd seen everything. There was no food here, no water.

I was going to die here.

My knees wobbled, almost buckling me to the floor. So thirsty. So tired. I wanted to sit.

Heading toward the big chair, I froze when the statue moved. Dust rained from it as it turned to look at me.

It wasn't a statue, it was an old man in long robes, skeletal and gaunt, flesh grey, but very much alive.

Sunken eyes examined me.

"Welcome back," he said. Dust fell from his bald head and sloping shoulders. He scowled and then shook himself raising a great cloud. "It's been a while."

"You know me," I croaked.

"Oh," he said. "I see."

He did? "Who are you?"

"Nhil," he answered, this time bowing low and cascading more dust to the floor. "At your service. As always."

I swallowed dust, coughed. I could barely speak. "I need water."

"There is none. Not after this long."

"I'm dying."

"I see," he repeated.

Knowing thirst and hunger would end me before long, I lost my fear. I moved closer. Something was wrong with the old man; he wasn't quite the right shape. His skull, a little too oblong, his limbs a little too long. He looked stretched. Eyes, too large, oddly oval, glowed violet as he studied me. He blinked wrong, liquid, one eye at a time.

"What are you?"

"I am your assistant, your confidant for many years. Your closest friend. At least until you left me here and never returned." He examined me, eyes doing that sliding, mistimed blink. "I waited for a long time." He shrugged, displacing more dust. "Eventually, I gave up hope."

"I have returned."

"Some of you."

Some of me.

"Can you bring me water?" I asked, hope making me desperate.

"No."

"I was in a wizard's tower with a woman. There was water there, food. I have to go back. Can you leave, can you get me back to the tower. She's alone. I have to…"

He waited with the patience of a man who stood motionless for thousands of years. "No."

"She's alone! The wizards will take her!" If she didn't die there first. My fists clenched. Tien did this. I'd take my time killing her, maybe bring her back here, show her the implements of torture—I stopped, swallowed the building anger. That wasn't me.

"I can't leave," said Nhil. "That is beyond my power."

"You have power?" Desperate hope. "What is your power? What can you do?"

He laughed, a deep sepulchral sound from such a slim old man. "I teach. I am a receptacle for knowledge. Ever was it my task to advise." Sunken, violent eyes watched me. "And I am your friend."

BLACK STONE HEART

My friend? Was he lying? I couldn't tell. Those eyes, those subtly inhuman features, told me nothing.

"That was a long time ago," he continued. "A different you."

"If you are truly my friend, help me. Please."

"It might be too late. But I shall try."

Turning, he approached the bookshelves, his gait strange and gliding, too graceful for one so old. Nodding to himself, he reached out a skeletally thin grey arm and selected a book.

"This one, I think."

"What is it?" I asked.

"A binding for water elementals." He turned to face me. "Normally it wouldn't work somewhere like this. Luckily there is a reservoir at the centre of this mountain."

"How did it get there?"

"You put it there." He cocked his head in thought. "Hopefully it hasn't gone dry." He grinned then, teeth too small and slightly pointed. "Of course, there was a fair amount of water in there and it's been a long time. It may have gone feral."

Feral water? I didn't care. I was thirsty enough to risk anything.

CHAPTER EIGHTEEN

"Normally," said Nhil, "a would-be-elementalist would spend two years learning about the elements, the strengths and weaknesses of each, their characteristics and personalities. They wouldn't begin even the simplest summoning until sometime into their third year."

"I'm not even going to make it to the end of your *Introduction to Elementalism* speech."

"Quite."

"You think I have the potential to be an elementalist?"

"Everyone does. Anyone can learn any branch of magic given the time and interest. That said, you were always drawn to the darker arts, the power and influence."

"Why 'darker'?" That seemed oddly judgemental, particularly from someone who I was pretty sure was a demon. "Magic is just a tool. The purpose it's turned to defines whether it's good or bad."

"Does it?" Nhil studied me. "I think, perhaps, we don't have time for that conversation right now."

I nodded agreement and set aside my curiosity.

For countless hours Nhil taught me the rudiments of the language of water, and the words of the ancient bargains.

I remembered Shalayn's question when I mentioned something similar regarding the summoning and binding of demons.

"Who created these bargains?" I asked.

"The gods."

"I was told there were no gods. That they were an invention of the demonologists, that religion was nothing more than a means of controlling the people."

"You were lied to." He shrugged. "Or misinformed by someone ignorant of the truth."

Had I worshipped these gods? I had so many questions. Exhaustion forced me to set them aside.

I felt drunk on lack of sleep, wrung hollow with thirst.

"I can't focus," I said. "Need sleep. In the morning."

"That concept has no meaning here."

"The sun never moves," I said, understanding. Swirling clouds, spiralling ever inward, devoured.

"That's no sun. It's a god, the Lord of this hell."

"Oh." I wanted to feel something. Shock. Awe. Horror. I was too tired.

Lowering myself to the floor, I looked up at this strange old man who claimed to be my friend and was clearly not human. Was he lying about that? Could he be lying about everything?

"You bound him," said Nhil as my eyes slid closed. "With the help of your god."

I slept.

Oceans of salt water drown my dreams. I sank in the brine. Far above, on the surface, fleets of warships did battle. We were losing here, as we were on the mainland. Wizards rained rocks from the heavens. Sorcerers sacrificed themselves, burning through years of life, spending their own muscle and flesh, to call colossal fire-storms. Lightning cracked the sky. It was so bright I saw it from the deepest depths.

Calling my demons to me, those of oceanic hells, I rode them to the surface. Kraken. Sea dragons large enough to swallow an entire man-o-war. Dark things, alien to the light, sickly white, savaged reality with their demonic power.

And still we were losing.

A thousand elementalists died waking the ocean. The wizards spent them at a terrifying rate and the fools, believing the lies of power-mad mages, let them.

The ocean was too big, too ancient, to ever be controlled. It was awake and it was angry. I knew it would be centuries before any man dared set keel in these waters. The wizards pitched the world into darkness. The Empire relied on the ocean for so many things. Food. Communication. Trade. The filthy wizards just toppled civilization and they probably didn't even realize it.

The ocean found me, sought to crush me.

I slipped away.

Thirst woke me, seized my throat, left me coughing and gagging. I rolled over and found Nhil standing exactly as he had when I fell asleep.

"Have you been there the entire time?" I asked.

"Where else would I go?"

"You don't eat or sleep?"

"If I did, I'd be long dead." He examined me with violet eyes.

Did he look younger, less wrinkled and ancient?

"If you're finished wasting time," he said, "we should return to your lessons."

"You love this, don't you?"

"Everyone needs a purpose," he said. "What's yours?"

"Kill Tien," I answered without hesitation.

"That will do. For now. Shall we begin?"

Rather than talk, I nodded.

We studied symbols, memorized chants and incantations—bargains, Nhil reminded me—until sleep claimed me. When I woke, we continued. We practised until my voice cracked and all sound was gone from me.

"Take a moment," Nhil said. "Find some saliva. Then we'll do this."

"Why do I have to do everything," I whispered. "Why can't you help?"

"The bargains weren't arranged for my kind. Now, no more questions."

Nhil watched as I chalked arcane symbols onto the floor. They were strange and alien, and achingly familiar. Careful not to scuff anything, I placed an empty bowl at the centre.

Sitting back, I worked to find even a drop of saliva. My tongue felt cracked, like leather left too long in the sun. There were things I knew, dark truths I had yet to examine. Unanswered questions flashed through my thoughts, scattering them. Waves of dizziness left me weaving and unsteady as I sat.

Why did demonic summonings and bindings require blood and souls? Why wasn't the same required of elemental summonings? Was interacting with elementals less evil than calling upon demonic aid?

Evil.

I didn't like that word. So judgemental. One man's evil was another's righteous. The world wasn't black and white, right and wrong.

That was what the wizard's preached. Evil, like beauty, was in the eye of the beholder.

I was not evil.

Sure, but was there a way to sacrifice a soul that wasn't evil?

There must be.

I shied from the thought. Were the wizards right? Was demonology inherently evil?

How many souls did it take to bind a god? This place, this bubble of reality, had been some kind of escape for me. There were enough rooms to host hundreds of friends or diplomats. Had I been the kind of person who had friends? Who carved this castle from the rock of this floating mountain? If there was a god here, was there also a native population to worship it? Where were they?

I had this sick feeling that I knew the answer.

I wanted to ask Nhil. Did I sacrifice the souls of an entire reality to bind the devouring god in the sky?

I couldn't spare the spit.

I coughed and hacked until I tasted sour bile. It was the best I could managed.

"Are you ready?" asked Nhil. "You drifted off there for a while."

Again, I nodded rather than speak.

"Begin."

The spell went on. I chanted until all I could manage was the ghost of a whisper. The chant built in me, filled my skull.

"Louder," commanded Nhil.

My voice cracked.

"Louder!"

I screamed the words, throat tearing, voice shredding apart.

I sensed it.

Deep in the heart of this floating mountain, was a reservoir of pure water. It was huge. It was thousands of years old. It sought to drown me, to douse the tiny spark of my life.

I hurled my will against the ancient intelligence. Rage burned away all doubt and fear. I *needed* this. No damned water elemental would be my death.

You. Will. Obey!

Fear. Terror.

The water elemental cowered. It remembered me. It remembered how I brought it here, how I bent it to my will.

"Fill the bowl," I commanded. "If I ask for water, you give it."

I opened my eyes to find the bowl filled with cool, clear water. I drank until I puked.

Then I drank more.

"Better?" asked Nhil.

"Yes," I answered, voice still raw.

"Good," he said. "Because we have another problem."

I lay back, belly distended. "What's that?"

"You're still going to starve to death before long."

"Oh." I released a long belch. "Fuck."

CHAPTER NINETEEN

"What are my options?" I asked Nhil.

He pursed grey lips, examined me with a judging eye. "When did you last eat?"

I realized I'd been so thirsty it dwarfed my hunger. Now, that need was sated, my belly was happy to let me know just how empty it was.

"It's been a while." First locked in the tower, and then here in the basement, I hadn't seen a moving sun in ages. Judging time was impossible. "It feels like at least three days." My fingers shook and I felt jittery. Hunger sharpened deep and ancient predatory instincts.

"Then I see one option," said Nhil. "A portal demon." He lifted a grey hand to forestall my inevitable questions. "They are immaterial beings existing in the space between worlds, between realities. As such, they can open temporary gateways from one world to another, or even from one location in a world to another in the same world."

"Why the hell didn't you teach me this first?"

"Ah, there we have a little of the old you. I didn't teach it to you first because it will take months to learn. You *might* survive that without food, but not without water."

My stomach rumbled complaint. It was not looking forward to starving for the next two months.

A thought occurred to me. "The ring that got me here. A portal demon?"

"Of course."

"Why can't it take me back?"

"Two problems," said Nhil. "That is a demon bound with very specific commands. All it does is bring people here, to your castle. I suspect it once belonged to a trusted advisor or friend."

"I had friends?"

"Everyone has friends. You gave them the ring so they might either visit you here, or escape to this place should they be in danger."

"Is that what happened to those corpses beyond the castle walls?"

Nhil pursed his lips. "Corpses? I didn't know. But probably. They likely came here to escape the war, only to find themselves trapped outside the tower and unable to leave. When the wizards betrayed you, you changed the orders at the gate. Where previously they opened to anyone on your short list of friends and advisors, you told them only to open to you."

I thought of these unknown friends thinking they were fleeing to safety, only to starve to death beneath a devouring sun. "I told the gate?" I asked.

"There is a powerful demon bound there. It recognized you and opened when you made it clear that's what you wanted."

"You couldn't get out, could you?"

"No. But even if I could, I could not have left this hell. There are no portal demons here to take me home."

I wanted to ask what he meant by *home*, but realized I needed to stay focussed on my own survival. Such questions could wait.

"I don't understand why I can't use the ring," I said.

"It was bound with a very specific set of commands. To change those commands, you'd have to break the binding, which would take half a year to learn, maybe longer. You would then have to rebind it using spells that would take another few months to learn. You don't have that kind of time."

"When I tried to bind it back in the wizards tower—"

"You failed. This demon is well beyond your current abilities. You were a thousand years old when you summoned and bound it. Perhaps not at the height of your power, but certainly more skilled and knowledgeable than you are now."

"Oh." I couldn't imagine how much someone might learn in a thousand years. "Let's get started," I said, deciding. Then, when Nhil turned to head off toward the bookshelves, I called out, "Wait."

He stopped, back to me.

"You said demon. I thought demonic summonings required souls."

"They do."

"Is there someone here other than us?"

"There is not." He turned to face me. "You have planned for such contingencies." He cracked a fractured smile. "Well, not quite for this. I don't think you ever imagined returning without your memories. But you left a Soul Stone here. It will provide the needed souls to power the summoning." When he saw I was about to ask more questions, he waved me to silence. "Soul Stones are receptacles. Lives can be sacrificed, their souls stored for later use."

"Did I sacrifice people to make this Soul Stone?"

"Of course."

I felt like that shard of obsidian in my heart grew a thousand times heavier and tried to drag me down. What kind of man casually sacrificed souls to store for later use? I knew the answer.

"How many souls?" I asked.

"I don't know. This one is a small stone; no more than sixty. Others were bigger. You were at war. Some carried thousands."

Thousands. I wanted to puke. "To sacrifice someone…"

Nhil waited.

"I killed them."

"Of course."

"Personally. Cut their throats."

"You were very good at it. Had it down to an art. I once watched you do hundreds in a single day."

My gut twisted, threatened upheaval. I bled hundreds of people in a single day, stored their souls in a stone, so I might later feed them to demons. How could this *not* be evil? How desperate would a situation have to be to justify such atrocity? Could anything justify murder on such a scale?

Shalayn was right.

The wizards were right.

"Ah," said Nhil. "I see you don't remember any of this. You are not the man you were."

Was that a bad thing? Hell, I wasn't even out of my teens, if I'd judged the age of my body correctly.

"I'm not him," I said, voice shaking.

"I know." Shoulders sagging, he gazed at the floor between us. Was that pity I saw in those demonic eyes?

This Soul Stone would save my life, assuming I learned the summoning and binding spells before I starved to death. But in using it I'd be feeding a soul to whatever demon I summoned. A soul *I* put there. A soul *I* tore from someone.

"It's too late," I said. "Those people are already dead. There is no saving them."

174

"A justification," said Nhil. "You're lying to yourself. Souls are eternal. People are reborn, over and over, to live different lives." He studied me. "Unless that soul is destroyed, devoured."

"If I shatter this Soul Stone?"

"The souls within will be freed to be reborn."

I broke, put my head in my hands, crushed my palms against my eyes until I saw red. "This is evil," I whispered.

"So be the good guy," said Nhil. "And starve to death."

"I hate you."

"Today you do."

And I hated that we both knew what I was going to do. Starving here meant an end. It meant Shalayn died in that tower or was taken by the wizards to die later. It meant I'd never see her again, and her death would be my fault. It meant Tien won. It meant a conclusion to my quest to regain my lost self.

That thought stopped me. I wasn't just some minor demonologist reborn. The dreams. The man with the stone eyes. The war. This place and the murals.

Nhil knew who I was.

"Who am I?" I asked into my hands.

"You know who you are."

And I did.

Who was the one demonologist the wizards would want destroyed?

"Khraen. The Emperor." I was the evil the wizards told everyone to fear.

I wanted to deny it. I couldn't.

It was too much. I couldn't comprehend the full import of what this meant. Whatever that man was, I knew I was different.

Pulling my hands from my eyes I glared at Nhil. "You said souls are eternal. If I die here, I'll be reborn."

175

He did that sliding blink. "Not quite. You dedicated your soul to your god. She locked it forever in obsidian. You've already been reborn." He shrugged. "Maybe other pieces of you have too. Perhaps, someday, one of them will come here and find your corpse. Maybe he'll cut that little shard from your chest and be one step closer to becoming the man you were."

That thought flooded me with rage. I was not part of someone else. They were all part of *me*.

"My god, what is her name?"

"No," said Nhil. "You are not ready for that."

I dropped it. Was the demon telling the truth about any of this? Who could I trust? He said that sky-devouring sun was a god, and then referred to my god as 'her.'

Some other version of me sacrificed the souls now in the stone. Would using those souls to save myself—to save Shalayn—be evil? How many souls would I sacrifice to save the woman I loved?

The question felt wrong, like I missed something.

I wasn't going to starve here. I knew that. I couldn't let Shalayn die. No way was I going to let Tien get away with this.

"We'd best get started," I said.

"Quite."

We spent weeks reading and rehearsing, memorizing lines of an ancient bargain Nhil claimed had been forged by gods. By the end, I was so weak I spent days and nights on the library floor. Nhil brought blankets and pillows from one of the bedrooms for me to sleep on.

Every night I dreamed of war. War on the oceans. War in the deserts. War in the jungles and on the plains. Dragons razed armies of demons to ash and I cried in sadness. Nightmares clawed through from other worlds. Ink flesh bled black light. They came at my call, obeyed my every command. I sacrificed thousands to summon them, spilled oceans of blood, and then set them upon my enemies. These things, all tentacles and split snake-eyes, shambling madness, devoured the souls of wizards and sorcerers. They crushed the mountains awoken by the elementalists, left dead rock in their wake.

The necromancers, once my closest allies, broke my demons. Battalions of dead giants pulled them apart. Stampeding elephant corpses trampled them in the dust.

Every morning I hallucinated. When awake, my hunger was everything.

The water elemental at the heart of this flying mountain refilled the bowl at my command. I drank until I was full. I drank until my belly stretched tight and the thought of more water nauseated me.

Hunger always returned, worse each time. Sharper. Deeper.

Finally, when Nhil was confident I'd memorized the bargains and could flawlessly paint the symbols of binding—or decided I'd never get any better—he brought out the Soul Stone. It was a diamond the size of my smallest fingernail. He lifted the rock, turning it to catch the dancing torchlight.

"Each facet can store a single soul," he said. "The number of facets limits the number of souls."

I remembered the fist-sized diamond in the wizard's tower, its thousands of facets. Was that a Soul Stone?

"How many does this one have?"

"Sixty."

Sixty. Sixty souls. Sixty people I killed, sacrificed so I might later make use of them.

"How many are in there now?" I asked.

"No idea." He lifted the gem, turning it, and peering into the facets. "The bargains were not struck with my kind in mind," he said, changing the topic. "No matter how much I learn, no matter my flawless memory or ability understand, I can't summon or bind."

"Souls were sacrificed to summon and bind you?"

"Many," answered Nhil. "For I am no minor demon."

"Really?" I eyed the old man. Even weak from hunger, I was pretty sure I could wrestle him to the ground and subdue him without much trouble. Remembering my dreams, the armies of monstrous demons, I said, "You don't look like much."

He darted a sly glance at me. "Looks can be deceiving."

"What are you capable of?"

Nhil shrugged.

"Tell me."

He grinned, showing those narrow teeth.

"You are a bound demon. I bound you, didn't I." It wasn't really a question. "I command you, tell me of your power!"

"I am not bound. You set me free."

"I did? Why?"

"Because, after thousands of years together, we are friends."

Were we? Was he lying?

"Ah," he said, "I see you are sceptical."

He didn't seem upset.

"When you are you again," he continued, "I will answer your questions."

"I don't want to be that man."

"Of course," he said, ignoring my words, "when you are you again, I won't need to."

"I will never be that man."

"And yet you seek out the shards of your heart."

I had no answer for that.

For the next week, he taught me how to access the souls in the stone. It required exactly the right frame of mind, a relaxed state of meditation, empty of worries and concerns. Not easy for someone starving to death.

"Hunger is a distraction," Nhil told me. "You will find this much easier once fed. You used to be able to achieve this state in an instant."

So, I was good at spending souls.

"Tomorrow," he said, "we will begin work on your visualization skills."

I was too tired to listen, too hungry to care.

When I awoke, I pushed myself to my feet and shuffled to the bowl. There was still water from the previous night. Nhil watched me drink.

During the day I worried about Shalayn, alone in the tower. I imagined finding Tien and killing her, the look of shock on her face at seeing me returned.

At night I dreamed of a world-spanning war and the fall of a ten-thousand-year-old empire.

My clothes hung off me. I was sunken, a man caving in on himself. My ribs protruded, ridges of bone in black flesh. My hip bones stood out, giving me a decidedly skeletal appearance. I stared at my arm. What muscle I'd possessed was gone. Day by day I wasted away. Hunger ate me, devoured me like the sun god devoured the swirling clouds.

I was always tired and never really slept. Emptiness was a state of being. Sometimes I drifted off, eyes open and seeing nothing. Nhil stood, patiently awaiting my return.

I told him of Shalayn and our time together. I told him I loved her, that she made me happy. I had to return to her. I had to save her.

He cried and I did too.

I told him I killed myself, cracked my ribs open, and dug out my own heart.

I told him of the people I murdered, the Septk youth. I wanted to tell him of the necromancer girl, Henka. I wanted to tell him how I hadn't killed her when I had the chance. I wanted to admit that I cared more about her and her stolen heart than I did for the people she would kill. But I hesitated, unwilling for him to know such things about me. Shame silenced me.

I asked if I was evil, if my choices were evil.

He asked what evil was.

Exhaustion left me stupid. I was too hungry to think. Surely evil didn't depend on perception or sides.

"Stop shying from it," he said. "You know who you are. You held an empire together for millennia. The world knew peace under your rule. There were no wars. The people were educated. Civilization thrived, working miraculous wonders the wizards only play at mimicking. There was a cost, there always is. Civilization comes at a price. If millions live safe, happy lives, is it not worth the sacrifice of a few?"

I didn't know. But in my gut, I thought he was wrong. A civilization that sacrificed human lives, be it to summon demons, or in fighting wars, was evil.

"The world needed you," he said. "Needs you still." He sighed, looking away. "The man you were."

"What do you mean?"

Offering a sad smile, he said, "Another time."

CHAPTER TWENTY

The Soul Stone, a small diamond, weighed nothing. And yet it weighed heavily on me. I held it between thumb and forefinger. How many destroyed lives were trapped within?

"The moment of truth," said Nhil, watching me examine the stone.

While I wasted away, melted to nothing, he remained unchanged.

"Smash the stone," he said. "Set the souls free to be reborn. I'll fetch a hammer if you wish."

The smug bastard waited.

I hated that he never ate, never drank, never felt hunger. Last night I dreamed I killed him, dragged his corpse to the kitchen, chopped him up, and made the most delicious roast.

"No?" he asked. "Then let's begin."

Crawling about the floor, I painted the symbols from memory. I screamed the chants, the bargains set down by unknown gods, until I was hoarse. I called the portal demon, offering it a soul from the Soul Stone, my end of the bargain.

It came.

It filled the circle with its ravenous presence. It hungered.

Next, I completed the Ritual of Binding and smashed my will against its own. Even weak from hunger I felt an exhilarating rush as it caved before my need. I crushed it, made it *mine*, owned it in every way.

Felkrish, it told me, was its name.

I locked Felkrish in a white gold ring Nhil provided me with.

Starved to the edge of death, barely able to stand, I gloried in the power.

I hated myself.

Opening my eyes, I saw Nhil watching me. "You feel it," he said.

I nodded, unwilling to speak.

"In the future," he said, "when you find yourself some sanctuary, such as this, memorize it. With practice, you'll be able to build rooms and places in your mind very quickly." He grinned narrow teeth. "I think we've spent enough time in this library—" I hadn't left the room in weeks. "—that you'll have no trouble returning."

I wanted to tell him I was never coming back, that everything here was evil. It was a lie. There were answers here. Nhil had answers. Somehow, Nhil *was* answers. And there was knowledge. Dark knowledge, to be sure, but things I'd need to know if I was to survive the wizards.

For two weeks Nhil taught me the skill of visualization. While I no longer felt hunger, concentration became an act of supreme will. My thoughts would wander, drift away, and Nhil would use sharp words or a slap to bring me back. Sometimes my vision blurred or suddenly doubled. Luckily, visualization was mostly done with one's eyes closed. I could no longer stand without help, and if Nhil released me, I crumpled back to the floor. Flesh continued to melt away as my body devoured itself. My breath stank of rotting apples, an incongruous scent for one starving. Soon, I spent more time comatose than alert.

I was dying, and dying fast.

And still Nhil continued. He talked even when I teetered on the edge of consciousness, his words creeping into my thoughts.

Portal demons of the type I summoned, he said, were only capable of taking me somewhere I had already been. Even then, I had to visualize it perfectly. Portal demons are telepaths, he told me, and rely on the demonologist to supply the location.

"And if I fail to remember something in enough detail?" I whispered.

"Either it won't work, or you end up lodged in some piece of furniture that wasn't where you thought. Or you disappear, never to be seen again."

Nhil told me to pick some simple place, not too busy, not too packed full of details to remember. A place unlikely to change. A completely unadorned stone box with no detail, he said, was a bad idea. They all looked the same. I wouldn't know which one I would appear in. A stone box with a single detail was perfect. I remembered the empty room off the master bedroom floors above me. The door closed, with the single table, empty, against one wall. Had that been the purpose of that room?

I chose one of the bathrooms in the wizard's tower, specifically the small room where water rained from the ceiling. I remembered the tiled walls and floor.

Nhil had me describe it over and over, narrowing in on different details each time. Were some of the tiles chipped? How did it smell? How did the floor feel? Did the room have interesting acoustics? On and on it went, always doubling back to confirm some detail, ask about the shape of some crack.

My memory was either better than I thought, or I was losing my mind and making things up.

"Now," said Nhil, once he was confident I'd mastered the skill, "you must visualize your destination."

I visualized the water closet and the rain room, taking time to focus on even the smallest detail until it existed in my thoughts. I felt the tiles under my bare feet. I breathed in the damp scent of ancient mildew. I imagined Shalayn there, naked. Water cascaded down her breasts, fell from her nipples, beaded on the muscles of her belly. Her hair, soaking wet and pale, framed her face. Those eyes, ice blue, promised fire. Her lips parted and she said—

"Pay attention!"

"What?" I looked around, confused, dizzy and disoriented.

Sprawled on the floor, I was still in the library.

Nhil stood over me, violet demonic eyes studying me with concern. "Pay attention or you'll die."

"Right," I croaked.

"Now, build the room again."

I built the room until I was there. It was real, solid,

"One more small detail," he added, voice distant, echoing off the tiles in the water closet. "Each time you use the portal demon, you must feed it a soul. And remember, each failed attempt still costs a soul."

"No."

"Then die here."

I fed the demon.

Opening my eyes, I found the rain room exactly as I remembered, right to the chipped corner of a tile, and the hairline cracks in the floor I lay sprawled upon.

Luke warm water poured down upon me and I lay there for a moment, enjoying the feeling.

Finally, I crawled from the room, dragging myself with weak arms.

"Shalayn."

Silence.

"Shalayn!" My voice cracked.

I dragged myself through the wizard's tower, calling her name. It was empty.

She was gone.

Dragging myself to the museum room on the ground floor, I found the door still unapproachable. The room no longer stank, the corpse of the wizard Shalayn stabbed in the throat was gone.

Surrendering to the obvious, I dragged myself back up the stairs to the kitchen. By the time I reached the top, the corners of the steps left me covered in bruises. Scores of empty wine bottles littered the floor. After my disappearance, she hadn't passed her time here in sobriety. Not that we'd been particularly sober together.

I crawled through the bottles to the cupboards and, with every last ounce of will, managed to drag myself upright using the handles. Though she'd made a dent in the stored food, plenty remained. I swept what I could to the floor and collapsed.

I ate cautiously, just a few nibbled bites. Still, I vomited. When the nausea passed, I struggled to decide what to do.

Had she found a way out?

No, the wizards found her here, alone. They took her.

How long ago?

The ceiling lost its glow, plunging me into darkness.

Was that an answer? Had I just missed them?

If that was the case, I should go after them now, maybe catch them unaware. My starved mind, thoughts sluggish and confused, wrestled with the problem. I had to save her, but I couldn't even walk.

Then it hit me. I had three places I knew well enough to use Felkrish, the portal demon: The rain room in this tower, the library in the floating mountain, and my wood and mud shack far to the north. I'd spent years there, knew it in intimate detail.

"No," I whispered. "There has to be somewhere closer."

I couldn't think. Months of starvation left me weak and stupid.

I ate a few nibbles of preserved vegetables, this time managing to keep it down, and slept alone in the dark, surrounded by the empty bottles of a woman abandoned to her demons.

Time had been difficult to judge in the world of the floating mountain. Here, in the perfect dark of the wizard's tower, it was impossible. I don't know how long I spent in that kitchen, eating and sleeping. At some point I barked at the elemental in the centre of that floating mountain to bring me water. It took several attempts before I remembered I was no longer there.

With nourishment and sleep, my senses returned. Scrambled as my thoughts were, I figured no more than a week passed since my return. No matter how much I wanted to rush to Shalayn, to save her from the wizards, I could not. I was still too weak.

I'd spent days building the rain room in my thoughts and it would likely take me near as long to create another place. But where?

The only place I could think of was the room Shalayn and I shared in the Dripping Bucket. We spent a fair amount of time there, either tangled in the sheets, or nursing hangovers. Could I remember enough detail to make it real?

I got to work.

Two days later, to my best guess, I thought I was ready. Drawing the Soul Stone from its place in my pocket, I glared at the damned thing, invisible in the perfect black.

Damned, indeed.

There was another much larger diamond down on the ground floor. Thousands of facets. How many souls did it hold? I wanted it.

"I will not be that man."

This small diamond with its sixty facets was already too much, too evil.

I laughed in the dark. I'd never find it anyway, and what would happen if I picked up the wrong stone and it had something powerful bound to it? So much potential power, so close and yet unattainable.

Nhil said every attempt to use Felkrish cost a soul, successful or not. The stone had sixty facets and could hold, at most, sixty souls. Unfortunately, I had no idea how many souls were actually in there. It was possible there'd only been one and I'd used it getting here. Should I wait, spend more time building the room in my thoughts?

Having found her in their museum of demonology artefacts, what would the wizards do to Shalayn?

They'd kill her. But first, they'd question her, torture her to discover how she got in there and if she had help. She'd talk, she'd tell them everything. Hurt someone enough, and they'll share their deepest secrets. Once they heard there was a living demonologist—thankfully Shalayn had no idea who I really was—they'd come for me in force.

I had to save Shalayn.

Soul Stone in one hand, white gold ring worn on the other, I built the room in my mind.

It didn't work. I didn't get sucked into some hell, and I didn't explode or die or appear stuck in a wall. I sat there, in the dark, on the kitchen floor.

"Idiot," I said. I'd rushed it. Even if it did work, I was still too weak to rescue her.

I tried again, spent days imagining the room, building every detail. I ate continually, washing every meal down with wine I barely tasted.

When I needed breaks, I exercised, first shuffling, later walking up and down the stairs. By the end of the second week I'd filled out a little and even managed to regain some small amount of muscle.

I searched for the lanterns Shalayn and I brought with us but couldn't find them in the dark. The wizards must have taken them. I existed in perpetual night, doing everything by feel. I bathed in the rain room in pitch black. Then I went in search of clothes, the ones I'd worn previously reeking of sour sweat and starvation. Dressing in the dark, I had no idea what I looked like. Sartorial splendour would have to wait.

My third attempt failed too, and I sat on the kitchen floor eating a jar of something slimy I hoped was preserved peaches. How long before they tortured and killed her? Was I already too late? Emotions warred within, each taking their turn to grind me down, to bend me toward submission. I felt rage at my pathetic helplessness, frustration at my inability to build the room in my thoughts, and the blackest self-hate.

Three souls. I spent three souls, fed them to a demon, and achieved nothing. How many times could I do this? What if the stone was full and there were sixty souls within? How many would I use? How many souls was Shalayn worth?

I realized the answer, and loathed what it said of me. No matter how many souls were within this stone, I would spend each and every one to get her back. And then I would wander blind on the ground floor until I found that larger diamond and spend a thousand more.

I imagined Shalayn asking, "Are you doing this for me, or for yourself?"

"For you," I answered, knowing I lied.

I hated myself for that too. Not for the lie, but because I was doing it for myself, for damned near entirely selfish reasons. I wanted her back.

"They took you from me," I told her.

The wizards would pay for that. Tien, first and foremost. Whatever she used to be to Shalayn, the little wizard would die. I grinned, imagining how I'd end her.

I spent days going over details of the room at the Dripping Bucket and worrying. What if they changed the blankets? What if they changed the curtains, or moved the furniture? What if I failed each time because someone was there, in the room, changing it with their presence?

"I'll try again in mid-afternoon, when the room is most likely to be empty."

Anger flooded me. It could be midnight now! I had no way of knowing.

I tried again and failed.

What if I'd used the last soul?

An hour later, I tried again. Again, I failed.

I waited, counting the seconds, the minutes, the hours. The room I'd built in my mind was perfect, I was sure.

I tried again.

Sitting in the dark, I cursed. How many souls were left? Would I even know when I'd used the last one? Nhil hadn't mentioned it.

I counted an hour, and tried again.

And found myself sitting in our room in the Dripping Bucket. It was clean, the bed made. Everything was as I remembered.

I realized suddenly I'd left my Septk knives somewhere. The floating mountains? The wizard's tower? I had no idea. Exhausted, I lay on the bed and fell asleep.

Hours later new tenants arrived and I left before the innkeeper was tempted to a more violent ejection. They watched me leave with their hating eyes and curled lips. Stained-soul they called me behind my back. Darker.

They had no idea.

Outside, the sky was thick with heavy clouds, billowing curtains of stained spider-silk, threatening rain. A storm brewed on the horizon. Flashes of distant lightning lit the clouds from above, a nightmare of warring colours. Cancerous yellow. The sick purple of old bruises gone gangrenous. Cold winds crashed in from the north, tearing the heat from me. I was, I realized, rather under-dressed. In my absence, summer had passed into fall. My clothes, chosen in the dark, were a gaudy clash of bright silks and jade green cotton pants probably meant as pyjamas.

I watched the crush of pedestrians, everyone rushing to complete their errands before the storm arrived.

Where would the wizards take Shalayn?

Probably to another damned wizard's tower I couldn't get into.

But which one? A dozen or more surrounded the city, and several more lay beyond the wall.

I turned, looking toward the colossal tower at the heart of Taramlae. Shalayn said it was the seat of government for both the capital, and the entire kingdom. I couldn't call it an empire; the wizards hadn't earned that.

The tower dominated the city. A lurking presence, its shadow crawling over all beneath it as the day progressed. Unlike the others, this one had windows, but I couldn't fool myself that it was any more accessible.

At least not to a long-dead demonologist.

But I thought I might know someone who could get me in. If she wanted to.

And if she didn't want to, I'd force her. She tricked us. Sending me to get that ring for her had been a trap. I had no doubt she knew it would take me away. After, when she was no longer useful, I'd take great pleasure in killing her. I'd do it once Shalayn was somewhere safe. She'd never need to know.

As I set off toward the cafe where Shalayn and I met Tien, lightning slashed the sky. Thunder shattered the air and the heavens unleashed their fury. In moments I was soaked and shivering.

I laughed as I walked. "Heavens."

Why could I readily believe in hells, but not in heavens?

I suppose having been to one helped.

CHAPTER TWENTY-ONE

With the onslaught of rain, the streets emptied fast. Those caught far from their destination ducked their heads as they ran, as if that might save them from a soaking. Wet as I already was, I maintained my pace. Rage warmed me. Against that, the rain was nothing. Lightning smashed the sky, licking at that lumpen turd of a tower at the heart of the city.

If the wizards hurt Shalayn, they would pay.

If they'd already killed her, if I was too late, I'd bring the tower down. I'd pull the entire city apart, bury them in the rubble of their pathetic kingdom. I'd drown them in blood. I didn't care how long it took. I could return to the floating mountains any time. I'd take a supply of food and study with Nhil until I knew enough to bring utter ruin upon my enemies.

And Tien. Even if she helped me rescue Shalayn, she would pay for her treachery.

Should I pretend naive innocence, act like I had no idea she tried to kill me by trapping me in some hell? Confronting her would tip her off that I knew the truth, make her wary. Better to be stupid so she underestimated me. That grated, but I was in no position to face a wizard, even a petty one like Tien. I felt sure her talk of boiling blood was bravado, but knew nothing of her power.

The storm turned the steps leading down to the cafe into a cascading waterfall of swirling mud. Ankle deep, it did nothing to cool my anger. Water poured through the ceiling, into the many buckets littering the floor and customers' tables. I didn't see the point.

Tien stood in her regular place, sipping coffee. Her eyes widened in shock when she saw me, but she recovered quickly.

"You've lost weight," she said. Glancing away and drawing a deep breath.

For an instant I saw something, worry or regret, and then it was gone, masked in the facade of uncaring she habitually wore. Eyes hooded, she watched me, waiting.

"They took Shalayn," I said. "The wizards."

She blinked and I caught a flash of confusion. "The wizards." She gnawed on her lower lip.

"Yes. We were trapped in the tower and they took her."

She studied me, weighing some decision. "But you got out. You got out before they came. You left her." An accusation.

"Not by choice." I locked my anger down deep, kept it from my voice and eyes.

"You've been gone months. I assumed you were dead." She snarled, bearing teeth. "I should boil your blood."

I raised my hand, showed her the ring she sent me to get, the one-way portal demon to the floating mountain. Her trap.

Her breath caught. "I knew it. As soon as I realized it was *that* tower, I knew it."

I didn't ask, didn't care. "Help me get her back, and it's yours."

She laughed without humour. "Can't use it. *I'm* not a demonologist."

I didn't bother to deny the accusation.

"It took me somewhere—"

"Where?"

"Doesn't matter. It took me months to get back."

She had questions, but swallowed them.

I told her about how Shalayn and I had been trapped inside the wizard's tower. I told her, without details, that I returned, starved and weak, and that the lights went out shortly after my arrival. Her eyebrows twitched at that.

"If you'd only been moments sooner," she said.

I nodded agreement, frustrated at my failure.

She stood in silence, examining her coffee, fingers drawing circles around the chipped edge of the cup. Looking up, she gestured at my famine-ravaged body. "You're rather thin on details."

"Very droll."

"You won't tell me where you were, how you got there, or how you got back."

"I'd rather not."

"But here you are. Asking for help, I assume?"

"Yes. I have to get Shalayn back. If you can get me into the tower," I nodded in the vague direction of the centre of Taramlae, "I can get her out." I prayed the Soul Stone had at least one soul left. Nhil said it would move me, and anything I was carrying. Would Shalayn count? My advanced state of starvation at the time of my lessons left those days a haze of unreality.

"You're insane," she said. "There are thousands of wizards in there including scores of Battle Mages. That's suicide. And if they capture you, they'll torture you, and you'll tell them all about me. No."

"If that happens, I'll tell them about you anyway, even if you don't help me. How do they feel about thieving wizards helping others break into their towers?"

"I should kill you now." She leaned back, took a sip of coffee.

"You're going to help me," I said, suddenly sure she would.

Tien grunted annoyance. "Maybe. But I'm not doing this for nothing."

Anger built in me and I crushed it, pushing it down deep. Rage wouldn't help me here. I needed this mage, and she knew it. Later, I reminded myself, once I had Shalayn back, I'd have my vengeance.

"Helping Shalayn isn't reason enough?"

She flinched a little. "No."

"What do you want?" I ground out.

"You bound a demon. I don't know how, but you did. I want a demon. You're going to command it to obey me."

That was a dangerous line of thought. "That's just it, that's why I got taken away. I couldn't bind it." It was only a slight lie.

She eyed me with distrust. "The ring," she said, leaning forward. "It teleported you somewhere."

"Sort of."

She glanced at the other ring on my hand, the white gold one I'd bound Felkrish to. "That's a different ring."

"It is."

"What's in it? A demon? What can it do?"

"It's just a ring," I lied. "I took it to sell. I have no money."

She examined me through disbelieving eyes.

"How about the other one then, the one I sent you to get."

That ring would only take her to the floating mountains, to my secret sanctuary. Did she know that? The thought of her there, a wizard in my castle, sent a shiver of revulsion through me. She'd likely starve to death beyond the walls like everyone else, but she was a mage and a thief.

"No," I said.

"No?"

She waved at the man behind the counter for another coffee. He brought her one, splashing through the water on the floor that now reached up to his shins, and ignored me. A dead rat floated past, carrying with it a faint sewer stench.

"It doesn't work like that," I explained. "The ring only goes to one place. You'd be stuck there. Like I was."

"You got back."

I definitely didn't want to tell her of Nhil and the castle, and summoning and binding a demon. "I had help. Help you would not receive."

"Why not?"

"Because you're a wizard."

She thought about that as she sipped her coffee. "So, it was either a demonologist who helped you, or an actual demon."

I shrugged rather than answer.

"I never believed all the demonologists were dead. There had to be some left, somewhere." Her attention locked on my hand, on the second ring. She put two and two together and got five which was a lot closer to four than I liked. "You lied about your new ring. This demonologist gave it to you. It has a demon bound to it, doesn't it? That's how you got back."

Hell. What could I tell her? "The cost of using it…"

"Cost?"

"Demons eat souls."

"I thought that was Guild bullshit."

"It isn't."

"But you used it to get back, and you're still wearing it. You're wearing pyjamas and you stink. You look destitute. If there wasn't something useful in that ring you'd sell it for the three hundred or so bronze it's worth and buy clothes and food and a nice room at the Dripping Bucket. So, there's a demon still in there, and you know how to use it." She grinned sweetly.

I opened my mouth to argue and she silenced me with a look of disgust. I was an idiot. I should have hidden the ring before coming to see her.

"You keep the ring," she said, "but you're going to use it to do something for me."

"You're okay with sacrificing a soul to do this?" I definitely didn't want to tell her about the Soul Stone.

"No, but you are."

I ground my teeth because she was right.

"What are you willing to do to get Shalayn back?" she asked.

"Anything."

She winced at that, a small stab of guilt cracking her uncaring exterior. "So, we have an agreement?" she asked.

"We do. But I get Shalayn out first." I stalled her argument by talking over her. "You know Shalayn won't let me renege on an agreement, so don't even bother. I'm not doing anything for you until she's been rescued. We don't have time for anything else."

Sipping coffee, she pursed her lips and stared into the mug, lost in thought. She closed her eyes, bit her bottom lip, and sighed. Finally, she nodded. "Fine." She looked like she wanted to change her mind.

"How are we getting in?" I asked.

"*We* are not. I like my life too much to do something this stupid." She smirked. "You will go in dressed as a wizard."

"It can't be that simple."

"It isn't. Guild members have a Chain of Office that gets them in. Without that, the Battle Mages at the gate will burn you to ash before you set foot within. We're going to have to steal one."

"Luckily, I seem to have fallen in with thieves."

Tien gave a mocking bow. "Now it gets ugly. There are ranks within the Guild, and the Chain of Office defines your rank. It also defines your access privileges. An acolyte's Chain will get you into the tower, but nowhere useful. We have to steal one from a ranked mage."

I cursed the delay, but saw no way to avoid it. I knew nothing of wizards and their Guild, and even less about their tower at the heart of Taramlae.

Tien glanced at me. "Will that new ring help with this?"

Assuming there were still souls in the Souls Stone, Felkrish could take me to any memorized location.

"Maybe," I said. "Is there a potential target with a predictable routine? Someone who goes somewhere we could access when they aren't around."

Tien considered this. "Master Thalman is a filthy old man with a weakness for whores. But it won't help. He's protected by a squad of Battle Mages. They search every room before he enters the brothel. And they use magic. They'd find you."

"I won't be there when they search, I'll arrive after."

"Right. Of course. If Thalman sticks to his usual schedule, he'll be there in an hour."

And therein lay the problem with the plan. "I need to get in there first and spend time memorizing the location. I'll need several uninterrupted hours. Some place small, like a closet, would be best. Some place that doesn't change."

She nodded, taking in the information. I wished I hadn't had to share it.

I wanted to charge into the tower now, cut my way past the Battle Mage guards, and rescue Shalayn. It would be suicide.

Another thought occurred to me. This plan involved using yet another soul from the Soul Stone. Two, actually. The more I thought about it, the higher the cost became. I'd need a soul to get in to the brothel, and one to get out. Then, once I'd used the Chain of Office to get into the tower, I'd need another soul to get Shalayn out. How casually I spent them now. I had to hope there were still souls to be used. For that matter, where was I going to have the demon take me when I left the brothel? My attempt at returning to the Dripping Bucket had met with many failures, and I knew there were new guests in the room now. I considered the floating mountain, but couldn't face the thought of more starvation if getting there spent the last soul.

Having spent years in my mud shack, I knew its every nook and cranny. Did I want to take her there? I'd been away for months, half a year or more. What if it had changed or fallen down? I'd continually been patching holes and maintaining it. What if I got into the tower, found Shalayn, and then had nowhere to take her?

I sagged. No way around it, I'd have to spend more time before I rescued Shalayn. There was little choice.

"I have to memorize somewhere in the city to escape to as well," I admitted. "Somewhere that won't change. Somewhere simple, without too much detail to memorize."

"I have the perfect place," said Tien.

Much as I hated to trust her, much as every part of me knew she'd betray me at the first chance, I had no choice.

"Let's do that first. After, you can get me into whatever room this Thalman will use?"

"Of course. And you will have to hire a whore while you're there. Otherwise people will ask questions."

I glared at Tien and she ignored me, examining her perfect fingernails. Something foul floated by, bumping against the leg of our table and leaving behind a brown stain.

"Why the hell do you hang out in this dump? You don't seem the type."

"Best coffee in Taramlae."

"Another problem. I don't have any money."

"I have to buy you a whore?"

I nodded.

She made a show of looking annoyed, but dropped a purse on the table.

After an hour of wandering through the torrential downpour, we arrived at a rundown home that would have been in the shadow of the outer wall had there been enough sun for shadows. It looked ready to fall in.

"It's a bolthole," she explained. "One of many."

Somehow, she'd managed to stay completely dry.

Tien led me inside, walking with an exaggerated strut, hips swaying and provocative. Having been alone with a demonic old man for months, I was unready to deal with the distraction, and unable to ignore it.

Tien glanced over her shoulder. "Hungry?"

"What? I…"

"You looked like you were in need of a little…something." An eyebrow twitched.

I'd been behind her, but staring at her ass. Somehow, she knew. Damn this teenage body! I blinked. Where had that thought come from?

I followed Tien through the dilapidated house. Rain fell through dozens of holes in the ceiling. The floor groaned and squeaked as we crossed. An odour of mould and rot filled the air.

"This looks abandoned," I said.

"Kind of the point."

She pushed open a door, exposing the room beyond. The floor had fallen in, and I saw the basement, rotting timbers and mud, through the gaping hole. It stank like death.

"Wrong room?" I asked.

Tien winked. The hole disappeared, leaving the floor flat and dry. The walls were painted a soft pink and the door Tien held open suddenly look very sturdy indeed. A single bed, big enough for two, sat in one corner. Shelves, laden with supplies of all kinds, and jars of preserved foods, lined the walls.

"Simple illusion," she said, entering.

Glancing back, I saw the rest of the house remained unchanged. I followed her in.

"Will this do?" Tien asked, hand on a cocked hip.

"Perfect."

"Shall I wait on the bed for you?"

She batted lashes at me and I felt a twitch of desire. She was small and cute, very much unlike Shalayn, but sexy as hell. At least to a nineteen-year-old who'd been alone for longer than he could remember.

"No. I need the room empty." I didn't want to explain why, or mention that if anything changed, I would be unable to return.

Heading to the door, she paused, plucking at her shirt over her heart. "What do you think, should I allow myself to get just a little wet?" She winked and wandered out into the rain, closing the door behind her.

I stared at the door, confused. Why the sudden flirting? It felt awkward. Was she trying to distract me, or did this have something to do with her past relationship with Shalayn, whatever it had been? Was she trying to see if I'd betray Shalayn?

Pushing Tien from my mind, I focussed on the task at hand.

Two hours later, I had a crushing headache but felt confident I had the room sufficiently memorized. Closing my eyes, I built the room quickly in my thoughts. If I didn't want to get caught in a whorehouse, speed was of the essence. When complete, I opened them, checking my memory against the reality.

Perfect.

Nhil said it would get easier, that I'd be able to do it faster, and he wasn't wrong.

I found Tien standing on the street. Though rain still pounded the city, she remained dry. I swallowed my disappointment.

"Done?" she asked.

"Done."

"Do you want to do a test, make sure it works?"

While a good idea, I couldn't risk using souls unnecessarily. "No."

She nodded. "I've talked with my contact at the brothel. Thalman has already been and gone, but I can get you in now."

My head hurt and I was tired from the walking. Two weeks of glutinous eating wouldn't undo months of starvation.

By the time we reached the brothel I staggered with exhaustion.

"What's wrong, old man?" Tien asked.

For an instant I thought she knew my past, but then she winked and gestured at the door.

"In you go. You look like hell and they'll probably want to throw you out, but show them the money and you'll be fine. Ask for Batrass. She's their star whore, the one Thalman always sees. She has her own room. She's expecting you and will leave you alone to do your thing."

Tien looked me over and for a moment I saw indecision war on her features, like she wanted to change her mind about all of this. Then she sighed and said, "If you finish early you can have Batrass for a quick roll."

"No thanks."

"Suit yourself. Either way, there's enough in that purse to buy you three hours."

CHAPTER TWENTY-TWO

I spent two and a half hours memorizing an empty closet, every crack in the paint, every knot in the wood trim.

Batrass, as promised, left me alone. She seemed more interested in doing her nails than in the black-skinned man in her closet. Apparently, compared to some of the things her clients wanted, this wasn't all that weird.

When finished, I found her having a glass of wine in her huge tub. She smoked as she soaked, the cigarettes dark and fragrant like a mix of cloves and roses. She watched me gawk at her glorious nakedness, the soap sliding from her, with an utter lack of concern.

"Yes?" she asked, sucking smoke into her lungs and holding it for a long moment. She exhaled it from her nose like a dragon.

"Does Thalman sleep here?" I asked. "After…"

"Half an hour. Then he leaves."

I wanted to join her in that tub, spend my own remaining half hour sliding around her like that soap.

"Thank you."

I left.

Tien caught up with me as I stumbled, exhausted, through the street on my way back to the Dripping Bucket. I thought to rent a room there with the coin left from her purse.

"Best not return there," she said. "Too predictable. People will recognize you." She gave me an appraising glance. "You do stand out."

The only man with midnight skin and black hair in a city of pale-skinned blonds. She was right.

I was too tired to think.

"Better to stay out of sight," she said. "At least for a while."

I let her guide me back to the rundown house with the illusory room.

"You and Shalayn stayed at the Dripping Bucket, right?"

"Yeah." I was hungry again.

"You stay anywhere else?"

I shook my head. "I need food. Still recovering."

"I'll fix you a meal. You look awful."

The rain let up before we made it back to the house. The sun made its much-delayed appearance and worms, pale and half-drowned, littered the street where they immediately began baking to hardened husks.

That night was too short. I woke once, when Tien brought me food—a loaf of bread, a selection of aged cheese, sausages and white wine—and then collapsed back into a dreamless slumber.

The next day I rose, still tired, to find Tien sitting on the edge of the bed.

Green eyes studied me. "You're really willing to do this?" she asked, gnawing on her bottom lip. "For Shalayn?"

I nodded. "It's my fault they took her." Which was true. But it was Tien's fault they found her alone. It was Tien's fault I was off starving to death in some floating hell.

She stared at her hands, examining her nails. "I'm sorry."

"For what?"

She blinked, darted a glance at me. "I misjudged you, thought you were just using her."

Her words left me uncomfortable. I couldn't shake the feeling something more was going on. Did she regret the stunt with the ring, sending me off to die?

"You know her well, don't you?" I asked.

"Better than anyone." Meeting my eyes, she added, "Better than you."

"Were you two together?"

She laughed, a soft grunt, and picked at a fingernail. "I might try a deeper red polish next time."

"You hurt her, didn't you?"

"Maybe something in a purple."

"You still love her."

"I had black for a long time. That seems childish now. Overly dramatic."

"Afterwards," I said, "maybe—"

"I don't want to talk about after." She tensed for a moment, and then said, "She deserves better than you."

"Can't argue that."

"Good. You should go now. Thalman's guards just finished searching the rooms."

"How do you know?"

She rolled her eyes. "Batrass will make sure the closet is exactly as it was."

"Tien?"

"What?"

"I know you don't like me or think I'm good for her—"

"You should go now," she repeated. Tien spun a dagger out of nowhere and offered it to me hilt first.

"It's not an assassination," I said. "I'm just going to steal his Chain of Office."

"If shit goes sideways and you don't have a knife, you're going to feel like an idiot for turning this down."

I accepted the knife and stuck it in the waist of my pyjama pants. I needed to buy real clothes at the first opportunity.

"If you're going to stay," I said, "I need you to be quiet while I concentrate."

She nodded.

"And remember to close the door on your way out."

Snorting wry amusement, she said, "I will."

This time it only took a few minutes to build the closet in my thoughts. Praying the Soul Stone had enough souls to get me in and out, I made the transition.

In the brothel, hidden in an empty closet, I listened to Thalman and Batrass talk for several minutes and then fuck for the best part of an hour. Soon after, the gentle snores of a spent man filled the room. Opening the closet door, I peered out. A young man, certainly not beyond his early twenties, slept on the bed. Tien called him a filthy old man. That mages held the keys to immortality seemed another reason to hate them. Then I remembered I'd ruled an empire for thousands of years. How had I extended my life? Had I sacrificed souls to demons for that purpose? It seemed likely.

Batrass sat beside Thalman, smoking one of her cigarettes. She nodded at me but seemed otherwise disinterested.

My hatred for the wizards soured. Maybe they *were* better than demonologists. Maybe they'd been right to topple my soul-devouring empire. Small and grubby as what they replaced it with might seem, at least when compared to my jumbled memories, I hadn't actually seen any signs of injustice.

I nodded to Batrass and she used her cigarette to point at a pile of clothes. Tilting her head back, she blew a series of perfect smoke rings. Crawling to the clothes, I searched through them. It took only moments to realize there was no chain there. Cursing, I approached the bed, staying low. Batrass watched, an eyebrow slightly raised. Thick waves of lustrous blond hair fell about her shoulders, framing perfect breasts.

Pointing at Thalman, I mimed a chain hanging about his neck.

She shook her head, gestured at her wrist, drew smoke, and blew a ring straight at me.

Rising enough to lift my eyes over the edge of the bed, I spotted the chain. It looked like a bracelet, and not at all what I'd expected. He wore nothing around his neck. Had Tien not known? Had she lied?

There was no way I could reach the bracelet from here. I'd have to stand over the wizard. Praying he was in a deep sleep, I stood.

Of its own volition, the dagger Tien gave me flashed from where I'd shoved it and jammed to the hilt in the wizard's neck. I stood, staring in stunned shock, as it sawed all the way around his throat.

The wizard's eyes snapped open. His mouth gaped as blood sprayed everywhere, showering Batrass and I in gore.

I couldn't understand what just happened.

Batrass screamed, scrambling to escape the fountaining blood, and distance herself from me. No doubt, she thought I'd just killed the man.

Beyond the bedroom door, someone roared in anger.

Snatching the bracelet, I dove into the closet, slamming the door closed behind me.

The door to the bedroom shuddered as someone crashed against it. Wood splintered.

Focus.

Block out the sound of half a dozen armed men battering in the bedroom door and filling the room. Ignore the screaming woman.

I built Tien's bolthole in my thoughts, piece by piece. The lone bed. The walls and floor. It was a simple room, easy compared to remembering the wizard's tower.

A thought twisted my stomach. Tien changed something in the room. She set me up, trapped me here. I was a dead man.

Beyond the flimsy closet door men yelled and smashed furniture and Batrass screamed, "He's in the closet!"

Silence.

I opened my eyes to find myself in Tien's room.

The knife killed Thalman, not I.

Tien gave me the knife.

"Fucking hell."

Knowing what I'd find, I crossed to the door. It was locked. After throwing my weight against it a few times I gave up. It was designed to withstand a far greater assault.

"You made it out," said Tien from beyond the door.

"You set me up."

"I had to. Thalman was blocking my entrance into the Guild. Your arrival, the timing, I couldn't pass up the opportunity."

I glanced at the bracelet I held. "This chain I took?"

"He actually had a chain? No idea what it is. Probably just jewellery."

"And Shalayn?" I demanded.

"Dead. The Guild found her in the tower. She fought them and they killed her." A moment of silence.

"You're lying."

"I fucking told you to leave! If you *really* loved her—"

"You're lying," I repeated. "You betrayed us."

"No!" The door shook as if she'd punched it. "I betrayed *you*, you damned stained-soul!" Her voice rose in anger. "She was supposed to leave! On her own!"

I listened to her sobbing through the door.

"It's my fault," I heard her whisper, voice cracking. "My fault." Again the door rattled, harder this time as if kicked. "You were supposed to die! Only you!"

"Had I been there—"

"You'd both be dead," she said, voice suddenly flat, drained of emotion. "You're nothing, could have done nothing." She cursed. "I wish you had been there. At least you'd be dead too."

"I'm not nothing," I whispered.

She was wrong. I would have figured something out, found some other demon to help us escape. I couldn't make myself believe it.

"I'm sorry," said Tien, voice breaking. "I really am. I never wanted anything to happen to her."

I collapsed to my knees, gutted. Shalayn was dead. Dead because of me. Dead because I wanted my past. Dead because I needed to know who I was.

Well, now I knew.

The wizards did this. All of this was their fault. They toppled my empire and they shattered my heart. Tien helped us get into the tower and sent me after a ring that took me from Shalayn. Because of Tien, I wasn't there when the wizards came.

All this was for nothing. Tien had known, and she'd tricked me again. She used me.

Molten rage burned in me, replaced the emptiness with searing heat.

"I'm going to kill you," I told Tien.

"Yes, well." She didn't sound concerned.

I tried to calm myself, pushing the hate deep. It festered in my gut, helpless, impotent. Anger would get me nowhere. "So, what's your plan, turn me in to the Guild?"

"Don't be stupid. You'd rat me out in a heartbeat. You'll die in that room. You're already half-starved, shouldn't take long. Sorry."

"You realize you're talking to someone who just teleported in with a demon, right?"

"Sure, but where can you go? You told me you had to memorize a place before the demon could take you there. And you told me the only place you'd been was the Dripping Bucket. I've made sure enough changed you won't be able to teleport."

Enough changed? "What did you do?"

"Burnt it to the ground."

Shit. Wait, there was the brothel closet. If I waited—

"The closet in the brothel has been changed," Tien said. "I had someone toss garbage in there."

I knelt, staring at the door.

"Yell all you want," she called from the far side. "No one can hear you from the street."

Rising, I returned to the bed and sat.

"Are you still in there?"

I waited.

"If you think I'm going to open the door to check on you, you're even dumber than I thought."

I waited.

"If you do teleport out," she called, "don't come back. I'll kill you. Shalayn's death is your fault. You deserve this. Think about that, while you're in there. Think about what you did to her. I told you it was suicide, and you did it anyway because you wanted whatever was in there more than you cared about her. You got her killed."

I ground my teeth, locking my rage down deep. I'd only left her there alone because Tien sent us after that damned ring. Somehow, I would have got us both out.

Eventually, Tien tired of shouting at me and left. I listened for a long time before trying the door again. No chance. This thing would take hours to get through with a proper axe.

"I'm not going to starve to death in here," I told the door.

CHAPTER TWENTY-THREE

Once I managed to calm myself enough I could think straight, the answer was obvious. My options were few: I could try to return to the Dripping Bucket, taking a chance that she lied. Each attempt would cost a soul, and I believed her. There was no way she'd leave me such an obvious escape in such close proximity. I could try the brothel closet, but I had no doubt she hadn't lied about that either. All she had to do was make sure someone left a broom in there, and it would be rendered useless to me. I could return to the library in the floating mountain, or the rain room in the wizard's tower, but both would be trading one prison for another.

My mud hut, far to the north, was my only option.

Yet, I hesitated. It was many weeks north of here. Sure, it was an escape—or would be, if it hadn't changed too much or fallen apart in my absence—but I didn't want to return. If I didn't stumble upon another caravan, it was a long and lonely walk.

Alas, I saw no other options.

I glanced down at myself and laughed. I was still wearing the mismatched pyjamas from the wizard's tower. Autumn in the far north was cold indeed.

After collecting the sheets from the bed, I searched the room for anything useful. There was nothing. Tien had stripped it of supplies, left the shelves barren.

Sitting on the floor, I began the task of building my mud hut in my mind. The years I spent there, staring at the walls, near mindless, helped.

I won't bore you with the details of my trip south after appearing in my hut. I made crude tools of wood and stone.

Sometimes animals, ragged and gaunt, wandered from the trees to stare at me. They always fled before I got anywhere near them.

Wearing the bed sheet and pyjamas, I stopped at small towns and begged or stole food. The one thing walking hundreds of miles gives you, is time to think.

Eventually, Tien would check the room. She'd wait a few weeks, until hunger would have left me weak and helpless, but she would check. When she found me gone, she'd wonder where I got to. Would she flee Taramlae, seek to escape my wrath?

Tien would worry, and she'd prepare. With me having killed the man who'd blocked her entrance into the Guild, I had to assume she was in now. Worse still, the Guild would no doubt believe *I* killed their wizard. Or was all of that stuff about the Guild a fabrication? Had I helped her murder a competitor, or some local politician?

None of this mattered. Nothing could save her. I'd get back to Taramlae eventually. I knew the coffee shop she frequented, and there were people there who knew her. Someone would know where she was. One way or another, they would answer my questions.

With a grin, I pictured the implements of torture laid out in neat rows back in the castle in the floating mountain.

Days of walking did nothing to cool my rage. I was not one, I discovered, to forgive. Not for this. Not for the death of the woman I loved. Tien tricked us, and she used us. I remembered the pain and the doubt in her eyes when I came staggering into the cafe, alone. In hindsight, it all made sense. She thought I'd touch the ring and get whisked away to wherever, never to be seen again. She effectively removed me from Shalayn's life. The more I thought about it, the more sure I was she saw me as a competitor for Shalayn's affections.

'I deserve better,' the damned trigger phrase for the levitation ring. And no doubt Tien thought she was the better Shalayn deserved.

Tien must have assumed that once I was gone, Shalayn really would be able to walk out the front door unhindered. She must have misjudged the wizard's security, must not have known what we'd face. The fact the little wizard hadn't intentionally killed Shalayn changed nothing.

She would feel my pain before she died.

I was going to return to Taramlae. I was going to make Tien pay for what she took from me. No one manipulated me. But I wasn't going back unprepared. I wasn't going back with a sharpened stick, decaying pyjamas, and a filthy bed sheet.

I wasn't going back alone.

I went in search of Henka, the young necromancer. Over the next week I managed to steal proper clothes, rugged hemp pants, a thick cotton shirt, and a pair of boots some farmer left unattended when he wandered into a stream to wash the muck from his body. Travelling from community to community, I asked about grave robbing, and people and animals going missing. When questioned, I claimed I was on Guild business and, for the most part, that quashed any further probing. I might not look like a wizard, but my black skin stood me out as someone clearly different, and that was enough.

Rumours led me further south and dragged me east, and I followed like a hound on a scent. When I first spotted a wolf dogging my trail, loping along, parallel to the path I followed, I wondered if I was going to have trouble with a pack. The beast looked desperately malnourished, its fur tattered. Wolves might avoid people, but desperation and hunger would drive any carnivore to pursue new prey. The beast reminded me of those mangy animals I used to see stalking the treeline around my old mud hut. Then the wind changed and I caught the unmistakable scent of death. Two more dead wolves joined the first, forming what I hoped was an honour guard rather than a pincer movement. They herded me south to an abandoned barn. The farmhouse looked to have burned down in the last year. I stopped just beyond the barn door and the wolves melted into the trees. Startling a necromancer seemed like a bad idea, so I called her name. Sure enough, the bear came out first. The beast looked somewhat worse for wear. Much of its hide had sloughed away exposing the rotting meat beneath. Sheets of tangled fur hung from its flanks, dragging in the dirt. Carrion insects, worms and grubs and maggots, writhed in the empty sockets of its eyes.

"Henka, it's me," I called out. "The man who spared you!"

The rest of the wolf pack exited next, a half dozen cadaverous beasts in varying states of damage and decay. They prowled circles around me but kept their distance. If Henka decided she wasn't feeling grateful, that I was more trouble than I was worth, this lot would have no trouble reducing me to an easily animated corpse.

The necromancer came last, sliding out of the barn, carefully closing the door behind her. It seemed an odd thing to do for someone who lived with a bunch of dead pets enslaved by her magic. Like it was the ghost of some long-gone life.

Henka was stunning. She'd cleaned herself up and showed none of the tangled, wild mess she'd been on our first meeting. Here, in the daylight, I could truly appreciate her beauty. Her skin remained the porcelain white I remembered. The dead don't tan, I supposed. Long, black, and gleaming in the sun, her hair hung like a curtain of ebony silk. Her eyes, however, gave me pause. While it had been night when last we met, I would have sworn they were dark brown. Now, they were ice blue.

Lifting a hand in greeting, I said "I'm glad you're still…around."

She smiled, a shy quirk of full lips. Her mouth looked different too, wider, more expressive. Though that might have been my imagination. Weeks alone on the road left everything looking good. Her clothes, too, had changed. She wore an expensive black dress. Low cut and revealing, it clung to her every curve. I couldn't imagine where she acquired it, out here on the frontier.

"I knew you'd return." She drank me with those blue eyes, taking in every detail, examining me from head to toe.

She'd changed somehow. Not just her appearance, but something else was different, too. She possessed a confidence, a presence I didn't remember. Had my earlier encounter with her done that? Was it something else?

I swallowed, suddenly feeling off-balance. She's dead, I reminded myself. But she looked very much alive. There was something here, something in her appearance, in what she was, that moved me in a way Shalayn's earthier, more wholesome beauty, had not. Pale hair, pale eyes. I realized I associated those characteristics with northerners, with wizards. I may have first awoken in the far north, but an island, far to the south, called my name.

I caught myself staring at Henka. She reminded me of someone I couldn't remember, but those ice eyes were wrong.

She waved a hand at her wolves. "Shoo."

They wandered off, tatty ears perking as they followed something I could neither hear, nor see.

"Do they still hunt?" I asked.

"They're still wolves," she said. "As I am still a woman." She watched her pets snuffle about in the grass. "Do you like my eyes?"

"Very striking."

"But you liked them better dark?"

I shrugged, unwilling to lie.

"I'll change them," she said.

How would she manage that? Could she work some kind of necromantic magic to alter her appearance?

"I'd like that," I said.

"Hmm." A small smile.

Her hand, which had been damaged last time we met, was whole and perfect.

"You seem to be doing much better," I said, nodding at the hand.

She glanced at it.

"I'd expected there to be a scar or something," I added. "Or stitches like…" I couldn't think of a polite way mention the crudely stapled wound between her breasts.

"Necromancy allows me to fix minor damage," she said.

The bear shuffled in a circle and headed back into the barn. It walked into the closed door a few times before Henka told it to stop and wait.

"Can you use it to repair his eyes?" I asked.

"Her," she said, shaking her head, not taking those startling blue eyes off me. "You were with a woman last time."

BLACK STONE HEART

Was her voice tense? "I was."

"I followed you for a while. I watched. I thought maybe you liked her for her eyes."

I did. Or I had. Somewhere, that started changing. My months starving in the floating castle changed me. Or maybe it was that shard of obsidian that retook its place in my heart. I was surprised that I was neither surprised nor bothered by the fact Henka had followed me.

"She was too…big…for you," said Henka.

I let that go without comment. Compared to Shalayn, Henka was tiny.

"Why did you come back?" she asked.

"I promised I would."

"You want to help me find my heart?"

"I do. And…I need your help."

She moved closer, slow, gliding steps. Flawless grace. "With?"

I was surprised to discover she didn't smell at all like a corpse.

"Wizards." I hesitated, trying to decide how much to tell her. She seemed young, naive, but if she survived out here alone, she was far from stupid.

Remembering Shalayn's reaction to the revelation, I decided to tell Henka the truth. "I am—or was—a demonologist. The wizards took my memories, broke them apart."

She blinked in surprise, a slight smile gracing those lips. "Did they?"

Not at all the reaction I'd expected. She showed no shock, no fear or outrage at my confession.

"Yes. Some memories are hidden away, in wizard's towers. Some might be more accessible. I want them back. I want to know everything about who I was. I want to know who I am."

She cocked her head to the side. "Do you want to be the man you once were?"

What an odd question, so close to so many of my own thoughts. Being dead, I suppose she understood the desire to return to a life long lost.

"No," I answered. "I don't think so." I couldn't tell her how evil that man was, how willing to sacrifice souls.

"If I help, I'll be with you?"

The question stunned me. I'd expected her to corner me on which we were doing first, her heart or my memories.

"Yes."

She slid closer, looking up at me. My breath caught.

Reaching out she touched my hand. "And after?"

My thoughts were so scrambled by her proximity it took a moment to understand the question. "After I have my memories and you have your heart?"

She nodded.

"I think I will still need your help."

"You will." She took my hand in hers, raised it to her face. For a moment I thought she was going to bite me, but she held it there, lips brushing my fingers like feathers.

"Alive," she said. "Warm."

Opening my hand, she kissed the palm. Startled, I realized she too was warm.

"You were cold last time," I said.

Henka smiled, a shy quirk of lips. "I've been taking better care of myself." Releasing my hand, she did a twirl, showing off the dress and the body beneath. "There are spells for hiding what we are. I never bothered before. I had no reason. But after you... after... You cared. I knew you'd return."

"All I did was offer some advice," I said, uncomfortable.

"More than anyone else has done. Where are we going?"

I couldn't tell her we were going to Taramlae to murder the wizard responsible for the death of the woman I loved. "I think I need more of my memories before I confront the necromancer who created you." I hurried to explain. "Right now, I'm weak, powerless. The old me, he knew things."

I waited for her to protest or complain, but she merely nodded.

"The next part of me is south of here," I continued. "A long way south. We will have to venture into cities and towns. I need supplies. Food. Weapons. Armour." I didn't mention I had no idea how I'd possibly afford this. "Are you alright with this?"

Henka nodded again. "I'll change my eyes. Make them the way you like."

CHAPTER TWENTY-FOUR

We travelled south together for weeks. Henka's beasts did the hunting, and between the walking and the near-carnivorous diet, I put muscle on fast.

After the third time the blind bear blundered into a tree, she called it to her. Henka whispered songs to the decaying beast. The bear listened, rotten ears turned in her direction. Sad rumblings burbled from its massive chest. She stroked those torn ears, not caring that her delicate fingers came away matted in dank fur.

"Lie down now," she told the bear. "Death can have you." Seeing me watching, she said, "She earned her rest."

That evening the wolves brought me three fat rabbits. After cleaning and gutting them, I impaled their naked carcasses on spits and roasted them over the fire, turning them often. Henka watched me eat, eyes intense, giggling when juices splashed down my chin and I yelped in pain at the heat.

"Do you want some?" I asked.

"No. I am dead."

"Can you taste things? Can you feel?"

"Sometimes. Those spells which give the me semblance of life bring those things back for a while. They fade. Most of the time my senses are muted." Rising, she moved closer, sat by my side. "I can feel some difference in temperature." She took my hand. This time her skin was cold. "You are warm." She sniffed my fingers again. "I can smell life. I smell death too." She gestured at one of the rabbits, still spitted, I'd set beside the fire to cool. "I know its death. I can see its last moments. Were I to breathe deep, I could tell you what corpses were nearby."

She inhaled, eyes closed, and I watched the interesting things it did to her chest.

"A baby goat died east of here," she said. "Foxes took it from its mother. There isn't much left of it now."

She opened her eyes, caught me staring, and bit gently at her lower lip.

"I…" I what? I was sorry for staring? I was sorry she caught me? I was neither of those.

"You can touch me, if you like," she said.

"No."

She sagged, staring at the ground between us.

I tried to explain. "You can't feel much right now, can you?"

She shook her head.

"But you could before, when you were warm?"

She nodded.

"It would be wrong," I said.

"Because I'm dead."

For some reason, that didn't bother me like it should. "Because it would be selfish, one-sided."

"Selfish?" She looked up, met my gaze. "When I can feel?"

I nodded.

"The necromancy requires some blood." She saw me glance at the rabbit. "Human blood." She turned away, ashamed, shoulders hunched as she awaited my recriminations.

Knowing who I had once been, and the terrible things I'd done, what could I say? I'd bled people to feed demons. More recently, I sacrificed countless imprisoned souls in my attempts to return to Shalayn. Henka needed some blood to work at least some of her necromancy. In comparison, my crimes were a thousand times worse. How could I judge this woman?

Her desperate need. Her flawless body. My own needs roared at me not to ignore them. She wants you to touch her! Touch her! She's beautiful!

I put a hand on her cold shoulder, turning her to face me. "Later," I said, "if you still want that…"

She sighed and said, "It would be nice to be touched. When you feel right about it. When I'm not disgusting."

"You're not."

She gave me a look of such heart-breaking desperate need, I leaned in and gave her a quick kiss on her cold cheek.

Henka sent the wolves out to patrol, keeping two back to guard her as I'd suggested all those months ago.

"When we reach civilization, you'll have to let them go," I said.

"I like letting them go. There's nothing scary about death."

Having an unknown number of souls trapped inside a diamond, I was less than sure.

"Life," she said, "even unlife, *that's* scary. I can't die unless I have my heart. When you caught me, you threatened to break me apart. I've never been so scared. I'd have been there, forever. Weeds would grow over me. Carrion creatures would pick the flesh from my bones. And I'd still be there. The earth would eventually swallow me, and I'd still be there. Forever. Buried. Helpless. Alone."

"I'm sorry."

She looked away.

"I won't let that happen," I said.

"Promise?"

My broken promises haunted me. This one, I swore, I would keep. "I promise." I had a thought. "When you have your heart, what will you do?"

"I don't know. That depends."

Rather than question further, I changed the subject. "I need to sleep."

"I don't. I'll stand watch."

I awoke the next morning to find her standing exactly as she had the previous night, staring at me.

After a breakfast of cold rabbit, we continued south.

When small farm communities became common Henka sang to her wolves, laying them to rest. I watched in silence, careful not to intrude.

While on the outskirts of civilization, the dirt roads looked to be at least occasionally maintained and were only washed out in some places. Most towns had an inn, and while the townspeople eyed me with distrust and thinly veiled loathing, they treated Henka well enough. We paid for rooms with money she'd collected over the years. At one town, I purchased a long knife. It felt better to walk armed, even if it wasn't much of a weapon. I thought we were safe enough then.

I was wrong.

Henka's silk dress spoke of wealth. Having spent months in the wizard's tower and in the floating castle, surrounded by that easy luxury, I didn't see it.

One morning, half an hour from the town where we'd spent the previous evening, men awaited us on the road. They were a rough bunch, broken noses and missing teeth, and I recognized two. They'd been in the inn's common room, drinking. I remembered the way they stared at Henka, eyes hungry. As they'd said nothing, made no attempt to bother us, I'd ignored them for the base peasants they were.

Chatting, Henka and I walked straight into their trap. Three men with drawn knives stepped out in front of us. When we retreated, two more exited the tress behind us with short hunting bows, arrows nocked and half-drawn.

I resisted the urge to reach for my own knife. Henka. I'd told her to send away her pets, and without them, I suspected she was helpless. What would these ruffians do to her? At some point they'd realize the truth. Would they break her apart then? I'd promised just a few nights ago I wouldn't let that happen.

I had to protect her.

A number of stupid things I could say passed through my head: This doesn't need to happen. It doesn't have to be this way. No one has to get hurt. You can take the money and leave.

But this was going to happen. There was no other way things would be. Someone was *definitely* going to get hurt. There was no way they'd be happy with just the money. The money was the excuse; they were here for Henka.

"It's alright," said Henka, grinning at the men before us. She ran a finger between her breasts, drawing the fabric tight. "I don't mind."

"Throw your knife down," said one of a men with thick hair and few teeth. "Toss it into the trees."

I glanced at Henka and she nodded. Grinding my teeth, I threw away my knife.

The two men with bows relaxed their draw and moved closer.

"I'll make you a deal," purred Henka, cupping a breast and sliding a finger between her thighs. "If you don't hurt him," she nodded at me, "I won't fight."

One of the men with the long-knives grinned brown teeth. "I want a fight."

"Then don't hurt him and I'll pretend to fight."

That confused him.

"Who's first?" she asked, gliding closer. "Or all five at the same time?"

Drawn by her promises, the bowmen approached, not wanting to be left out.

"Kantz," said the hairy toothless bastard. "Watch him. Put an arrow in him if he moves."

Kantz looked unhappy, but did as instructed. The other four closed in on Henka.

"How are you going to fuck me with all those clothes on?" she asked.

When one sheathed his knife and started fumbling with the draws of his pants, she reached out as if to help, plucked the knife away, and stuck it in his neck. He gurgled, eyes wide, hands clawing at the knife, and fell backward.

Pulling the knife free, she stabbed another in the belly as he came at her. He crumpled as the blade came free, curling about his wound and sobbing.

An arrow appeared in her back, and I turned to see Kantz fumbling to nock another. Rushing him, I tackled him to the ground. The other two went after Henka. She made no attempt to defend herself as they stabbed her over and over. Then I was fighting for my life, too busy to watch her get slaughtered.

Though shorter, Kantz had twenty pounds of muscle on me. I realized just how much of my former strength I had yet to regain. For a moment we wrestled over his knife, but we fumbled it and it landed in the long grass. Twisting my arm, Kantz rolled me off him and pinned me face down in the dirt. A knee in my back, a hand keeping my arm bent so far up my back I thought the shoulder would pop, he drove punches into my ribs with his other fist. Squirming and kicking, I failed to dislodge him.

Hot blood splashed me from above, showered me in gore. I heard Kantz's choked gurgling and his weight fell away. Groaning, rubbing my shoulder, I rolled onto my back. Henka stood over me, her beautiful silk dress shredded. Through the torn fabric I saw many knife wounds. None bled.

"Are you hurt?" she asked, reaching back to pull free the arrow. She tossed it aside like it was nothing.

I laughed, and then grunted at the deep pain. "Only my pride." I winced. "And my ribs, and my arm."

Kantz rolled around in the dirt, making quiet wet sobs. Glancing at him, Henka strode over, pulled the knife from his neck, and then put it in his heart. She showed no hint of emotion.

"Are you…hurt?" I asked.

"They ruined my dress." She wrapped her arms around herself, hiding the wounds. "They damaged me."

"I thought I had to protect you," I admitted.

"That's sweet, but I'm dead."

"Can your necromancy heal the damage?"

She nodded, studying the scattered corpses and turned back to me. "Not here, though."

I understood. It was a grizzly scene, and the dead would draw animals.

"If we dress you in some different clothes," I said, gesturing at the dead, "you can pass for living, if somewhat pale. We could go to the next town, get a room. Would that be better?"

She wrinkled her petite nose. "Yes. But..." She hesitated, teeth worrying gently at her lip. "I need privacy." She flashed a glance at me.

"Can you do it in the room? I could leave."

"It would be too loud, draw too much attention."

I remembered her singing to the bear. Did the volume of the song depend on how much power she needed? "Can I help?"

She shook her head. "No." She pulled the wreckage of her dress tighter. "I don't want you to see me like this."

We stripped the smallest of the men and she made me turn my back as she peeled away the tattered dress and donned his clothes.

Collecting a pair of long-knives and scabbards, I hung them from my belt. Then I selected a shortbow and a quiver with a dozen steel-tipped hunting arrows

"Perhaps we were a little premature in releasing my pets," she said, eyeing the corpses. "We could still use guards. I'd rather not get stabbed, if I can help it."

"They're a little rough," I said. "They'll never pass as living." She'd stabbed three in the throat, leaving gaping wounds. "Unless they start wearing scarves."

"That one is fine," she said, pointing out a man she'd only knifed in the belly. "A new shirt and he'll be perfect. At least until he rots." She shrugged. "I can maintain him too, keep him fresh."

The idea of having a little extra muscle around appealed. An undead body guard wasn't a terrible idea. I nodded agreement. Truth be told, I wanted to see if she truly could raise and control a dead man. Animals were one thing—not without their uses—but a man was something very different. I imagined an army of obedient corpses, all under the control of a loyal necromancer. Could she be that? Sometimes I saw such utter love and devotion in her eyes. Worship, even.

Was there a difference between love and worship? I wasn't sure. Both seemed useful.

Useful? I twitched. Who was that? What kind of man thought like that? Was that the old me?

"I'm selfish," I said, admitting my flaw aloud.

"We all are," Henka answered. "But if you can get what you want, and I can get what I want… Maybe we can be selfish together."

"I'd like that." I studied the corpse of this man who tried to kill us and rape Henka. "Is this evil?"

"Bringing a man back from the dead?" she asked.

"Yes."

"The wizards would say yes. They would say my very existence is evil, that I am a foul creature deserving of utter destruction." She glanced at me, searching for censure. She found none. "They'd say the same of you, destroy you in an instant, given the opportunity."

The wizards.

She shrugged. "We do what we must to survive. What is evil? Is the wolf evil for devouring the lamb?"

"Let's do this."

She smiled that shy smile and for a moment I forgot she just killed five men without a hint of emotion.

But she had. She was perfect for what I planned.

Staying out of her way, I watched Henka lay out the body. Peeling off his torn and bloody shirt, she carved strange symbols over his heart.

"This is different than making a necromancer? You aren't going to cut his heart out?"

"Very different."

A thought occurred to me. "How did you get a pack of wolves?"

"I found one already dead and used it to hunt and kill the others. There were more. Most got away."

"And the bear?"

"Found it dead. No more questions."

Henka sang as she worked, dirges of incomprehensible gibberish. I resisted the urge to ask if this was part of the necromancy.

An hour later, she stopped.

The man's eyes snapped open and he said "No" in the most heart-breaking tone of sadness. "Please, no."

"Silence," commanded Henka. "You will answer questions and say nothing else."

He nodded, face miserable.

"Stop looking so miserable."

He managed a broken smile.

"Never mind," said Henka. "What's your name?"

"Chalaam."

"Is he still…him?" I asked. "He's not a mindless zombie?"

"Different spell," she said. "He's more useful like this."

"He remembers what he knew, who he was?"

"Everything."

I saw how that would be infinitely more useful. I also saw how unhappy he was. Turning away from his look of purest misery, I felt a pang of guilt.

This was his fault. He shouldn't have attacked us.

Who was that, the old me, or the new? I wasn't sure.

"Should I raise the rest?" Henka asked. "They can scout ahead and follow us in the woods. Stay out of sight."

Useful as that sounded, I didn't relish being followed by so many corpses. "Best we stay with just the one."

Shrugging, she turned back to Chalaam. "Find yourself clothes without too much blood."

Once he was dressed, we headed south.

Walking at Chalaam's side, I asked, "Is it really that bad?"

He glanced at me, eyes bleeding depression, and said nothing.

"Answer Khraen's questions," said Henka. "Obey his commands as if they were mine."

Had she ever said my name before? I liked hearing it on her lips.

"There is something after," said Chalaam. "It was awful." Eyes closed, he trudged on. "Because of all the terrible things I've done. It was hell."

He spoke like there was only one hell instead of many. Was that a local belief? Could the actions of the living decide where their souls went? I'd ask Chalaam, but doubted an ignorant peasant would have any real knowledge.

"Had you been better, you'd have gone to a heaven?" I asked.

"I don't know." He turned a bruised gaze upon me. "But that hell was better than this. Death separates me from the world. I can't *feel*." He broke his smallest finger to demonstrate.

"Don't damage yourself," said Henka, shooting him a look of weary annoyance.

Bending the finger back into place, he said, "I'm rotting. That I do feel. I'm decaying inside."

"I won't let it get too bad," said Henka.

"Gee, thanks," he muttered.

"You were going to rape her," I said. "After, you were going to kill us both."

Chalaam sagged. "I deserve this."

Henka rolled her eyes. "Stop being so melodramatic."

We walked on in silence.

That tiny diamond with its burden of souls weighed heavily on me. Chalaam all but confirmed Nhil's claim that souls existed after death. It was no great stretch to believe they might be reborn. The wizards were wrong. There were gods. I had a god. If only I could remember her.

How many souls had I fed to Felkrish, my portal demon? I realized I had no idea. Not knowing how many there were to start with, I'd made no attempt to keep track. I remembered being appalled at the thought of sacrificing souls, but could no longer find the horror in me. Now, I was more worried about how many remained in the stone.

The thought of sacrificing a living person, however, still filled me with revulsion. I wasn't a monster. A soul in a stone is a difficult thing to relate to, to think of as a human life.

I couldn't make the distinct personalities in me coexist. I remembered the young man I thought I was, the youth who lived for years in a mud hut. That was *me*. But sometimes flashes of the ancient emperor slipped through. He considered Chalaam an ignorant peasant. He saw Henka's power as useful. I couldn't bring myself to hate him. I understood his drive to succeed, his willingness to do anything do win, all too well. Yet his self-centred manipulation of people disgusted me.

Did it disgust me enough to stop what horrors were to follow?

No.

CHAPTER TWENTY-FIVE

The town of Willows on the Ridge had neither willows, nor a ridge for them to be on. The land was rolling fields of clover for as far as the eye could see. At best guess, a thousand souls called Willows home, with a few hundred more in the outlying farmsteads. An ancient cobbled road, very unlike the rough dirt paths we'd seen up until now, passed through the centre of town. The stone buildings looked old enough, I suspected this place may have been here back when I was emperor. A wizard's tower, windowless and filthy from neglect, walls sprouting moss and lichen, sat in the centre of town. I wanted to knock it down, melt the stone.

Though they stared at us, Henka still beautiful in her rough clothes, and my black skin standing me out as a foreigner, they left us alone. Chalaam shuffled along behind us, depressed and silent, the only one of the trio not drawing attention to himself. Misery, apparently, is more acceptable than being different.

The inn, a two-story stone building that looked like it used to be part of a larger castle—of which there was no sign—was called Willows Inn. The main room held a dozen round tables, each big enough for six men to sit at with ample elbow room. The innkeeper, a huge woman with pale hair tied back in a loose bun that most of it had already escaped from, bustled to our table as we sat. Aside from one man nursing a whiskey at the bar, the place was empty.

"How can I help you, honeys?"

I choked down a laugh. A necromancer, a demonologist, and a dead man, and she calls us 'honeys.' If my black skin bothered her, she hid it well.

"I'll have a heaping plate of whatever is cooking, and a pint of something delicious." Our four would-be-robbers had added a bit to our purse.

"Kidney pies, today," she said. "And we brew our own beer right here in the basement. Willow's Ale, we call it."

"Great name."

She blinked at me before turning to the others. "And you, dears?"

"Nothing, thanks," said Henka, flashing that shy smile.

"But you're a waif! You need some meat on those bones!"

Henka rubbed her belly. "Not feeling well."

"Poor dear." She glanced at Chalaam and he glared sullenly at the table.

"He's not feeling well either," I said. "We'll need a room."

"Just one?"

Looking up from the table, Chalaam stared at her until she left.

"Are you going to wait until dark?" I asked Henka after the innkeeper delivered a huge wedge of pie and a pint of dark red ale. The pastry was thick and buttery, golden brown and flaky. Dark juicy mushrooms, butter-fried kidneys, and wedges of soft yellow potato, filled the pie.

I tried not to think about drunkenly asking Shalayn to eat pastry with me.

"Yes," said Henka as I shovelled pie into my face. "I don't want to be interrupted, and these small towns turn in early. It should be easy to find somewhere secluded."

"Will you be gone long?" I worried about her wandering the streets alone. Chalaam and his friends came from just such a sleepy village.

"Not long. A couple hours at most."

"Perhaps I should come with you."

She shook her head, huddling her over-large clothes tighter. "You can't see me like this. I'll be fine."

I wanted to argue, but hesitated. "Where will you go?"

"I'll find an empty barn, somewhere quiet and out of the way. Perhaps Chalaam can ask around, save me time searching."

I examined the dejected corpse. "With his social skills? Might arouse suspicion."

Henka glanced at the man sitting at the bar. "I'm going to go talk to him." She darted a quick glance at me. "I'll have to flirt a bit to distract him. Don't be upset."

"If it will keep you safe and bring you back to me sooner, I'm fine with whatever you need to do."

Flashing a look of gratitude, Henka unbuttoned her shirt a little more, exposing cleavage, stood, and walked to the bar. Sitting beside the man nursing his whiskey, she leaned in close and whispered something to him.

I pretended to focus on my meal and they had their quiet conversation. The man checked to see what my reaction was and, seeing me occupied and uncaring, returned his attention to Henka.

"Prolly Kamdi, Panfis' daughter," I heard him say. "She's only eighteen, but she's a looker awright."

The conversation once again dropped in volume.

"Thank you, kind sir," Henka finally said, leaning in to kiss him lightly on the cheek before returning to our table.

"Cold," I heard him say as she left, though I don't know if that was in reference to her lips, or her abrupt departure.

The whiskey-drinking man followed her with his eyes until he noticed me watching him. He abruptly returned to his drink, back hunched.

"Done," she said, joining us. "There's an abandoned farmstead on the edge of town."

"Kamdi?" I asked.

"He started comparing me to other girls he knew."

"Are you sure you won't at least take Chalaam with you?"

"Would you like me to have dark eyes again?" she asked, ignoring my concern.

I did. The blue eyes were disconcerting, reminded me of Shalayn. But more than anything, I wanted her to once again resemble that ancient and deep-buried memory of a specific woman. So selfish. I stared at the remains of my pie. An eyeball-sized mushroom protruded from one side, round and glistening in dark gravy.

"I would like that," I said. "But you don't have to. Not for me."

"I'd do anything for you. You know that."

"I do."

"Anyway," she said, "we're being selfish together. I want this too."

Selfish together. Was that possible, or was I letting her believe the lie?

So beautiful. So desperate to please. Was I using her, abusing her trust and her feelings for me? And what were her feelings? Did she feel she somehow owed me just because I didn't kill her when I had the chance? Did she feel indebted because of my small act of kindness when others would have ended her?

When you don't know yourself, sometimes it takes a while to comprehend your choices. Understanding crept up on me: I wasn't helping Henka for Henka. I was helping Henka for me. I needed her. I needed her undead. She would not only make for me an army of corpses unlike the world had ever seen, but she'd also make an army of necromancers, for me. Enslaved necromancers, their hearts under my control. I would not make the mistakes I'd made in the past. None of this, however, could happen until we had her heart back. I couldn't chance the necromancer who created her showing up and claiming control.

My self-loathing sank deeper as I realized that once I had her heart in my possession, I'd likely be unwilling to give it up. I knew from my fragmented memories that the necromancers had joined the wizards in their war against me. I could avoid that this time, if they were all under my control. I couldn't understand why I hadn't done it this way last time. Why had I left the necromancers such freedom? I wouldn't make the same mistake again.

For a mad instant, the young man I was wanted to confess everything to Henka, to tell her she couldn't trust me, that I planned betrayal. The old man, the fallen emperor of the world, the demonologist who spent souls like bronze pieces, squashed the urge. We needed her. If we told her the truth, she'd leave, and neither of us would get what we wanted. He knew me, knew I wanted her. I hated him.

I hated me.

Unsure if I was lying, I told myself the decision had not yet been made. I could still tell Henka later. Or, maybe, if I was sure she wouldn't betray me, I could leave her in charge of my necromancer army.

When had I started thinking of the emperor and I as separate people? Were there two distinct personalities in me, or was I simply a young, naive version of the manipulative old bastard I would become?

I promised Shalayn she could shatter my heart if I became someone she didn't like. She wouldn't like the emperor. She wouldn't like *me*.

Were she not dead, would I have kept my promise?

Were she not dead, everything would be different. I'd be different. All this was Tien's fault. I couldn't wait to see the look on the little wizard's face when I found her, when I cut her down, when I took everything she had like she'd done to me.

I hid all this from Henka. She didn't need to know.

Burying my anger, I forced myself to focus.

The real question: Knowing who I had the potential to become, could I change?

Yes, I decided. Yes, I could.

Wanting what I once had, wanting my memories, wanting to know who I was, did not mean I had to *be* that person. Yes, I desired something of my old power as well. Once the wizards realized I was alive—if they didn't already know—they would hunt me. I needed to be able to protect myself. They would not break me a second time.

We retired to our room, me collapsing on the lumpy bed as Chalaam stood sullen guard at the door. Henka sat at my side, careful not to touch me. She chattered on about the dress she wanted to buy, how she'd need a proper seamstress to make it for her.

I wanted to see her in it. I wanted to see her out of it, once her necromancy had repaired the damage to her body.

When the sun sank and the town fell to silence, she touched my hand, the slightest caress, her flesh cold.

"I won't be long," she said. "Get some sleep. We'll move on first thing in the morning. I want to see the capital." She flashed a smile of embarrassed excitement at the prospect.

I watched her leave.

Chalaam said nothing, stared at the door with the patience of a corpse.

I didn't think I could sleep with her gone, but I woke when she slipped back into our room.

She was stunning, eyes dark and bright, just like I remembered from our first meeting. Her skin, however, was an odd patchwork of tones, some pale white, some more pink.

Noting my attention, she said, "It will fade. A week, and I'll be as you remember."

As I remember.

Those words, and seeing her like that, shook something loose, deep inside. Though I still lacked most of my memories, she reminded me of someone. Someone I loved. Someone I lost thousands of years ago. But much as I searched through my disjointed recollections of the past, I found nothing more. Only distant longing and sadness remained of that unknown woman. And now Henka subconsciously remade herself to fit my desires.

The past was dead. I had to focus on the moment, and on the future. If I regained my skills, my knowledge and power, surely, I would regain my immortality. Henka, too, possessed an immortality of a sort. She'd make the perfect partner, I realized. Gorgeous. Never ageing. Powerful.

And, if I found her heart, enslaved.

CHAPTER TWENTY-SIX

It's not just lies that fester inside you. Half-truths and omissions do the same.

I told Henka we were going to visit Taramlae for supplies, food preserves, and a better sleeping roll to ward off the night-time chill. It was all lies. Or at least half-truths. I could have purchased what I needed at any number of the towns we passed through. I had but one reason to go to the capital: Find and kill Tien.

Her first betrayal led to Shalayn's death. Her second betrayal nearly cost me my life. I wanted my bloody vengeance and nothing would stop me. I'd see her dead at my feet. Until I achieved that, I could not move on, could not put Shalayn and that part of my life behind me.

Henka never argued, never showed a hint of doubt. Dark eyes watched me with love, and she agreed to everything I suggested.

We travelled south, stopping at small towns and villages, taking rooms in quaint inns and taverns. Each night Henka slipped away for an hour or two to work her necromancy. Each time she returned more perfect, more beautiful. She became flawless, a walking goddess. She sparked such an inferno of desire in me I had trouble concentrating. I choked it down. I would not take advantage of this young woman. I would not abuse her obvious worship of me.

For all my plans of using her to create an enslaved necromancer army, sometimes it felt like I was the one caught in a trap. But what a beautiful trap. I didn't even want to escape.

We passed through the gates of Taramlae unnoticed by the Battle Mages. We were nothing, a trio of peasants with little beyond what we carried on our backs. I laughed at them, mocking the filthy wizards in silence. What use were guards who let the long dead emperor, a necromancer, and an undead rapist into the city? Demon guards would do better.

The Dripping Bucket, I saw, was fine. Tien lied about burning it to the ground. I stifled another laugh at my own gullibility. Unwilling to waste souls, and worried what would happen if I tried to go somewhere that no longer existed, I hadn't even tried going there. Had I, I could have caught her then. She'd already be dead. On the other hand, in spite of my promise to help Henka find her heart, I'm not sure I ever would have returned to the north. My path was a dangerous one, and with the wizards against me, the chances of death and failure were high.

Unwilling to return to a place with so many memories of Shalayn, I found us another inn. Once again, I was the centre of attention. This was a city of hate. Anyone who noticed me glared with disgust and sneered revulsion. Henka they treated somewhat better, but she was clearly stained by her association with me. She made no mention of it, didn't seem to notice. Perhaps, after having lived in the wilds for so long, she didn't know what to expect of city life. Chalaam, for the most part, was ignored.

Our funds being limited, I found us a room at a dingy inn called the Dragon's Cave. I suspect dragon caves were likely both more inviting and more comfortable than the inn. The room was dirty and reeked of sweat and stale sex. The food was plain and boiled tasteless, the whiskey cheap and harsh. Rough and lumpy, the mattress seemed to be constructed of a bag of sharp rocks. The clientele, what little there was, stank and looked like they were succumbing to their various vices.

I learned something then: No matter how low their station, no matter how poor, how desperate, how close to the pauper's grave, everyone in Taramlae thought themselves above me. Even the oldest whore, taking customer after customer to scrounge enough bronze to buy himself a drink, eyed me like I was the squirming worm he found on the heel of his decrepit boot.

The next morning, I asked Henka to take Chalaam and go shopping for food preserves. I told her I knew a place where I could purchase a decent sleeping roll. She agreed without question and led her dead slave out into the street. Without me in their company, no one would pay them any mind beyond Henka's unearthly perfection.

I went to the cafe where Tien liked to take her morning coffee. With any luck she'd be there and I'd kill her before she knew I'd returned. If not, I'd ask after her. Someone would tell me what I needed to know. Along the way, I purchase a large floppy sun hat and pulled it low to hide my features. It looked ridiculous, but did the trick. Leaving the millinery, I noticed I was suddenly no longer an object of hate. With the colour of my skin all but hidden, I was suddenly just a man with a poor taste in hats.

The sky grew dark and heavy with cloud. A storm was coming. Icy winds snapped from the north, chilling me, tugging at my hat and clothes as if they sought to strip me naked, expose me for what I was.

I hated Taramlae, hated the cold and the weather. Hated the pale-skinned people and their loathing. I wanted to bring it all down, burn it to ash.

Checking the long-knife, I made sure it was loose, ready.

The building hadn't changed since my departure. It still looked like it might fall in at any moment. After several days without rain, the steps were dry. No doubt that would soon change. The rank carpeting at the bottom, however, still squelched beneath my feet. I doubt it ever fully dried out. The same man, still looking trampled, worked behind the bar, cranking away at a hand grinder to reduce coffee beans to the grit that would soon scum someone's chipped mug. No one looked up when I entered and I saw immediately Tien was not at her usual table. Two other women, however, were. I recognized them as the two Tien had been talking with when Shalayn and I first visited the thieving wizard. They might know something.

I heard the rumble of thunder and then the patter of rain. It grew steadily in volume.

Head down, I weaved through the tables, unhurried. Sliding the knife free, I held it behind my back. From under the brim, I examined the two women as I approached. One was older, maybe in her thirties. The other looked to be in her early twenties. Both had the pale hair and eyes of northerners, though the younger woman's eyes were more green than blue. She was pretty, in a freckled waifish kind of way, though she had none of Shalayn's muscled solidity. The more mature of the two had a presence to her. She stood at the table, poised and regal, like she owned the place. The tables around them were all empty as if no one dared encroach on their space.

What were the chances at least one of Tien's friends was also a wizard? Quite high, I decided, studying the woman. I hated her instantly.

"That is the silliest hat I have ever seen on a grown man," said the older one as I arrived.

I looked up from under the brim and she added, "Oh. You're just a boy," in a dismissive tone.

Her eyes widened as she recognized me. Hand lifting, her fingers twitched, drawing invisible shapes in the air. Remembering the wizard Shalayn killed in the tower, I stabbed her in the throat, angling the long-knife upward. She gagged, spewing blood. Ripping the knife free, doing as much damage as I could, I grabbed her by the back of the head and slammed her face into the table. The table broke under the impact, as did the wizard's regal nose, and the two crumpled to the sodden floor. The mage lay twitching and retching, clawing at the savage wound in her throat.

I stared at her, stunned at what I'd done, horrified by the sudden brutality. It had been easy, so easy. It almost felt like someone else had done it, like I'd stepped aside while an older, more experienced man, did what needed doing.

The other woman squeaked.

Turning my attention on her, I said, "If you move, or try to cast a spell, or run, I'll kill you." I flashed her a cold grin, all teeth and rage. My god, it felt good to finally kill a wizard. "And leave your hands where I can see them." She held one of those small chipped cups clutched in both hands like she'd been using it to warm them.

Frozen in terror, she didn't move. Blinking back tears, she gaped at the woman on the floor, watching the last shudders run through her as she died.

By the time the wizard stopped moving, the cafe was empty. Happily, there were no heroes, no one rushing to this woman's aid.

"I have questions," I said. "Questions you will answer."

Clutching the mug, tears streaming from green eyes, she whispered, "You… You killed her."

"She was a wizard," I said, as if that justified my actions. "Are you?"

She shook her head, blond hair moving about her shoulders.

"Then perhaps I won't have to kill you. Answer my questions, and I'll be on my way. Stall or lie, and I gut you here and now."

She nodded quickly. Staring at her mug, she took a sip as if to bring some normality to the situation.

"Tien," I said, "the wizard you were with when I first came here."

She looked at me now, eyes desperate.

"Is she still in Taramlae?"

Apparently too scared to speak, she shook her head.

Holding the bloody knife before her face, turning it so she could appreciate its brutal simplicity, its defining purpose, I asked, "Where did she go?"

"South. Nachi, on the coast."

"Why?"

She gaped at me, baffled. "I... I don't know. Sometimes they go south for the winter."

"They?"

"She and her sister."

"Is her sister a wizard?"

She shook her head again. "No."

"Good."

She wasn't lying, I felt sure; she was too terrified.

I had what I needed. It was time to leave.

Yet I hesitated. This girl could describe me in detail. To the rest of the patrons, I was probably nothing more than a silly sun hat and a knife, but she'd seen my face. She could connect me to Tien, might even have some way of warning the wizard. If Tien knew I was coming, I wouldn't have a chance. I wondered if she really could boil a man's blood as she so often threatened.

I killed a Septk boy because I was unwilling to leave an enemy behind me. This young woman associated with wizards and was a friend of Tien's. Was she my enemy?

She watched me, tense.

"I'm not going to kill you," I told her.

When she sagged with relief, eyes closing, I stabbed her. I tried to do it fast, to make it a quick and painless death. Inexperience betrayed me. Instead of stabbing her in the heart, sliding the blade neatly between ribs, the knife tore a long gash in her, skidding off bone. Screaming, she flailed at me, retreating. I followed, stabbing and slashing, wanting to tell her not to fight, that it would be quicker if she didn't, but knowing how insane that would be.

By the time I left the cafe I was splashed in gore and shaking at the horror of what I'd done. I butchered a woman who fought for every last second of life. Long gashes left by sharp fingernails raked my arms. My face burned where she clawed me, blood trickling down my neck. I'd lost the stupid hat in the struggle.

Staggering up the steps, wading through the waterfall cascading down them, I stood in the icy rain, face turned up to the sky so it might cleanse me of my sins.

Soaked through, I found a shop selling sleeping rolls and purchased one. The shop-keep looked like she wanted to spit on it, but seeing my fresh wounds, wisely decided not to.

By the time I returned to the Dragon's Cave I was shivering from the cold, deep bone-shaking shudders. My wounds still felt hot and raw. In our room I found Chalaam staring glumly at a wall. Henka sat on the bed waiting with that infinite patience she had.

"You're soaked. Oh!" Leaping up she came to my side, checking the lacerations, making sure none were serious.

"I'm fine."

"These were left by fingernails," she said, watching for my reaction, gauging.

I forced a rueful grin. "I ran into a woman I knew last time I was here."

"Oh?" she asked, an eyebrow lifting.

"She was a wizard. I killed her."

The tension left her and she returned to fussing over my wounds.

Tien went to Nachi, a city on the southern coast. Did she know I was coming for her? When I found her, I'd have to kill her fast.

"Tomorrow we leave for the coast," I said.

Henka nodded without looking up.

"We're going to Nachi. We should be able to hire a boat to take us south from there."

"It'll be nice to get away from the cold," she said.

Her hands, I realized, were warm with life. Leaning close, she licked the blood from my arm with her hot tongue.

CHAPTER TWENTY-SEVEN

After Taramlae, we followed my heart, its pull dragging me like an ocean current stealing a ship. Having come this far south, I no longer felt like I was going to freeze to death every night. Winter, however, followed close in our footsteps.

The weather held, favouring us with blue skies and the rare cloud of brilliant white, glowing in the sun. The land changed, becoming greener, more vibrant. Shards of memory bubbled up and I realized how much I missed the bright life of the south. Gloriously colourful birds, blue and gold and crimson, replaced the dark and drab birds of the north.

The people changed, too. Their skin faded from the bright pink of folk who saw little sun, to the tanned brown of those who lived their lives beneath it. I still stood out, my jet-black flesh much darker than anyone else, but the further south we got, the less hostile the stares became. Not that the hate ever completely went away. We were still days from the coast, but I wanted to be there. I wanted to board a ship, feel the familiar rise and surge of the ocean beneath me. I wanted to hear the gulls and taste the salt air. Somewhere out there was an island. My island.

PalTaq.

It would have to wait.

In the last day, the call of the nearest shard of my heart grew louder. We were close. Somewhere far to the south, I heard the call of another piece. A large shard, if the volume and pull was anything to judge by. It, too, would have to wait.

Early one morning I spotted the ruins of a much larger city to the east of us. Unlike the wizard's capital, this city had no wall. Colossal towers stabbed into the sky. Sweeping bridges, mere spiderwebs at this distance, connected them a thousand feet above the ground. From here I saw no obvious signs of damage.

Over the next several days we moved closer, our route taking us past it. I made out more detail. While the city was overgrown, vines crawled over everything, and trees and plant-life had long erupted through the stone of the streets, it seemed otherwise untouched by the passage of time.

"What is that place?" I asked Henka.

"Kazamnir. A city of the old empire."

"Kazamnir," I repeated. The name meant nothing, twigged no memories. "It dwarfs Taramlae."

"It's been abandoned since the war."

"Why? It looks to be in good shape."

"Demons. It's inhabited by thousands and thousands of demons. They're bound to objects and walls, right to the very superstructure of the city. They maintain and repair it, even now. No one knows how to command or control them. It was easier for the wizards to abandon and ignore the old cities than to destroy them."

"Are there many cities like this?"

Henka shrugged, staring wistfully at Kazamnir. "So I've heard. The further south you go, the more you'll find." She glanced at me. "Apparently PalTaq still stands, untouched by time."

PalTaq. The capital of the old empire. An entire island given to city. And she still stood? I wanted to rush to see her, my bright gem.

"Every now and then," said Henka, "some adventurous idiot wanders into one of the old cities. Most are never seen again, their souls —or so claim the wizards—devoured by demons. But every now and then one returns with fantastic tales and some demonic artefact." She laughed, a soft, breathy sound. "The wizards then hunt and kill them, and hide away whatever they brought out. Still, there's always another adventurer willing to risk certain death."

When I was ready, when I had something of my old power, I would plunder these cities. They were, after all, mine.

The pull of the nearest shard of my heart had drawn us south for weeks, but I awoke the next morning to discover I suddenly wanted to veer east. Closing my eyes, I examined my feelings. That larger shard remained, far to the south, likely somewhere in PalTaq. But the closer shard had definitely moved.

"We need to go east now," I told Henka.

I rarely bothered talking to Chalaam. He tended to be uncommunicative, answering in grunts and baleful glares. His skin grew greyer with each passing day, and I caught the first wafts of decay. Soon Henka would either have to work her necromancy to repair him, or let him die. We could do much better, I thought, if we hand-picked a guard. Perhaps someone educated, and more skilled in combat.

Hand-pick. Kill. Murder. Was I really contemplating killing someone so they might be enslaved as a bodyguard? And yet, it made so much sense. My experience showed me that people could not be trusted. The wizards betrayed me all those millennia ago, and more recently Tien betrayed me. Why trust someone when you could own them? Why give them the chance to betray me the way Tien did?

I still couldn't believe she played me so well, that I hadn't seen it coming. Certainly, there had been clues. My naivete embarrassed me. Had all this happened before? Was that why I'd previously ended up the kind of person willing to spend souls and enslave innocents?

We walked another day, and I still felt no closer to the shard of my heart. If anything, it was farther east now.

"It's moving," I said. "The piece of my memories is moving. Someone is trying to take it away from me." I considered the possibilities. "Wizards."

"Wizards?" asked Henka.

"It's the only answer. Somehow, they know I'm coming."

Had the wizards realized someone had been to their tower and taken something? Did they know what was missing, what it meant? They must have taken my heart from wherever they'd previously stored it, thinking to move it somewhere safer. I couldn't let that happen. My one advantage was that they apparently didn't realize how close I was. If they did, they'd be moving faster.

"We need to catch them," I told Henka.

"We need to kill horses."

Seeing my confusion, she explained. "The dead never tire. You can ride them hard all night." Then she winked.

It took a moment for her words to sink in.

I remembered the way she licked the blood from my wounds, the sensuous heat of her tongue.

The pieces clicked together, things I'd avoided thinking about.

'Necromancy requires some blood,' she once said. 'Human blood.' She'd been talking about the spells that warmed her body and allowed her to pass for living. Every time she was warm, she'd somehow made use of human blood to achieve that.

I'd seen the implements of torture in my floating castle. I'd seen the rooms where the sacrifices took place, the floor carved deep with runnels for the blood. Most damning of all, I'd sacrificed an unknown number of souls, fed them to Felkrish, my portal demon. Me, not some forgotten past. *I* did that.

Who was I to judge?

She needed a little blood. That hardly made her a monster.

I surreptitiously studied Henka's form-fitting dress, the way it clung to every curve, accentuated her perfection. She was not at all dressed for travel, and yet seemed perfectly comfortable.

Confusion tore through me. Every time I looked at her I saw fragile beauty and gorgeous eyes. And then part of me would whisper, *she's a corpse.*

"Let's find horses," I said. "Lots of farms around here."

Late in the afternoon, we found a farmstead with a paddock of four horses. Huge grey and black beasts, well over seventeen hands high, they looked more suited to pulling ploughs and wagons than running. Henka assured me that, once dead, it wouldn't matter.

The farmhouse, a rough-hewn log cabin, sat atop a slight rise in the ground. A second building, larger than the house but less sturdy-looking, served as a barn. From within I heard the gentle bleating of sheep. A score of chickens wandered the space between the two buildings pecking at the dirt as if eating pebbles. Smoke wafted from the cabin's smoke-hole in lazy curls, filling the air with the rich scent of birch. I saw no sign of the family living there. This late in the day, they were likely taking their dinner.

The horses shied as we approached, moving to the far side of their enclosure.

"Animals don't like the dead," said Henka. She watched the beasts with longing.

Their manes and tails, lustrous black, swayed in the wind, twitched at flies. Muscle rolled under grey hair. They were beautiful. I didn't relish the thought of murdering such fine creatures.

"What's the best way to do this?" I asked.

"Use the bow," said Henka. "Minimal damage. No one will even know they're dead. At least, not for a while."

Was I really going to hesitate at killing a couple of horses?

I needed them. I needed to catch the wizards moving my heart.

Unslinging the bow I'd taken from Chalaam and his companions, I nocked an arrow and shot the nearest horse. One arrow from a shortbow will not kill a horse. Though maybe a better archer than I could manage it. It took three arrows before I managed a lucky shot and the horse dropped. They aren't stupid creatures; they understood immediately. But the poor beasts were trapped in their paddock. Still, I missed as often as I hit.

The second horse staggered about, bleeding profusely from the many arrows puncturing its hide. Its screams drew the farmer from whatever field he'd been working, an event I'd rather foolishly hoped to avoid. He must have been somewhere deep in the corn as I had no idea he was there until he suddenly appeared, roaring and charging straight at us. Spinning in surprise, I loosed an arrow that went over his shoulder. With a knife clutched in one fist, he rushed me. I fumbled for a weapon of my own, but Chalaam stepped forward and chopped into his neck with a long-knife as he passed. Eyes wide, the farmer fell.

Chalaam raised his weapon to finish the man when Henka said, "No." She darted a look to me, hesitating. "I…" She looked away. "I need the blood."

The man writhed at our feet, desperately trying to stanch the wound. It was futile, the wound too wide, too deep. He was a dead man.

Nothing I could do would save him, and Henka needed the blood to pass for living.

"I need the blood to be warm for you," she added in a small voice.

I wanted that. I wanted to touch her. I wanted her warm and alive, not cold and dead. That hot tongue licking the blood from my wound.

I nodded. This man was dead anyway, I told myself.

"Collect as much as you can," she ordered Chalaam, handing the dead man a wine skin.

A scream came from the farmstead. A woman stood there, a small child in her arms.

"Kill her," commanded Henka.

The woman fled inside, banging the door closed behind her.

Chalaam set off, pace even, unhurried.

"No," I said, grabbing a cold arm to drag him to a halt.

Shaking me off, he continued up the hill. I knew then who his real master was.

"We have to," said Henka. "She'll tell people. The wizards will come after us. They'll break me apart. They'll bury me."

"I won't let them. We'll be on undead horses. No one can catch us. Call him back."

She watched Chalaam march up the hill a moment longer. "Chalaam," she finally called, "come back."

He did as instructed. I'm not sure if I imagined it, but I thought he shot me a look of gratitude as he passed. With his unquestioning obedience and apparent lack of personality, it was easy to forget he was still the man he'd once been. Not that he'd been a paragon of virtue, but a man willing to rape and kill might still baulk at murdering babies. Henka could command him to do anything, and he had no choice but to obey.

What cruel hell would that be?

He hadn't wanted to kill that woman and child any more than I wanted him to. Yet he set off without a word of complaint.

And here I was, planning to create battalions of enslaved necromancers who would enslave countless dead to make me an army unlike anything the world had seen.

Not evil. Not evil at all, I chided myself.

Chalaam bent to the task of bleeding the dying man into the wine skin.

Shaking the image off, I returned to the business of killing the horses. The desire to be moving grew in me. The wizards were fleeing with my heart. If they got to wherever they were going, I had no doubt retrieving it would be markedly more difficult.

Henka approached as I killed the third horse. "Not killing the woman, this may come back to haunt us later."

It might. I understood all too well that the 'wise' thing to do was kill any and all witnesses. The old me wanted to. That woman, her child, they were nothing. Small lives, easily crushed.

"I'm not that man," I whispered.

"Pardon?"

"I'm not that man," I repeated, not caring if she understood.

Maybe she saw something in my eyes, because she stepped close and pulled me into a tight, cold, hug.

"You're better," she whispered into my ear.

CHAPTER TWENTY-EIGHT

After sending Chalaam to the barn to fetch saddles, we rode hard through the rest of evening. Night fell, clouds swooping in as the sun picked up speed in its mad plummet into the western horizon. The horses, raised by Henka's necromantic magic, never slowed nor tired. We only reduced our pace in the dark for fear of them tripping on an unseen hole and either killing me or damaging the others. In the end, it was my own exhaustion that drove me to call a halt. If I didn't get an hour of two of sleep, I'd surely fall from my undead mount. My weakness disgusted me.

After shovelling some hard biscuits and salted meat into my mouth, I cleared an area of stones and curled up in the grass.

"Wake me in two hours," I instructed.

Henka sat, cross-legged, beside me. With the clouds growing ever thicker, she was rendered to a curved slice of shadow.

"I could kill you," she said.

Curled in my sleeping blanket, I froze.

"I could cut your heart out. I could make you like me. You wouldn't tire. I could teach you necromancy. We'd be together. Forever."

I lay in the dark, contemplating this. While shedding the weaknesses of life held some attraction, I saw problems. Would it even work with my incomplete obsidian heart? More importantly, could I trust her to give me my heart after? In raising me, she'd have complete control. I'd be her slave.

I couldn't chance it.

She shifted in the dark, touching the ground between us with a pale finger. "You don't trust me with your heart. I understand."

"I'm not ready to die."

She brushed cold fingertips across the back of my hand. "I could never hurt you. You saved me."

That wasn't quite true, but I saw nothing to gain in correcting her.

Rain, pounding the earth to mud, woke me less than two hours later. Crawling from my sodden blanket, I rang it out as best I could before stuffing it into my pack. Henka stood watching, motionless as stone. Even in the dark I saw how her wet clothes clung to her. Water ran down her face like tears, dripped from her petite nose. She showed no hint of discomfort. I, however, shivered uncontrollably.

Seeing me examine her, she smiled, a slight quirk at the corner of perfect lips. "Will you hold me? Just for a moment?"

I nodded and she stepped into my arms. Our clothes soaked, I felt her against me, every curve, every softness. She was so different from Shalayn's muscularity. I hated myself for comparing the two. Though she melted into me, no warmth came from her. Wrapping her arms about my neck, I felt algid lips against my throat.

"I'm sorry I'm cold," she whispered.

I pulled her tight, kissed her neck.

Corpse. No pulse. No heat of life. A side of rain-chilled meat.

"You're so warm," she said. "Like a fire." She licked water from the hollow of my throat. Dead tongue.

"We should keep moving."

Remounting our horses, their ears drooping, we rode east, though at a safer pace. The rain broke just before dawn. Clouds fled the morning sun and for the first time in hours, I thought I might not freeze to death. Our mounts looked miserable, dejected.

With every passing hour we closed the distance. The call of my heart thrummed through me.

An hour later we passed the remains of a sodden campfire. At Henka's command, Chalaam dismounted to search the ground.

"One person," he said. "Mounted. Rode east."

One? Had the Guild only sent a single wizard to move the shard? Did they think so little of me, or did they not know how close I was?

Or, was the single mage more than enough to handle a demonologist who knew almost nothing of his power? They must not know of Henka. The thought made me feel better, though I wasn't sure what she could do against a Battle Mage.

With the sun up, we pressed the horses hard, thundering across the grasslands and cutting through tilled fields of wheat and clover. My chest tightened with every passing mile, hunger and excitement building. What would I learn? Who would I be? I had no real plan. Without knowing what we faced, it was difficult to decide how to approach.

"What are we going to do when we see him?" Henka asked.

Him? Why was she sure the wizard would be a man? It didn't matter.

I shrugged and said, "Ride him down before he can cast a spell."

Hopefully we'd catch him off-guard and unprepared.

We caught sight of him mid-morning. His horse plodded east, sagging with exhaustion. Its head hung low, swung back and forth with every step, ears flat. The rider didn't look much better. Shoulders hunched, long black hair hung down his back in tangled knots. Riding at speed, the wind had dried us somewhat. He looked sodden.

I knew that shape.

While we were still a distance off, he reined his horse to a stop, wheeling it about to face us.

Midnight black skin. Obsidian eyes that drank light.

"Don't kill him," I said.

We approached, slowing, fanning out and surrounding him with our much larger mounts. His horse hardly noticed us, it was so tired. There would be no mad attempt to escape, no dash for freedom.

He eyed me with distaste. "Hello, Khraen."

"Hello," I answered, "Khraen."

I stared at myself. Unlike me, he had not suffered recent starvation, the effects of which I was still working off. Yet he remained gaunt and thin.

"What do you remember?" he asked.

I dismounted. "Enough."

"Were that true, you wouldn't be here."

What did that mean?

"You know why I'm here," I said.

"Don't do it. Let him die."

I knew he meant the Emperor.

"The wizards seek to destroy me," I said. "I won't let them break me again."

"The wizards?" He laughed, a mirthless chuckle. "Ride away. You have a new life." He glanced at Henka and his eyes narrowed. "You look familiar." He shook his head as if trying to dislodge a memory. "Ride away and be with your woman. You can be happy. If you succeed in bringing him back, you'll find only misery."

"How do you know? What do you remember?" Hunger ate at me.

"We did terrible things. I know nightmare truths. He was evil. If the wizards did this to us, they did so with good reason."

Unslinging my bow, I strung it and nocked an arrow. He watched.

"I need to know everything you know."

He turned pleading eyes on Henka. "You love him. I see it in you. Don't let him do this. It will end whatever you share. It will end any chance at happiness."

Henka studied him, head tilted, the ghost of a smile dancing her lips. "You're wrong. He will be better than he was. I am his. He is mine. Always and forever."

"You…I almost remember…"

I knew what he meant. I too had fleeting memories of a woman with pale skin, dark eyes, and long, straight black hair.

Henka shrugged, unconcerned at being compared to someone from our past. She turned to me. "Shall I have Chalaam kill him?"

Dismounting, Chalaam drew his long-knife. Unless this piece of me was more skilled in combat than I, this corpse would have little trouble dispatching him. The dead had too many advantages.

"No," I said.

I put an arrow in his chest and he grunted. He tried to wheel his horse about to flee but the beast staggered. I put another arrow in his back. He fell to the ground.

Drawing my own blade, I approached cautiously.

He watched me, eyes slitted, lips peeled back in a grimace of agony. "Don't."

"You know I'm going to."

"You'll bring nothing but misery to the world."

"That's not true, I—"

He lunged awkwardly at me, slashing at my legs with a knife he'd kept hidden.

I danced back beyond his reach. "I know you at least that well."

He sagged back, closing his eyes, and I kicked the knife away. After making sure he didn't have any other hidden weapons, I crouched at his side. Opening his eyes, he stared up at me. I saw no fear, only sorrow.

"You aren't going to die," I said.

"I am. This me will die. The me that was happy. The me that doesn't hurt people." He coughed blood. "The me that chose not to rip people's souls out so he might feed them to demons."

Hunger pulled me closer. "You know how to do that?"

"Have you not wondered that the obsidian heart holds *his* memories but not ours?"

"No. You know how to harvest souls, don't you?"

He glared loathing at me. "Stop now, before it's too late. It's evil—"

I stabbed him in the chest.

Again and again I stabbed him, splashing myself with gore. I hated him.

Henka watched, pale and beautiful, as I hacked at his chest, driving my knife into the cartilage in the centre to open his ribs wide. She watched me cut his heart free and then carve away the excess meat to expose the shard of obsidian. She watched as I cupped it in my hand. She saw it sink into my flesh and tear its way through my body.

I wanted the pain.

I earned it.

I deserved it.

I screamed and screamed, and she comforted me, my head in her lap. I had no memory of falling.

Other things, however, I did remember.

CHAPTER TWENTY-NINE

PalTaq. The capital of the world. The centre of an empire so large, so all-encompassing, it didn't need a name. The Empire.

My empire.

The empire I built from a thousand warring kingdoms. The empire I carved from chaos. The empire I held together for ten thousand years before the traitorous wizards brought me down.

When someone said 'the palace,' there was only one place they could mean. My palace, the beating heart at the centre of my empire.

Every branch of magic contributed to the empire, but demons were the cornerstones upon which civilization rested. Spirit demons, bound to every wall and door, warded the palace. Manifestations, physical demons called from other worlds, guarded the streets, patrolled the city. Demons maintained the aqueducts. Bound elementals lit the streets each night. The main thoroughfare was called the Street of Eternal Day. Water elementals turned mill wheels and kept wells potable and full. Demons and earth elementals laboured together to work mines, supplying the empire with steel and iron. Air elementals kept the breeze fresh, blew away the odours of civilization. Fire elementals powered forges.

Demons maintained the roads that kept the Empire together. They were our means of communication. They chilled our drinks, built and protected our cities. And when the wizards killed the last demonologist, when they shattered my heart, they shattered my empire.

Though I still had no memory of that moment when they broke me, I remembered so much more.

Beneath the palace lay the catacombs, basements beneath basements. Some were libraries, some were prisons. Every empire, no matter how grand, has its malcontents. In most civilizations, such people were a burden. They fought to overthrow governments, they interrupted communications, practised foul acts of terrorism, all with only the vaguest idea what they'd replace the current regime with. Such people fed my empire. The dispossessed were the souls we used to strike bargains with demons. The enemies of empire kept it running.

And we never ran short on souls.

In the very deepest basement sat my personal sacrificial chambers. There were rare times when it was necessary to harvest a great many souls to bind a single, powerful demon.

I remembered the room.

Shallow trenches, blood runnels, lined the floor in twisted mind-shattering symbols, directing the spilled life into a single great bowl set deep in the stone. To look at them, to truly comprehend their meaning, was to crack one's sanity. There were no shackles here. By the time the would-be sacrifices made it this deep, they were broken souls, long past struggling. My demonologists made sure of it.

On this day, thousands of men and women knelt on the floor, leaning forward, necks held waiting over the runnels. No one stirred. No one shifted or coughed. Silence reigned like a terrible god.

I stood, demon-bound knife in hand, surveying the room. This particular chamber was for the summoning of gods and Lords of hells.

Today I planned the latter. With the help of my god I would bind this Lord to my service. Forever.

There, in the centre of ancient runes carved in stone, lay the sword. The ore it was made from had been mined by demons, transported be demons, forged by the greatest demon smith the world had ever known. No mortal hand had ever touched any part of the weapon. Even the leather wrapped around the hilt came from an animal no man had ever seen. It was slain and harvested by demons, cured by demons.

This would be a sword to kill gods, to end worlds.

Even without a Lord of Hell bound to it, the blade was already a work of art, already the greatest sword ever forged in a thousand realities.

The will of my god filled me. I did her work. I was her intent given flesh. She defined me. What I would do here, was right. It was necessary. She made it so. Unknown forces plotted against me. Hidden armies gathered. War would soon come to my empire. A war to end all.

I would wage that war with a god's weapon. I would smite mountains, sunder the earth, split the sky.

Drawing breath, I let it out in a slow sigh. I would not sleep for days. The blended narcotics pulsing through my veins ensured my alertness. Killing this many—for I had to bleed each one myself—was a near impossible task. If I faltered, if I missed a syllable, stumbled a moment of the sacrifice, or wavered during the summoning and binding spells to follow, I would fall prey to this Lord of Hell. He would devour my soul. My god might back me here, but this, I had to do myself. She could not protect me.

For three days I slashed throats, my demon-bound dagger never losing its edge. For three days I chanted impossible words seared into my brain through decades of repetition. When my throat grew dry and raw, I drank the blood of those I killed. With no pause for water, no chance at rest, I had no other choice.

BLACK STONE HEART

By the end of the third day, I was soaked with blood, much of it already dry and brown, turning my red robes into gore-encrusted armour. I stank like an abattoir, staggered with exhaustion. With the last throat cut, I paused for a moment to gather my strength. Chest heaving, I stared at my reflection in the black-veined red granite of the polished floor. An ebony-skinned nightmare looked back at me. Blood caked my hair, dripped from my chin. My eyes were gone, replaced by two gemstones of different sizes. The larger one looked to have cracked the orbital bone when driven into place, leaving my skull slightly misshapen.

I had no memory of that incident, no idea what the stones were, or when it happened. They appeared to be fused to my skull, the flesh around the sockets melted and ridged with ancient scars.

So much remained lost to me.

I remembered the huge bowl in the floor, brimming with blood. Demons, set in the stone, warmed the blood, kept it from clotting. I remembered the bodies, lying where they fell. By the third day, those I killed first were already beginning to stink. Though the labyrinthine basements were cooler than above ground, here, in the tropics, they were still stifling hot.

Arms numb and shaking, I lifted the fist-sized diamond I'd carried with me for the last three days. Cut by a demonic jeweller, it bore thousands of perfect facets. Part of my incantation had been aimed at capturing the fleeing souls of those I killed. The Soul Stone was full, loaded with the souls I would feed to this Lord of Hell.

I summoned him. I named him.

The End of Sorrow.

It was a joke born in the horror of my actions. Killing so many left me teetering at the brink of madness. Calling upon a Lord of Hell, and forever binding him to a sword, shoved me screaming over that edge. Alone, surrounded by the thousands I sundered, I laughed, cackling insanity. This sword would end everything. There would be no more war. No more pain. If I couldn't have the world, no one could.

I understood the joke. The Lord of Hell's name: Kantlament.

But what went wrong? I'd bound the Lord. I remembered the finished sword. Yet here I was, thousands of years later, in a world ruled by wizards.

What stayed my hand?

CHAPTER THIRTY

I woke in the dark, the stars above bright sparks torn in the curtain of night. No clouds. No moon. That diamond in the wizard's tower Shalayn and I broke into, was that the one from my memories? Did it, even now, bear thousands of souls?

I wanted it.

I wanted to destroy it, to free any souls within so I wouldn't be tempted to spend them.

I could return to the wizards tower. Should I go get it?

What if only one soul remained in my stone, and the other turned out to be empty or something completely different? Dare I chance it?

I don't want it, I told myself, knowing I lied.

Henka sat beside me. Porcelain skin glowing pale in the starlight, round face framed in black hair, she was ghostly beautiful.

"What do you remember?" she asked.

She wasn't upset that I'd hunted and killed a man who looked just like me. Seeing me cut his heart out hadn't bothered her. That obsidian shard sinking into my flesh, and my resulting screams and loss of consciousness, left no trace of concern on that perfect brow.

Parts of my heart might be missing, but she completed my soul.

I sat up, glancing around. Two dozen paces away, Chalaam stood alone, still as only a corpse can be. He stared off into the dark, lips moving in silent argument with some imagined opponent. Or perhaps he talked with himself, battling loneliness the only way he could.

"I had him drag the body away," said Henka. "So we wouldn't be bothered by scavengers." She put a hand on mine, her skin warm, alive. "Chalaam," she called to the dead man, "go for a walk. Be back in two hours."

Chalaam wandered away without a word.

Blood.

"You used necromancy to make yourself warm?" I asked.

She nodded, eyes locked on mine. "Waste not want not." She squeezed my hand. "And I have wants."

She crawled on top of me, robes falling open to expose perfect breasts and the terrible steel-stapled scar running between them. She pulled my hand close, placing it on a breast. Flesh warm, the nipple hardened under my fingers. She ground against me, throat loosing a low, animal growl.

"What do you remember?" she whispered in my ear.

No matter the confusion in my thoughts, my body reacted to her proximity, to her heat and her need. I grew hard against her and she shed her robes, dropping them from her shoulders to puddle about her slim waist.

"What do you remember?" she asked again, voice husky.

I pulled her close, kissed her neck. "I remember how to collect souls. I can store them in Soul Stones."

"That's good." She gasped as she writhed against me.

"I remember a sword."

"Where is it?" She fumbled with the drawstring of my pants.

I shrugged, helpless. "No idea."

Henka pushed me flat, dragged my pants open, and I was inside her. She groaned as I gripped the cheeks of her ass.

She leaned forward, nipples brushing my chest. "What else?"

"Killing. Thousands."

She moved, rhythmic, hot and wet, above me. "What else?"

I searched my memories. "I remember the basements in PalTaq."

"What else?"

What did she want from me? What was she hoping to hear?

"Do you remember women?" she asked.

"What?"

"Other women?"

"No." That wasn't quite true. Even in the beginning there'd been some deep memory of a pale woman with black hair and dark eyes. But acquiring this shard changed nothing. I knew no more of her now than I had before. Whoever she was, the memory of her lay ahead of me, in some other shard. And it didn't matter. Like the sword, she was thousands of years gone, long dead.

"There's only me," Henka whispered, licking my ear. "Forever. Only me."

"There's only you," I agreed.

And Shalayn. Had the wizards tortured her? Had she spoken of me, broken by agony? Had she died cursing the day she gave me her shirt?

I was going to bring the Guild down. The only wizards left would be the dead ones enslaved to me through Henka.

I woke the second time to the smell of meat cooking on open flame. Chalaam bent over a small fire, turning two spitted birds above it.

"Breakfast," he said.

"Thank you."

"She told me to," he said, gesturing at Henka with a thumb. She sat on the far side of the fire, once again dressed. "I had no choice."

"He's quite good with a bow," she said, flashing a shy smile at odds with her behaviour of the previous evening.

I remembered the heat of her. Her orgasm locking her body rigid, mine whiting out all thought.

'What else do you remember?' over and over. And she asked of other women. Was she jealous that I might remember some woman from three millennia ago? Who could know the hearts of women?

The scar. She had no heart.

"Henka."

"Yes?"

"Come sit with me." I patted the ground at my side.

She rose, circled the fire, and sat beside me, leaning her head on my shoulder. The heat of her had faded, though she wasn't yet cold.

I shifted, uncomfortable with her presence, uncomfortable with what I had to say. "I have to go to PalTaq."

"I know."

"I mean…" I hesitated. "I made you a promise."

She stared up at me, eyes huge.

"I promised we'd find your heart."

"Later," she said. "PalTaq first. The gods know I trust you."

"I'm sorry."

She smiled, and my heart broke. I hated myself a little more.

Why? Why should my desire to find myself come before fulfilling my promise to her? Why should she be all right with this? What or who did she think I was that she would trust me so completely?

"Maybe—"

She silenced me with a cool finger on my lips. "PalTaq first. My heart can wait."

"Gods," I said, remembering Shalayn's claim there were no gods, that they were inventions of the demonologists, tools for compelling the populace.

I knew now she was wrong. Though I remembered little of my god, I knew she was real. Or should I say she *was* real? What happened to gods when their worshippers ceased to believe or were killed off? Had my god died, faded to nothing?

Or was she still here, even now waiting for me to once again feed her souls?

Henka waited, eyes wide and trusting.

"You said gods," I said.

She nodded.

"I was told there weren't any."

"Who told you that?"

Shalayn. Another woman. Remembering Henka's questions, I said, "It doesn't matter."

"They were wrong. There are gods. There are demons. There are heavens and hells." She squeezed my hand. "I know, because I was in hell for a long time. And then you found me. You saved me."

I wanted to deny her words. I'd done no such thing. In not ending her existence on the night we first met, had I done a terrible evil? Where I fed souls to demons, she called them back from wherever they went and forced them to inhabit their rotting corpses. She enslaved them. It took a conscious effort not to look to Chalaam.

"We'll go to PalTaq," she said. "We'll get every shard of heart along the way. We'll make you whole. We'll find your sword."

"Kantlament."

"The End of Sorrow," she agreed. "You're important. I'm nothing, a corpse."

"You're not nothing. I need you." I wanted to tell her I loved her, but Shalayn's death was too recent, too raw.

"I know you do," said Henka. "Your need keeps me… alive." Again, she lay her head on my shoulder. "Your need gives me purpose. Without you, I would revert to the animal I was already well on my way to becoming when we met. Eventually I'd lie down in the dirt. Let the earth bury me. I'd be so close to nothing."

Her voice broke and I realized she was crying, though no tears fell. I pulled her close, an arm around her slim frame.

"Nothing," she said. "That's what scares me. Nothing is more terrifying than nothing." She shuddered against me. "Sometimes I want it, I crave it. An end. But I can't. I'm too scared. How long would I lie there, bones in the earth, helpless, alone, waiting? What if it never happened? What if I never became nothing?" Words spilled out of her, a torrent of emotion. "What if I was stuck there forever, slowly sinking deeper, further from the light and life of the world, unable to return?" Squeezing my hand hard she said, "I can't chance it. I need purpose."

"I'll never leave you," I swore.

Henka said nothing, her silence damning me with her doubt.

"The man I was," I said, "he was immortal. I won't die."

"Together? Forever?"

"Forever."

The nineteen-year-old in me meant every word. The ancient man, the Emperor of the World, mocked my naivety. The man I killed yesterday knew how to sacrifice people, how to store their souls. Yet he made no use of his knowledge. He said he was happy. He said that by continuing on my path, I would bring misery to the world.

He was right. I would make use of that knowledge. I would hurt people. I would harvest them for their souls.

Shalayn used to worry I'd become someone she didn't like, someone who didn't like her. Henka had none of that fear. If anything, she seemed excited by the prospect, like there was no way I could not love her.

Maybe we were perfect together.

"The difference between me and him" I said, "is that I remember more of Khraen. He knew more demonology, but I know more of the man." Was this all an excuse, a pitiful justification for my actions? "He was only happy because…" I saw it, I understood. "…because he wasn't me."

"Happiness is fleeting," said Henka. She seemed to have relaxed, loosening her grip on my hand. "The longer you go on—the older you are—the more fleeting it becomes."

How old was she? I didn't know, had never asked. When I met her, I'd assumed she'd only recently been turned into a necromancer. I decided that if I could have my secrets, she could have hers. She'd tell me when she was ready.

"Can we build a lasting happiness?" I asked. "Together?"

"We can build something lasting," she said, not quite answering my question.

CHAPTER THIRTY-ONE

Chalaam returned from hunting rabbits, hobbling on a crude crutch he cut from a branch. Shattered at the knee, his right leg dragged behind him. A single rabbit hung limp over his shoulder, a breeze ruffling the powdery grey of its fur.

"Vicious rabbit?" I joked.

He stared at me, unblinking.

"He's damaged," said Henka, leaning close to examine the knee.

"Look at him. He's miserable. Let him go."

"He's useful. Who will hunt for you? Who will light fires? Who will stand watch at night while we're…" She gave me a smouldering look which lit a fire of its own.

She was right. He was useful. "I can hunt for myself. I can light my own fires. I've done these things for myself for a long time." Years in the north.

"But you shouldn't have to." She straightened, tutting at the damaged joint. "We could, I suppose, replace him at the next town, find someone more useful."

While I agreed, and it had been nice having someone do all those menial tasks, I couldn't condone murder for the simple expedience of convenience.

Demons sweeping the streets, working the mines, slaving at every task imaginable. I pushed the thought aside.

"Please," I said. "Let him go."

"Please," echoed Chalaam.

"He was going to hurt you. He deserves this."

"He has suffered enough."

Chalaam looked awful. In some areas his skin had sloughed away, exposing grey muscle. Countless scratches laced his face and arms where he'd blundered, unheeding, through thorns in pursuit of my next meal. With a little work, he could still pass as a living man, though not in the best of health. Soon, that would no longer be true.

It hit me then. I'd been thinking of using Henka to create armies of enslaved necromancers who would, in turn, create armies of enslaved undead. Why was I concerned with this one man who'd tried to kill me, and rape Henka? If I couldn't stand to see him enslaved, how could I do it to thousands?

Would I be someone who didn't hesitate to spend souls, or cut the throats of thousands to make a sword? Would I be the ruler of a world-spanning empire? Would I be powerful? Strong?

I didn't want to be a victim ever again. What Tien did to me, using me and leaving me to die, that was that last time anyone would ever use or take advantage of me.

The wizards betrayed me, too. They would pay for that. I would topple their pathetic kingdom, bring down their towers. The empire of demons would return. I'd show the world sights unseen in millennia.

This time, it would be forever.

Shalayn was right. I would become someone unrecognisable to the man she knew.

"End him," I told Henka. "We'll find someone better in the next city."

"Thank you," he said, tossing the dead rabbit at my feet.

Nodding acceptance, Henka led Chalaam away.

Shalayn. I knew she wouldn't like this choice, wouldn't like this me. I made her a promise.

"She's dead," I told the rabbit's corpse. "What's a promise to a dead woman worth?"

What were any of my promises worth?

By the time Henka returned, I'd cleaned and gutted the rabbit and had it turning over a fire. I was getting tired of rabbit, but it was a damned sight better than bugs and roots. I turned the spit occasionally, not caring if I burned the meat a little.

Henka stepped across the fire and examined me. "Are we really going to replace him?"

"And then some," I said, hesitating to tell her of my plans.

"And then some," she repeated, grinning.

Maybe I didn't have to tell her. Maybe she already knew.

"South?" she asked. "To the coast and beyond?"

"South," I agreed. "Though we have to make another stop first. I sense another shard of my heart nearby."

"How close?"

I looked east. "Hard to tell. A couple of days."

She seemed to relax a little, nodding as if pleased with herself. Was she less excited about going to PalTaq than I thought?

"Is this one moving?" she asked.

"Not that I can tell." I hesitated. "Henka, you don't have to come to PalTaq with me." She froze. "Not if you don't want to."

"I'm coming," she said in a way that left no room for argument.

"You seemed happy that there was a diversion, something I had to do first."

Glancing east, she shrugged, wrinkling her nose. She was quiet for a while, unmoving and unblinking. You don't realize how accustomed you are to the regular movement of people drawing breath until they don't do it.

"Oceans scare me," she said, finally. "Sinking away from the light. Eaten by fish."

"I'll keep you safe," I promised, not at all sure I could.

She flashed a look of purest gratitude. "I thought you were going to leave me, were looking for a reason."

"Never."

She pulled me into a cool hug. The heat from the blood magic she'd worked the previous night had almost completely faded. She must have sensed my discomfort because she backed away, eyes downcast. I felt like an ass.

"I'll get more blood," she promised. "With Chalaam gone I won't have to use so much maintaining us both. It'll last longer." She met my eyes. "I'll be warm for you."

How much had she needed to maintain them both? I'd never thought to ask.

"I'd like that." I meant it.

Three hours east, Henka reined her dead horse to a stop. I pulled up alongside her.

"I have a confession," she said, looking back the way we came.

I couldn't imagine what she might have done.

"I left Chalaam. I didn't end him. I told him to lie down on the ground and never move. I wanted to punish him for trying to hurt you." She glanced at me, biting her lower lip. "I'm sorry."

I thought about Chalaam lying there, slowly going mad, someday to be buried in the earth or pulled apart by scavengers. I found no anger in me at Henka's choice.

"Perhaps," I said, "when we venture north, we can try and find him. End his misery." I took her hand. "If you want."

"Perhaps." She smiled, happiness lighting her face, making her beautiful beyond words.

We rode east, Henka chatting happily about everything and nothing, while I enjoyed the strange normalcy of the moment.

Those people back in Taramlae who flinched away from me, glared barbs of loathing at the colour of my skin, they showed me something. They showed me how much rejection hurt, how deep it sank into you, poisoning your perceptions. Somehow, I suspected, it was a lesson I hadn't learned in my previous life. I wouldn't do that to Henka. I wouldn't reject her because she was different. I would hold on to her for who she was, not because of the shell she wore. Henka was the woman inside the corpse, gorgeous as that corpse might be.

"Do you ever think about memories?" she suddenly asked.

I laughed. "All the time."

"When we're born, we follow a path, even if we don't see it. As adults, that path, each step a decision, shapes us. Our memories define who we are."

I wasn't sure I agreed, but kept silent. If my memories defined me, I had no choice but to once again become the man I had been. I didn't want that. I wanted his power. I wanted to protect myself from those who spat at me on the street, and from the wizards, but I didn't want to be the man who cut thousands of throats for a damned sword. Much as I now wanted that sword.

I didn't want the diamond in the wizard's tower, because spending those souls was evil.

I was excited that I now knew how to store souls in a stone.

I'd wanted Henka to free Chalaam, but wasn't bothered when she didn't, and was already planning on replacing him with a better undead slave.

I was appalled at the number of souls I'd fed Felkrish, and couldn't be bothered to keep track of them.

I loved Henka and wanted to be with her forever.

I wanted to enslave her so she could never betray me.

I didn't want to be the man I was, and yet I planned to rebuild his empire.

I was, I realized, at war with myself. Every time I did something righteous—like telling Henka to free Chalaam—some part of me sabotaged the act. I didn't even see it happening.

Conflicting desires tore me apart.

"What if those same memories—that same path, those steps, those choices—were walked in a different order?" asked Henka. "What if you only knew love *after* suffering pain and betrayal? What if you only knew victory *after* suffering defeat?" She darted a glance at me. "Would that change us? Would we end up different people?"

We rode on in silence, me lost in thought.

Was she on to something? Would the order I took on shards of my heart, and the memories they contained, define who I became? How could I do that? I had no idea what memories resided in each piece. Could I collect all the pieces together, without taking them into myself, and then make educated guesses as to what was in each? Or was there some branch of magic that could tell me? I had few memories on the topic, but knew powerful shamans were capable of reading souls. Those pieces of my heart found in other versions of me offered some hope, as that Khraen might be able to tell me what he knew. Of course, the fact I planned to cut their hearts out might sour the relationship.

It was hope. A sad, desperate hope, but better than nothing.

I clung to that pathetic hope like a drowning man.

"It's a good idea," I told Henka. "But we have no way of knowing what memories are in each shard." I felt oddly comfortable discussing this with her.

"But if we could," she said, "if we knew?"

"I think it might work."

"I think so too."

Two days later, it became clear we were riding toward the ruins of an ancient village. Not nearly as impressive as the demon-haunted city I saw earlier, it still was very different from the many wizard-ruled towns I'd seen. Every night, fire sparked to life within bulbs mounted on tall poles, lighting empty streets. The flames danced in a familiar pattern. Swirling mini-tornados, little taller than a dog, swept the streets free of dust and debris, dumping it in fields long gone wild. No one lived here. We hadn't seen another human in days. Though nothing looked wrong with the surrounding grounds, what wild plants there were grew tall and strong, yet no one was interested in farming them.

This village could have housed five thousand or more souls, but stood empty. The buildings weren't simply in good repair, they looked new. No blemish marred a single stone. Windows, unbroken after thousands of years, glinted bright and clean. It was beautiful, orderly.

We stopped beyond the town's limits. The sun would soon slip beneath the horizon and the town's elemental lights would spark to life.

"Is it really as dangerous as people say?" I asked Henka. "Or is that another lie told by the wizards, often repeated and never questioned?"

Henka examined the town. "A bit of both, I suspect."

We watched as, in a heartbeat, the streets were suddenly lit.

"Elementals," I said. "I bound all the branches of magic together in the greatest civilization the world has ever seen. Why do the wizards not make use of elementalists?"

"Fear. Paranoia. A need for dominance and power."

Henka dismounted. Her horse, hair fraying under the saddle where it chafed, stood motionless. It didn't look around, showed no interest in the rich grass between its hooves. It looked as sad and depressed as Chalaam had.

"Even horses don't like being dead," I said.

Henka frowned at the beast. Reaching out, she touched its nose, a soft caress. "Have you ever cared about the feelings of a horse before?"

I hadn't done much riding since my return to life, but suspected the old me wouldn't have concerned himself with the feelings of beasts of burden. Was this progress? Or had I not yet found enough of my heart to lose empathy for these noble creatures?

I examined the village. Who would I find in there?

"Do you feel strongly enough that I should send these horses back to the earth?" asked Henka. "We could walk."

Would I walk all the way to the coast just to prove I wasn't the old me? "No."

She gestured at the town. "Then shall we?"

I dismounted to stand at her side. "In the morning."

We lit no fire that night, not wanting to draw attention to ourselves. There was no knowing who, or what, might live out here.

After I finished my meal of cold rabbit, Henka shuffled closer. She leaned against me as she often did, cheek cold even through the cotton of my shirt.

Part of me stirred at the proximity of her shapely body. The rest of me twitched in revulsion at the thought of cuddling a corpse.

"I wish I could make myself warm for you," she said, dark eyes downcast.

CHAPTER THIRTY-TWO

I dreamed of dead lips and a gelid tongue, chill fingers fumbling at my pants and working me to hardness. I dreamed of a cold mouth and entering a corpse slick with rot. I woke, sweating, to find myself alone. The eastern sky showed the faintest flush0 of dawn. It was still an hour or more before sunrise.

I squinted into the dark. "Henka?"

Nothing.

Sitting, I looked toward the horses. Hers was missing. Where would she have gone? Was she out hunting for food, or had she left in search of blood? After that dream, I had mixed feelings. I wanted her, alive and warm, but wasn't sure I could forget the thought of her corpse flesh against me.

Henka returned as the sun crested the horizon.

"Everything alright?" I asked, as she dismounted.

"I wanted to make sure we weren't being followed."

Followed? By whom? We hadn't seen another living soul in days.

"And?"

She grinned, pale and beautiful in the dawn light. "I was being silly. There was nothing."

I remembered how sometimes, back in my mud shack, I got the feeling I was being watched. Those desperate starved and ragged animals would stumble from the forest to stare at me before once again disappearing. I understood her paranoia. Out here, far from everything, with a demon-infested town less than half an hour away, it was easy to think others must be here too. We had, however, seen no evidence of life.

"Let's leave the horses here," I suggested. "We'll go in on foot."

One of the many advantages of dead horses was knowing they wouldn't wander.

Henka agreed, and we set off together. She made no attempt to touch me.

We walked through fields ripe for harvest. A warm breeze, sweet with the raucous profusion of life, turned the landscape into a calmed ocean of gentle waves of soft clover. Butterflies, some ghostly white, others a mad riot of bright colour, danced in drunken pirouettes. They reminded me of Shalayn and I stumbling up the stairs to our room in the Dripping Bucket. Two lightning fast swallows darted about above us, chasing a huge hawk that was weaving in stately grace with wide-spread wings. Though they went for its eyes, it seemed somehow unworried.

A herd of wild goats, brown and black, long ears flopping as they cavorted, stopped to watch us, heads tilted, inquisitive. How many generations had they wandered free? They showed no fear of us. We continued past, and two broke from the group to follow. Now and then, they bleated something that might have been a warning or a question. Eventually they turned back, either having given up on us or grown bored.

The village began with a cobbled street, stones gleaming, polished clean.

"There are demons here," I said. "Many."

"Elementals too," Henka agreed. "The wizards tell everyone to fear demonology, that it's all evil, can only be used for evil. This town…"

I saw something in her I didn't understand, a longing. She saw this abandoned village as more than just a proof of the wizards' lies, more than just a reminder how far we'd fallen from our former glory.

"We should be safe enough," I said. "Most will have been bound in such a way they couldn't hurt the non-demonologist population."

"The Empire made use of necromancers too," she said. "Or so I read. Undead were used for unpleasant or repetitive menial tasks. Citizens were raised after death to serve in armies. One could sign contracts stipulating terms of service at the end of which they were released, their souls freed to go elsewhere."

Elsewhere. What differentiated heavens and hells? Was it simply a matter of perspective? Was one man's heaven another man's hell? What —or who—decided where souls went after they died?

We entered the village side by side, close, but not touching.

People could live here, I was sure they'd be safe. Why didn't they? Was it fear, or wizard propaganda?

"Folks used to buy themselves out of debt," continued Henka. "They'd sign contracts for decades, even centuries. Some did it to ensure comfortable lives for their children." She looked about the town. "What parent wouldn't sacrifice themselves to guarantee their child's future?"

Had I ever been a parent? Had the dark-eyed, pale-skinned woman I almost remembered been my wife? My lover? Ten thousand years I walked the earth. Surely, I must have fathered children in that time. How many of my descendants were out there, ignorant of their past? Did I owe them anything? How many generations had come and gone since my death? Sixty? One hundred?

"The Empire's armies were swollen with corpses," said Henka. "Millions and millions of dead, marching to the command of the necromancers. We conquered the world."

I examined a mill as we strolled past it. The huge millstone turned, a rumble more felt than heard, even though no water moved it, and no millwright required its use. More demons. Bound, they followed their last commands and would until the end of time. Or until the wizards worked up the nerve to come and destroy them. Truly, I had made an empire for the ages.

Yet, it fell.

"*They*, I mean," corrected Henka.

Lost in my own thoughts, I'd only been half listening. "They?"

"They conquered the world. For the Emperor."

They also turned against me, sided with the wizards. I'd given them too much power, too much freedom. A mistake I would not repeat.

Henka. Could I do that to her? Could I enslave her? I didn't want to. The thought twisted my gut with guilt. But I also had to protect myself from betrayal. Whatever happened last time, could never happen again.

"You know a lot about history," I said.

Focussed on a burnished bronze weathervane shaped like a strutting rooster, mounted atop a stone house, she didn't seem to have heard.

"The necromancers had their own libraries. They were the keepers of the past. It's all gone now, burned by the wizards. Every now and then a book turns up. I read everything I can find."

Keepers of the past. Did the necromancers remember me? It occurred to me it was entirely possible that some among their numbers might be old enough to have known me. The dead never die.

"Do you suppose there are any necromancers left from the old Empire?" I asked

"After the Great War, the wizards hunted them down. The mages turned on everyone, not just the necromancers. Elementalists, shamans, sorcerers. There must be some left, hiding far away, but not many. Anyway, it's too long." She flashed a quick smile at me, winking a dark eye. "That kind of time would drive anyone mad."

Would it? I was ten thousand years old when the wizards turned against me. I remembered my sacrificial chambers, the abattoir stench of thousands of dead, the copper reek of blood. I remembered the sword, Kantlament. An end to sorrow. A war to end all. Had I gone mad at the end? Was that why they rebelled?

No. They were power-hungry, hated not being at the top. And wizards could be immortal too. Surely, then, they'd have been just as mad.

"We have company," said Henka.

At first, I thought it was a huge man, half again my height and wrapped in thick ropes of muscle. Like mine, his skin was black. As he moved closer I saw my mistake. His knees bent the wrong way, giving him a chicken-like bobbing gait. A monstrous axe, steel stained crimson, haft of ebony, hung in one massive fist. His eyes were all black, lacking whites.

"We should run," I said, retreating.

"No," said Henka, eyes fierce. She made no move, stood her ground without flinching.

I couldn't leave her, couldn't abandon her to this demon. Drawing steel, the knives felt small in my hands.

The demon lumbered to a halt ten paces away, and I realized it was female. Or at least guessed it was by the curve of its hip and chest, though it wore a kilt of leather hiding any real proof.

It stood, examining me, slit nostrils flaring as it tested the air, milky membranes flicking across black eyes. The beast ignored Henka.

"You," it said.

"Me," I agreed.

Slinging the axe over its shoulder, it called out, "I can't kill him!"

Relief sighed through me. I was damned sure I couldn't kill it.

"Khraen," said the demon, again facing me, "I can't take sides in this. Though he bound me, you are shards of one soul."

Shards.

A young man dressed in black pants and a red shirt reminding me of the sails on the Habnikaav, the flagship in my dreams, strode from a nearby building. Black skinned and dark-eyed, he had a couple of years on me. He hadn't shaved his beard either, though it looked well maintained. I liked it that way. His hair, like mine, hung thick and black around his shoulders. Though we were the same man, he was bigger, better fed and more muscular.

A sword hung at his hip and my heart skipped a beat. But it was just a sword, not *my* sword.

"Khraen," he said, grinning bright teeth.

"Khraen," I answered.

"I've felt your approach for days."

"You didn't come out to meet us."

"Safer here," he said.

"And you didn't run."

"Why would I?"

Glancing back the way we'd come, I said, "The last one did."

He gave me a confused look. "I've been waiting. I want what you want."

I nodded at the demon. "Did you summon and bind that, or find it?"

"Summoned and bound, though I had to find a Soul Stone to do so. Harvesting souls is beyond me."

It was my turn to smile. "I know how to do that."

We stood for a moment, grinning at each other. This was not at all what I'd expected.

"What's its name?" I asked, nodding at the demon.

"You'll know soon enough."

"Its name," said the demon with a sigh of annoyance, "is Valcarb."

"She gets a little touchy," he explained. He drew his sword. "Shall we?"

A shock of fear ran through me. "I rather thought to take *your* heart."

"And trade this strong and healthy body for your scrawny malnourished one?"

He had a point.

"We could fight," I suggested.

"And risk injury? Why?"

Damn, he had another point. We did want the same thing, and he was me. What did it matter who took whose heart? And he was right, his body looked to have suffered fewer hardships and was in much better shape. While I'd filled out since leaving the north, he had eaten well and been strong his entire life. Not to mention the great beard.

Henka moved close, pulled me into a hug. "Kill him," she whispered into my ear.

"Who is that?" asked Khraen, as if finally noticing her. "She looks familiar." He examined her, dark brows furrowing as if trying to retrieve some deep buried memory.

"Kill him" she whispered again. "When he gets close, kill him."

"Why?" I asked. "We're the same man. Or parts of the same man."

"Why is she whispering?" called the other Khraen.

I knew that distrust. Had he, too, known betrayal? Or was it perhaps deeper, written into our very blood?

"Please," she begged, still whispering. "You have to kill *him*."

There it was. Who did I trust more, Henka, or myself? If I asked more questions, I might give something away, lose any chance of killing this other me. On the other hand, why was it so important I took his heart instead of the other way around? If we both wanted—

That was it. What if he had no intention of taking the stone from my heart and joining it with his own? What if he, like the last me I met, didn't want to change? But he'd spent souls to summon and bind a demon. And I saw the hunger in his eyes when I mentioned I knew how to harvest souls. He wanted that. He needed it. Soul Stones still carrying their burden of souls must be terribly rare. There hadn't been demonologists in thousands of years.

Henka released me, stepped away. Dark eyes watching, she left me to make the decision.

Who *did* I trust more, me or her?

But he wasn't me, not really. Not quite. His past, the years since waking, would have shaped him as mine shaped me. They'd have been different. How long had he hidden here, safe and comfortable in this demonic village? How different from mine were his early years? I murdered a trapper for his boots and clothes, scraped out a meagre existence in a hut of mud and sticks. I split my own head with an axe.

Shalayn.

Tien.

Henka.

Nhil.

When we took on shards, we learned of our ancient past, but nothing of the experiences gained since our rebirth. He wouldn't remember Shalayn. Tien would forever go unpunished. He wouldn't know about Nhil, or the floating castle.

Turning, I examined his clothes. They were spotless, new. Were they made here in this town, or did he travel to nearby villages to purchase them?

"You and I are the same," I said. "We want the same thing." I held my hands away from my weapons.

"Good." He raised his sword, moving closer.

"Do you know how to use that?" I asked.

"I woke knowing."

"Good. I learned these knives the hard way." I moved to meet him.

"Khraen," said Valcarb.

"Yes?" we both answered.

The demon's nostrils flared. "Someone is out there. Something," she corrected.

Henka cursed under her breath.

"Go find out what it is," commanded Khraen.

Valcarb set off, backwards knees propelling her from sight in an instant.

Closing the distance, I asked, "Should we wait until she's dealt with whatever is out there? We might need two of us, and the pain of taking on a shard incapacitates us."

"It does?"

Ah. He hadn't killed any of us yet. That other shard hadn't been far from here, days at most. And I'd sensed both. Even now I could already feel another shard calling me south. Why had he stayed here? Why hadn't he gone after the others? Had he not known they were there, or did he have reasons for not leaving?

Was he afraid?

I nodded. "Takes us out for two days."

"Valcarb can handle anything out there," he said with utter confidence. "And anything she can't kill would make short work of us."

Drawing my knives, I lunged. He spun away, slapping a knife from my hand.

"I know you at least *that* well."

Hadn't I said something similar to the other me before I killed him?

He advanced, sword ready, moving with relaxed confidence. With only a single knife, I retreated.

"Why?" he asked. "I thought we want the same thing."

"I think we do."

"Then why?"

I glanced at Henka. "Because I trust her more than I trust me."

"Your trust is going to get you killed."

CHAPTER THIRTY-THREE

I faced myself, wondering if, for reasons I couldn't comprehend, this was exactly what Henka wanted. It made no sense. If she wanted me dead, she could have stabbed me a thousand times as I lay sleeping. What could she possibly hope to gain?

Khraen lunged at me and I retreated. Between his greater skill and the reach advantage the sword gave him, my future looked grim. Except, of course, I was pretty damned sure he'd cut my heart out and join it to his. If we wanted the same thing, why were we fighting?

Henka.

I darted a look at her but she seemed more interested in where the demon had gone off to. Eyes narrowed, she watched the streets around us. She looked more annoyed than scared.

My distraction cost me. Not only was he stronger and more skilled, but he was faster, too. Steel tore a line of fire along my ribs. I tried to back away but found my legs unwilling to move. My knees buckled, dropping me to the cobbled street. I knelt, looking up at him. I'd dropped my knife when I fell.

Khraen stood over me. "Why?" he asked again. "It didn't have to be like this. I would have made it painless."

That would have been nice.

"I know," I said. I sat back, stanching hot blood with a hand.

"Then why? You can't possibly trust her more than you trust yourself. Look where it got you!" He shook his head in disgust. "How could we be so different? How could you be such a fool?"

"I don't—"

An arrow stood in his chest. Then two more.

He, too, crumpled to the road. We knelt there, looking at each other, seeing ourselves and seeing someone completely different.

He laughed, coughing blood. "See where trust gets you?"

And yet, I still trusted her.

"She betrayed us," he said, looking over my shoulder at the woman I loved. "I wish I could remember where—"

An arrow took him in the throat. He gurgled and fell dead.

I toppled to the side and lay groaning, pouring my blood out on the clean stone of the street. Shadow fell across me and I looked up to see Henka. Kneeling at my side, she fussed with the wound.

"You'll be fine," she said, pressing a handful of material against me to slow the bleeding. "You heal quickly."

"How do you know that?"

She blinked dark eyes at me. "My rotting mountain lion tore open your back. You should have died then, either of the wound or from infection. At the least it should have crippled you."

I'd forgotten about that.

Valcarb returned, blade sheathed, half a dozen arrows sticking from her. Too weak to do anything less embarrassing than crawl away, I lay watching. Henka, unworried, ignored the demon.

Valcarb stopped, stood over me with narrowed eyes of black. "There was a score of corpses running around with longbows," she said, glancing at the other me. "Where do you suppose they came from?" she asked, pointedly ignoring the necromancer as she pulled arrows free and tossed them aside.

A score? I looked to Henka.

"I worried," she admitted. "I've been gathering a small army of dead to keep you safe." She touched a cold hand to my cheek. "I'm sorry."

"A small army?"

"I had Chalaam wander at night, kill anyone he found and drag them back. I raised them while you slept. Sent them to get more. They hunted. Brought down wolves and rats and rabbits and I used those as spies."

She saw something in my face. "I was afraid you'd tell me to release them, but Chalaam and I weren't enough. I couldn't risk losing you."

Would I have done that? I wasn't sure. "You sent them ahead of us," I said.

"They reported the demon to me. I didn't know she wouldn't be able to hurt you. I had to be ready for anything."

"But he'd take my heart, or I'd take his. It didn't matter."

Anger flashed across pale features. "You know me, he does not. What am I to him?"

"He's me. He would have loved you just as I do."

"You don't know that." Cold fingers brushed hair from my face. "And it does matter. He isn't you, hasn't lived your life. This way," she nodded at his corpse, "when you take his heart, it is your life that will be the base, your memories that will continue on. He had it easy. He was cruel and self-centred. He never knew love, or the pain of betrayal."

While I could assume she meant my love for her, I'd never spoken of Shalayn, or of Tien's betrayal. Could she mean something else?

"The order matters," she said. "It has to be you taking the shards. Your experiences in this life will shape the man you will be."

The order matters?

"By deciding the path of one shard," she said, "we can exert some control over who you become."

Decide the path? Exert control? "Why?" I asked.

"Whoever you were, ended up like this." She waved a hand as if to encompass all the shards of me littered about the world. She looked miserable beyond words but no tears fell. The dead don't cry. "If I let you become that man again, the same fate awaits you."

"If you *let* me?"

If she heard the anger, she ignored it. "I love you too much to hurt you. You must know that by now. You know I would do anything for you. You trusted me, you killed him. I know you love me too."

I did. Blood loss left me weak and confused, my thoughts fraying apart with pain. Her plan seemed impossible, but ever was I the kind of man who wanted control. Even if it was somewhat illusory. Maybe I couldn't guarantee what kind of man I would be at the end, but I did prefer the idea of being the consciousness that survived. Of course, the others, assuming others lived, would likely feel the same. I realized, when I faced Khraen moments ago, that neither of us had truly been willing to sacrifice himself. And she was right: The old me died. The old me failed. I couldn't be that man.

I grimaced a fractured smile at Henka. "Thank you."

"You're not angry?"

"I am, but you're right. So, I'm mostly angry at myself." Mostly. "Every piece we meet would rather die than give himself to me."

I looked over her shoulder at Valcarb. The demon stood watching. "So?" I asked. "What now? Will you kill us to avenge your master's death?"

Valcarb snorted through the vertical slits of her nose. "You're still alive." She tilted her head, examining the corpse. "That's why I couldn't kill you when he wanted me to. You and he are the same. Were the same."

"You're bound to me now?" Having a demon in my service could prove handy.

"I am."

"Good." I crawled to Khraen's body. "I'm going to cut his heart out and take the shard in. I'll be unconscious for a day or two. Protect me. Do whatever Henka says."

"As you wish." The demon bowed low.

Finding the knife I dropped during our struggles, I eyed Khraen's corpse. I wasn't at all sure I was up to cracking his ribs open.

"Valcarb, can you open him for me?"

She did so with ease, sliding clawed fingers under the lower ribs and then snapping them apart in a single pull.

Setting aside my regret at the waste of such a good body—it would have been nice to wear that muscled form—I cut free his heart. The obsidian shard was the largest I'd yet seen. What had he been like? How had his life of ease and safety here shaped him?

I'd never know.

Henka, I decided, was a lot smarter than I gave her credit for. She clearly thought all this through long before I. She loved me, and yet she wanted me to be a certain kind of man, someone different than the man I'd been. That was fine. Someday I would once again be the emperor, but I would not make his mistakes.

Where Shalayn would have hated the man I was becoming, Henka loved him. Where Shalayn would have shattered his heart, broken him back to a simpler man, Henka wanted to make me whole. Which woman, then, truly loved me?

The answer was obvious.

With the beautiful necromancer at my side, nothing could stop me. She'd lead my undead armies and together we'd conquer the world, rebuild my empire.

I remembered her heart. I'd planned to find her master and destroy him. I'd planned to take her heart for myself. My intent had been to use it to command her and the necromancers she'd make for me. I was going to control her, enslave her so she couldn't betray me.

Shame ate me.

This other Khraen, he wouldn't have hesitated. I didn't want to be him.

Henka deserved better.

Taking the shard in my hand, I pressed it against my chest.

I screamed and screamed and—

The Emperor rode a mountain. The undead elementalist commanding the mountain, an ancient man who looked to be carved from grey stone, stood a single pace behind him. Before them a great host gathered, a world of monstrous demons bound to a single purpose: War.

A Lord of Hell commanded the army, awaiting the Emperor's orders. A minor godling, the Lord was ready to bring his demons into the Emperor's world. The wizards had rebelled, uniting the necromancers, elementalists, shamans, and sorcerers against the Emperor. They'd gathered their armies and declared war. The fools. They had no understanding of the power they faced. Hosts from five worlds stood ready to answer the Emperor's call. They would crush the rebellion.

With a flicker of will, the Emperor moved himself, his enslaved elementalist, and the mountain, to another world. The larger of the two stones driven into his eye sockets glowed hot, the scarred flesh surrounding it burning.

Another gathered host of demons, mind-twisting nightmares with faces of writhing squid-like tentacles, huge glistening bulbous skulls, and colossal wings of membranous leathery tissue, tattered and torn. A world of mad gods, all loyal to Khraen's god.

From world to world Khraen travelled, appraising the armies gathered, ready and waiting to invade his world at his command. With each new hell the stone in his eye grew hotter, charring the flesh around it.

Finally, abandoning the dead elementalist and his mountain in some distant hell, Khraen returned home to PalTaq. The island was besieged, surrounded by the fleets of the wizards. He laughed, striding the long halls of the palace. They thought they'd won. They had no idea.

Their fleets were doomed.

Their armies were doomed.

Their rebellion was doomed.

One word—one command—would bring through the hosts of demons.

Yet, he hesitated.

He could end this struggle, bring peace once again to the world. He could rebuild his great civilization from the ashes left by the wizard's betrayal.

Or he could go out, face them in person.

Bring an end to sorrow.

Bring an end to everything.

Forever.

Khraen touched the hilt of his sword, Kantlament.

A soft hand on his shoulder.

"My love," she said.

He turned—

Waking, I found Valcarb standing over me. Henka sat nearby. The necromancer shot me a look of nervous expectation. I flashed her a smile to let her know I was fine.

"What do you remember?" she asked, brushing long strands of sable hair from her eyes.

She was so beautiful, heartbreakingly fragile. I felt like she'd always been a part of me.

My chest ached where the two shards had come together. The arrow-riddled corpse of the other Khraen was gone.

Had she bled him first? The thought of her, warm with life, stirred lust in me.

It was us against the world.

Henka stood, unfolding in one smooth, graceful motion, and crossed to me. Offering a hand, she pulled me to my feet.

"You're stronger than you look."

She shrugged. "There is strength in death. You can push muscles to tearing."

Valcarb stood silent sentry, head in constant motion as she scanned for enemies.

"How long was the other me here?" I asked the demon.

"I was with him for seven years. Before that, I cannot say."

"His clothes and sword were all made here?"

"The demons here remain bound. He spoke the languages necessary to communicate his needs."

BLACK STONE HEART

It was true. I realized I now spoke a dozen demonic languages. Not having known that demons might speak different tongues, I laughed. "This is why the wizards stay away. They can't command the demons."

Valcarb, once again scanning the horizon, ignored me, as I hadn't asked a direct question.

A tornado of memory pulsed through me with each beat of my heart. There were two basic types of demons. Spirit demons could be bound to objects like swords and armour and, as in the case of this village, walls and buildings. The other type, manifestation demons, came from their home realities wearing their own flesh. Valcarb was a minor manifestation demon from a reality alien to our own. She'd been bound, permanently, to Khraen's service. Anything I commanded, she would do. If I told her to fall on her axe, she would do so without hesitation.

She was a slave, the cruellest kind. A slave who had once been free. She knew what freedom was. She remembered her previous life, and had no means of escape, no choice but utter loyalty.

I'd set her free, but I needed her.

Eventually, I promised. Eventually I would free her and return her to her own world. It occurred to me then that I didn't actually know how to do that. I would learn.

Had the Emperor ever done that? Had he freed demonic servants who performed well? The thought reminded me of Nhil, the old man in the floating mountain. He claimed we were friends, that I freed him.

He was still there, and now I could return. I had a Soul Stone, and I knew how to harvest souls and store them within.

Soon, I would return. Nhil, I felt sure, still knew more about me than I did. Searching my memories, I found I still knew nothing of him. Had he lied?

How had the wizards broken my heart apart? Why had they scattered the pieces, and what had they hoped to achieve? Too many mysteries remained. I was impatient to be about solving them. However, something was missing, something critical. Had I made a wrong assumption somewhere?

"Henka, why would the wizards scatter bits of my heart?" The more I thought about it, the less that idea made sense. The piece I retrieved from the wizard's tower hadn't grown into a man. Shouldn't all the pieces be locked in towers?

She raised an eyebrow, shrugging. "Maybe they thought it would destroy you, like scattering a victim's ashes in the wind."

Ashes in the wind? I'd never heard of that, had no memory of such a practice. Now that she mentioned it, it did seem a good way of disposing of necromancers. I kept that thought to myself. Did her suggestion make sense? Did they know so little of their enemy they all but guaranteed my return?

I laughed. "Fools."

Henka grinned and pulled me into a hot kiss. She was warm with false life. Lips met. Wet tongues. Her body melted against mine. I knew where the blood came from, and tried not to think about it. He was dead anyway, why not make some use of the corpse?

"Come," she said, voice husky, as she dragged me into a nearby building. It looked to have been a shop of some kind. The shelves were empty, clean of dust. It looked ready for a business to move in.

We made love on the floor while Valcarb stood guard in the street beyond. Henka took every thought from me, left me emptied of worry.

Once we were dressed, we made our way back to the street, hand in hand. Henka leaned against me and I drew strength from her.

"Valcarb, show me where the clothes are made."

The demon nodded and held out Khraen's scabbard and sword. "Please wear this from now on. Clearly I cannot protect you from everything."

As I took the sword, felt its familiar weight in my hand, I realized I knew how to use it. Trained by the best, the Emperor had thousands of years of practice, taken thousands of lives in battle. Unfortunately, the other Khraen remembered only the tiniest sliver of that. It was still more than I'd known. I was now a reasonably skilled swordsman.

Examining the weapon, I found it the crude work of a rank amateur. The blade was pitted, the edge notched and imperfect. Judging from the colour of the steel, stained with swirls of brown and yellow, it was brittle and would likely shatter in a serious fight. He had been no master smith. But an inferior sword was better than no sword.

Though demons maintained much of the village, ready to do my bidding, they didn't do everything. The people who once lived here had worked the fields, harvesting grain and crops and cotton. Demons might power the mill to grind the grain, and fire elementals burned low, waiting to heat ovens and bake bread, but without someone to harvest the fields and make the dough, nothing happened. There were no free and effortless meals to be had.

Khraen, Valcarb told me, learned how to work the fields and figured out enough of the demons in the town to produce passable clothes and a bread that tasted like sawdust. That knowledge, unfortunately, was lost when he died. Were I willing to stay long enough, I could do the same. But I was not that man. I would not cower safe in the town. Far to the south, another shard of my heart called for me.

Valcarb showed me the house Khraen claimed as his own. It was small and simple, lacking anything that might give it character. She also brought out his longbow and quiver of viciously barbed arrows, designed more for punching through plate armour than bringing down rabbits.

She informed me that she did most of the hunting and gathering of crops and wild vegetables. When first summoned, she found him rail-thin and on the edge of starvation. He filled out in the following years, after his diet improved.

"How did he summon you?" I asked. To complete a summoning one required blood and souls, runes and symbols, to call and then trap a demon.

"He found a Soul Stone," she said. "Stealing a child from a nearby town, he brought the boy here to be the blood sacrifice."

He killed an innocent child? I was suddenly glad I didn't have his memories. I could never do that. *Would* never do that. Once again, I saw the wisdom in Henka's plan. It had to be this me who lived through to the end. I had to be the consciousness that rose to become the new Khraen. The man who died here, shot through with arrows, was a monster. He would have either risen to become much like the old me, or hidden here in this safe haven until old-age claimed him.

Leaving Khraen's home, I turned in a complete circle, examining the town. "Where did he do the summoning?"

"At the church in the centre of town." Valcarb gestured toward what was easily the tallest building in the village.

Spires stood at each corner, turreted openings at the top that would serve for lookouts, and for raining arrows on those below. I'd assumed it was the centre of government or a defensible position for the town to retreat to. Maybe it was both.

The meaning of the word *church* sank in, an ancient word. A place of worship. A place where people went to pray to gods and show their devotions. It occurred to me that in all the small towns and communities I walked through, I had not seen a single church.

"What gods did they worship here?" I asked.

"This particular church was dedicated to Yahaarn, a demon lord."

"And he was real?"

"She would manifest at certain times each year, bless the town's folk, and devour a few souls offered in tribute."

I knew nothing of these gods. *Pantheon*, another ancient word. How many gods were there? Were they all real? Where were they now?

My questions would wait. I wanted to see the inside of this church.

We approached along the main street, and I realized I'd misjudged both the size of the town and the church. The four spires towered at least sixty feet over us. Huge oak doors stood twice the height of a man and swung silently open as we approached. They moved with effortless ease, as if weightless.

"Demons?" I asked.

Valcarb nodded.

"Someone bound demons to doors just so people wouldn't have to push them open?" The cost in souls represented by this town both staggered and appalled me.

"And for security. Those doors are warded, likely impervious to fire and axes."

Inside was a cathedral with forty-foot ceilings. Tall as it was, this was actually a single-story structure. From inside I saw that the spires were purely decorative, hollowed, with no means of access. The ceiling *was* the roof, massive panels of some translucent material letting the sun fill the church with golden light. From outside, the roof looked like shingled clay.

Torches lined the wall and they all sparked to life as we entered, leaping into that now familiar synchronized dance. The floor looked to be a single piece of red granite polished to a mirror-like sheen. I saw no seams. At the front of the room was an ornate pulpit carved from a single block of marble. It looked something like a swarm of snakes mobbing an octopus, and it glistened, black and crimson. Behind the pulpit stood a twenty-foot-tall statue carved in the same stone. It depicted a woman, buxom and round everywhere Henka was slim, caught in the middle of a sinuous and sensuous dance. Her ruby eyes, almond shaped and wicked, glowed red in the firelight. Jewels decorated her, drawing the eye to her curves. This goddess would bounce in so many interesting ways when she walked.

"I don't like her," said Henka, moving to stand at my side.

Not knowing how else to react, I shrugged non-committally.

Valcarb stood at my other shoulder. She ignored the statue, eyes always scanning for threats. "There are summoning supplies and everything you might need in the basement. Except blood and souls."

"She was really real?" I asked again, not sure what I believed.

"*Is* real," said Valcarb. "True gods don't die. She's probably off torturing the inhabitants of some other shitty reality with her demands for worship."

"Show me the basement."

The demon led us to a door in the far wall. Stairs, still that gleaming red granite, still showing no seams, spiralled down. We descended, and once again the torches lining the walls joined the dance as we approached. Air sighed past us, a cool breeze of lost souls, whispers teasing my ears.

"Is there another exit?" I asked, wondering at the moving air.

"Air elementals," said Valcarb. "Bound and commanded to keep the place clean and well-ventilated."

Elementals were as much a part of the old empire as demons. And yet I'd seen no sign of elementalists in the wizards' kingdom. Henka said there were still some out there, hiding. Perhaps, when I retook the world, they would welcome the chance to once again hold positions of power instead of lurking in the shadows. Though I wouldn't soon forget their betrayal.

Henka would give me the means of controlling the necromancers. I'd make her Queen of the Dead and their hearts would be hers. She would command them. She would own them. I had no memories of such an arrangement, and that suited me fine. I had to think differently than the old Emperor—act differently—if I was to survive and build something truly lasting.

Remembering the dead elementalist from my dream, I asked Henka, "Is an undead elementalist still an elementalist?"

"Yes."

"And a wizard?"

"Still a wizard."

"Interesting."

Valcarb led us to a set of rooms two floor below the church. The first basement level, chambers for the resident priest and a library I wanted to spend the rest of my life studying, once again reminded me of the floating mountains. The civilization I built had been one of wonder and wealth. Even the wizard's capital, Taramlae, had nothing like this one small farming town. I remembered dirty streets, rain pouring down the steps into a decrepit cafe, and the mouldering stench of rotting timbers. Though a few of the main streets were lit with crude oil lanterns, most of the city fell to the dark each night. The wizards' refusal to make use of the other branches of magic doomed their civilization to poverty and decay. In Taramlae, a city a fraction of the age of this village, buildings were already falling down, crumbling from age.

Thinking of the coffee shop reminded me of Shalayn and I pushed her from my thoughts.

I wanted to see more.

CHAPTER THIRTY-FOUR

The summoning chamber was a smaller version of the one I remembered from beneath the palace at PalTaq. Binding symbols, madness scarred deep in stone, troughs waiting to be filled with blood. A calligraphy of coercion. Everything a budding young demonologist could want lay here, perfectly maintained, ready for use.

Except blood and souls.

I realized, with a start, that might not quite be true.

Withdrawing the Soul Stone, I held it up to examine the diamond's facets in the dancing torchlight. How many souls remained trapped within? I wanted desperately to attempt a summoning—any summoning—just to prove I could.

No, I decided. Souls should not be spent so lightly.

In any case, what would I summon? I dug through my memories. I could summon a few minor manifestation-type demons like Valcarb, all of a similar strength. I also knew how to bind them. My hand fell to Khraen's sword, which I'd strapped to my hip. I also knew how to summon some spirit demons. I could bind a demon to this crude weapon making it virtually unbreakable. With some effort, and a few souls, I could make a weapon capable of cutting through plate armour, shearing off limbs with ease. Had I many souls at my disposal, I could make something truly terrifying. Then again, it might be smarter to make something more defensive in nature. I could bind demons to clothes or armour.

All these summonings, I realized, were of a similar nature, called creatures of a similar power.

That stopped me. Was this a coincidence, or could someone have broken my heart with foreknowledge of what memories would be in each shard? Was it simply that I learned all these summonings at the same point in my old life? Why could I remember making Kantlament, but not where it was? Why could I remember a few minor summonings, but not my god? Why couldn't I remember the castle in the floating mountains, or Nhil? Who was this dark-eyed, pale-skinned woman who seemed to haunt every shard of me?

Questions without answers.

Maybe I worried about nothing. Maybe there was no invisible hand guiding me along this obsidian path.

I set aside my questions. Either way, I needed demonic weapons and armour. I needed souls. I felt exposed, weak and vulnerable.

After exploring the basement and discovering it large enough for several families to live in comfort, with many of the same amenities I found in the floating mountain, we retreated to the surface.

Henka watched, expectant and waiting, as I paced the cathedral. Valcarb, unhappy with not being able to see any approaching enemies, left to patrol the perimeter outside.

"Why did he stay here?" I asked as I stalked past Henka. "He knew summonings that I didn't, and yet the only demon he called was Valcarb. She hadn't even really had to protect him until we showed up."

"And then she failed," said Henka.

"True." But that wasn't what bothered me. "He had a demon to protect him, and yet he hid here."

"If he set out, and the wizards found him, a single demon wouldn't save him."

"I left the north with much less. Was he so afraid? He wasn't startled when I arrived; he knew there were other pieces of me out there. Yet, he stayed. He could have hunted through abandoned cities until he found another Soul Stone and made demonic weapons and armour for himself." I stopped in front of her and she looked up into my eyes. Words poured out of me with mounting frustration. "He should have been hunting other fragments. Hell, the last one I killed was only a few days from here. They must have known about each other. Certainly, I felt their presence. The fragment who knew how to make Soul Stones was within reach."

"He spent a soul to summon Valcarb," Henka pointed out.

"But he made no effort to get more souls."

Had he wanted to?

I remembered being appalled at the idea of spending souls. Now, however, I wanted a demonic sword. I wanted demonic armour. I was at war with the wizards.

Henka stepped closer, touched me with warm fingers. "It doesn't matter. He isn't you. You killed him. You took *his* heart. You are the path."

I breathed deep, calming. "I am the path." Hadn't I just been thinking something similar? Either way, it sounded right. *I* would decide who the new Khraen was.

"Stop worrying about why others made different choices," she said. "They aren't you."

She was right, of course. The other Khraen hadn't possessed the knowledge to harvest souls. Maybe he hadn't even known it existed. I was continually learning things I'd never previously thought to question.

Leaning close, standing on her tiptoes, Henka kissed, me, her tongue hot and wet. "What's your plan?"

"If I run into a wizard now, I'm a dead man."

"You need weapons and armour."

"I need weapons and armour," I agreed. "I'm tired of being helpless."

"We'll go to the nearest town and take a few souls?"

There was a town not more than two days distant.

"We'll bring them back here. It's a rather elaborate ceremony, not something I can do in a filthy back alley." Though that wasn't quite true. I had ancient memories of working dangerous magics in less than optimum circumstances.

Unlike the other Khraen, I wouldn't take children. I'd find criminals if I could, murderers and rapists. Failing that, at the least I'd take the elderly, those who'd already lived full lives.

"Khraen, my love?"

"Yes?"

She hesitated. "These people… The ones you take… Can I…" She looked away, eyes downcast.

I saw it. She wanted their blood to maintain herself, but was too ashamed to ask. She worried I'd turn on her, judge her evil, and reject her. If I was going to take their souls, why could she not have their blood? They were going to die anyway, I told myself.

"I need some of the blood for the summoning," I said, turning her so she faced me. "The rest is yours."

She grinned thanks and gave me a quick kiss. Already she was cooling.

A thought occurred to me. "These corpses, after I've harvested the souls, can you raise them?"

She shook her head, dark hair sliding across slim shoulders like a silken waterfall. "No. Raising the dead means recalling their souls to inhabit the corpse."

"Too bad."

She touched my chest, drew a line over my heart with a fingernail. "I can be warm again for you."

I grinned. "Not a total waste then."

My words hit me like a slap. Harvest. Blood. Not a total waste. I was going to this sleepy farm town to commit murder, to harvest people for blood and souls.

"It's alright," said Henka, moulding herself against me. "You have to. You *need* to. Someday, the wizards will find us. They'll break you apart again."

"Never again," I swore.

"Never again."

I called Valcarb inside and explained the plan. We'd take our two undead horses—the demon could easily match their pace—to the nearest town. If we were extremely lucky and stumbled across some criminals or otherwise disreputable folks, we'd take them. Failing that, we'd find a homestead on the outskirts with an elderly couple living alone. Depending on how things went, we might stop by two or three homes. A half dozen souls, I decided, should give me enough to summon the demons I wanted and leave me a couple to spare in the Soul Stone.

I swallowed my doubts. This wasn't what I wanted, but the wizards left me little choice.

"I need these people alive," I told the demon.

Valcarb bowed acceptance. "If there is trouble, something unexpected?"

"Keeping me and Henka safe is your priority."

It took a day and a half to reach the town. From the hill I selected as our vantage point, we looked down into a sleepy farm community of five hundred souls. I realized there was little chance of finding criminals of the type I sought here.

Plenty of farms lay beyond the town proper offering us many to choose from. We watched, keeping a tally of how many were in each house, looking for places where the elderly lived alone.

Valcarb, who saw better than Henka and I, spotted a family of seven at one house. When I realized one was a child of less than a year, and another not more than two, I discounted it. That was an evil I would not commit.

As the sun sank toward the horizon, I realized what I'd first taken to be a church at the centre of town was actually a small wizard's tower. Like the others, it had a single door and no windows.

As I watched, that door swung open and a woman, dressed in robes of pristine white, exited. She crossed the town's central square and entered a small inn.

"A wizard," said Henka.

Cold rage.

The fucking wizards ruined everything.

Reining in my frustration and anger, I thought it through. "This changes everything."

"Why?"

"If anyone notices people are missing before we've returned to our village, the wizard might come after us."

Getting caught by a wizard before I had a chance to summon and bind demons, would be the end of me.

"We can find another village," said Henka.

What were the odds the wizard just happened to be in that tower when I was here? Did things like this happen all the time? In Taramlae, the wizards lived in mansions and houses, not in the towers. Had she somehow followed me here? Had Tien sent her? Did the mages already know where I was?

I wanted to question the wizard, but that was insane, too dangerous.

I hated that the wizard was here, spoiling my plans. Rage boiled deep within me.

There was, I realized, a way I could safely question the mage.

"What if we surprise her?" I asked, thinking of how Shalayn stabbed that wizard in the throat when we were stuck in the tower. "If we kill the wizard, no one will dare follow us."

Henka, staring down into the village with narrowed eyes, said, "An arrow will kill a wizard, just like anyone else."

"We get close. Wait for her to come out of the inn."

Henka nodded, licking her lips. Perhaps she shared some of my hatred for wizards. No doubt the millennia of wizardly rule hadn't been easy on the necromancers. Had the wizards lied to them all those thousands of years ago? Was that why the necromancers turned against me?

"This is a bad idea," said Valcarb. "Even a lone wizard is not to be trifled with. This will draw unwanted attention to this town, to us."

Valcarb was right, but I didn't care. I was tired of running. I wanted a taste of revenge. They broke me, it was long past time they paid for that. Even if just a little.

"Henka, if I kill the wizard, can you raise her?"

Henka nodded, eyes bright.

"And she'll still be a wizard, but under your control?" I'd asked earlier, but wanted to be sure.

Again she nodded.

A pet wizard. She could get me into the towers. I could plunder their secrets. Were there other museum towers, like the one Shalayn and I had been trapped in back in Taramlae? I thought of that fist-sized diamond I suspected was a massive Soul Stone. Should I return there with my enslaved wizard and see what other demonic artefacts lay waiting for someone who knew what to do with them?

My mind whirled with possibilities. Why stop with one wizard? Why not have an army of enslaved wizards? Much as I loathed their filthy chaos magic, they were powerful. They were useful. I knew better than to trust them ever again. When I once again rose to power, what reason had I to leave a single wizard free? They would *all* be mine.

One thing at a time. First, I had to kill this wizard.

"Let's go," I said. "Stay close. Not you," I told Valcarb when she moved to follow. "You stay with the horses."

"I cannot protect you from here."

"The wizard will be dead before she knows I'm there. I'm going to have to be right in town to get close enough for a decent shot. Henka will watch my back." I examined the demon. "You stand out too much."

The demon didn't argue, though I didn't know if that's because she agreed with my reasoning, or if it was because she was bound and had no choice but to obey.

"Did the other me talk to you much?" I asked Valcarb on impulse.

"Yes. Though, in truth, it was more like he talked *at* me."

What did that mean? I'd ask later. "We'll be back when she's dead."

"If things go wrong," said the demon, "should I come to your assistance?"

"Of course."

Henka and I strode through a field of soft, waist-deep clover. Bees, fat and slow, lumbered from flower to flower, ignoring us. A cool breeze rippled waves in the alsike and we floated in an ocean of green and lavender.

Alsike? I could differentiate between types of clover? It was, I remembered, poisonous to horses. Not that this mattered, with our undead mounts. What kind of man tore souls from people and knew about flowers?

Henka took my hand in hers. Cold, dead flesh.

"Do you mind?" she asked. "You're not disgusted by the feel of me?"

"Of course not." I lied to avoid hurting her.

She extricated her hand and walked in silence at my side.

She'd have blood again soon. Thoughts of her, hot and wet, stirred deep desires in me. My nineteen-year-old body was a constant distraction and I found myself missing the focus of a much older man, even though I remembered little of his life. That woman with the dark hair and eyes and pale skin who haunted my memories, had she moved him as Henka moved me? Picturing what I remembered, a man splashed in gore, his eyes torn from their sockets and replaced by strange stones, I couldn't imagine it. The older people I'd seen in my travels all seemed so lifeless, without passion.

We found a spot not far from the inn's entrance where we could wait within sight. Night fell fast. Candles and lanterns within various buildings lit the street with golden patches filtered through curtained windows. I worried for a moment that, in the gloom, I might mistake someone else for the wizard.

I grinned at the thought. Their love of white robes made them easy targets.

Keeping the bow in my left hand and the arrow ready in my right, I waited.

"I wonder if she's powerful." Henka sounded excited at the prospect of owning a wizard.

"I doubt it. She's out here, after all. Wizards like their comforts. She's probably a messenger or something."

The tavern door swung open and two drunks stumbled out, a man and a woman leaning heavily against each other like either would topple without the other's support. They paused in the street to grope each other. Henka and I watched them kiss and nibble and fumble at each other's clothes.

Shalayn and I used to do that at the Dripping Bucket, making out halfway up the stairs, annoyed patrons squeezing past. It was so different with Henka. There was a familiarity, a comfort between us. With Shalayn, everything was new and exciting. We shared meals and drinks. Now, when I ate, Henka often sat and watched.

I lost Shalayn to the wizards because of Tien's betrayal. Had she planned it from the beginning? I couldn't believe she duped me so easily.

Again, the tavern door swung open and this time the wizard strode out. Ignoring the two drunks, she went around them, no hint of intoxication to her movements.

Raising the bow, I sighted along the arrow. At this range, with these viciously barbed arrows, it was an easy kill. I loosed, the bowstring thrumming a deep bass note through my arm. The arrow cracked and splintered apart before reaching her, peppering the drunks with sharp slivers of wood. One screamed and the wizard lashed out in thoughtless reaction. The lovers came apart in a bloody explosion like someone shoved them at high speed through a fine mesh filter. A red mist hung in the air, blood falling around the mage in a pattering rain, staining her pristine white robes crimson.

Loosing another arrow, I again heard it shatter in the air. Bubbling fire raged toward me and Henka. Spinning me with surprising strength, she put herself between me and the mage. Flame ravaged her, turned her beautiful hair to ash and boiled the flesh from her back. Those dark eyes never left me, showed no hint of pain or fear.

Charred to the bone, Henka dropped as the wizard's fire abated. I caught her as she fell, dragging her ravaged body around the corner and out of sight. She weighed nothing. Flesh and muscle, cooked to white ash, fell away where I touched her. I saw the burnt ridges of her spine.

Something passed us in the night. Black, knees reversed, that odd bobbing chicken walk replaced by a deadly speed no horse could match. Valcarb passed the wizard, axe swinging in a decapitating arc. Light exploded with an air-shattering *crack* and the wizard was sent cartwheeling into the night. The force of the explosion buckled the nearest wall of the inn. With a long groan of tortured beams, the building crumpled. The wizard, clearly having survived being tossed like a doll, lashed out with twisting tongues of fire, stabbing blindly in the dark. The panicked screams of those trapped within the fallen inn rose in terror as her attacks lit the ruin ablaze.

Scooping up Henka, I threw her over my shoulder and sprinted back to where we left the horses. Swirling whips of flame lit the sky behind me and then another explosion flattened several houses.

We made it to our undead mounts, the sounds of battle echoing behind us. Her limbs a charred ruin, she couldn't possibly ride. I climbed awkwardly onto my horse, damaging Henka further in my clumsy efforts. She made no sound of complaint. Directing the beast back toward the demonic village, I kicked it into motion, urging it to ever greater speed. We left the other horse behind.

Riding hard in the dark is stupid. Riding hard in the dark on an undead horse who'd lost all sense of self-preservation, is suicidally stupid. When the beast found the inevitable gopher hole, there was a loud *snap* of breaking bone and we pitched forward, thrown from the saddle. I broke two ribs and one of Henka's ravaged arms snapped off at the elbow with a sickening crunch.

Wheezing, sobbing in pain, I staggered around in the dark looking for the missing limb.

"Leave it," she said, voice less than a whisper.

Lifting Henka, cradling the ruin of her against my chest, I carried her from there.

CHAPTER THIRTY-FIVE

I walked, stumbling and often falling. Every time I tripped on some unseen obstacle and crumpled to the ground, some part of Henka broke and I cried. Exhaustion emptied me, left me a husk of flesh driven by will alone. At first, she tried to talk, offering soft encouragement, but her lungs were damaged and soon she trailed off into silence. Only her face, porcelain perfect, remained untouched. I saw fear in those dark eyes, horror at her helpless condition.

"I'll never leave you," I told her.

Hadn't I said something similar to Shalayn? I pushed the thought away and staggered on.

Sometimes weakness or exhaustion stopped me and I'd collapse to the ground, lie there breathing until I felt ready to move again. I kept turning to look back the way we came, hoping to see Valcarb, expecting to see the wizard.

It took two days to carry Henka's burnt remains back to the demonic village. I brought her to the church, and then carried her into the cool of the basement. Already, my ribs were beginning to heal.

"Valcarb would have caught up with us by now," I told Henka, laying her down on a soft bed in one of the bedrooms.

She nodded.

"My hatred of wizards cost us everything. No souls for summoning. Valcarb is likely destroyed. You…" I looked down at her, failure twisting my gut.

She said something, lips clicking. I had to lean close, ear against her mouth, before I heard the words, "I'm still here."

Henka was right. I hadn't lost everything. Not yet.

"Can your necromancy repair this much damage?"

I hated asking, feared the answer.

She hesitated, examining me with her own desperate fear. Finally, closing her eyes, she nodded once.

Relief surged through me. "You'll need some blood?"

She nodded, a near imperceptible movement of her head. But her eyes remained closed. She wouldn't look at me.

"A lot?" I asked. "How much?"

She opened her eyes but turned her head, facing away. Her lips moved, dry clacking.

Again, I leaned close. "I couldn't hear."

"You'll hate me," she whispered, attention locked on the wall.

"I won't. I could never hate you."

"You will. I'll lose you."

"This is my fault," I said, desperate. "All my fault. You have to let me help you."

Meeting my eyes, she seemed to cave in on herself. "To repair. Not just blood." Voice barely a breath. This close, the stench of charred flesh, rotting meat, and burnt hair overwhelmed my sense of smell.

Not just blood? "What else do you need?"

She hesitated. Finally, "Parts."

That one word connected the last piece of the puzzle that was Henka. I remembered how she'd changed as we travelled south, the way her flesh became a patchwork of pink and white.

'Would you like me to have dark eyes again?' she asked at the Willow's Inn.

The man at the bar told her about someone's beautiful daughter. He hadn't just brought that up, she'd asked. The next morning, she had dark eyes.

Parts.

She harvested people to repair herself. No, more than that. She harvested people to remake herself for me.

Every time she changed, every time she became more beautiful, more flawless, more the woman I wanted her to be, someone died.

She'd taken some girl's beautiful eyes.

Parts.

She harvested flesh from gods knew who.

No, I knew who. That flesh had been smooth and perfect. She must have carved it from young women.

How many had she killed? How many flayed and dismembered corpses did we leave behind us?

Parts.

And now she lay here, utterly helpless, a charred ruin, because of my stupidity. The only way I could have her back was if I got her the parts she needed. I'd have to harvest them for her. It was that, or abandon her.

She stared up at me, watching, waiting, no doubt seeing my thoughts writ plain on my face. The horror. She knew me too well.

"I promised I would never abandon you," I said.

She didn't move, didn't blink.

I swallowed my revulsion. "Tell me what you need."

I went to that town to take people, to harvest them for their souls so I could summon demons. I was going to give their blood to Henka. How was this different? How was this any more evil than what I already planned?

"Tell me what you need," I repeated, voice steady this time. "I'll get you everything you want."

This was all my fault. She suffered this horrible damage protecting me. She saved me from the wizard's fire

Henka flashed a wan smile full of heart-breaking misery. "Full body," she whispered.

"What's better, alive or recently deceased?"

"Fresh dead. Fresher better."

"I'll find you a girl, a woman," I corrected, though I wasn't sure why. "I'll bring her back here for you."

"You'll have to kill her for me," she breathed into my ear.

"I will." My stomach churned.

"I need at least two," she whispered. Dark eyes bore into me. "Beautiful. Young. Perfect."

I swallowed. Kidnap two or three young women and bring them back here to be slaughtered. Why should it make any different that these would be pretty girls? Why was I hesitating?

I was a fool, letting my conscience get in the way of what I wanted. I wanted Henka, whole and unharmed. I wanted her beautiful and warm. I did this to her. She was damaged protecting me. I owed her this, and so much more.

Conscience. The Emperor of PalTaq would never hesitate, of that I was sure.

I needed Henka. My plan, vague as it was, depended entirely upon her necromantic skills.

If I wasn't quite lying to myself, I wasn't being entirely honest either. I needed her beyond my plans for an undead army. I needed *her*. Her strength. Her support. Without her, I was alone. Khraen, the Emperor, had been alone. And he fell alone.

Except that ghost of a memory, a face seen and forgotten. Pale skin. Dark eyes. Black hair. Perhaps he too had known love. I couldn't imagine it, this man capable of cutting thousands of throats, sharing a tender moment with a lover.

Maybe even the worst people need someone, need to know they aren't alone in this world.

"This isn't going to be easy," I told Henka.

No horses. No demon. Even her undead were gone, dismantled by Valcarb as they filled Khraen with arrows. As I recently visited the nearest village and attacked a mage, returning there would be stupid.

"Damn. The village. The mage."

Henka stared up at me.

"I don't know if Valcarb managed to kill the wizard. Did they both die, or did the mage survive? She may have reported the attack and called for more wizards."

I thought it through. There was nothing like Valcarb natural to this world. The mage would know she'd been attacked by a demon. Where, then, would such a demon come from? The nearest demon-infested ruins seemed a safe bet.

"Oh hell."

The more I thought about it, the worse my situation looked. Assuming the mage I attacked survived, she'd definitely return with backup, and they'd definitely come looking here in case there were more. Would they dare enter the village? Would they search every house, or settle for patrolling the perimeter? Were we safe here, under the church?

"We should run," I said, then glanced guiltily at Henka's charred legs. My stupidity did this to her.

Felkrish, the portal demon, I could use it to get us out of here! I considered my options.

The floating mountains? We might be trapped there if the Soul Stone ran out of souls. There was no food. The place was a potential grave. Henka would be trapped there forever with Nhil and my own corpse. She'd likely raise me from the dead, if possible, if only for the company. We'd fall apart together, slowly decaying. I wasn't ready for that.

The Dripping Bucket in Taramlae? Tien lied about burning it down, but what were the odds the room would be as I remembered it? And last time I'd used several souls before succeeding.

My mud shack in the far north? Back where it all began. The thought of returning there hurt my heart. No one would be looking for us there. It might work, if the hut hadn't fallen in by now. And there were plenty of towns I could raid for parts.

Parts? People, I corrected. I'd turn them into parts. People like the woman who fed me in spite of her husband's distrust. People like Shalayn who talked to me in spite of the fact everyone loathed me for the colour of my skin. I remembered the smell of her, the blue of her eyes, and the way she flushed pink when orgasming.

"I'm going to get us out of here," I told Henka. "I can take us back to the north."

She shook her head, eyes wide with fear. "No!" Though almost inaudible, I heard the vehement denial.

"I can do it, I think. I have a portal demon."

"No!"

I didn't understand. Sure, it would delay us, but it wasn't like we were working to a plan or a schedule.

"We can be back in the south by next spring."

"No!" she croaked.

I wanted to ask why, but that single word tore what remained of her voice. She watched me, eyes pleading.

"You want to stay here?"

She nodded.

"I suppose we can hide in the church."

Again, she nodded. The effort cost her, ashen flesh and bone flaking away with every movement.

I swore. In truth, I didn't want to flee to the north any more than she.

"We'll stay," I said.

Relief and gratitude poured from still beautiful eyes. "Thank you," she mouthed.

After making sure she was comfortable—a useless effort, but it made me feel better—I hurried about the abandoned town gathering what supplies I could. I found several loaves of stale bread that the other me must have made in the bakery. It felt so strange that he'd stayed here, learning to harvest wheat and bake bread, instead of searching out the shards of his heart. I tasted one, tearing off a corner, and it was terrible. There was also a small garden that offered up a selection of carrots and potatoes. They grew in orderly lines, carefully weeded. I couldn't imagine myself kneeling in the dirt.

Once I had an armful of vegetables and hard bread, I returned to the church's basement. Water wouldn't be a problem as the same water system that fed the town serviced the church.

Henka watched as I sorted my supplies.

"I don't have any meat," I told her.

After my time in the north, and trapped in the floating mountain, I was damned tired of starvation. The thought of wizards causing me even the slightest inconvenience filled me with a deep anger. They took my world and now I cowered in a basement.

How long would it take the wizards to get here? Would they come cautiously, in force?

They were cowards, I decided. They'd be days getting here. First, they'd search the town where Valcarb fought the wizard. Only when they were sure there weren't more demons, would they come.

Collecting my bow and arrows, I returned to Henka. "I'm going hunting. I won't be long."

Killing a goat or two should be easy.

"Be careful," she mouthed.

Leaning forward, I kissed her cold lips.

CHAPTER THIRTY-SIX

The goats frolicked about the field, ears flapping as they jumped, calling 'Maaaaah! Maaaaaaaaah!' When they spotted me, they stopped playing and gathered around to examine me. I remembered Valcarb saying she'd done the hunting. Apparently, they hadn't seen enough of the other Khraen to learn to fear men.

Nocking an arrow, I drew back and shot one of the goats. At this range, I couldn't miss. The goat stared at me, blinking in shock. The rest wandered over to sniff at the arrow protruding from behind its left shoulder. As its legs gave I shot a second. For an instant they turned looks of hurt reproach in my direction, appalled at my betrayal, and then all was chaos. Goats scampered, bleating, in every direction. Next time it wouldn't be so easy.

Movement in the air caught my attention and I dropped into the long clover. Distance made it impossible to judge size, but a tiny dot floated toward the demon village from the direction of the town we visited. Staying hidden, I watched it grow in size until I saw it was a man in white robes, standing upright, floating through the air. I hated him instantly, his superior 'arms crossed over chest' pose. His perfect goatee, long and braided with some trinket dangling at the end. His hair was blond, shot through with hints of red. His eyes, blue like the deepest lake, scanned the ground.

Crouched in the clover, I studied my enemy. His gaze slid past me, slowing as he spotted the fleeing goats, and then moving on. Had he been a hunter, he'd have wondered what spooked them and come looking. Instead, he didn't appear to give them a second thought. Fool.

After hovering for a few minutes, a dozen paces in the air, a hundred paces from the edge of town, he flew in a slow arc, circumnavigating the village. I watched him disappear from sight behind the church. Should I chance a run for the nearest building? While the clover offered cover, beyond that lay fifty strides of open ground. Perhaps, if I stayed here, stayed hidden, he'd see the town as empty and go back to report the lack of activity. It wasn't until he appeared at the far end of town, that I realized his path would take him directly over top of me. While his focus appeared to be on the village, only an idiot would miss a man and two dead goats in the grass

Unless... I watched for a moment, trying to judge his speed. He was taking his time, studying the houses.

Working quickly, I tore up fistfuls of clover and tossed it over the goats. Then I tore up some more and covered myself as best I could. Lying in the dirt, covered with sparse camouflage, I watched his approach through the grass. The bow I kept clutched in my left hand, an arrow in the right. If he spotted me, I'd take a shot, pointless as it likely was.

His hovering flight bothered me, niggled at my mind. The woman I'd loosed an arrow at in that village possessed some kind of protective shield, and yet her feet touched the ground. Did that mean the shield ended there, that she wasn't protected from beneath? This man flew. Would his shield, if he had one, now encompass him, or would he be vulnerable from below? If the hovering spell exerted some force on the ground to keep him airborne, then surely any shield must not interfere with that.

I cursed my ignorance.

The wizard flew closer.

An all-encompassing shield would make a lot of sense for someone flying.

The mage passed overhead and I learned, too late, just how difficult it is to draw a bowstring when you're lying flat on your back. My movement must have alerted him, because he glanced down, eyes wide and startled.

My half-drawn arrow took him awkwardly in the thigh. He screamed, wobbled, and plummeted to the earth with a flailing crash.

Nocking another arrow, I ran to where he fell. I found him clutching his ribs, teeth gritted in pain. Only now did I realize how young he was. He couldn't have been much more than a year or two older than I. Seeing me, he screamed and held out a hand. Thinking he was about to blast me with fire, I kicked it away. Nothing happened, and he hugged the kicked hand against his chest with a wail of pain. One of the fingers jutted at an odd angle.

"No!" he screamed as I stood over him, drawing back another arrow. "I don't care if you're working these fields! I'm looking for demons!"

Working the fields? Did the wizards have some law against people getting too close to the abandoned demon villages? Could I use this?

His eyes widened as he focussed passed the tip of the arrow and saw me clearly. Darker. Ebony soul. Stained. I remembered all the hateful words they called me.

Mouth opening, he raised his other hand. I put an arrow in his chest. He grunted, blinking. Again, he lifted that hand. As I'd left my other arrows lying in the grass, I grabbed the one in his chest. Twisting it, I drove it deeper.

The young wizard coughed blood.

He stared past me, at nothing, mouth slightly open. Not blinking. No movement. Perfect stillness.

I twisted the arrow and he didn't react. In case he hadn't been alone, I searched the skies, finding them empty.

Pulling the arrow free, I watched the wound for a moment to make sure it didn't suddenly start healing. Nothing happened.

"Dead," I whispered.

My breath caught. Maybe I wouldn't have to kill two young women. At the very least, this might postpone the need for murder. Grabbing him by the ankles, I dragged him back to the church.

Henka watched me, dark eyes bright, an eyebrow raised, as I lugged the dead wizard down the steps. His skull bounced off each step with a dull *thonk*.

"It's a mage," I said, dropping his legs to leave him on the floor by her bed. "What do you think?"

Eyes narrowed, she examined me.

"We need to get out of here and we need to move fast. When he doesn't return, they'll send more. I got lucky this time."

She darted a glance at the corpse.

"I see two options. Either you raise him and he flies us out of here."

She shook her head, just the slightest movement, and I guessed she wasn't capable in her current state.

"Or you use him for parts, repair yourself enough we can run."

Henka closed her eyes.

"He's not that bad," I said. Looking him over, I added, "Maybe a little hairier than you'd like—"

Her eyes flashed open.

"Not in the mood for jokes, fine. We need to move."

She stared at the dead wizard for a long time before finally nodding.

"You're going to need help, aren't you?"

"Yes," she mouthed.

First, she had me drain the wizard of blood, collecting it in buckets I found elsewhere in the village. I then spent hours carving him like an uncooked roast. Starting at the legs, I peeled away flesh and then muscle. Draping them over the charred remains of Henka's legs and dribbling the gathered blood on them, I watched in amazement as she closed her eyes and focussed her power. Her mouth moved continually, singing whispered enchantments. The end result wasn't pretty, but she could walk.

Next, I cut the mage's arm off at the elbow, careful not to damage the bone. Holding it against the stump of her charred arm and pouring more blood on the joint, I watched flesh, muscle, and sinew fuse together as she sang. After harvesting the upper arm for what it had to offer, she now had one working arm. Muscled and hairy, it looked out of place, clashed jarringly with the lithe body of my memories.

Twice, I went outside to vomit, excusing myself, and dashing up the steps. I felt her eyes on me each time, and apologized for my weakness upon my return.

By late afternoon Henka had four working limbs and I'd peeled the young man to replace the skin on her back. I decided not to tell her just how dark and curly the wizard's back-hair was. With his flesh flayed away and added to her own, covering her burnt skull and torso, she could now pass for a living being. Albeit one with a strange haircut.

She couldn't, however, speak yet. The wizard's fire had burned her organs and damaged her lungs.

"Can we harvest those too?" I asked. "So you can speak?"

She pointed at the hole in the mage's chest where I'd pulled the arrow free.

"One of the lungs is ruined," I agreed. "But the other—"

She crossed her arms over her chest. Though burnt and bubbled, the flesh was basically whole and we hadn't yet replaced it. The stapled wound between her breasts remained closed.

"No," she mouthed.

"No, you can't, or no, you won't?"

She stared at me, eyes pleading.

"No, you won't," I said. "Why not?"

She huddled her arms tighter.

"A hairy chest isn't the worst thing."

That earned me a sharp look. But there was something more, something in the way she held her arms crossed over her chest. For a moment, I thought it was fear of losing her breasts, but that wasn't it. Right now, most of her looked like a hairy young man. She knew she could replace herself with whatever she wanted at some point. This was temporary.

"Heart," I said.

Her eyes locked on mine, terrified.

"You don't want me to see where it should be. Because it's empty." I touched her cheek. "I don't have a heart either. Not a whole one. Not even close. And then, when I do, it'll be black stone."

She watched me, eyes softening. A hand, knuckles hairy, reached out to touch my arm.

"What does that say about me?" I asked. "Why do I have an obsidian heart?" Worries I'd kept buried bubbled to the surface. "People don't have obsidian hearts! What *am* I?"

Henka pulled me into a hug and kissed my neck, lips corpse cold.

"Fix lungs later," she whispered. "Must flee."

Rising, I pulled her to her feet. "We'll get you fixed up as soon as we're clear of the mages. I really think I should use Felkrish to take us north again."

She shook her head, no give in her, and pointed south.

The wizards would likely catch us, but at least we'd be together.

After butchering the two goats for whatever meat I could get quickly—an unnerving experience so soon after having butchered a young man—we put the demon-infested town behind us.

While the wizard I shot out of the air seemed content to fly the town's perimeter, I suspected this time they'd complete a more thorough search. Would they dare enter the buildings? Would they find the harvested mage, and what would they make of that? I got the impression necromancers were as rare as elementalists. Would they understand what they saw, or assume someone carved him for food? By the end, he and the goat looked awfully similar.

Early in the afternoon we found a farmhouse. A small barn, red paint now peeling with age, resounded with the sounds of goats and chickens. Two horses, swayback mares, watched us from within a shoddily fenced paddock. Only laziness kept them there. Henka gestured at the house, a log cabin with shuttered windows.

I knew what she wanted, what she needed.

Parts.

"I need your help," she whispered.

Flaying flesh. Peeling muscle.

This was my fault. She saved me, sacrificed herself to keep me safe. Swallowing bile, I nodded.

Decision made, my thoughts raced. I didn't like it, but this had to happen. Henka needed working lungs. I couldn't stab whoever lived here in the chest for fear of damaging them.

"Do you need other internal organs?" I asked.

She nodded.

So, I couldn't stab them in the gut either. How the hell was I supposed to kill them?

Blood. Henka needed blood as well. It played some part in how she fused new pieces to herself. I'd watched as she used the wizard's blood to work her magic.

Whoever lived here, I'd either have to beat them to death or suffocate them. The thought reminded me of the young woman I killed in the cafe, the way she fought, desperate for life.

When we reached the front door, I knocked. There was, I decided, no point in chatting with someone I planned to kill. It would only make the grizzly work of harvesting them more difficult.

A woman, middle-aged and plump, opened the door. Her eyes widened as she saw me, sword drawn, Henka huddled in her robes, the patchwork quilt of her skull's flesh visible.

The woman opened her mouth—to speak greeting or call out a warning, I don't know—and I hit her. I felt the crunch of her nose breaking beneath my fist. Bulling my way into her house, I slammed her into the wall. She hit with a wheeze of air and slid to the floor.

Unsure what I'd face, I spun with my sword drawn and held at the ready. Sitting in a chair at the dining table, a spoon of porridge halfway to his mouth, was a chubby man into his forties. Short hair, jutting out at all angles, added to his look of surprise.

"Stay," I said. "Stand, and I'll cut you down."

He glanced to his wife, sobbing on the floor, hands trying to stanch the flow of blood from her nose, and back to me.

"Stay," I repeated, putting stern warning in my voice.

I saw it in his eyes. I hit his wife. No sword-wielding teen would get in his way.

He stood.

"Sit," I said. "Sit down."

Meaty hands bunched into fists.

"We're not here to hurt you," I lied, which might have worked better if I hadn't just broken his wife's nose.

Stalking around the table, he collected a chair, hefting it like a club. Only now that he stood did I realize how big he was. I retreated before his rage. How could I fight him without damaging him? Then I remembered two things: We had his wife, and didn't need him. And I remembered I was a swordsman with years of practice and war.

Letting him get close, I feigned retreat before suddenly stepping forward and lashing out with the sword. The tip scored a deep gash in his wrist causing him to drop the chair. In one smooth motion I stabbed him in the chest. He grunted in surprise. All the strength in the world is nothing with a foot of steel in your lung. Coughing blood, he swung a clumsy punch at me. Twisting the blade, I ducked under his attack, pulled it free, and stuck it in his other lung.

He bared teeth at me in an animal snarl. Again, I twisted the sword, doing more damage, causing terrible agony. Pinioned on my blade, he couldn't move forward to reach me with those huge hands.

I watched him blink, his slow farmer brain not yet understanding he was dead.

He tried to speak. Frothing blood bubbled from his lips and he cursed me with his eyes. Withdrawing the sword, I was deciding where to stab him next when his knees folded, dropping him to the floor. He lay there, twitching, clinging desperately to a life already lost.

I stood silent witness.

Why had I twisted the sword? Why cause unneeded pain when I could have ended him much quicker? I knew a dozen places to stab a man that were near instantaneously fatal. Why had I toyed with him?

That wasn't me. I took no pleasure in the suffering of others.

It was *him*, the old me. The Demon Emperor of PalTaq.

Demon Emperor?

Henka's touch interrupted my thoughts. She gave me a hug and another cold kiss, though I wasn't sure why.

Taking a deep breath, preparing myself for what was to come, I said, "I'm ready."

She shook her head and pointed at the door.

"You're sure?"

She nodded.

Sitting on the front porch, I watched the sky for wizards. I enjoyed the breeze on my face, the dusty smell of the nearby barn, and tried not to think about what went on in the farmstead behind me.

I knew Henka would never be happy with what she'd get from the woman. Middle-aged, and beginning to sag, the farmer's wife would be a temporary measure at best.

"She won't be content until she's perfect," I told the frogs and crickets. "She won't be happy until…until I'm happy."

Henka wouldn't be satisfied with her body until she was my perfection, until she'd become everything I wanted in a woman.

It was my fault she'd been damaged, and then the repercussions—what it would take to repair her—would be my fault too.

That wizard's arm didn't match, was longer and more muscled than the other. It would have to be replaced.

Patchwork skin, wrinkled and old.

How many young women died, flayed and dismembered, until Henka achieved her goal?

I laughed, a humourless chuckle. I'd been concerned about how much blood she needed to maintain the semblance of life. What a fool.

"She's a monster," I told the frogs.

But I was a monster, too.

I was going to help her. I was going to get her whatever she wanted, whatever she needed. I was going to do it because I owed her, because she sacrificed herself to save me without hesitation, and all of this was my fault. But I was also going to do it for purely selfish reasons. I wanted my Henka back. I wanted that flawless perfection.

"Is this who I was?" I asked the crickets.

No, they said, this is who you are.

"Were the wizards right to destroy me?"

Do you care?

By the time Henka finished, the sun had fallen and the creatures of the dark took up their ancient chorus. Stars burned sharp holes in the blanket of night. A warm wind whipped up from the south, bending fields of corn, dry leaves sounding like the whispers of a thousand lost souls.

Though her pale face remained mostly untouched, Henka had shed the hairy limbs. Her torso looked subtly wrong, breasts a little too big, her skin that of a woman in her forties. A vast improvement over the hairy wizard's flesh, but a long way from the flawless girl I knew.

"How are you?" I asked.

She shrugged with a rueful smile. "Better. But not..." She looked down, shying from my eyes.

"We'll find you others as we go south," I promised, and my guts writhed.

Taking my hand in hers, she led me into the cabin, her flesh warm from whatever necromantic magics she worked. The wife lay sprawled on the floor, splayed and open, a terrible sight, blood splashing everything. Ribs cracked and spread wide, Henka had harvested her lungs and several other internal organs. The husband lay where I left him, though he looked sunken and drained.

"Is this alright?" she asked, tentative and timid.

For a moment, I thought she meant the murder and butchery of these people and I wanted to laugh and scream as my mind wrestled with an answer. But then she opened her robes to show me what lay beneath and I realized that wasn't what she meant at all. She wanted to know if I was satisfied with her new body.

The stapled scar remained. Everything else was different. With Shalayn, by the end I knew every freckle and dimple, every curve and crease. Henka kept changing. I felt off-balance. In fact, I'd felt strangely unbalanced since our second meeting.

"It's you I love," I told her. "Not the shell."

We slept together in the farmer's bed, curled around each other, though she refused to remove her robes. Well, *I* slept. The dead don't rest. I woke sometime late in the night to the distant howl of wolves. Henka lay beside me, watching me sleep, eyes unblinking shards in the dark. She kissed me, lips hot, and I returned to my slumbers.

CHAPTER THIRTY-SEVEN

After killing the farmer's horses, we rode them south, exchanging our dead mounts for new ones whenever their appearance decayed to the point they became recognizable as corpses. We stopped at each farming community and village. Henka would ask after the prettiest girls, and we harvested them. We flayed their perfect flesh. We drained them of blood, filling wine and water skins with the precious liquid. Watching Henka work was like witnessing a master butcher. How many had she harvested to get this good?

I claimed their souls, tore their eternal spirits from their bodies and locked them away in my Soul Stone to be later spent, fed to demons.

We left a trail of tears and nightmares behind us as families found the husked remains of their loved ones.

My stomach turned sour, felt like it was trying to consume itself. I envisioned that sky-devouring god from the floating mountains and felt like he was nested in my gut. I swirled around that sinkhole sun, falling forever inward to be annihilated.

Appetite dead, I lost weight, my ribs once again showing.

Nightmares shattered my sleep. Skinned corpses, peeled in great bloody sheets. Odd bits harvested as Henka searched for exactly the right part to build the woman she wanted to be, the woman *I* wanted her to be. Empty bodies. When I wasn't haunted by images of butchery, I dreamed of Tien. I dreamed of finding her, of crippling her so she couldn't cast spells, fingers sliced away, tongue torn free. I dreamed of telling her exactly who I was, rubbing her little snub-nose in the fact she helped bring back the Demon Emperor. I dreamed of torturing her, punishing her for her part in Shalayn's death. I dreamed of killing her.

Henka became perfect once again, her flawless grace returning with each harvest. Though if I looked close enough, when the light was right, I saw thin lines where the skin tones didn't quite match. Those lines faded with each day. The cost appalled me, and yet I helped pay it. Guilt ate me from within, forgotten only when we made love and she took me from myself. Henka knew me so well, knew me better than I did. She knew when my thoughts grew dark enough to blind me to the beauty of what I had.

"Life feeds on life," she said. "Why should death be any different?"

She was right. What were those young women to me? Nothing. Small, pointless lives. They possessed no destiny, certainly not like mine. They would build no empires, found no eternal civilizations.

Still my guts roiled. Snakes nested in my bowels, twisting and coiling and fighting.

I was two men. I was the ancient emperor, inhuman and immortal, a servant to some foul god I could not remember. And I was a nineteen-year-old boy who knew right from wrong, good from evil. The boy despised what I was becoming. The old man rejoiced. Both of us loved Henka. Both of us would do anything for her. Where the Emperor acted without a twinge of conscience, the boy drowned in self-loathing.

I learned something of myself. I wanted to escape into the man I had been. I wanted his cold, his distance. I remembered the dreams, those gemstone eyes fused into his skull. How did the world look through stone?

Henka hoped to make me something better than what I had been—though how she'd know if I succeeded, I had no idea—but the crimes I committed for her were doing more damage than my memories.

I wanted to tell her, to ask her to stop. I couldn't. I wanted *her*, the warm sensuous woman her necromancy made her, not the ever-decaying corpse she, in truth, was.

The days grew hotter and longer the further south we travelled and, for the first time, I was almost comfortable. The majority of the population was still pale-skinned, blond-haired and blue-eyed, though many looked closer to red from their time in the sun. Every now and then, however, I caught sight of skin brown beyond a tan. No one was near as dark as I.

Even with the increasing number of brown people, I drew glares of loathing and disgust as we rode our latest undead mounts into the port city of Nachi on the southern coast.

Beginning high on a steep hill that fell only short of being a cliff, the city tumbled toward the ocean. The highest homes were palatial, sprawling wings spread wide. As the streets wound their way chaotically down, the buildings became smaller, simpler. Dirtier. Down by the docks, where the land finally flattened out, most were little more than sheds and shanties, leaning out into the ocean like they might fall in at any time. From up here, among the mansions, I saw evidence that many already had. It looked like the coastline crept ever closer, claiming the next line of shacks. Someday, thousands of years from now, these huge homes would fall into the ever-encroaching ocean.

Was Tien still here, or had she already moved on? Had she boarded a boat bound south, or travelled by land? There were spirit demons skilled at hunting and finding things, I suddenly recalled. Unfortunately, I didn't know how to summon or bind them. That knowledge lay somewhere further down my path.

I prayed to the god I couldn't remember that the little wizard was still here.

Dismounting, Henka and I led our recently deceased mounts down the steep winding paths and slick cobbled streets. Even up here, Nachi stank like fish, saltwater, and sweating men. Screaming gulls turned the air above the city into a churning cloud of stained white and grey. They shat on everything. They fought each other, a raucous, never-ending battle over the scraps of civilization.

The wizards, I decided, chose the wrong shade of white.

Far below us, in the harbour, a profusion of log jetties stabbed into the ocean like splayed skeletal fingers. Boats of all sizes rocked with the waves and tide. Under the screeching gulls, I sometimes caught the groan of ancient timbers swollen with rot, the low grumble of wood on wood.

"I want to get closer," I told Henka. "I want to see the harbour, walk the docks. I want to see the ocean up close."

She stood, looking out over the sprawl and confusion of Nachi. Then she gave me that shy smile and took my hand, her flesh warm but cooler than yesterday. We spent the last of the blood the previous night, and the wine skins hung collapsed and empty from our saddles.

If the looks I received earlier were dark, now that Henka and I held hands, now that it was clear we were together, they were black with revulsion.

Alert, constantly scanning the crowds for Tien, I noticed a trend as we walked: The deeper into Nachi, the lower down the hill, the darker the people were. I, with my sable skin, remained the darkest by far, but the looks of loathing faded. They transformed into something else, something very different. As we reached the harbour the men and women working the docks, brown skinned, long of limb and lithely muscled, watched us pass. Many froze, stopped whatever they were doing, and stared. Some few, the darkest workers, dipped shallow bows, something close to worship or adoration painting their faces.

When I realized I hadn't seen a pale face or blond hair in several minutes, I stopped. Henka stood with me, still holding my hand. She seemed utterly unconcerned by the attention.

"Why no northerners?" I asked.

She studied the boats moored out on the docks, eyes sad. "The ocean is dangerous. After the Great War, it never returned to its previous state. The elementalists woke its fury, turned it against the Emperor's fleets, but there was no way they could control it. The depths are still plagued by monsters and demons, remnants from the war. Ships disappear all the time."

I watched her, struggling to understand.

"Sailors are the scum of the earth," she said, "the lowest class in society, loathed by everyone. Islanders. Darkers. Ebony souls. Only these people sail the seas. No one cares if they disappear. No one cares if they die."

So it was unlikely Tien left by boat. I glanced back up the hill. If the wizard was still here, she'd be up there somewhere. Unless there was a decaying cafe serving the best coffee in Nachi somewhere down here.

"The people in Taramlae hated me because they thought I was a sailor?" I asked.

I knew there was more to it than that. I knew that my pitch-black skin reminded them of their ancient foes, of everything they lost during and after the Great War. I couldn't even blame them. The irony that here I was, the Demon Emperor reborn, was far from lost on me.

They had reason to hate.

They had reason to fear.

My soul was indeed stained.

But their hate fuelled my hate. I, too, lost everything in that war. My empire. My life. My memories. My heart, and the woman I loved.

The woman I loved?

That memory of a memory, the ghost of a recollection lost.

"Are we going to book passage to the islands?" asked Henka.

"Yes, but not yet." I wanted to find the wizard before we left. "We're going to rent a room." Laughter burst from me. In spite of everything, I remained destitute. I had little to my name beyond the clothes I wore and the crude sword I took from the other Khraen. "I may have to sell the sword first," I said. I wouldn't get much for it, inferior work that it was.

"No need," said Henka. "I have money. I've been taking it from those I kill. A little each time, but it's been some years."

She travelled light, a small pack with only a few changes of clothes, and the pouch with the tools she used to harvest bodies. I almost asked where she kept it, but luckily figured it out before I made an ass of myself. Of course she hid things in the cavity of her chest, where her heart should be. Where her heart would one day again reside.

One day. Was I lying to myself?

"I need to find somewhere that won't change," I said. "Somewhere I can memorize."

A look of tension crossed her flawless features and was gone. "Memorize? Why?"

"I have a place I'm going to take you. It's safe, but I need to have somewhere to return to so we don't get trapped there. To do that, I need to—"

"Where?" Her eyes never left mine.

"It's a castle in a floating mountain in some kind of hell."

"How did you find it?"

"I stumbled across a portal demon in a wizard's tower."

She cursed and looked away. "Was anyone there, in the floating mountains?"

"No." I don't know why I lied, but I did. It was something in the way she snapped questions at me. Maybe I didn't want her fretting about me learning demonology from a demon. Suddenly I was less sure about bringing her. Should I find some excuse to go alone? Should I surprise her, introduce her to Nhil without warning? I was damned sure she wouldn't like that.

Staring out over the ocean, she said, "Why do you want to go?"

"I have souls stored in my Soul Stone now. I know summonings and I know bindings. I can make even a crude sword like this a dangerous, unbreakable weapon. Maybe I can even bind a demon to some clothes as armour." I recalled the red armour, how it terrified me. I wasn't ready to touch it, much less wear it.

"How long do you want to be there?"

The way she said that made me wonder if maybe she didn't want to join me there after all. That would certainly make it easier to keep my secret. And I really did want to keep Nhil and the floating mountain a secret.

"I don't know," I said. "A couple of weeks. Maybe a month."

Henka turned away from the ocean, once again faced me. "I'm sorry, I can't go. With no people there, I won't be able to maintain myself. After a month, I'd be a frightful sight indeed."

Was that why she asked who was there?

"I'll rot," she continued. "Without blood I'll be corpse cold in a day. I will not have you watch me fall apart." She raised a hand to forestall my argument. An argument I had no intention of making. "I have a better idea. We'll book passage to the islands, take a private cabin. I'll tell everyone you don't feel well and keep the room unchanging so you can come and go as you please. You won't have to spend the entire time alone in that hell." She smiled that shy smile, the corner of those perfect lips turning up, eyes all promise and heat. "You can return to me when you need release and distraction."

That was, I had to admit, a lot more appealing than spending a month with only Nhil for company. I stared up the hill at where all the pale-haired blue-eyed people lived. I wanted Tien. I wanted to punish her. But here, on the coast, the shards of my heart to the south called to me. What did I want more?

A single visit would cost two souls, one each way. How had I gone from loathing the Soul Stone and its burden, regretting and hating the cost of each use, to contemplating spending them for sex and companionship?

"Each time I use the portal demon it costs a soul," I told her.

Henka examined me, head tilted. "Saltwater is hard on the dead. I will have to kill a few on our trip south to maintain myself." She looked away, stared out to sea. "It's what we are."

What we are. A necromancer and a demonologist. Blood and souls. The hated of the world.

But when everyone hates you, either for the colour of your skin, or for a history you don't remember, what was the point of fighting it? Guilt? Why not embrace the truth of what I was?

No. I had to be a better person than the man I had been. Why was it so difficult to stay focussed on that? Why did I so easily slip into behaviour most would call evil?

Most? I stifled a laugh.

What if that was me? What if *I* was evil? Could someone want to be better and still be evil? Did the attempt matter for anything?

I shook off the thoughts. The need to move grew in me. Here, on the southern edge of the continent, I felt many shards of my heart to the south, somewhere out in the ocean.

What if the wizards tossed fragments of my heart into the water? Come to think of it, why hadn't they done that? Why didn't they smash it to dust? What would happen then, would there be thousands and thousands of me, each with only the tiniest sliver of memory? The more I thought about it, the less sense it made. If the wizards had my heart, they could have kept it safe, kept it somewhere with no chance of it growing. With no life to feed off, the shard I took from the wizard's tower hadn't become a person. If the wizards just left the entire thing there, I'd still be dead.

"Why do you think the wizards shattered my heart?" I asked Henka.

"What do you mean?" As always, she accepted my sudden change in topics without question.

"Why break it? Why litter it about the world? Part was in a tower, imprisoned. Why not do that to the whole thing?"

She shrugged, the slightest twitch of a slim shoulder. "Maybe they never had the whole thing. Maybe they didn't know what it was."

"Who broke it then? Who scattered the pieces?"

"Perhaps it broke during the Great War. Maybe your followers or demons escaped with parts. Maybe the wizards only got that one shard."

Did that make sense? It held together better than my original theory that the wizards were behind my every woe. What if they had no idea I'd returned? Even Tien assumed I was some minor demonologist.

"If my followers had parts of my heart, they would have taken better care. I could have been back thousands of years ago."

"There was a war going on, a war they were losing. Perhaps there was a schism, some wanting your return, others happy with your demise."

My own people? Certainly, the wizards and necromancers turned on me. Could I have been so terrible the demonologists turned on me as well? I had no memory of that one way or the other.

Something felt wrong. For reasons I couldn't defend, could hardly verbalize, I felt like one person was responsible for my current state. But who, and why? What could anyone hope to gain by bringing me back? Were there still those out there who longed for the return of the old empire? Having seen the splendour of the abandoned villages and cities, I could understand that. But who would be old enough to remember my empire? I remembered Shalayn telling me that many of the high-ranking Guild members were immortal.

It hit me.

"A wizard did this," I told Henka. "They've found something they want controlled. A demon. Or they want access to something only a demonologist can get to. Maybe something warded by demons. Maybe something like the floating mountains. Hell, maybe even that specific fortress. Something must have gone wrong with their plans though."

"Could be," agreed Henka. "But it doesn't feel quite right."

Damn. She was right again. What wizard would be so sloppy as to litter my heart about the world?

Henka took my hand in hers. Little trace of last night's heat remained. She was insatiable in so many ways, an eternity of need. But aren't we all? Doesn't everyone want one more breath, one more meal?

"Let's go find a ship," she said. "We'll get to the bottom of this in the islands."

And turn my back on vengeance? What if Tien wasn't even here? All I had was the word of one terrified young woman. Would I lead

Henka off on some prolonged hunt just so I could kill this wizard? How would I explain that, without telling her about Shalayn? No. I wanted my heart more. The wizard could wait. My vengeance could wait. I'd find her. I had all the time in the world.

"There are many pieces to the south," I said. "A large one in PalTaq, I think."

"We'll work our way south, island to island. PalTaq will be our last stop. Before we get there, you need to know as much as you can. The palace will be dangerous."

She was, as always, correct.

CHAPTER THIRTY-EIGHT

Boats, crammed tight in the docks, moved together with each swell of the ocean, groaning like old lovers. Brown skinned men and women hustled about, shoulders stooped under sacks of grain and other assorted sundries. Everywhere I looked I saw goods being removed from ships and loaded onto wagons drawn by short but sturdy oxen to be hauled up the steep hill. Apparently, nothing went south beyond what supplies the crew needed to make the voyage.

Steaming mountains of ox shit, circled by swarms of fat flies glistening rainbows of green and blue in the sun, littered the docks. Teams of children scampered about, shovelling it into wheelbarrows. I seriously doubted ox shit was something worth collecting in *my* empire. With fire elementals supplying light and heat for every purpose, what use would it be beyond fertilizer? Even then, earth elementalists could likely solve that issue without stooping to hauling shit everywhere.

Filthy wizards with their filthy chaos magic and their filthy little kingdom.

The docks stank. Rotting fish. Sweating men and women. Decaying grains and damp wood. The harbour was raucous with life, people pushing and shoving, voices raised to be heard over the yelling of everyone else doing the same thing. So much brown skin. Not a blond-haired pink person to be seen. Even the harbour master was a deep mahogany.

I loved it. I loved the stink. I loved the chaos. I loved these people, the way they saw me, the way they stared with awe and moved from my path instead of glaring and spitting.

"That one," said Henka, pointing out a ship. "It's already loaded. She'll be leaving soon."

I studied the massive carrack, fat-bellied and low in the water. Three masts carried sails of stained cotton, but she also bore banks of oars should the winds die. The sheets hung slack, moving sluggishly in the ocean breeze. The crude figurehead, carved in wood and sloppily painted, portrayed a mermaid with breasts large enough to make swimming impossible. Men and women crawled over the vessel like a plague of locusts, small and dark. By my best guess, she had a crew of thirty souls and most were already aboard. A few still worked at loading supplies up the gangplank. A man, the darkest I'd yet seen, though still paler than I, stood at the railing. He barked orders in a harsh and booming voice, an unlit cigar clamped between his teeth. He was huge, easily six and a half feet tall, barrel-chested and bow-legged. A thick black beard, braided and plaited in what looked to be gold, hung to his belt.

"Come," said Henka.

Releasing my hand, she led me up the gangplank, sailors parting before us. I'm not sure who drew more attention, Henka, gloriously beautiful and the only pale-skinned person down here, or me. The captain watched us, face expressionless.

"Captain," said Henka, dipping a quick bow as we reached him.

"Off my fucking ship."

"We require passage south," she said, unperturbed.

"No. Off." Pulling the cigar from his mouth he gestured at the gangplank with the much-chewed and soggy end.

"We will pay well. Very well. We need a cabin and we are not to be disturbed."

He turned dark eyes, haloed in blood-shot yellow, in my direction. "The boy is a long way from home."

Anger bristled in me at the casual dismissal. *Boy.* If this man had any idea who he addressed he'd grovel on the deck.

"And that's where we're returning," said Henka, calm as death.

"And you, boy?" said the Captain. "Does this pale-skinned cunt speak for you?"

Rage pulsed through me. "You would be wise to show her some respect," I ground out.

"Fuck wise. Off my fucking ship before I have you thrown off." He eyed me, judging my reaction with a jaundiced eye. "*Boy.*"

"We're going to PalTaq," said Henka as if the Captain hadn't spoken.

He blinked, examining me, and then turned his attention back to Henka. Some of his certainty seemed to have shrunk and crawled away. "No one goes there."

"He does," she said, nodding at me. "He's going home."

"Home." There was something wistful in the way he said that, but I had no idea what it meant to him. "It's haunted." He looked over her shoulder, staring at the hill, at the sprawled city of Nachi, but not really seeing it. "It's death."

"Captain," said Henka, drawing his attention back to her. She showed him a pouch full of gold, careful to keep her body between it and the rest of the crew. "This again when we reach the islands."

"Maybe I'll toss you overboard once we're at sea," he mused, eyeing the gold.

"Maybe. But look at his skin," she said. "When is the last time you saw skin like that?"

Eyes narrowed, he looked me up and down. "A stained-soul. Black deeds writ in flesh. I've only heard stories." He lifted a hand like he was going to touch my arm to confirm the reality of me but let it drop. "I thought… It's not possible. They're all dead."

"Not all," said Henka.

"Just a boy," said the Captain, speaking as if I wasn't right there in front of him.

I forced myself to remain silent.

Henka tossed him the pouch of gold and he snatched it out of the air.

"We'll take a private cabin," she said. "No one is to disturb us. Khraen will remain there for much of the voyage."

The Captain's breath caught. "Khraen?"

"Khraen," repeated Henka.

Tucking the pouch of gold into his shirt, he turned and shouted at a nearby crewman to show us to a private berth.

"Welcome to the Habnikaav," he said.

Habnikaav. That name sent shivers through me. It was an ancient name, important to me. Hadn't I dreamed about a ship? But this wasn't her. My Habnikaav had been a colossal warship, twenty times the size of this vessel, demons bound to every plank and trunnel. She'd been the queen of all the ocean, the greatest ship ever built. The wizards sank her. They'd pay for that too.

An omen, no doubt.

"It's a good name," I told the Captain.

"Named after the Empire's flagship," he answered.

"Which was named after the demon bound to her hull."

Chewing on his cigar he stomped away, shoulders hunched, muttering under his breath.

A youth of maybe eighteen years approached us. His face, pocked by acne and weathered by a life at sea, displayed raw curiosity. Under a mop of curly brown hair, eyes, dark as night, widened as he approached. Henka, as always, was stunning in her form fitting dress. And her porcelain skin stood out more here than anywhere. But in spite of her unearthly beauty, he only had eyes for me. Upon reaching us, he stopped. Unlike the Captain, he did reach out and touch the exposed flesh of my arm. Scraping at me with a fingernail, he then checked to see if any of the black came off.

"You finished?" I asked.

Swallowing nervously, he nodded.

"Show us to our berth, please," said Henka.

Finally noticing her, he blinked, nodded again, and led us below decks without a word.

Descending thick steps of heavy oak swollen with damp, we found ourselves in a long hall. The sun pouring down the steps at both ends provided the only light. Closely spaced doors lined the walls.

"Guest berths," said the boy. "All empty. Always empty."

He pushed at a door and it didn't budge. Throwing his shoulder against it several times, he managed to wedge it open far enough we could squeeze in.

"I'll get oil for the hinges," he said, waiting in the hall, happy to do nothing while we examined the cramped quarters.

It was small, more like a closet than a room. A single filthy portal let in a brown stain of sunlight giving the room a leprous pallor. A single cot, big enough for two only if you piled one of top of the other, sagged against the far wall. The mattress, mouldering and concave, looked ready for a cleansing fire. Thick spider webs, heavy with dust, clogged every corner. Corpses of beetles and gods knew what other insects crunched beneath our boots.

"I love it," said Henka. "Though I do feel we may have overpaid."

"Are you sure you want to stay here?" I asked in a whisper. Should I invite her to the floating mountain? I'd lied, told her no one was there, and that shamed me.

"Insects don't bother me," she said.

I imagined returning to find her rotting, crawling with maggots, and crushed the thought.

The boy coughed. "I'll bring blankets and water and something to eat. The Captain says it's best if you remain below decks until we leave."

When had he talked to the Captain?

"I need to refresh my store of blood before we leave," Henka whispered into my ear.

I saw an opportunity: One last quick look around the city. Maybe ask a few questions, see if anyone knew which way Tien travelled. And the longer we could stave off murdering and harvesting the crew, the better.

"How long before we reach the islands?" I asked the boy.

"Once we depart, three weeks if the weather holds. A month or more if the winds change."

"When do we depart?"

"Tomorrow morning."

"We have things to do in town first," I said. "We'll be back before he sets sail." I considered the Captain. "And tell the Captain if he leaves without us, I'll send something after him."

"Right," said the boy.

"What's your name?" I asked.

He dipped a sloppy bow. "Brenwick Sofame, at your service."

"Brenwick." I tossed him a coin. "Clean this place up while we're gone. New mattress. Fresh sheets."

He nodded and departed.

I turned to Henka. "No point in staying in this dump any longer than we have to. We'll get a room in town, one last night of luxury, and return first thing in the morning."

She gave me a cold peck on the cheek, but her eyes promised warmth. "Let's go."

We walked back up the hill, away from the brown folks of the ships and docks, and back into the world of pink-skinned blonds. Where did I fit in? The pale people loathed me and, apparently, the brown feared me.

"What does the colour of my skin mean?" I asked Henka as we strolled crowded streets. They watched us, hate in their eyes. Hate for my black skin. Hate for the fact we were clearly together. "Why did the Captain call me a stained-soul?"

"Superstitious nonsense. Islanders believe consorting with demons stains a person physically."

"Are there others like me?"

"Farther south, in the centre of the world. After the war, the wizards all but wiped out your people. The survivors fled to the archipelagos around PalTaq. There are thousands of islands, many places to hide. I doubt anyone this far north has seen skin like yours in two thousand years."

My people. What would it feel like to fit in? What would it feel like to walk into a room and not be loathed?

Selecting an upscale inn that looked out over the ocean called Hawk's Landing, Henka led me inside. The interior was finished entirely in white marble veined with gold. The floor, the walls, the pillars, the desk behind which sat a sneering old man, all were immaculately carved from cold stone. A dozen pink-skinned fair-haired men and women lounged on huge chairs of soft leather, smoking cigars and drinking coffee from tiny cups. Narrowed eyes followed us. Seeing the coffee cups, I scanned the room for Tien. She wasn't here. Either the place was too nice, or the coffee not good enough.

Approaching the desk, Henka smiled sweetly at the old man. Most people melted at her smiles, she was gorgeous and young. The old man's sneer sank deeper into the crags of his ancient features.

"We'd like a room, please," she said.

"We're booked."

"The sign outside says otherwise."

He stared at her, not answering.

Placing a gold coin on the counter, enough to buy us a room for a month, she said, "We have money."

He eyed the coin with clear distaste. "We do not accommodate ebony souls and we certainly don't serve whores." He eyed her slinky dress. "Even expensive ones."

Henka stopped me reaching for my sword with a hand. "Then good day to you, sir," she said, collecting the coin and leading me back out into the street.

I bottled my rage, shoved it down deep, swore vengeance. Someday I would return to that inn and paint the white stone red.

It took three more attempts before we found a place willing to take us. I knew that when I returned to repay these people for their rudeness, I would be busy indeed.

The Sleeping Inn wasn't much compared to Hawk's Landing, but it was still palatial in comparison to our berth aboard the Habnikaav. With the room secured, Henka and I did some shopping. We collected a supply of preserved foods, vegetables and dried meats, as much as we could carry. Every shopkeeper we interacted with made no attempt to hide their loathing. Darker. Ebony Soul. Stained. All the hurtful words muttered just loud enough to know I heard. They wanted our coin, but wanted me to know I was not welcome, would never be welcome. Someday I would return, I would repay them in kind.

Once we had enough to keep me alive, if not well-fed, for several weeks in the floating mountain, we returned to leave our purchases in our room. With the bound water elemental beneath the castle, water wouldn't be a problem. In the morning we'd lug the supplies down to the Habnikaav.

Unbuckling my sword, I tossed it onto a chair. Hate exhausted me, theirs and mine. It was a constant weight on my soul. Placing a pillow against the headboard, I collapsed onto the bed. I sat, watching Henka.

Crawling across the bed like a lithe cat, Henka sprawled out beside me, back arched slightly, nipples showing through the thin silk of her dress. Obsidian eyes, filled with promise, watched me. I cupped a breast, found it cold, and released it.

"Sorry," she whispered.

I shook my head. "No need to apologise."

"Do you want to eat first, or shall we procure ourselves a supply of blood?" She lifted a suggestive eyebrow.

Lust, revulsion, and excitement warred within me. Kill someone. Drain them of blood. I couldn't eat. At least, unlike the harvesting for parts, the blood didn't have to come from beautiful young women. Henka didn't care what the source was, as long as it was human.

I hoped I might get a chance, if Henka and I separated briefly, to ask around after Tien. Maybe I could come up with an excuse.

"Blood first," I said.

The hint of a smile ghosted her lips. She slid from the bed, smoothing the dress and examining herself in the mirror.

"You're perfect," I said to forestall any additional butchery. And she was. Every curve and contour, flawless, as if custom built to my every desire, my every want and need.

"We'll find an old whore," she said. "Get a second room in a hotel down by the docks, the kind of place that doesn't ask questions. We'll drain her there."

"One will do?" I asked, knowing the answer, but hoping.

"Three would be better."

Three more murders. I'd add their souls to the stone. The thought reminded me of the butcheries I'd seen in Taramlae, how nothing was left by the end. Every organ, bone, muscle, and sinew, every drop of blood, was turned to some purpose.

Like somehow, by not wasting our victims, I might be less evil.

"What we do," I said, "you and I. Killing. Murdering. Draining people of blood, harvesting them. Stealing their souls to feed demons. Is that evil?" Such a stupid question. "Are we evil?"

I knew the answer, but wanted to be proven wrong.

"Evil," said Henka, with a slight shrug. "If a wolf eats a rabbit, it is evil?"

"Wolves are carnivores. If they don't eat meat, they die."

"Think of me as a carnivore. I might not eat my prey, but it's the same in the end. Dead is dead." She turned away, suddenly shy, eyes downcast, perfect brow crumpling, retreating from my questions. A pang of guilt stabbed me at hurting her like this. At forcing her to defend her very existence. "I need blood to maintain myself. And for us."

Us. I wanted her to have the blood. Perhaps I'd asked the wrong question. What I really wanted to know was if *I* was evil.

"Without the blood," she said, "I must exist outside, hidden away from civilization. Like you found me. More animal than human. The longer I go the worse it gets. I become feral. I forget what I was." Her shoulders sagged. "I don't want to be like that. I don't want to *be* that." Reaching out she touched my chest with cold fingers. "I want to be real."

She needed the blood, and surely need must separate evil from necessity.

"What about me?" I asked. "I don't need to spend souls."

"You do if you're going to protect yourself from the wizards. You do if you're going to reclaim what was yours. You do if you are going to rebuild your empire, the greatest empire the world ever knew. This," she gestured at the window and the city beyond. "This is pathetic. A mockery of what we had. The wizards think small. They don't dream. They're content to rule this filthy hovel of a civilization."

A mockery of what we had? Somehow it felt like she meant *us*, rather than civilization. She was too angry at what was lost. I remembered the wistful way she stared at the abandoned village.

"How old are you?"

She looked away. "Not as old as you," she answered, voice soft. "If you are doing something grand, building something more than yourself, if you better the state of all humanity, how can you be evil?" She turned back to me, eyes intense. "Surely the end justifies the means."

Was that why I was doing this? Was I going to bring down the wizards to make people's lives better?

I closed my eyes. I might be willing to lie to myself, but I would not lie to her. Which was, of course, a lie. I hadn't told her of Nhil.

"Henka, my love, that's not why I'm doing this. The wizards took what was mine. Maybe they didn't scatter my heart, but I have no doubt they broke it. If they find out I'm alive, they'll hunt me. They'll destroy me again. Power is the only way I can protect myself."

"I know." I felt her cold hand in mine. "It's you and me against all the world."

CHAPTER THIRTY-NINE

Evening claimed Nachi as the sun sank and lit the clouds from beneath in a gorgeous swirl of red, yellow, purple, and orange. The western sky burned like it was on fire. A full moon grew in brightness as night fell.

The docks, I discovered, weren't the only part of Nachi populated by those of darker complexion. Even among the mansions of the upper town, narrow alleys lurked behind ostentatious wealth. A hidden no-man's land of whores and thieves and cutthroats existed in the shadows cast by marble and gold. A slurred blend of skin and hair colours suggested centuries of interbreeding.

It didn't take long to find a rundown hotel where no one asked questions and rooms could be rented by the hour. Enough other patrons came and went, whores of varying age and appeal on their arms, that no one would notice us returning with one. Or that we would do so several times throughout the course of the evening. That wasn't quite true. People noticed us—my midnight skin and Henka's unearthly beauty—but gold purchased inattentive eyes and failing memories.

At least that was the plan.

After taking a room of stained sheets and cockroach-killing spiders for the entire evening, Henka and I descended to the streets to begin our own hunt. About to exit the front door, I stopped, half in, half out of our decrepit tavern. There, exiting an equally seedy establishment across the street, was Tien. The wizard—thief, whatever the hell she was—glanced up and down the street, eyes sliding past the inset door in which I stood without pausing. Nodding to herself, she selected a direction and set out. Though short, she walked fast, hips swinging in a confident strut. She looked just as she had, even wearing the same unassuming clothes.

My god, whoever, whatever, wherever she was, smiled down on me.

"What is it?" asked Henka from behind me. I felt her hand, a gentle touch on the small of my back. "You saw something?"

How to explain? I turned to face her. "Someone. A wizard."

"A wizard? From before? Someone you remember from a long time ago?"

I shook my head. "I met her in Taramlae. She's a thief."

"She?" Henka's eyes narrowed.

I couldn't explain Shalayn and I, our weeks in the wizard's tower, or her death and the part this wizard played. Back then I hadn't known Henka beyond our very brief first meeting, and yet my time with Shalayn made me feel like I'd somehow been unfaithful. The knot of warring emotions confused me. In a time when I was lost and alone, Shalayn showed me kindness. God it hurt.

"I hired her to help me get into the wizard's tower where the shard of my heart was." Not a lie, not the whole truth.

"It shouldn't have been there," said Henka. I saw in doubt her eyes.

Her words sunk in. "It shouldn't have been there?"

She looked annoyed at the change in topic. "None of the others are in towers. How did they find that one?"

Good question, but it felt like an evasion.

Henka watched Tien. "The wizard you hired—the thief—she's cute. Petite."

Cute. True, Tien was extremely cute, though not at all my type. At least Henka wasn't digging deeper into what happened at the tower.

"Not my type," I said. "And you know that. You have no reason to be jealous." Not of Tien.

"Jealous?" She hmphed.

"We should follow her."

"Really?" She gave me a hard look. "Why?"

"Why is she here? What if she's somehow followed us? What if she's here on behalf of the Guild?"

"And kill her?" Henka asked.

"And kill her," I agreed.

I reminded myself not to be stupid. Though I had no idea of her power, Tien was a wizard and not to be underestimated. There'd be no time for questions. No time for all the torments I dreamed up for her. But there would be time for a fast and brutal vengeance.

"I want her," said Henka. "An enslaved wizard will come in handy. How else will you get her to answer your questions?" She examined me. "You don't mind? She doesn't mean anything to you, does she?"

Oh hell. She might learn of Shalayn.

I grinned at Henka. "I could never deny you anything."

"You never could," she agreed.

We followed the diminutive wizard at a safe distance. She weaved through knots of people, her confident strut never changing. When she ducked into a narrow alley, I hesitated, wondering if she spotted us. She hadn't glanced over her shoulder at any time, but I had no idea what wizards might be capable of. Arriving at the corner, I peeked around to see her, still strutting, turn another corner. If she was worried or aware of us, she hid it masterfully.

Remembering the cafe hidden in the warrens of Taramlae, I wondered if there was something similar here. I had no doubt Tien either knew where it was or had some means of finding it.

After the second corner, the alleys were empty of people but littered with trash. I followed Tien, and Henka remained a few steps behind me. Where I was quiet, the necromancer was silent as the grave.

The sun disappeared and the world fell dark, these narrow back streets lit only by the light struggling past stained windows and gauzy curtains, and the bright moon above. Nachi became a city of ashen slate.

Carefree, the wizard whistled a jaunty tune. Drawing my crude sword, I closed the distance. If Tien had some kind of magical shield, all this would end very badly indeed. I found I didn't care. The thief stole from me. She stole Shalayn and she stole my chance at happiness, at a different life. I knew in my blood that if Shalayn and I had remained together, I would be a different person than I now was. I could have been someone Shalayn loved instead of loathed.

The thought gave me some pause, though I didn't allow it to slow my approach. The person I'd become, this man who loved Henka, who helped her kill and harvest, who was to blame for him? I knew killing was evil, even if there were reasons. Even if there were good reasons. Yet here I was, a murderer several times over, planning on killing again. And I was definitely going to kill Tien. Nothing would stay my hand. Shalayn was dead because of her. Tien tricked me, manipulated me. No one does that. But this man I'd become, this murderer, could I lay that on Henka? Had she somehow shaped me?

I remembered how she said we had to collect the shards of my heart in a certain order, how it mattered that *I* was the one to take in the other pieces, the constant personality.

It felt like ducking responsibility, a cowardly escape. But it also felt true. To be fair, however, she made no attempt to hide her plan. She wanted me to be someone different than the Demon Emperor who failed, who died, betrayed by the wizards.

But why? Was it love?

My own wash of torn emotions—love for Henka, rage at Tien and the wizards, pain at Shalayn's death—left me unbalanced, confused.

I closed the distance.

Tien spotted someone ahead and raised a hand in greeting. Seeing my chance, I dashed forward, drove my sword into her back. It entered near her liver, to the right of her spine. Angled up, it punched out between two of her lower ribs in the front.

Vengeance!

My horribly beautiful god it was glorious!

She stood, transfixed.

Behind her, so close, almost a lover's embrace, I whispered in her ear, "I got you."

Tien coughed blood, twitching. Twisting the sword, savaging her insides, I ripped it free. Gore came with it, spattering the earth and my boots. I'd gutted her.

Tien said something, her knees folding, and she fell dead. Just like that. So simple. Done.

Triumph and glee filled me. I did it! I killed the—

"No!"

The shout, voice cracking with agony, shattered my victory. I finally saw who Tien waved at.

Shalayn stood at the front step of yet another dingy coffee shop. She was as I remembered, wearing her armour, sword at her side, as always. Beautiful and strong in the moonlight.

She saw me, screamed utter heart-rending pain, drew her sword, and charged.

"You killed my sister!"

Her words froze me for an instant and she damned near ended me with her first frenzied attack. Only instinct, honed over forgotten years, saved me. I defended myself, knocking aside her wild decapitating swing. Sparks and slivers of my crude sword flew as she hacked at me like she meant to chop down a tree.

She stopped, sword held ready, death in her pale eyes.

"I didn't know," I said. "I thought—"

She attacked again, this time with finesse. Again, I parried, retreating before her wrath. Eyes narrowed, searching for a weakness or an opening, she followed. Already my sword was nicked and pitted.

"Tien told me you were dead," I said, backing away.

Shalayn's sword, licked out, snake fast, opening a wound along my left arm. I might be the better sword fighter, with my years of practice, my centuries of war, but she was faster. And my shoddy sword would only take so much abuse.

"Liar," she said, feinting, opening a cut along my thigh.

Wincing in pain, I retreated. Blood ran free, the wounds burning like fire.

"Kill her!" Screamed Henka from behind me.

Shalayn saw her and those beautiful blue eyes bled hate. "You abandoned me for *her*?" she growled.

"No, I—"

BLACK STONE HEART

Shalayn slashed my ribs and I gasped in pain. She followed, blade stabbing and feinting, looking for openings. She meant to bleed me, to see me suffer.

"I came back to the tower," I blurted as fast as I could. "You were gone."

"Stop talking to her and kill the bitch before she guts you!" yelled Henka.

It was good advice. It was advice I ignored. I had to explain, to make Shalayn understand.

"Tien tricked me," I said. "I—"

Pain lit my gut as she drew a line across my belly. It was a shallow line, drawn with precision, cascading blood. I was better than this, better than her. But I didn't want to kill her. I couldn't.

"Liar," Shalayn ground out between clenched teeth. "Tien rescued me and you never came back. She said you abandoned me once you had what you wanted."

Of course it looked like that. I get the shard of my heart, I put the ring on, and I'm gone.

"No, I—"

This time I blocked her attack, steel singing harsh echoes in the stone alley. The force of the blow bent my blade.

I saw in her eyes she wanted to believe me. I also saw she could never forgive me for killing her sister. Only one of us would walk away from this fight.

Fast as Shalayn was, I had years of skill writ deep in every bone and muscle. This time, when she attacked, I riposted, sending her sword skittering away into the filth and detritus littering the alley. My own sword shattered with the manoeuvre and she had a knife drawn, lightning fast, when my left fist clipped her chin.

She crumpled, unconscious.

"Kill her," said Henka, approaching.

"No."

"Do you love her?" she asked, watching my reaction with those knowing eyes.

She saw inside me, knew me better than I did.

"I did. She…"

Shalayn wasn't dead. Tien lied about that. She wrote 'I deserve better' on the table top, the words Shalayn was to use to trigger the magic ring. The thief used me and lied about her sister to separate us, to protect her. I couldn't even be angry.

"She betrayed me," I lied to Henka. "Back in Taramlae."

"I want her eyes," said Henka.

"No you don't. You know I love you with dark eyes."

"Why won't you kill her?"

"Because *he* wants to, the old me." It was true. The Demon Emperor knew better than to leave an enemy alive. He railed at me to stab her while she lay helpless. "I need to be different than him. I need to be better."

Henka looked thoughtful, staring at the unconscious woman. "Fine. Bring the wizard. She'll be useful."

"No."

"Why not? With an enslaved wizard—"

"No." This time I offered no explanation. Tien may or may not deserve such a fate, but I could never do that to Shalayn. Raising her sister as an undead slave would forever ruin me in her eyes. Stupid, but the truth.

Shaking her head in disappointment, Henka said, "Fine."

She gave in too easily but I was grateful she didn't push me to kill Shalayn, to harvest this woman I did, in fact, still love. It felt like my stone heart cracked anew. My chest hurt and I wanted to sit somewhere and cry.

Tien's only real crime was trying to save her sister from me. She saw what I was: Evil. She knew Shalayn's self-destructive bent, the way she was drawn to me. Tien knew I'd eventually either hurt Shalayn or get her killed. Hell, I almost did. Had some wizard other than Tien found her in the tower…

I had to turn away, to keep moving. If I hesitated, if I stayed here staring at Shalayn, Henka would know the truth. And if I was still here when Shalayn regained consciousness, then I really would have to kill her. Still, I hesitated, not wanting to leave the woman unconscious in this filthy alley. She didn't deserve this. She didn't deserve any of this. Her skin glowed pale in the moonlight, that dusting of freckles. She was beautiful, a luminescent ghost. She'd been kind to a stranger. Where everyone loathed me for the colour of my skin, she found something to love. She took dangerous risks to help me. She trusted me.

And I murdered her sister.

Taking Henka's cold hand in mine I pulled her away. "Come, let's go."

"We don't have what we came for." She walked, unresisting, at my side.

More killing. "I can't. Not now."

"I can, I suppose, make do with what's onboard the Habnikaav," she said, squeezing my hand.

"I'll need blood and souls for the summoning and binding rituals. We'll harvest some of the crew together. The floating mountain has everything else I need."

I wanted to flee there, to escape myself. I needed time and space to think. And I wanted to test the skills I'd learned from the last shard. Anything to distract myself from what I'd done.

"What," I said, "is a demonologist without demons?"

"True," she said, giving me a quick kiss on the cheek.

Henka and I returned to the ship.

The Captain, standing at the rail, watched us ascend the gangplank, eyeing the blood leaking from my many wounds. I nodded as we passed and he said nothing.

Back in our cramped, stinking cabin, I collapsed onto the bed with a groan, uncaring what insects I shared it with. Light-headed from blood-loss, I was exhausted and shaken with the horror of what I'd done.

Shalayn was alive.

I, however, gutted her sister right in front of her. I knew Shalayn; she'd hunt me to the ends of the world and beyond. No hell was safe.

Part of me hoped she found me. I promised her she could break me back to someone she loved.

She deserved her vengeance.

I deserved her wrath.

I slept.

When I woke, I found Henka sitting on the edge of my bed, watching me.

"I returned to town," she said. "I got the supplies we purchased." She nodded at the heaped sacks crowding the small room."

I wondered how she managed to carry it all back here but didn't ask. Instead, I kissed her cold cheek and told her, "Thank you."

CHAPTER FORTY

For the next two days, I spent my time standing at the bow, feeling the salt wind on my face and in my hair. In the evenings I memorized the cabin we shared. Gods, I missed the ocean. The gentle rise and fall of the ship beneath me, the rhythmic *slap slap* of the waves against her hull. Gulls followed us, calling and screeching, and fighting over our scraps.

Henka remained below decks, claiming the salt water and strong winds were murder on her skin. I didn't argue. I valued my solitude. For years it had been just me, alone in my mud shack. I missed the simplicity. I missed being an animal, empty of thought.

Shalayn.

I recalled our stay in the tower. Looking back, that was the best time of what little of my life I remembered. While we'd been trapped there, we'd been together. We ate and drank together. We bathed and slept together. She'd been my world. When I thought she died because of me, it broke my heart. The flesh, not the stone.

I loved her. I loved her and I missed her. I loved her, and if she ever saw me again, she wouldn't hesitate to kill me.

I knew I'd see her someday. Or maybe I'd feel her sword in my back as Tien felt mine. Hopefully the latter, for if the former, I'd kill her. I'd have no choice. Though she still lived, I felt the loss of her in my chest. Shame soured my gut. I hadn't been honest with Henka. Much as I loved her, I saw now that some part of me always held out some impossible hope for Shalayn.

That hope was dead. The man that held that hope was dead too. I was Khraen. I would be the Demon Emperor once again.

It was past time to set aside my doubts. It was time to stop allowing myself to be distracted. I needed a demonic host. I needed armies of the dead. Dead wizards. Dead elementalists. Dead shamans. Dead sorcerers. Dead necromancers.

Frustration ate at me. I wanted it all. I wanted everything, the whole world. I needed the shard of my heart residing in PalTaq. I needed to know what it knew. Summonings. Bindings. My most ancient secrets. My god. My sword, Kantlament. The End of Sorrow.

On the second day the Captain joined me at the rail, ocean breeze tugging at the thick coils of his black beard. For several minutes we stood in silence.

Finally, he said, "For over two decades I've captained this ship."

I grunted something non-committal, waiting for him to get to the point.

"In all that time, we've never taken on passengers." He turned to face me. "And now I have two berths rented out."

"Two?"

"A young lady joined us the morning we set sail, before you rose."

My heart dropped. "A swordswoman?"

He raised an eyebrow at that. "Hardly. She paid well and said she didn't want to be bothered."

Relief flooded me. It wasn't Shalayn. She would never travel without her sword.

"Should I be worried?" asked the Captain.

Had someone followed us from the town? There'd been the fight with Shalayn, but I hadn't seen any witnesses. The law would have grabbed us before we set sail.

"I don't think it has anything to do with us," I told the Captain.

He grunted doubt.

Leaving the bow, I joined Henka below decks.

"Apparently a woman took a berth just before we left," I told her.

"I saw her." Unconcerned with the revelation, she studied me with loving eyes. "How are you?"

I grinned and took her cold, dead body into my arms. "I am good as long as I am with you."

She hugged me tight. "I worried I lost you. I know…" She pulled back so she could look me in the eye. "I know you loved her. I know she meant a lot to you."

"I killed her sister," I said, as if that explained anything.

"You had to. She was a wizard. If not now, then in the war to come."

The war to come. And there would be war.

"The floating mountains have almost everything I need to summon and bind demons. I have souls, but will need blood. I'll return when I'm ready, and we'll harvest a few crew members."

"We'll share the blood," she said. "So I can be warm for you."

I nodded agreement. I wanted that more than I could say. I wanted to drown myself in her, forget Shalayn. "I want a demon-bound sword, and demon-bound armour." Suddenly, I wanted her to meet Nhil, the ancient demon who claimed to be my friend. "Come with me. Escape the harsh sea air and the damp and this insect-infested berth."

"No. I have work to do here."

Work? I didn't ask.

Releasing her, I collected the preserved foods we purchased. Staggering under the weight, I turned to face her. Luckily, as I planned to arrive in the library this time, I wouldn't have to carry it far.

"I have enough for maybe three weeks," I said.

"If you run out sooner, come back to me. I'll collect what I can, tell them it's for our meals." Her eyes twinkled mischief. "And come back for visits when you need to relax or take a break."

I knew then she'd collect blood in my absence. Was the Captain already short one crewman, or had she harvested someone when she returned to collect the food? I decided not to ask.

"I will," I promised.

She kissed me on the cheek. I stood for a long time, envisioning the library in the mountain keep. The weight of the pack faded, forgotten, as my focus became absolute. I saw the library, the thousands of books, the huge leather chair.

Felkrish, my portal demon, took me there.

"Welcome back," said Nhil, standing behind me. He sounded utterly unsurprised.

Had he known I was coming, or had he simply been waiting there since I left?

"What kind of demon are you?" I asked.

"Manifestation."

"Obviously. Where are you from, what hell? What is your real name? What purpose do you serve?"

"I see you have regained some of your memories. Clearly you still lack many."

"That's not an answer."

"No, it isn't. But it's the best you'll get."

"Listen, demon—"

He stalled me with a raised hand. "Fine. My purpose was to provide you with knowledge and information, both magical and mundane. These books," he gestured at the walls of bookcases, "are but a fraction of my reading. I have unimaginable sources of knowledge. This flesh," he gestured at himself, "is but a sliver of the being that I, in truth, am. I exist in countless realities, fragments of my soul seeking out information, pursuing ever more convoluted pathways to ultimate wisdom. You can't command me, and you can't bind me because you released me over five thousand years ago. Lucky for you, I remain a loyal friend and will always assist you however I can."

I gave up. I needed Nhil's help and antagonizing the demon would get me nowhere. And I believed him.

"We'll finish this discussion later," I said.

"Perhaps."

Another thought occurred to me. "You're free. Why do you not return home?"

"I cannot."

"You aren't capable?"

"It's gone. Destroyed." Seeing the question on my lips, he said, "She destroyed it."

She. I knew he referred to my god. Dreading the answer, I asked, "Why?"

"To weaken me. To ensure I had nowhere to escape to."

I had the horrible feeling she did this for me, that my god killed Nhil's world to bind him to me.

"However," said Nhil, "you did not come to discuss the ancient past."

"No." I dropped the bag of supplies to the floor and left my questions unasked. "There are three weeks of supplies here. Less, if I don't feel like going hungry." My last visit remained fresh in my memories, an experience I didn't care to repeat. "I need your help. I must summon and bind demons. I need a demonic weapon, and demonic armour. Once I have those things we can discuss next steps."

"Your armour is upstairs."

I shuddered. "I'm not ready for that." The thought of touching the red armour terrified me.

"Probably wise." Nhil rubbed his chin in thought, did that weird mistimed blink. "How many souls in the Soul Stone?"

"I can't be sure, but at least twelve," I said. "Maybe more."

"You don't have enough for something of real power. I'd suggest prioritizing, weapon or armour."

Defence or attack.

"Can I summon something that will protect me from wizards?"

"Nothing can protect you from everything. A wizard could drop a rock on you, cook you with fire, boil your blood, or a thousand other things."

Boil my blood. Tien had threatened me with that. I crushed a pang of guilt.

Cowering behind demonic protection didn't seem right. I wanted a weapon. I wanted to kill wizards.

"A sword then." A thought occurred to me. "The End of Sorrow."

"Kantlament."

"Do you know where it is?"

"Of course. It's in PalTaq, where you left it."

Where I left it? Hadn't I had it at my side during the final battle? But if I left it somewhere, that must have been *after* the war. Why had I set it aside? Had I surrendered? That definitely didn't sound like me.

So many questions and so little time. I had to focus. Once I had a sword, I'd question Nhil at length.

"Let's get started," I said. "Henka is all alone on that ship. I want to get back to her as fast as I can."

"Henka," said Nhil. He sighed and rubbed his face. "I'd worry more about the ship's crew."

His words slammed through me, took my breath. "You know her?"

"Of course," said Nhil. "She's your wife."

CHAPTER FORTY-ONE

I blinked at him, mouth opening and then closing when it realized it had nothing to say.

My wife.

All those times I'd been teased by memories of pale skin and dark hair and there she was, right beside me. So many questions fought for dominance, but one crushed the others with its need for an answer: Why?

Why hadn't she told me?

Did she not know?

I felt certain she did. Too often she seemed to know me better than I knew myself.

Pieces fell together.

The dead man, killed with an arrow, dragged onto my grave, whose blood brought me back. I never questioned how he got there, who killed him. When I first clawed my way free of the earth, a gaunt wolf stood there, its fur hanging in tatters, watching me. The ragged pack I kept seeing in the far north. They never came too close, never stole my kills no matter how starved they looked. They'd been dead. I was positive. I remembered the scream of the Septk man who hunted me after I killed his boy, the trail left as something dragged his corpse away, the lingering taint of rot on the air. Had that been the dead grizzly bear, fleeing with its kill lest I see it? So many times, I saw animals and felt like they were watching me. Those tattered birds circling above Taramlae, had they been spying on me even while I was with Shalayn?

I staggered, found my way to the huge leather chair, and collapsed into it.

The way Henka and I met, the attack on the caravan. That had been no coincidence. She planned it, staged everything. She knew exactly where I was. She must have lost me briefly when I fled Tien and escaped back to the far north. I felt sure she'd picked up my trail quickly enough. When I eventually found her, she'd been ready. She'd been perfect, the woman of my dreams, the woman written so deep in my blood I could never forget her, though I remembered nothing else. Pale white skin, in contrast to my own. The sable silk of her hair. Those gorgeous obsidian eyes. She made herself that way for me. After thousands of years as my wife, Henka knew *exactly* what I liked.

"She manipulated me," I said.

"You were always blind to her."

But why?

She made no attempt to harm me, no attempt to hinder my quest to find myself. In fact, she'd assisted me in every possible way, looking out for me, protecting me. She suffered vicious wounds when Chalaam and his friends attacked us. She defended me. When the mage lashed out with fire, Henka sheltered me with her body. She'd been charred to the bone, burnt to nothing, utterly helpless. She did that for me.

"Why didn't she tell me?"

Nhil did that sliding mistimed blink. "She remembers everything you do not. Unlike you, she knows what happened at the end."

It was an answer. It was no answer. I couldn't even be sure it was true.

The end. What had happened? Had she betrayed me? Was that what this was, did she manipulate me for one more great betrayal?

But then why save me?

Because she had something more final in mind, more crushing than death at the hands of a mage.

"If she had nothing to hide," said Nhil, "she would have told you. If she could be trusted, she would have told you. We can't know her plans, but we do know she has lied, she has concealed the truth from you." He sighed, shaking his head sadly. "Remember, she disappeared before the end. Why would she leave you?"

I didn't know. I couldn't even be sure that Nhil wasn't lying. I had no memory of the end.

Emotions surged through me, a maelstrom of confusion. Henka was my everything and she was not what I thought. I trusted her utterly and she repaid me with lies.

I loved her, nothing could change that. But could I trust her after learning the truth?

Why hadn't she told me?

This betrayal hurt a thousand times more than Tien's. More, even, than when I thought I'd lost Shalayn.

How could I trust her to join me on my quest to find the rest of myself?

Was she waiting to find a specific piece of me so she might destroy my chance of discovering my past?

I'd grown increasingly sure the mages had not broken me. Now I saw it in a new light. What if Henka broke my heart? What if she destroyed my empire, scattered me about the world? Had she thought that would kill me? Had she been surprised when her spies announced my return?

"I have to go back," I told Nhil.

"Is that wise? She is ancient and powerful. Don't be fooled by her appearance."

I didn't care. I loved her and nothing would change that. I had to see her, to talk with her. I had to know the truth.

And if she planned betrayal?

My heart hurt. My skull ached. I wanted to scream and do terrible damage to something, anything.

If she betrayed me, I would end her. I would toss her into the ocean, damn her to an eternity in the darkest deeps. She would rot to nothing, flesh devoured, scoured away by the tides. Her skull would sink away, disappear into the ocean floor, buried in silt.

I rose from the chair.

"Henka, my love, I'm coming for you."

EPILOGUE

This is only the beginning.

I pray the memory of these thoughts—this knowledge—is in one of the first shards you find, if not *the* first. But our god, she doesn't answer prayers. At least, not that kind.

She dreams.

She dreams in blood.

She dreams in blood, and she waits.

She waits for you.

She waits for you to be whole.

She waits for you to bring her back to this world.

You must not become the man I am.

I have done terrible things. I harvested entire worlds for our god. I tore the very fabric of creation, shattered the laws much as our heart was shattered. There were rules governing reality and I cracked them wide open. Nightmares spilled forth. I hunted gods and lords of hells and bound them to my purpose.

You must be better.

I pray you find this memory before you find the stone eyes, before you reach PalTaq. Before you find your sword, Kantlament. You'd be better off knowing nothing than everything.

There is so much you don't yet know, but if you continue along the Obsidian Path, this trail of cleverly laid crumbs drawing you south, you will find only sorrow. You must understand what I failed to learn: There is no end to sorrow.

Death is no escape. Not for us.

In finding what you seek, I promise you, you'll lose that which matters most.

There are gods and demons.

There are heavens and hells.

But there is no fate, there is no force of destiny.

Only you can decide who you are.

Your actions will define you.

Printed in Great Britain
by Amazon